The Big Adventures of Majoko

5

Original Illustrations
Mieko Yuchi
("Majoko Series" published by Poplar)
Manga
Tomomi Mizuna

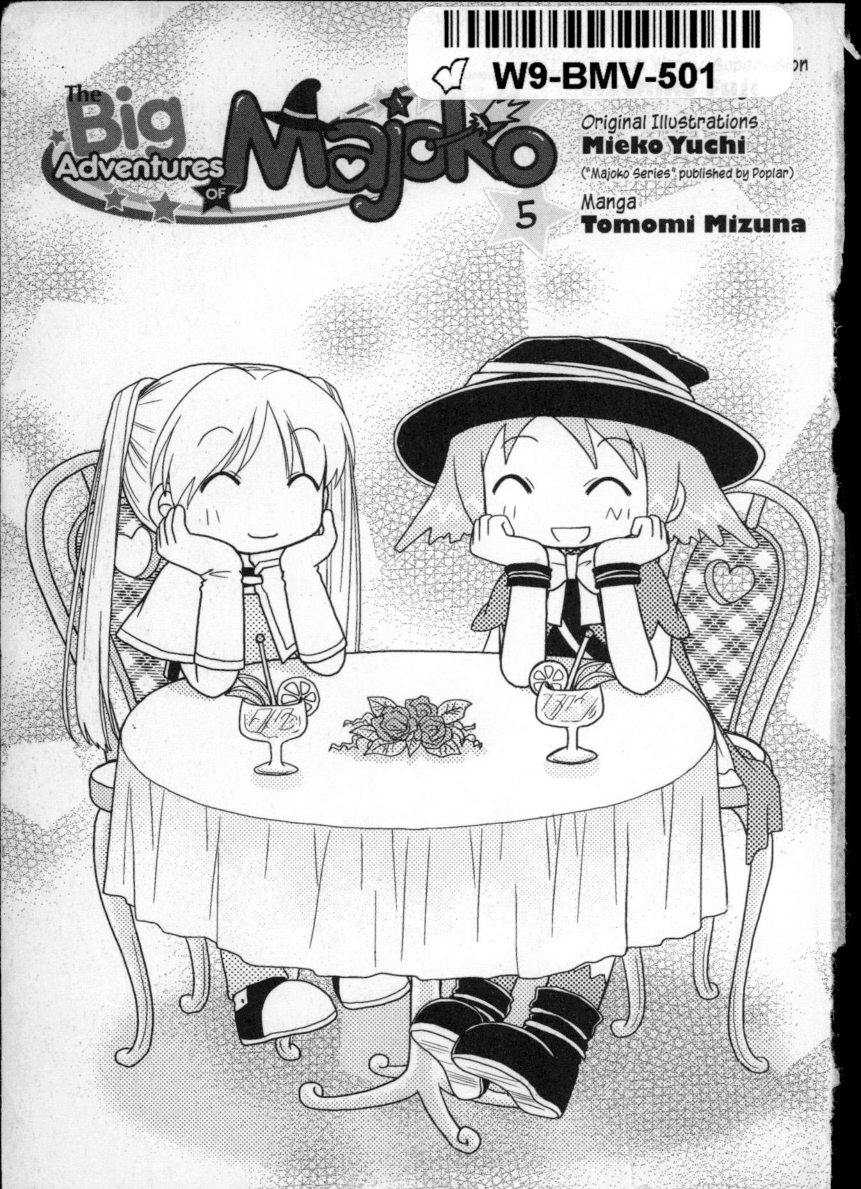

HOW TO READ MANGA!

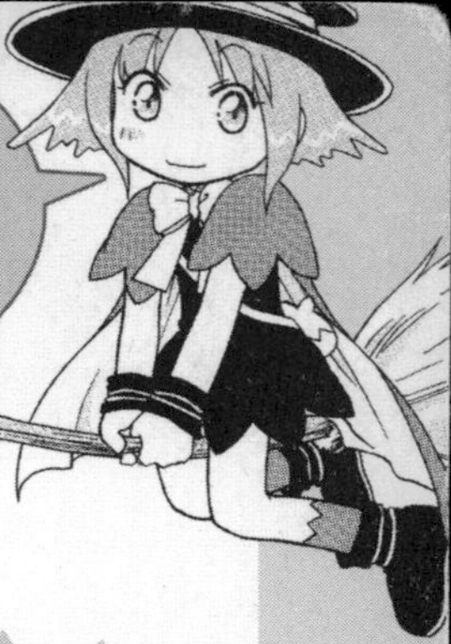

Hi there! My name is **Majoko,** and this is my book - **The Big Adventures of Majoko**! It is a comic book originally created in the country of **Japan,** where comics are called **manga.**

A manga book is read from **right-to-left,** which is **backwards** from the normal books you know. This means that you will find the first page where you expect to find the last page! It also means that each page begins in the top right corner.

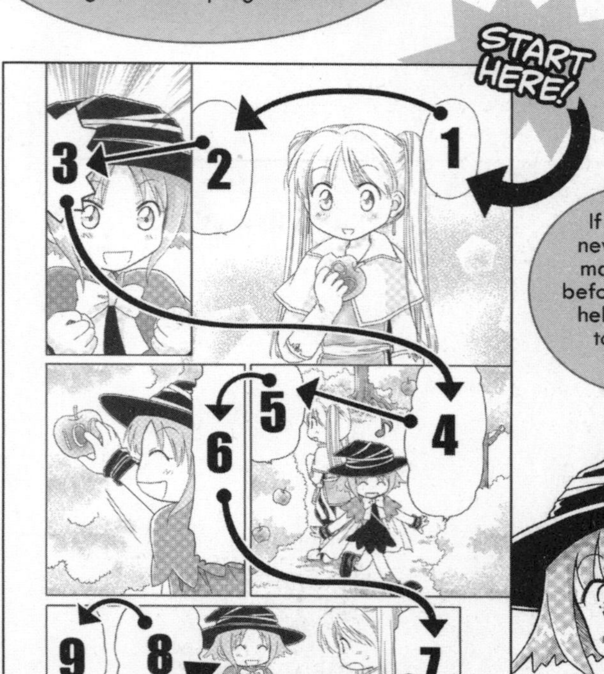
START HERE!
1
2
3
4
5
6
7
8
9

If you have never read a manga book before, here is a helpful guide to get you started!

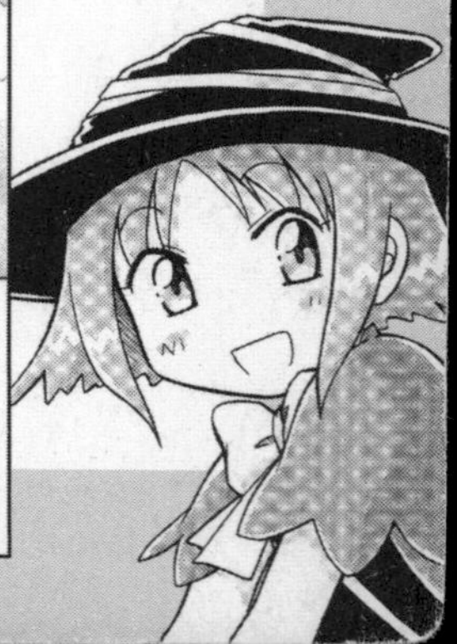

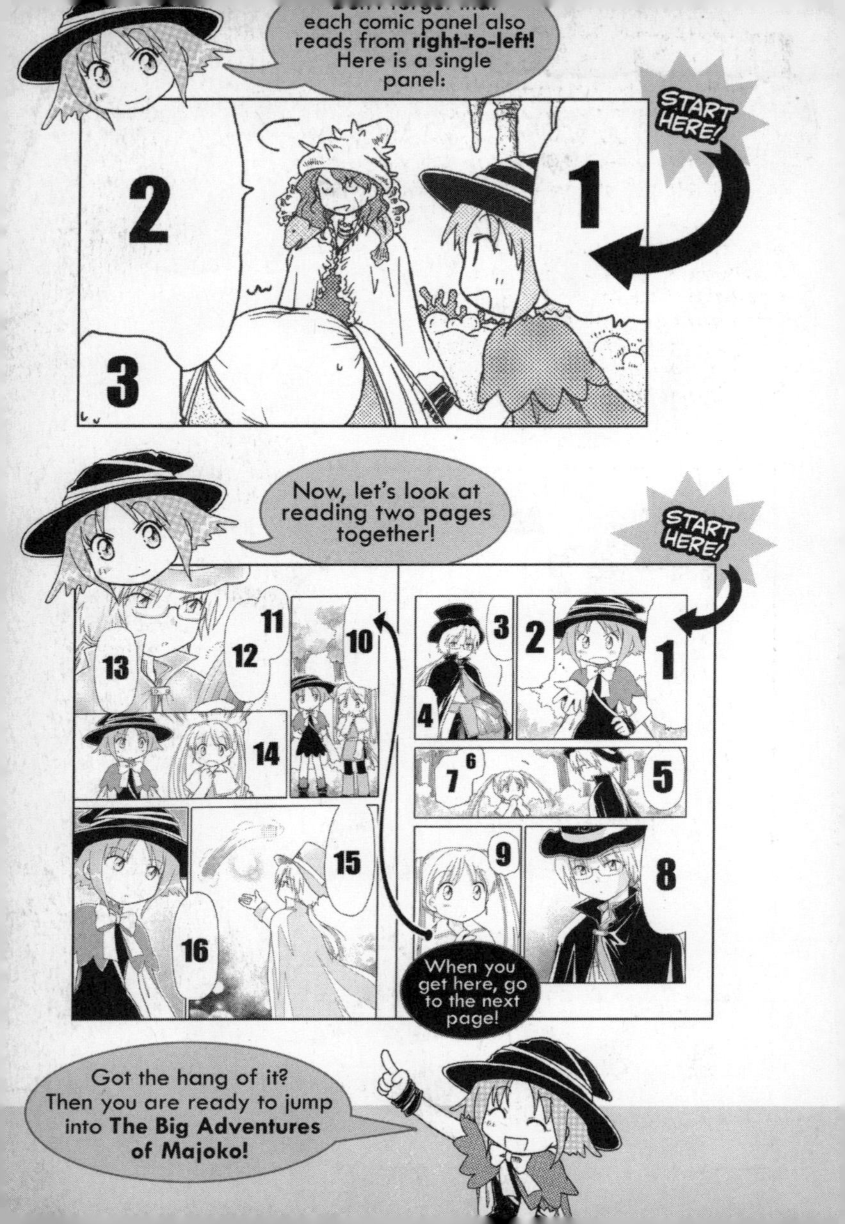
each comic panel also reads from **right-to-left!** Here is a single panel:
START HERE!
1
2
3
Now, let's look at reading two pages together!
START HERE!
1
2
3
4
5
6
7
8
9
10
11
12
13
14
15
16
When you get here, go to the next page!
Got the hang of it? Then you are ready to jump into **The Big Adventures of Majoko!**

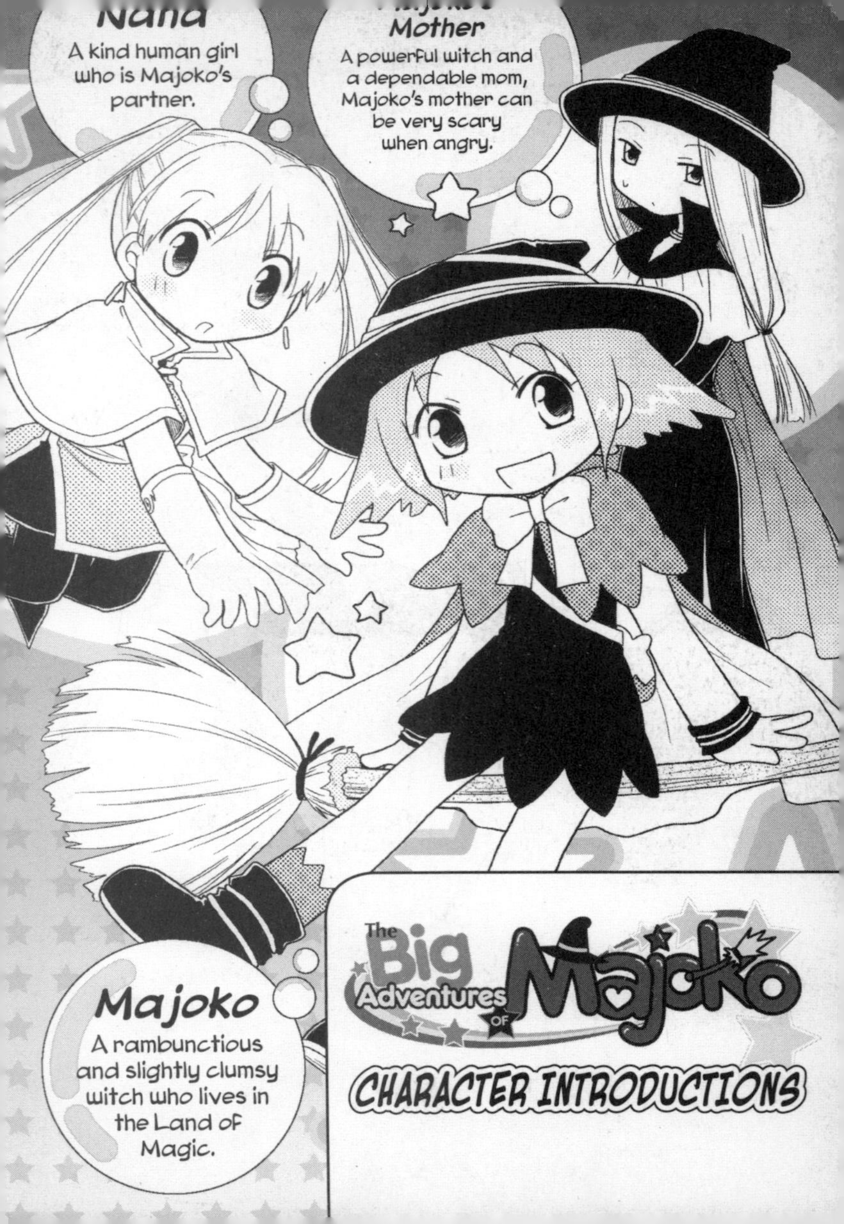
Mother
A powerful witch and a dependable mom, Majoko's mother can be very scary when angry.
Nana
A kind human girl who is Majoko's partner.
The Big Adventures of Majoko
CHARACTER INTRODUCTIONS
Majoko
A rambunctious and slightly clumsy witch who lives in the Land of Magic.

THE STORY SO FAR

One day, Nana found an unfamiliar diary in her room. When she opened the diary, a girl came flying out! The girl was Majoko, a witch. The two quickly became friends, and the two of them have since been having mischievous adventures all over the Land of Magic!!

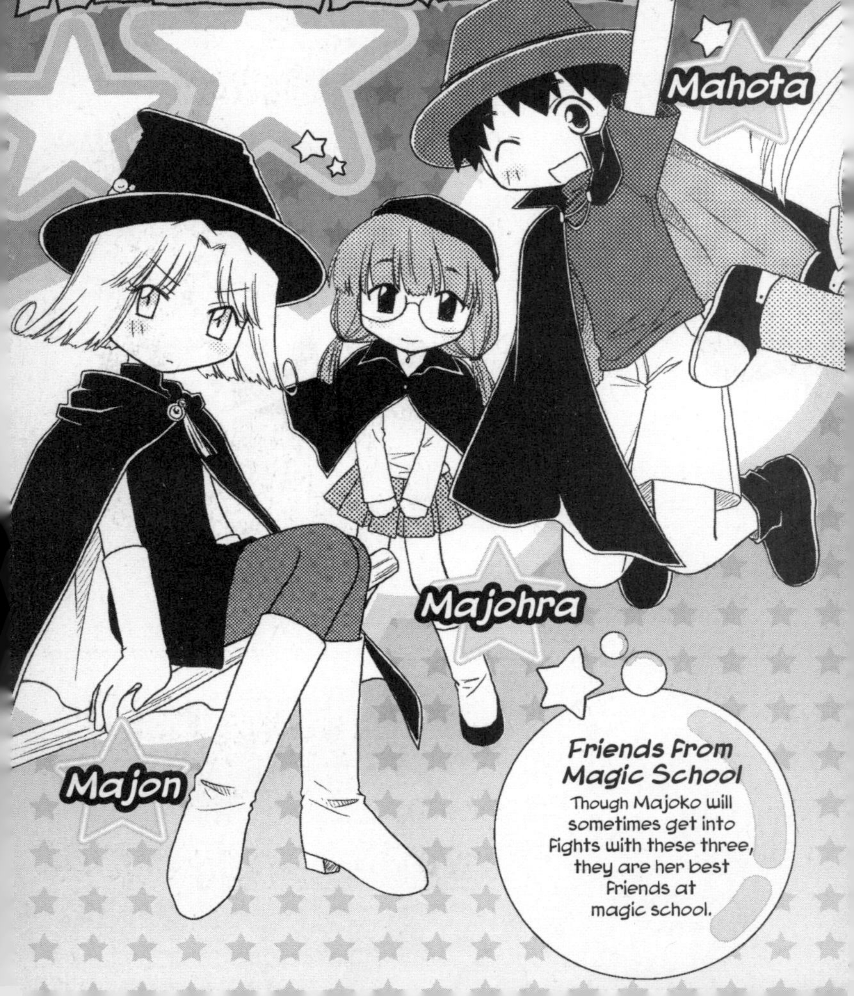
Mahota
Majohra
Majon
Friends from Magic School
Though Majoko will sometimes get into fights with these three, they are her best friends at magic school.

Majoko's Diary

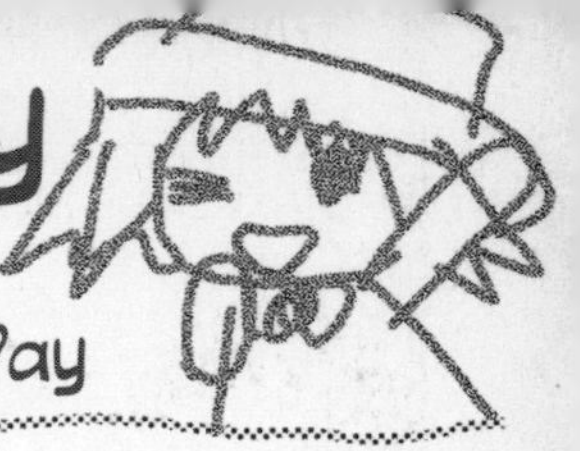

Month Day

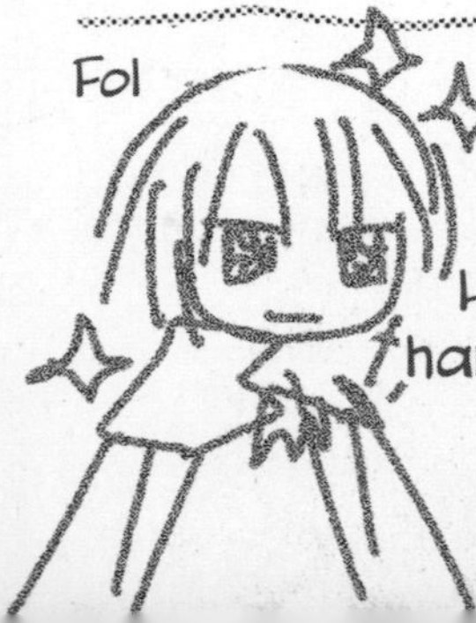

Fol
He's so handsome!

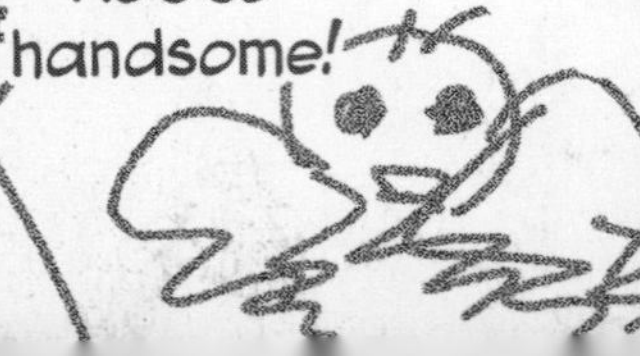

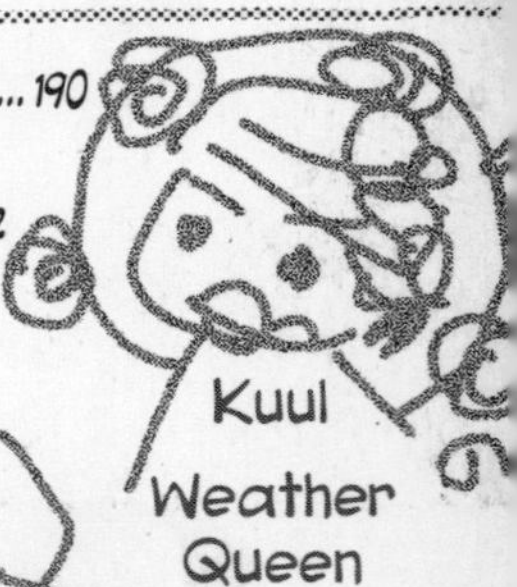

Kuul
Weather Queen

Chapter 30
A Promise Under Starry Skies

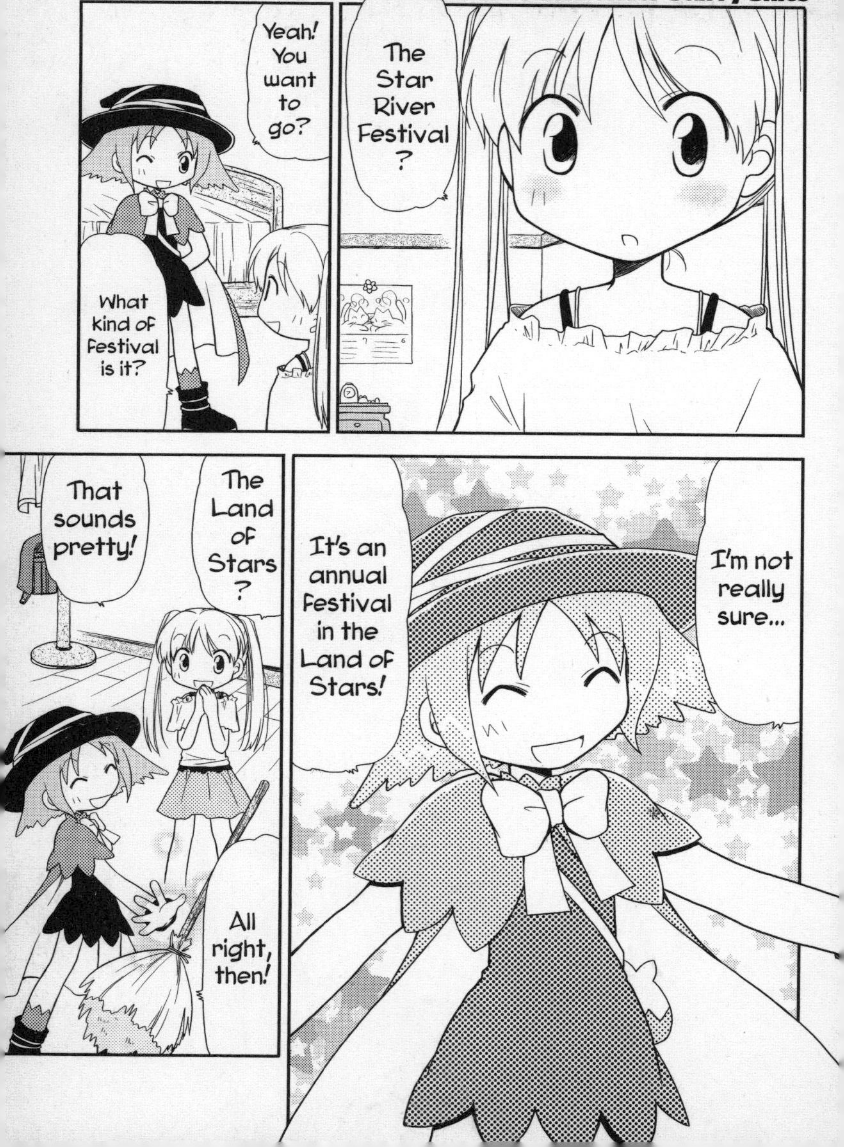
The Star River Festival?
Yeah! You want to go?
What kind of festival is it?
I'm not really sure...
It's an annual festival in the Land of Stars!
The Land of Stars?
That sounds pretty!
All right, then!

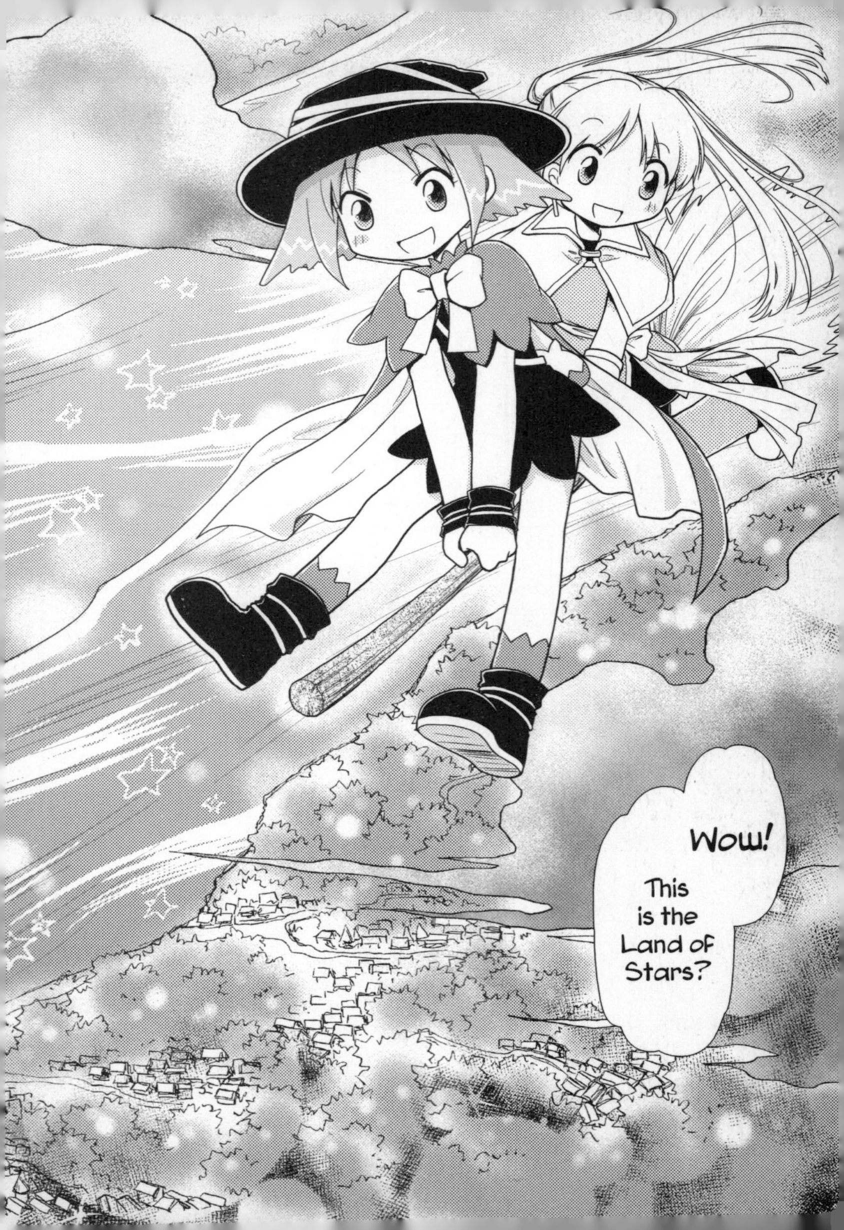
Wow!
This is the Land of Stars?

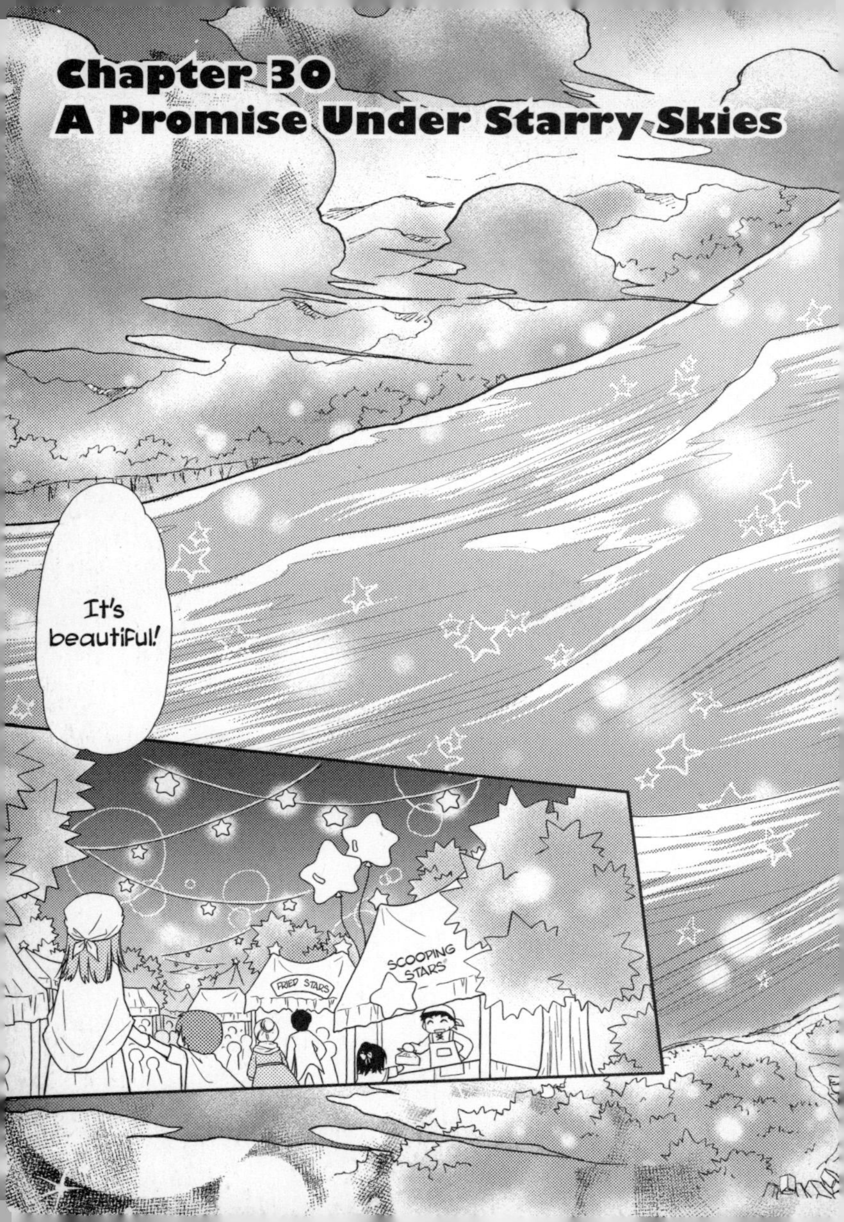
Chapter 30
A Promise Under Starry Skies
It's beautiful!
SCOOPING STARS
FRIED STARS

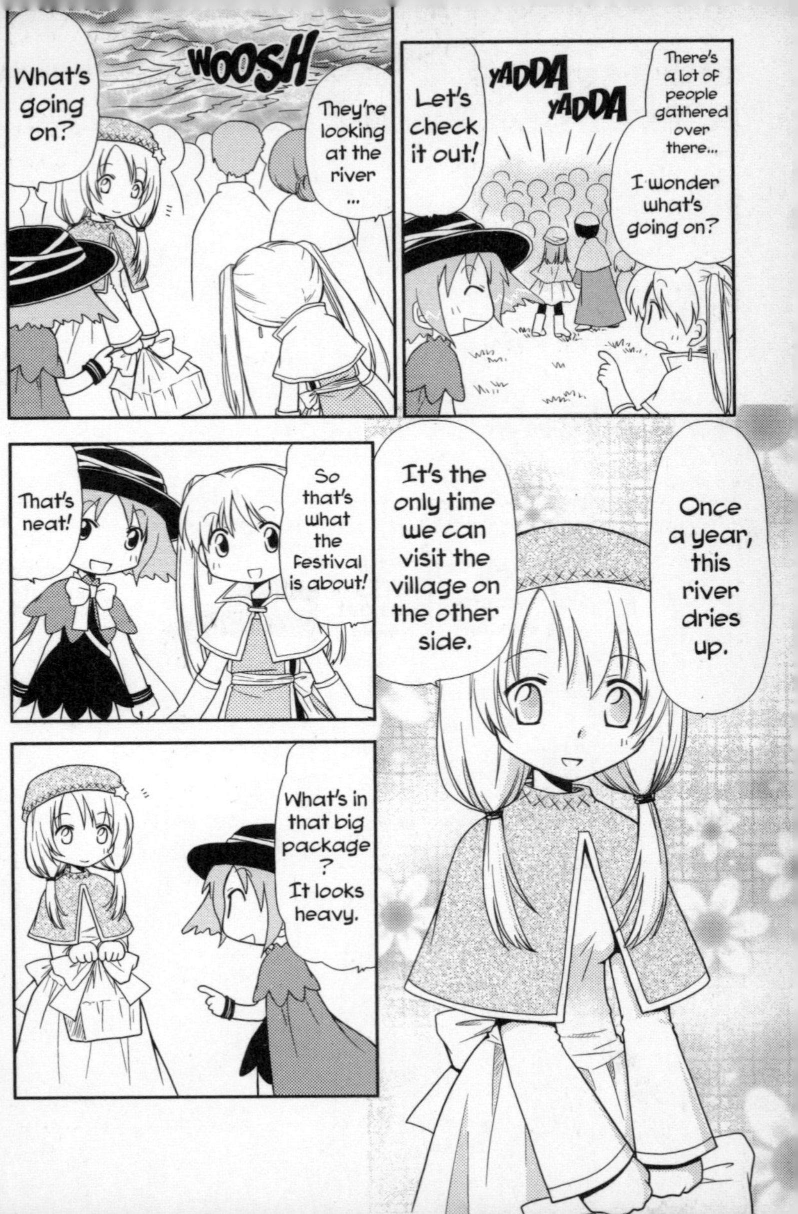
There's a lot of people gathered over there...
I wonder what's going on?
YADDA YADDA
Let's check it out!
WOOSH
What's going on?
They're looking at the river ...
Once a year, this river dries up.
It's the only time we can visit the village on the other side.
So that's what the festival is about!
That's neat!
What's in that big package? It looks heavy.

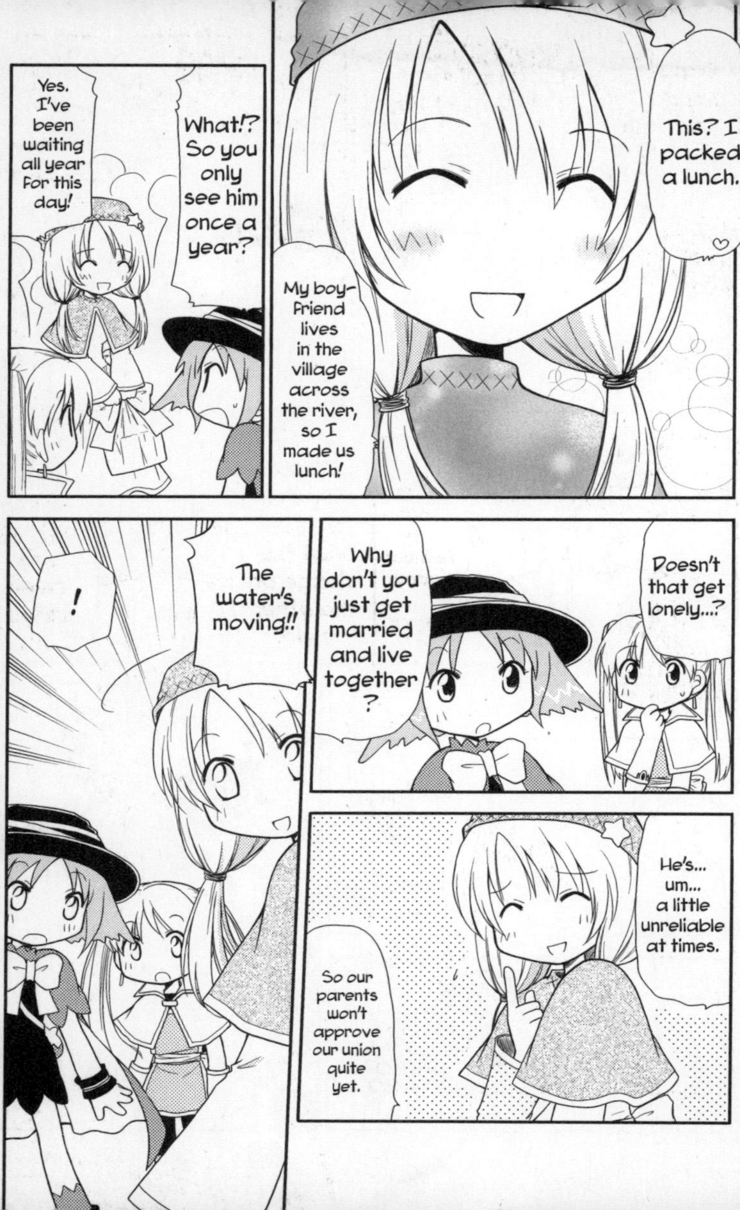

This? I packed a lunch.
My boy-friend lives in the village across the river, so I made us lunch!
What!? So you only see him once a year?
Yes. I've been waiting all year for this day!
Doesn't that get lonely...?
Why don't you just get married and live together?
He's... um... a little unreliable at times.
So our parents won't approve our union quite yet.
The water's moving!!
!

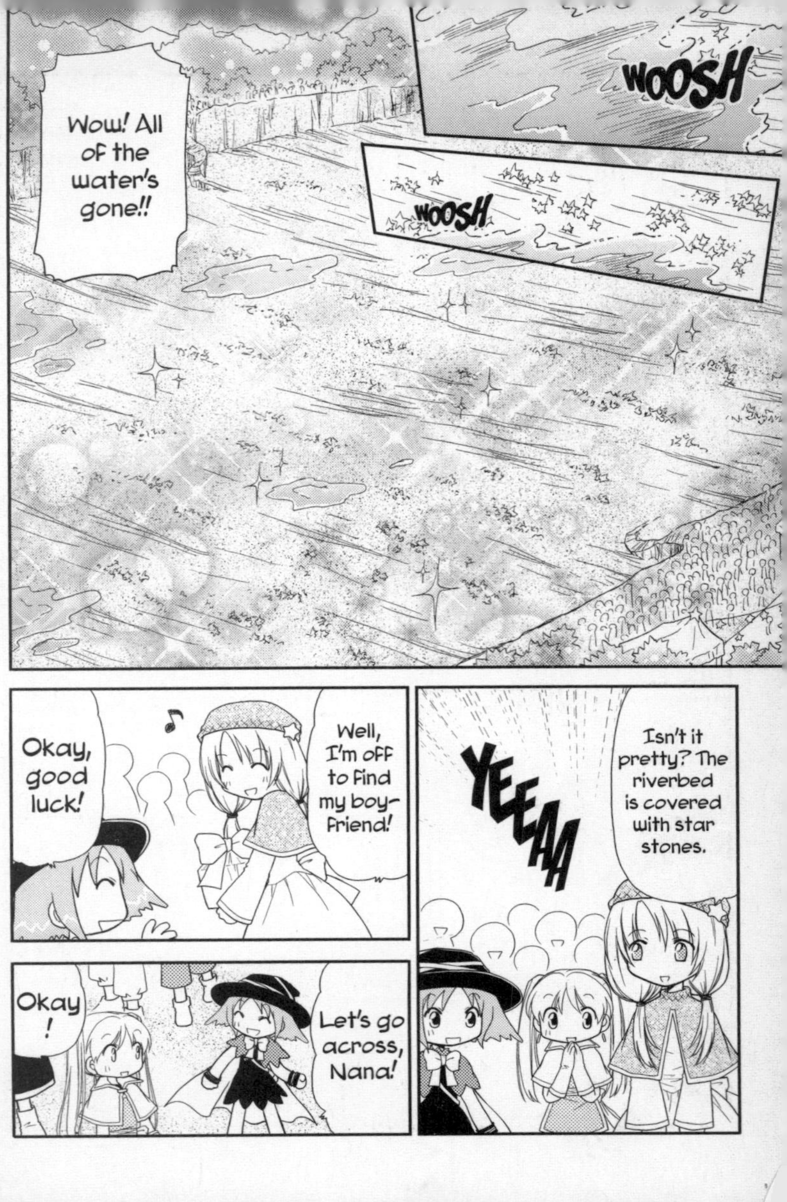
WOOSH
WOOSH
Wow! All of the water's gone!!
YEEAAA
Isn't it pretty? The riverbed is covered with star stones.
Well, I'm off to find my boy-friend!
Okay, good luck!
Let's go across, Nana!
Okay!

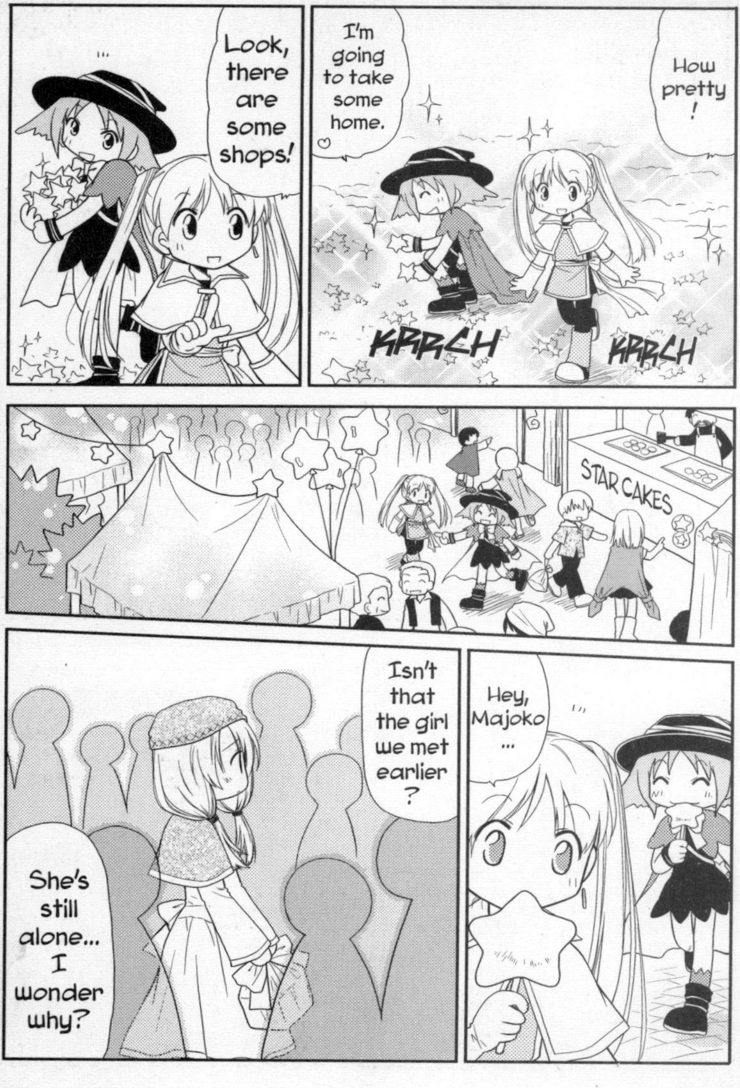
How pretty!
I'm going to take some home.
KRRCH
KRRCH
Look, there are some shops!
...
STAR CAKES
Hey, Majoko ...
Isn't that the girl we met earlier?
She's still alone... I wonder why?

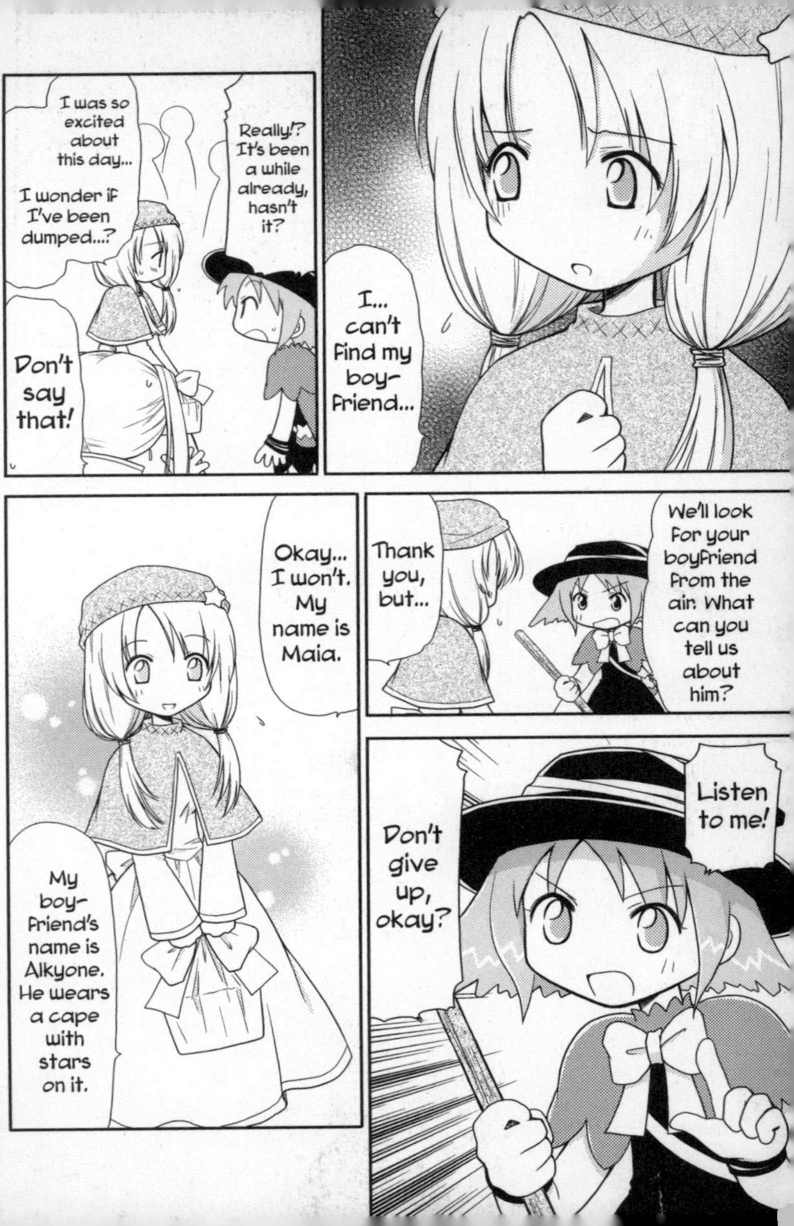

I... can't find my boy-friend...
Really!? It's been a while already, hasn't it?
I was so excited about this day...
I wonder if I've been dumped...?
Don't say that!
We'll look for your boyfriend from the air. What can you tell us about him?
Thank you, but...
Listen to me!
Don't give up, okay?
Okay... I won't. My name is Maia.
My boy-friend's name is Alkyone. He wears a cape with stars on it.

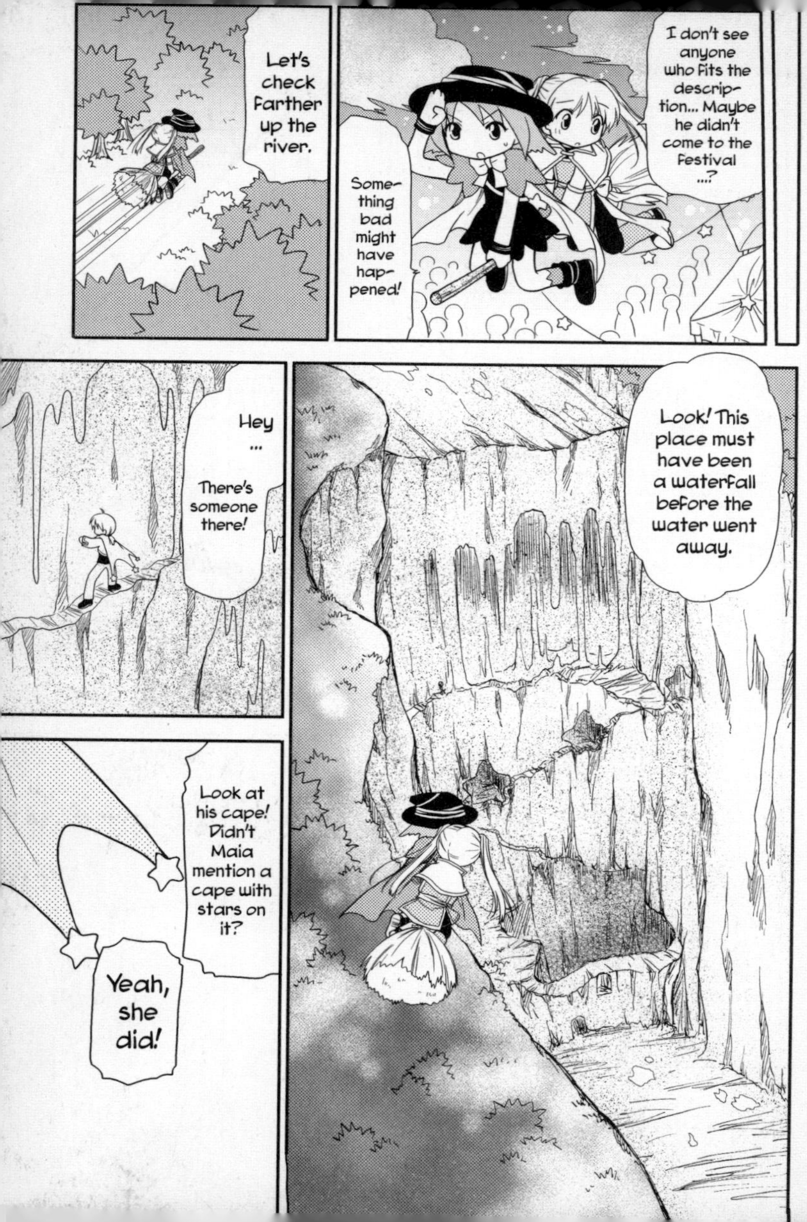
I don't see anyone who fits the description... Maybe he didn't come to the festival ...?
Something bad might have happened!
Let's check farther up the river.
Look! This place must have been a waterfall before the water went away.
Hey ...
There's someone there!
Look at his cape! Didn't Maia mention a cape with stars on it?
Yeah, she did!

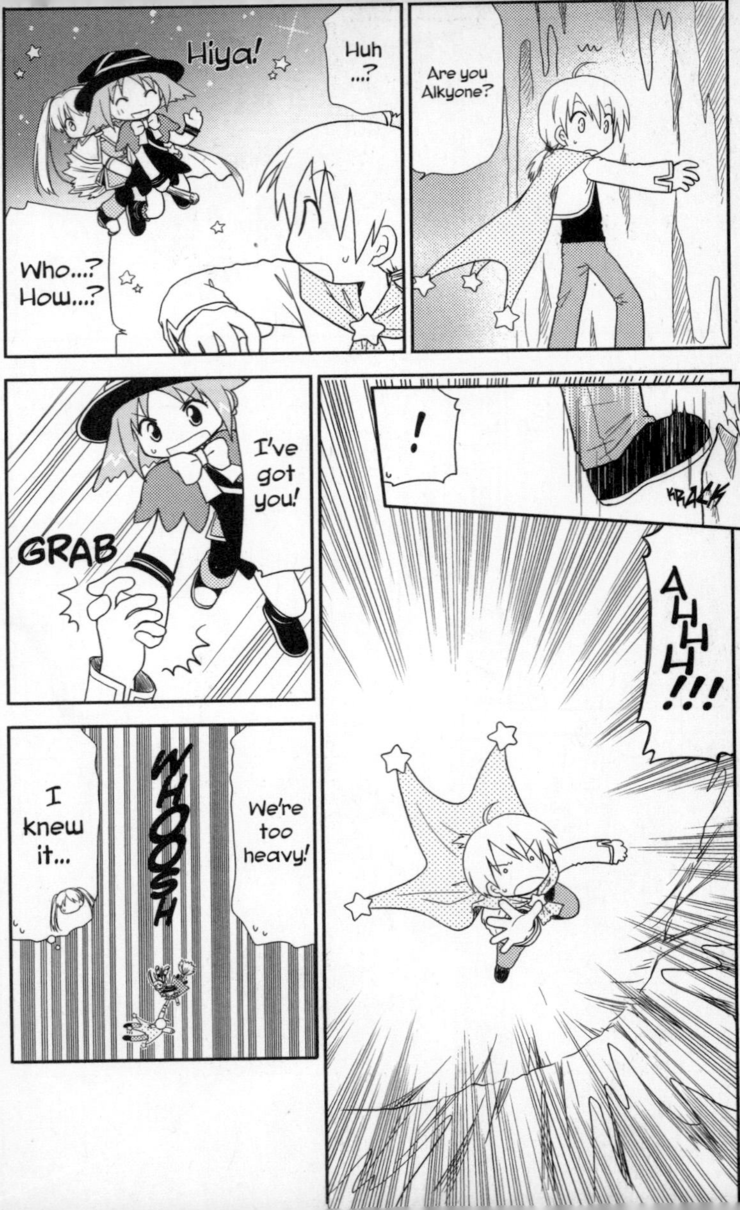
Are you Alkyone?
Huh ...?
Hiya!
Who...? How...?
!
KRACK
AHHH!!!
I've got you!
GRAB
We're too heavy!
WHOOOSH
I knew it...

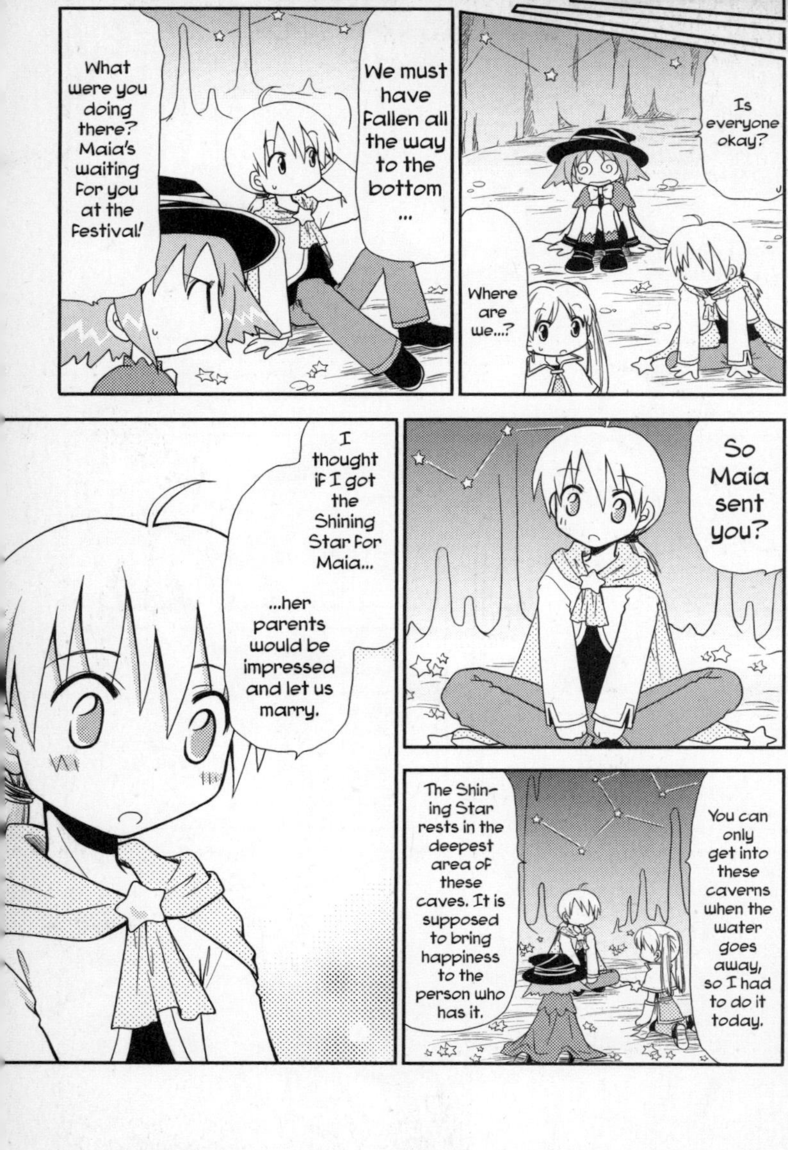
Is everyone okay?
Where are we...?
We must have fallen all the way to the bottom ...
What were you doing there? Maia's waiting for you at the festival!
So Maia sent you?
The Shining Star rests in the deepest area of these caves. It is supposed to bring happiness to the person who has it.
You can only get into these caverns when the water goes away, so I had to do it today.
I thought if I got the Shining Star for Maia...
...her parents would be impressed and let us marry.

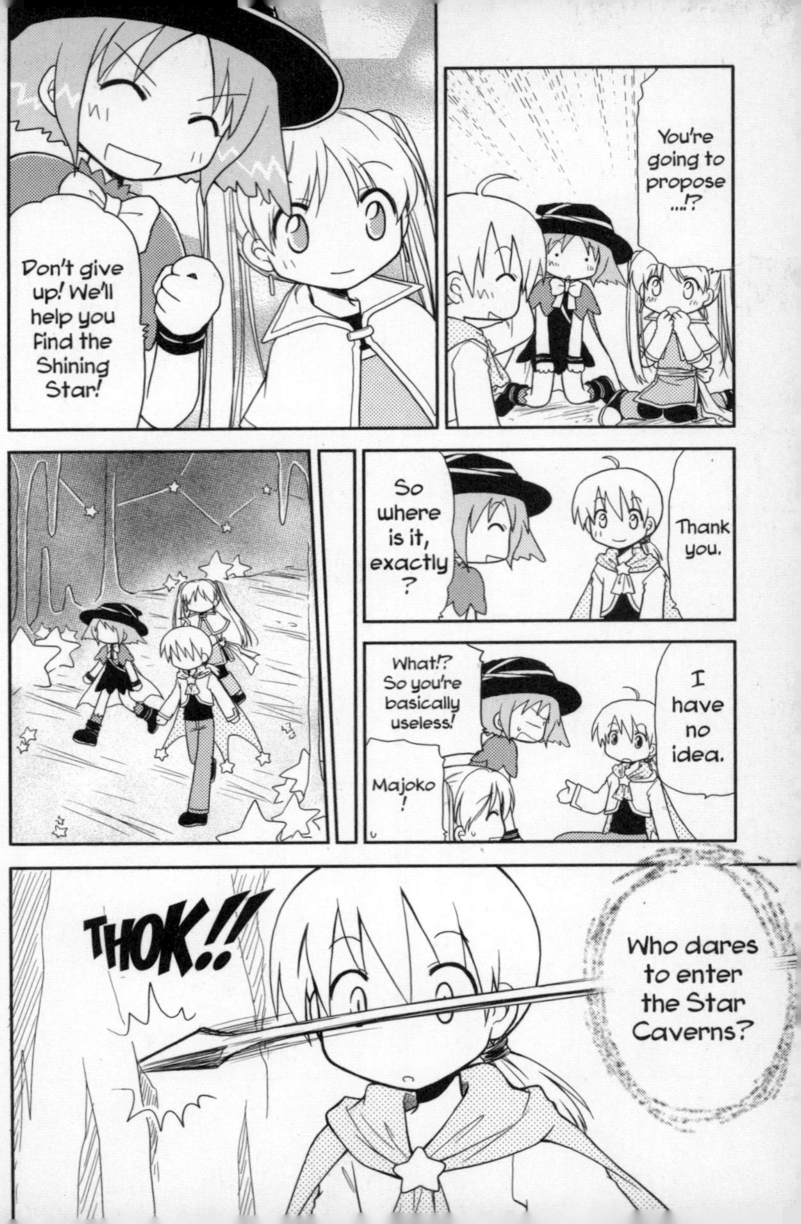
You're going to propose ...!?
Don't give up! We'll help you find the Shining Star!
Thank you.
So where is it, exactly?
I have no idea.
What!? So you're basically useless!
Majoko!
Who dares to enter the Star Caverns?
THOK!!

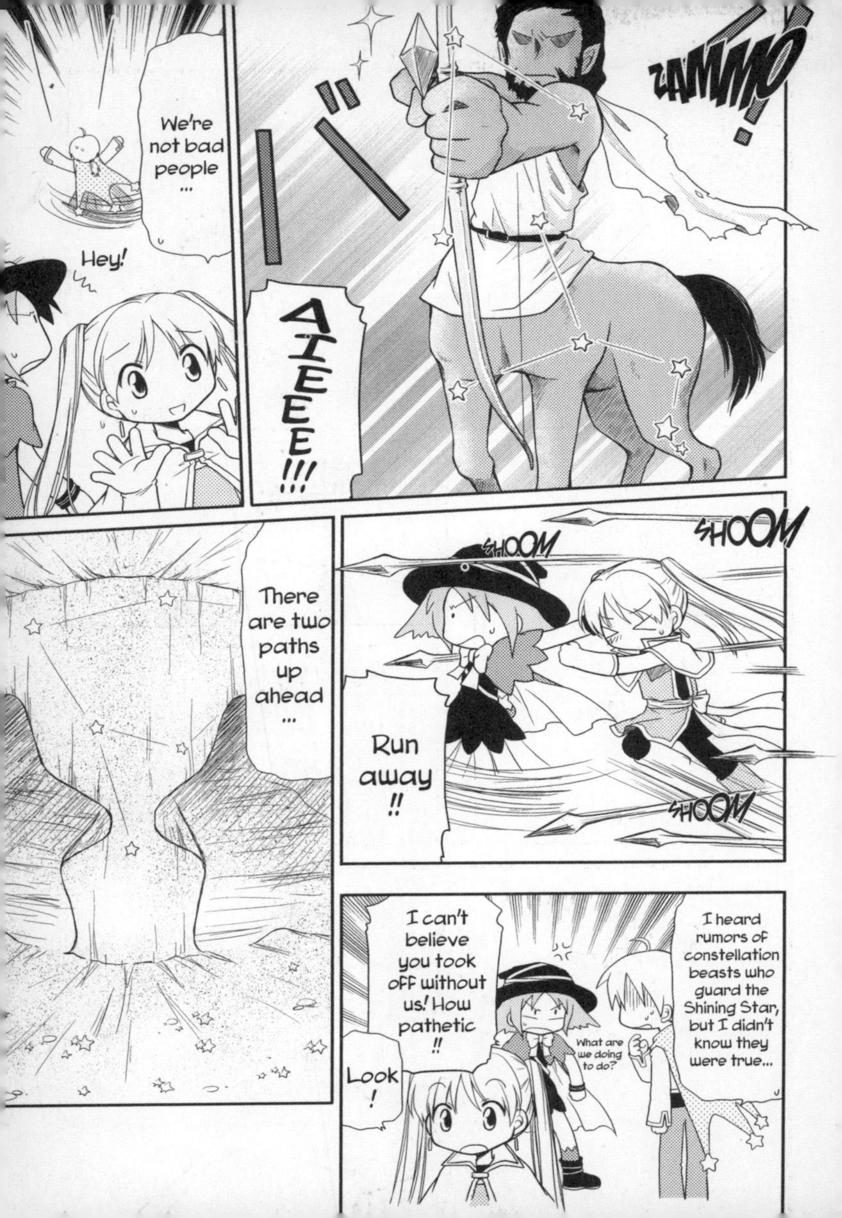
ZAMMO!
AIEEE!!!
We're not bad people ...
Hey!
SHOOM
SHOOM
Run away !!
SHOOM
There are two paths up ahead ...
I heard rumors of constellation beasts who guard the Shining Star, but I didn't know they were true...
I can't believe you took off without us! How pathetic !!
What are we doing to do?
Look !

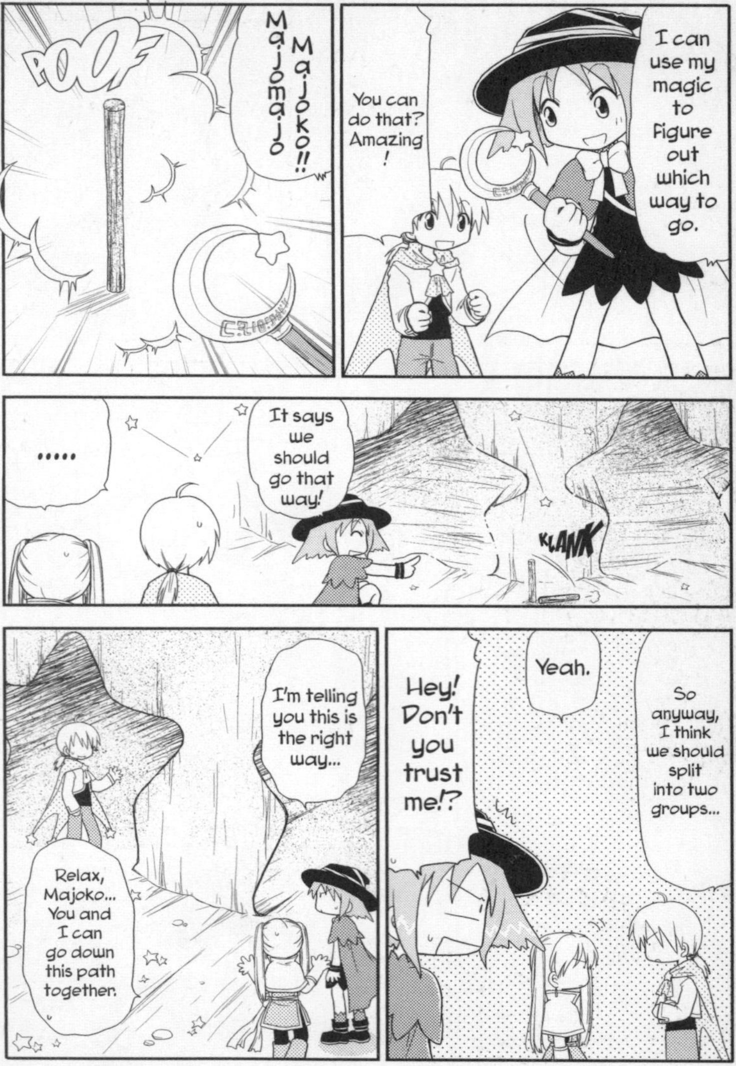
I can use my magic to figure out which way to go.
You can do that? Amazing!
Majomajo Majoko!!
POOF
It says we should go that way!
KLANK
.....
So anyway, I think we should split into two groups...
Yeah.
Hey! Don't you trust me!?
I'm telling you this is the right way...
Relax, Majoko... You and I can go down this path together.

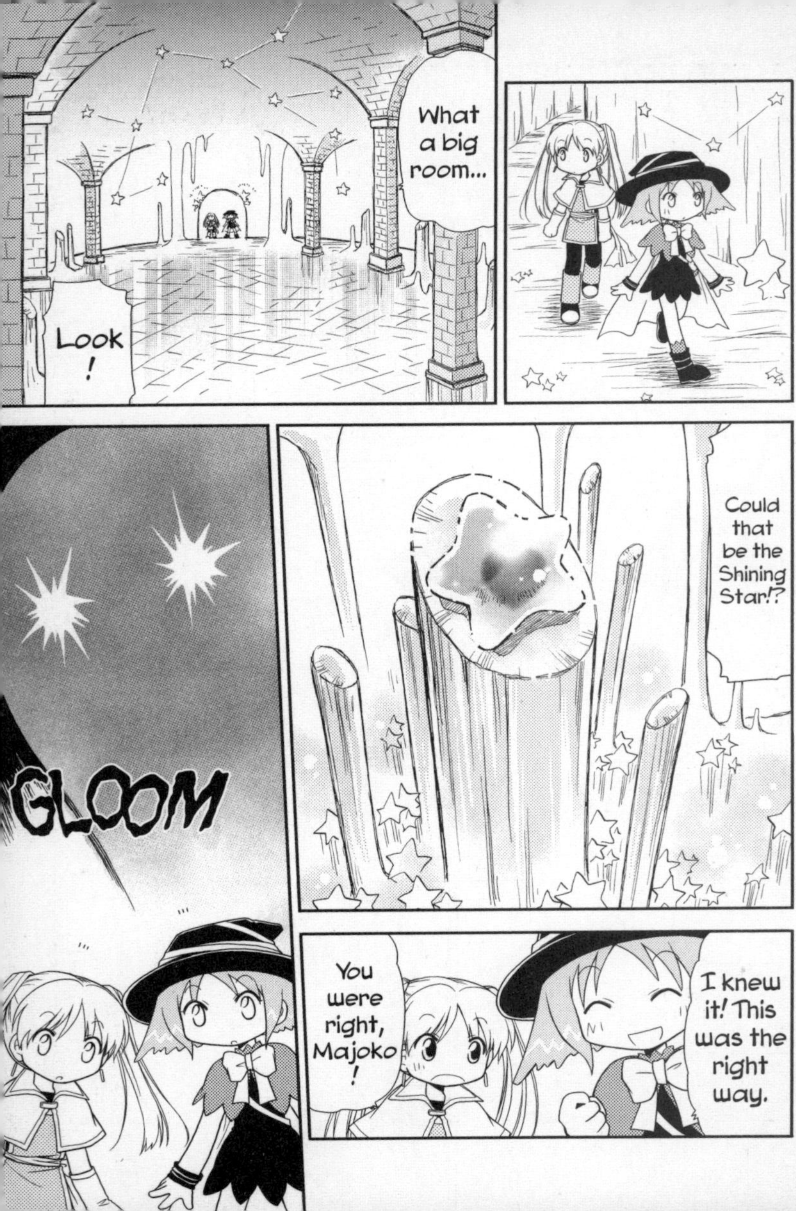
What a big room...
Look!
Could that be the Shining Star!?
I knew it! This was the right way.
You were right, Majoko!
GLOOM

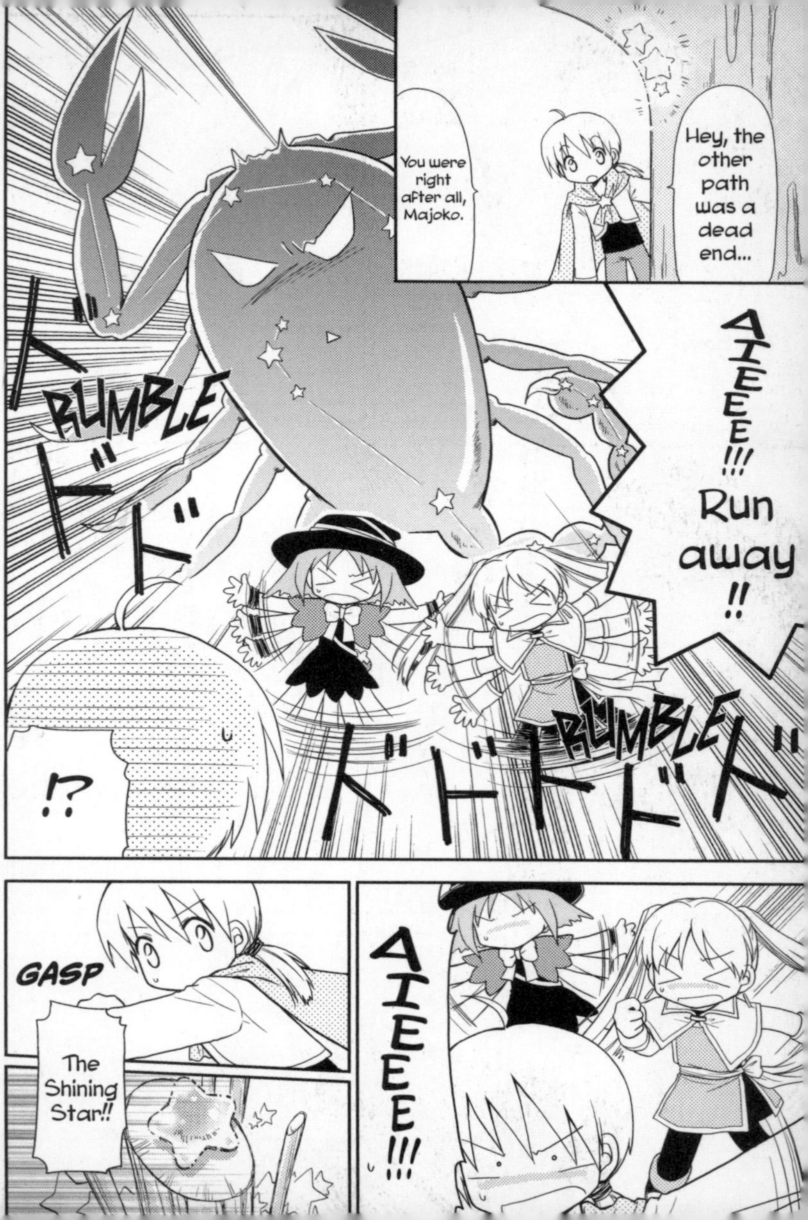
Hey, the other path was a dead end...
You were right after all, Majoko.
AIEEEE!!! Run away!!
RUMBLE
RUMBLE
!?
AIEEEE!!!
GASP
The Shining Star!!

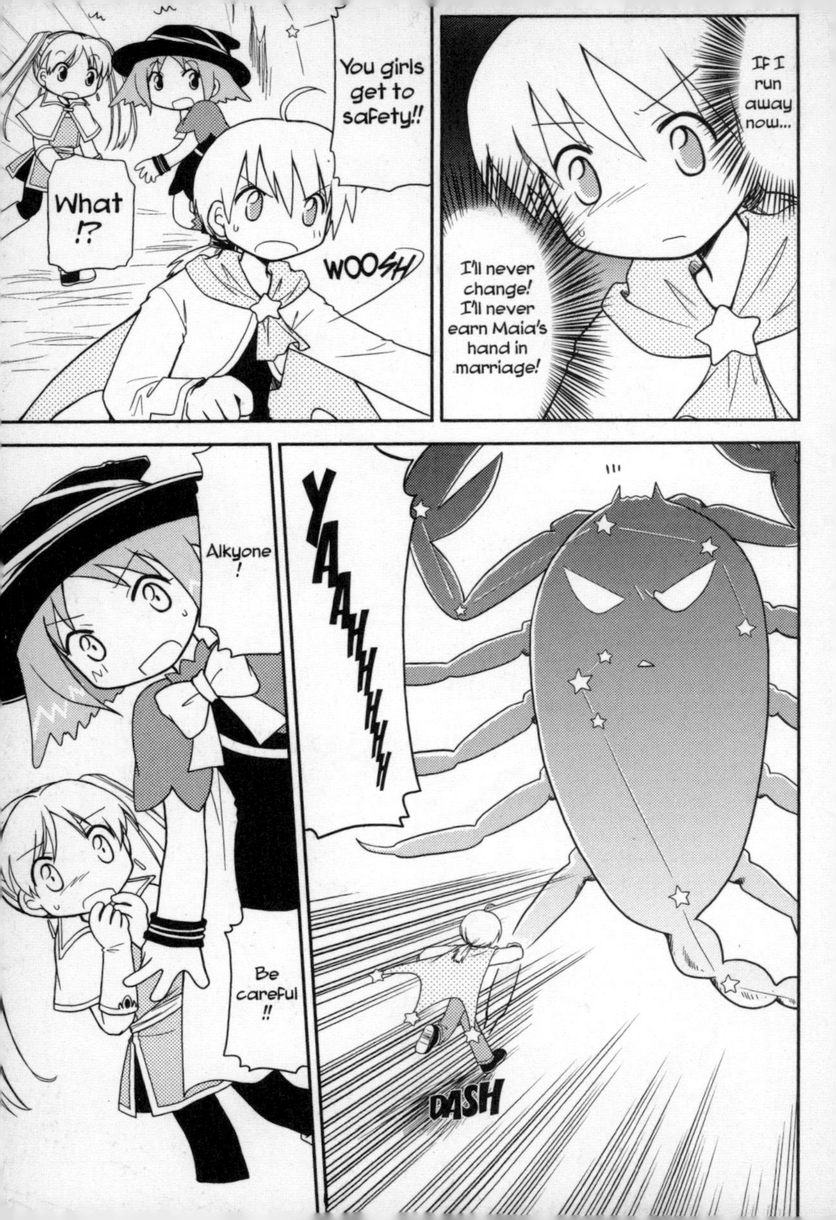
If I run away now...
I'll never change! I'll never earn Maia's hand in marriage!
You girls get to safety!!
What!?
WOOSH
YAAHHHHHHH
!!!
DASH
Alkyone!
Be careful!!

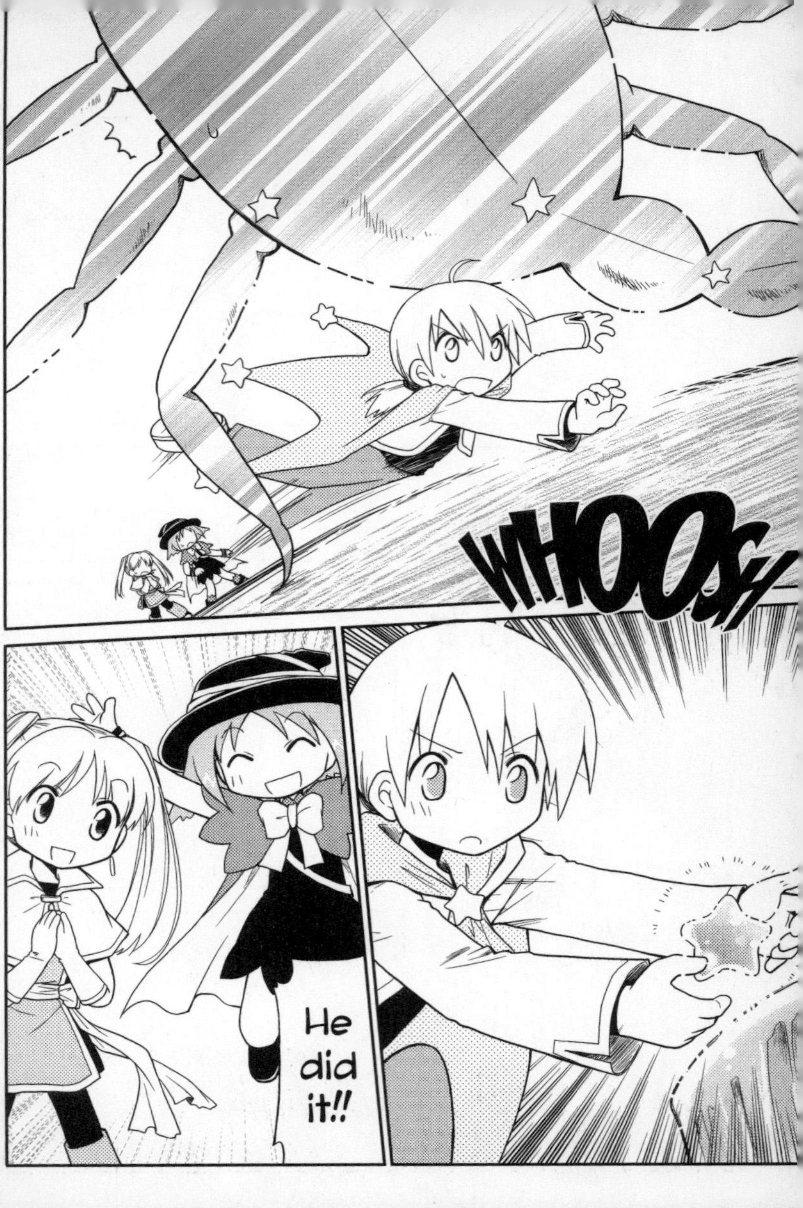
WHOOSH
He did it!!

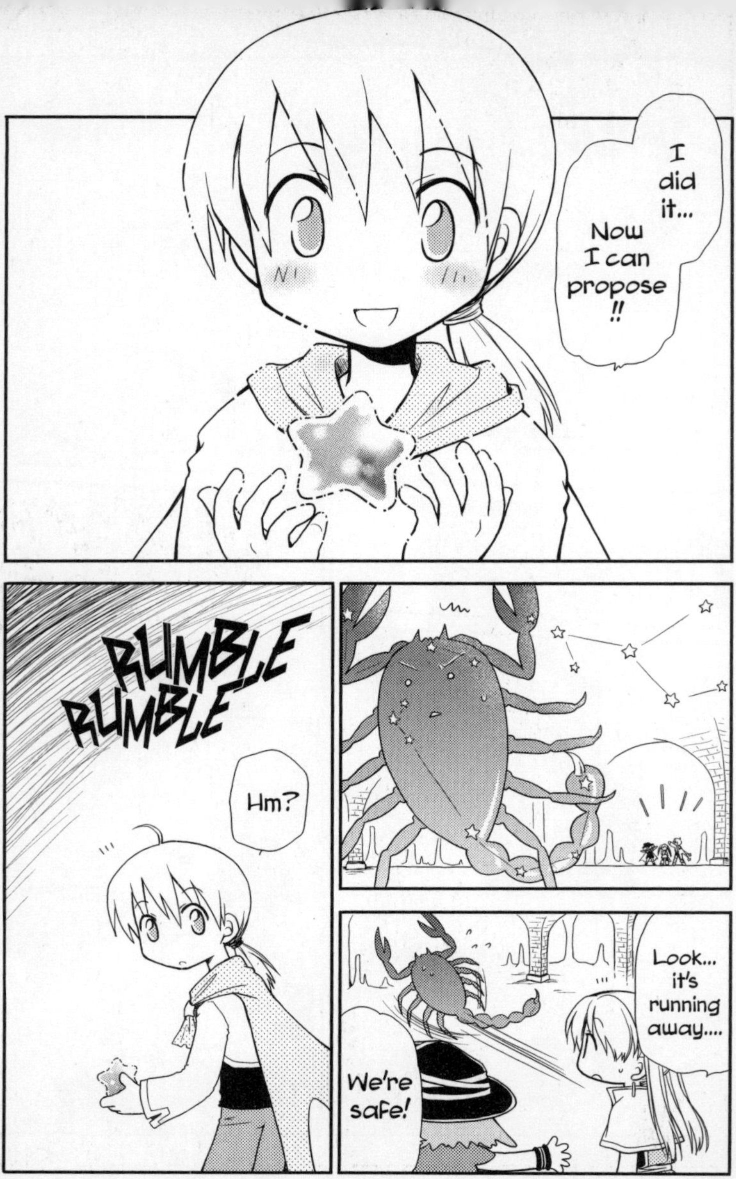
I did it... Now I can propose!!
Look... it's running away....
We're safe!
RUMBLE RUMBLE
Hm?

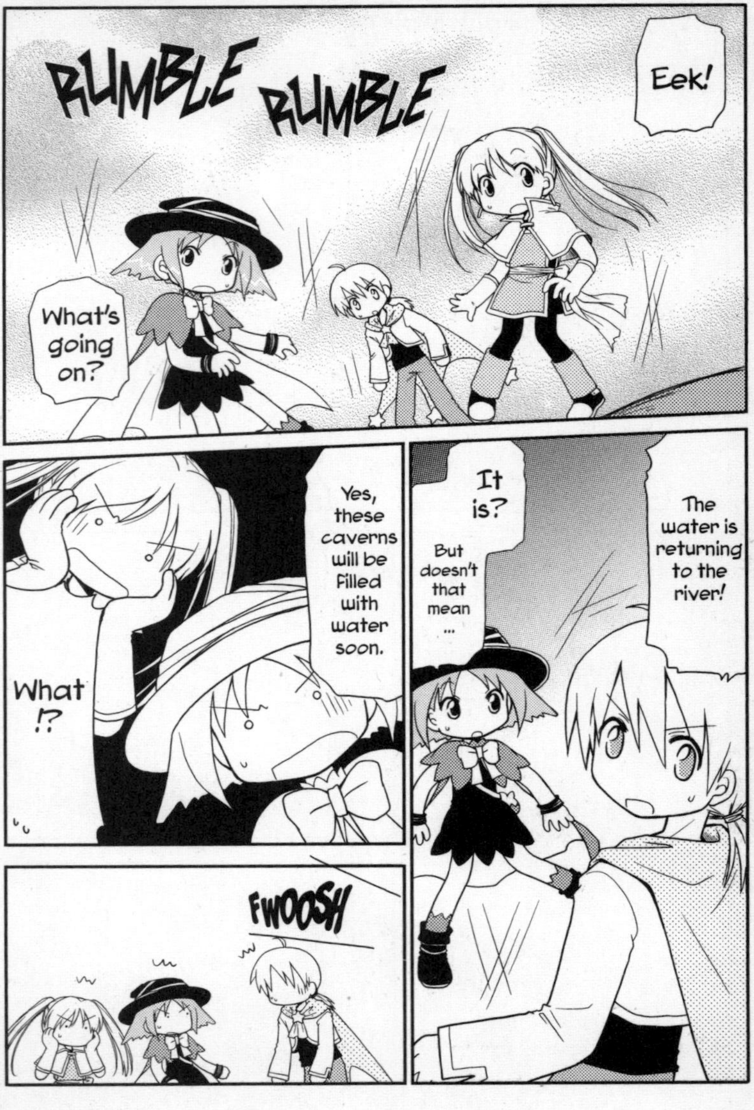
Eek!
RUMBLE RUMBLE
What's going on?
The water is returning to the river!
It is?
But doesn't that mean ...
Yes, these caverns will be filled with water soon.
What !?
FWOOSH

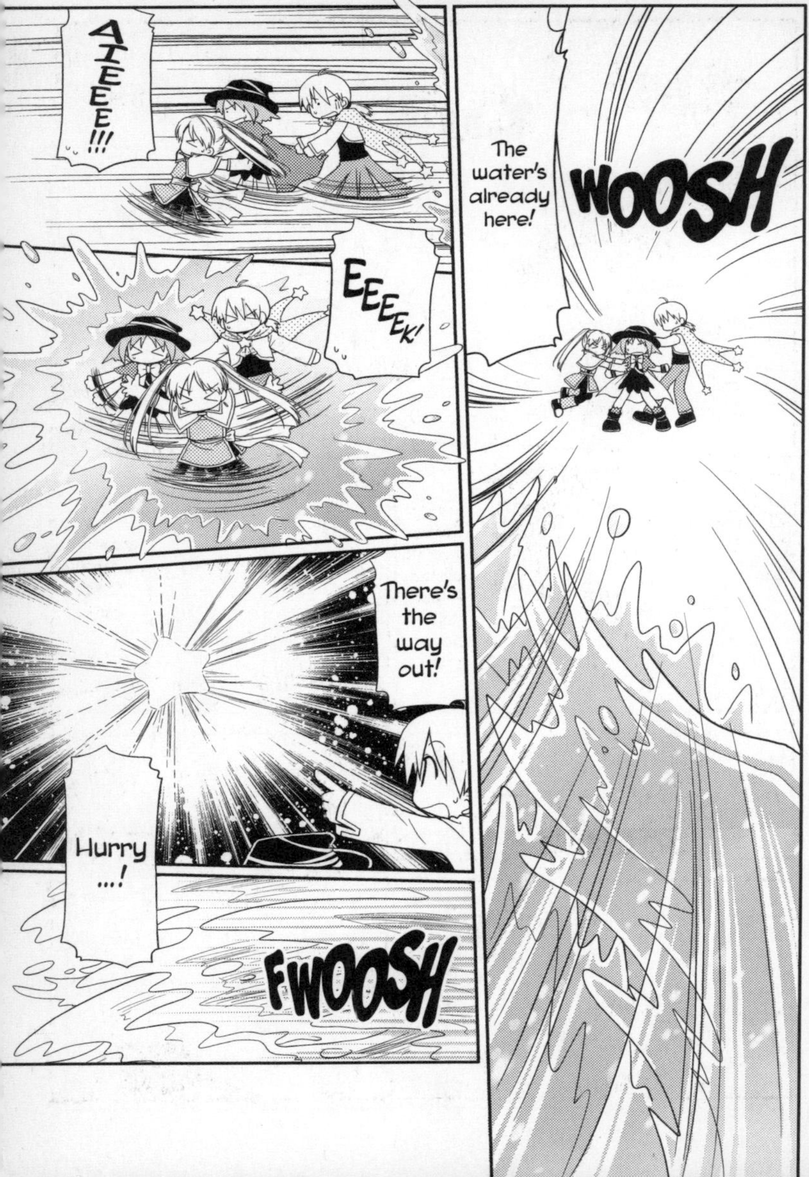
The water's already here!
WOOSH
AIEEE!!!
EEEEK!
There's the way out!
Hurry ...!
FWOOSH

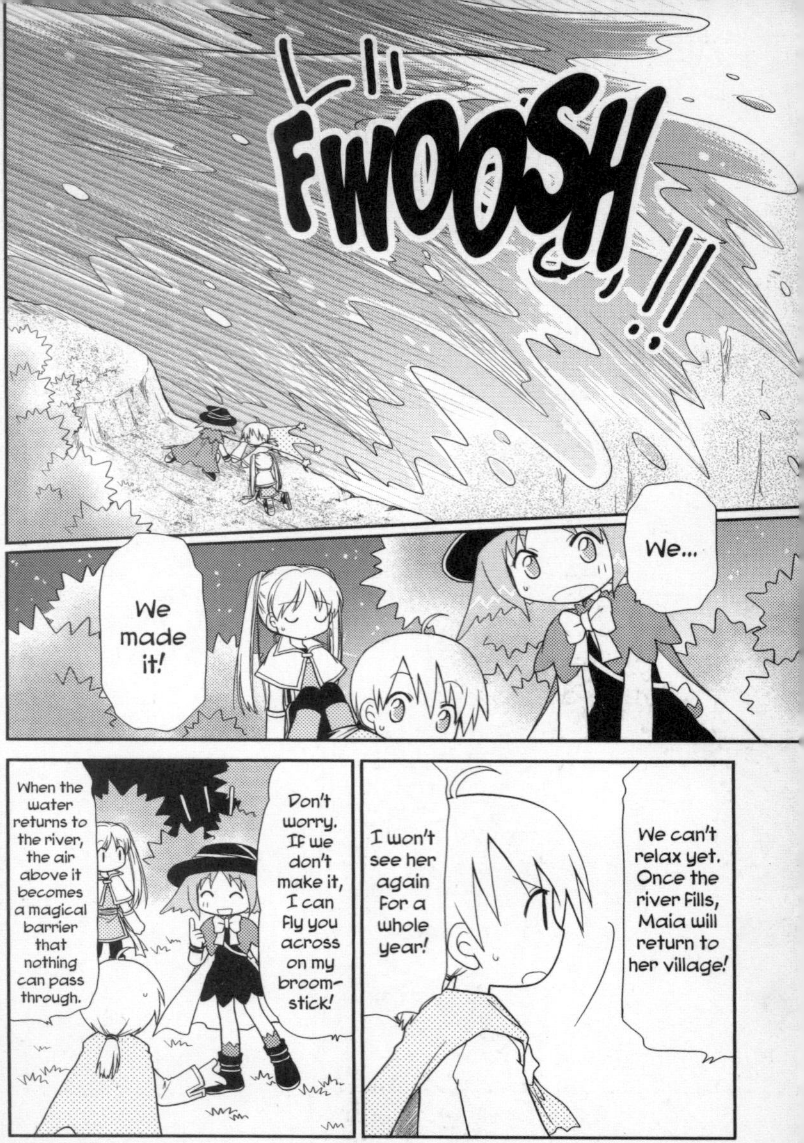
FWOOSH!!
We...
We made it!
We can't relax yet. Once the river fills, Maia will return to her village!
I won't see her again for a whole year!
Don't worry. If we don't make it, I can fly you across on my broomstick!
When the water returns to the river, the air above it becomes a magical barrier that nothing can pass through.

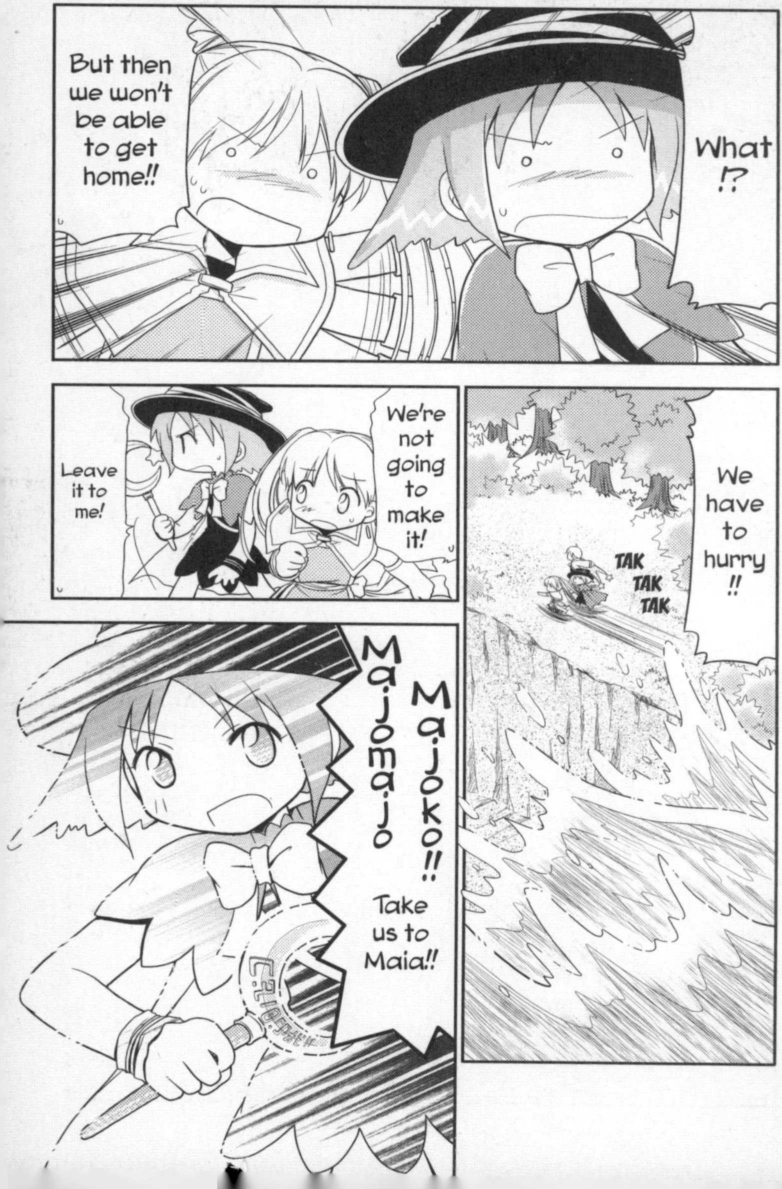
What!?
But then we won't be able to get home!!
We have to hurry!!
TAK TAK TAK
We're not going to make it!
Leave it to me!
Majomajo
Majoko!!
Take us to Maia!!

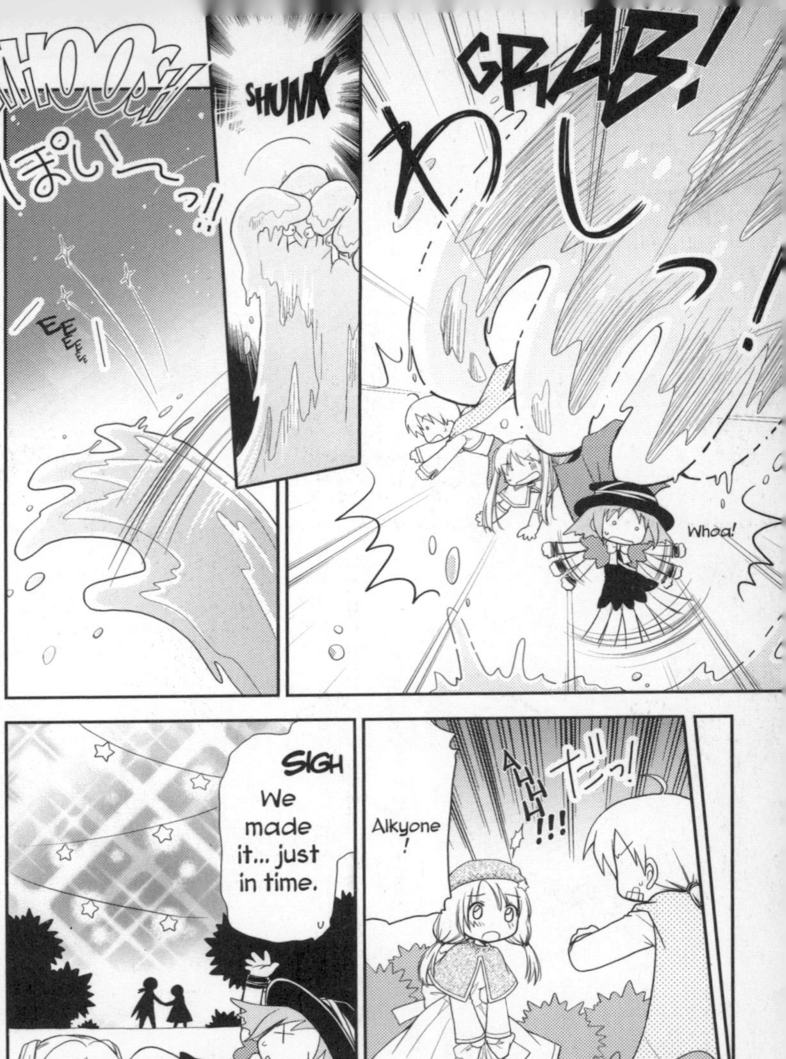
GRAB!
わしっ!
Whoa!
SHUNK
WHOOSH!!
ぽしーっ!!
EEEEE
AHHH!!!
だっ!
Alkyone!
SIGH
We made it... just in time.

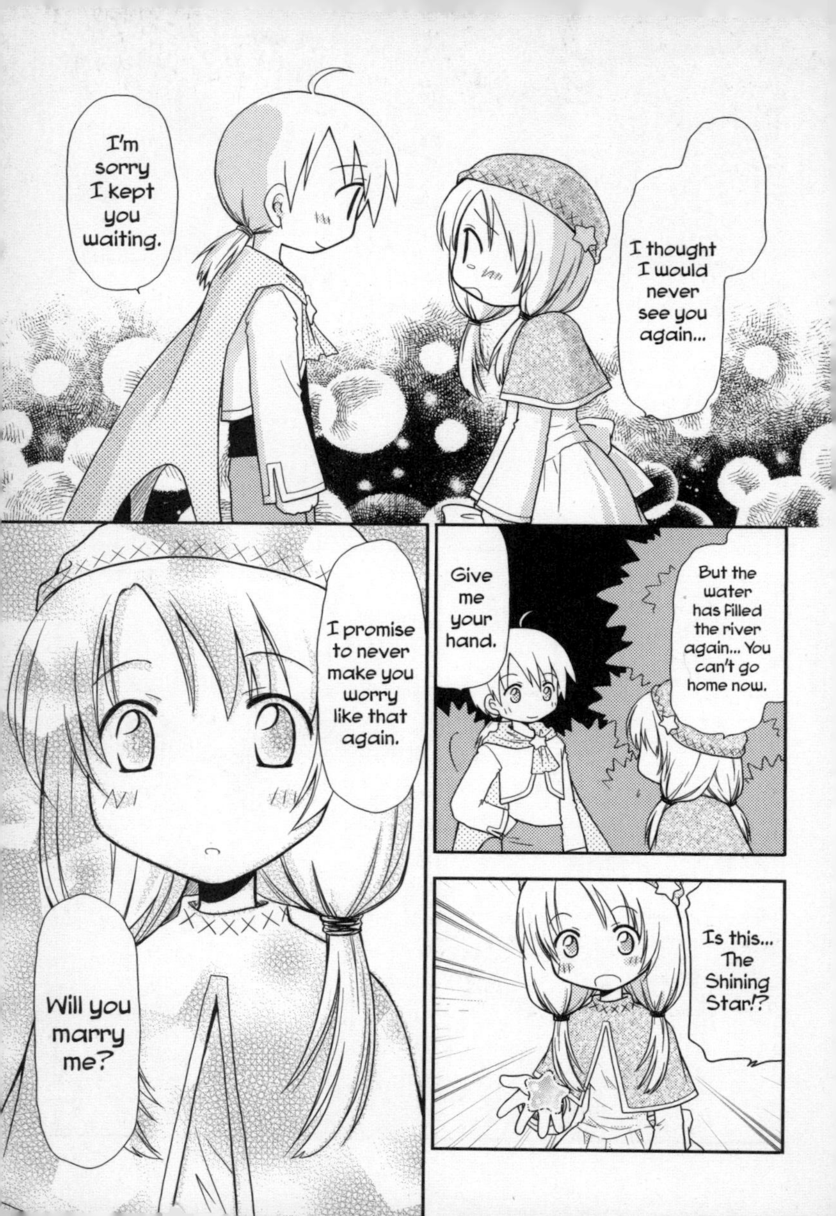
I thought I would never see you again...
I'm sorry I kept you waiting.
But the water has filled the river again... You can't go home now.
Give me your hand.
Is this... The Shining Star!?
I promise to never make you worry like that again.
Will you marry me?

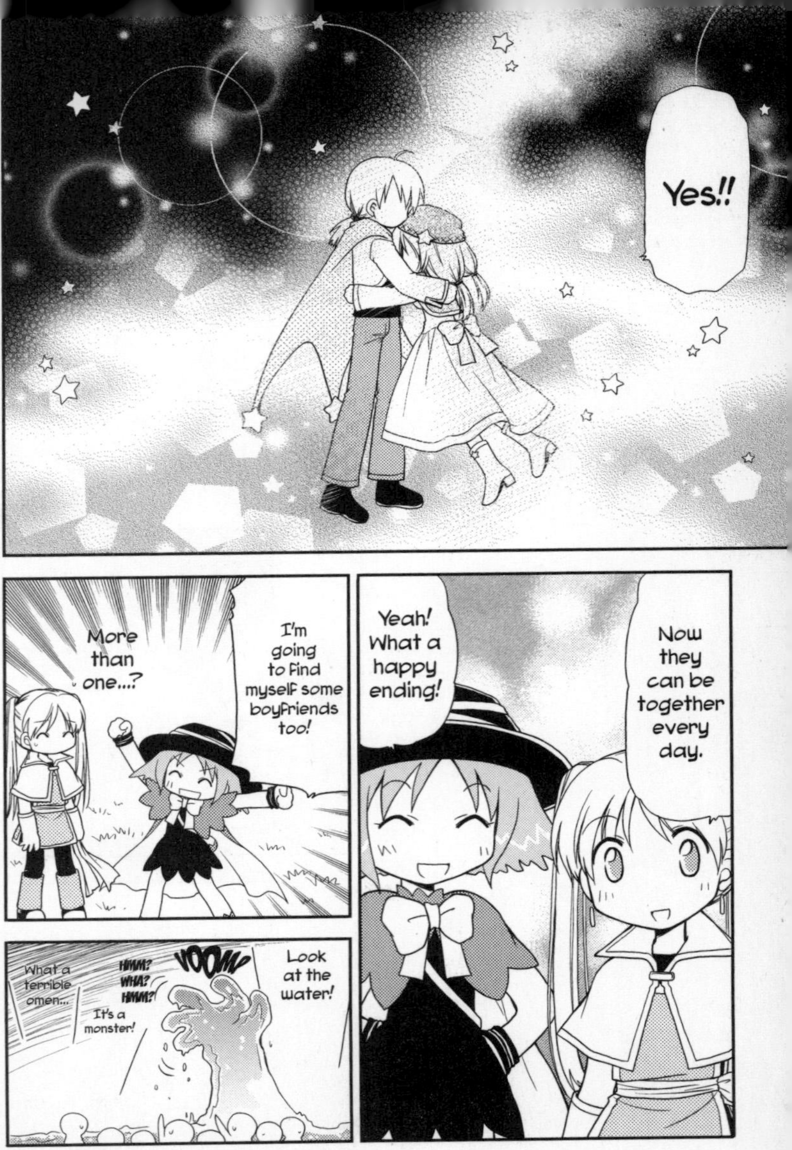

Yes!!
Now they can be together every day.
Yeah! What a happy ending!
I'm going to find myself some boyfriends too!
More than one...?
Look at the water!
VOOM
HMM? WHA? HMM?
It's a monster!
What a terrible omen...

Chapter 31 A Big Fuss Over a Special Mushroom!?

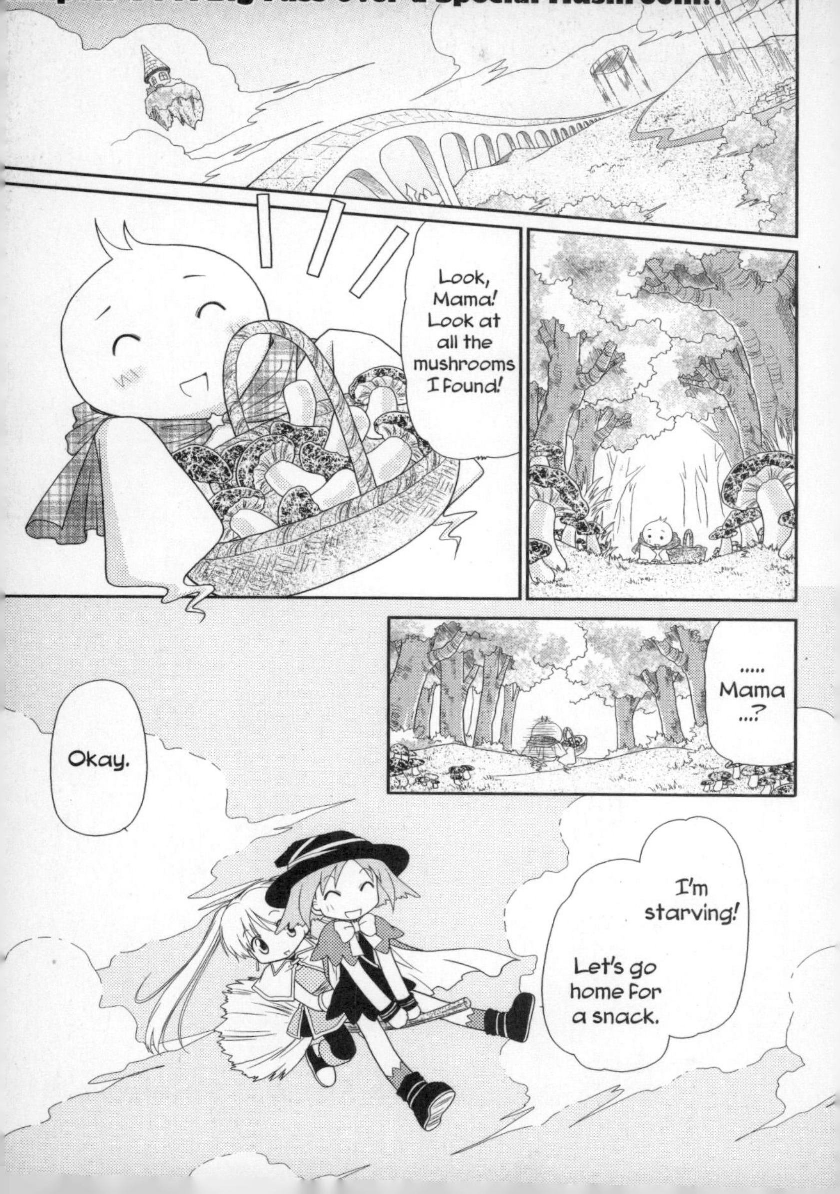
Look, Mama! Look at all the mushrooms I found!
..... Mama ...?
I'm starving!
Let's go home for a snack.
Okay.

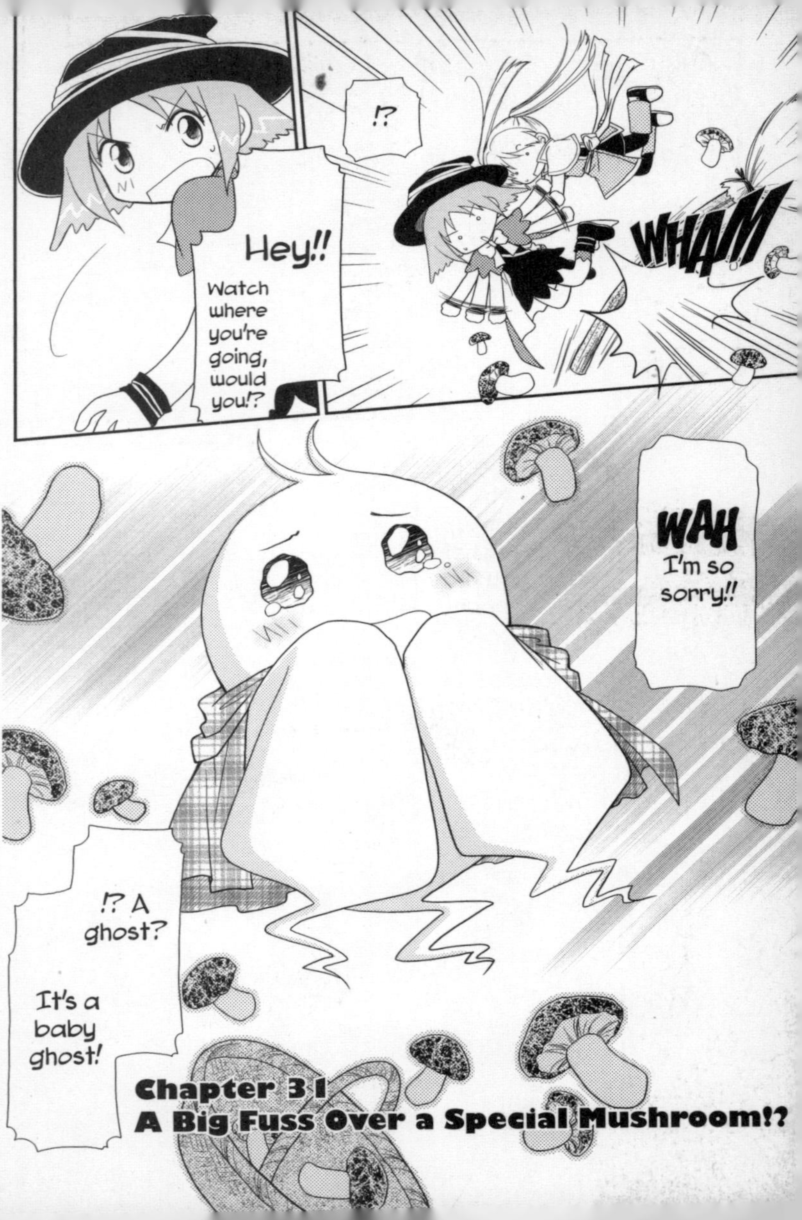
!?
WHAM
Hey!! Watch where you're going, would you!?
WAH I'm so sorry!!
!? A ghost?
It's a baby ghost!
Chapter 31
A Big Fuss Over a Special Mushroom!?

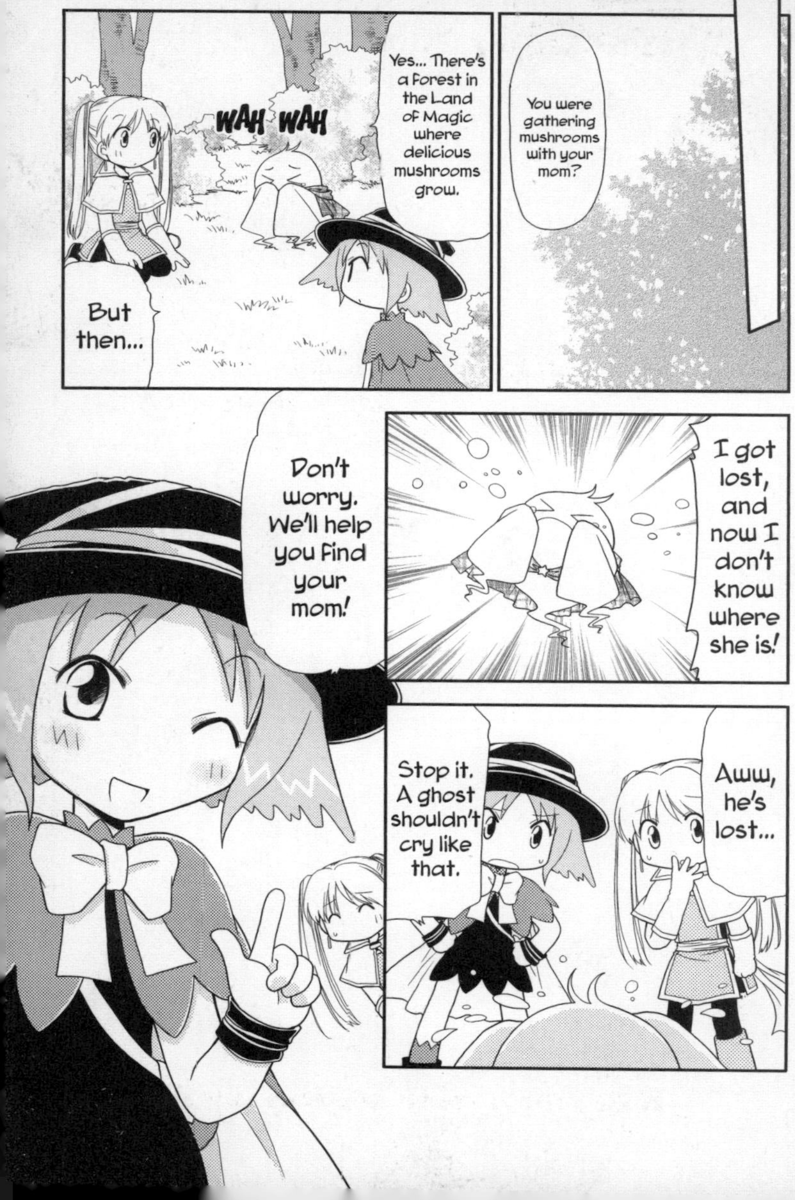
You were gathering mushrooms with your mom?
Yes... There's a forest in the Land of Magic where delicious mushrooms grow.
WAH WAH
But then...
I got lost, and now I don't know where she is!
Aww, he's lost...
Stop it. A ghost shouldn't cry like that.
Don't worry. We'll help you find your mom!

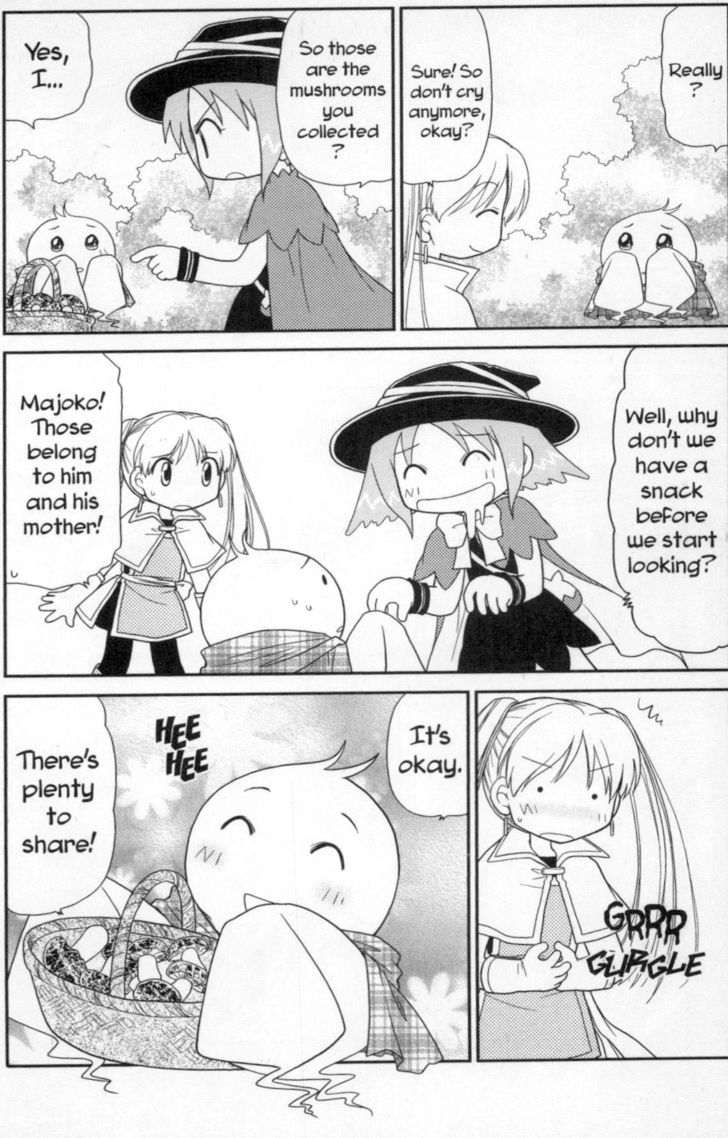
Really?
Sure! So don't cry anymore, okay?
So those are the mushrooms you collected?
Yes, I...
Well, why don't we have a snack before we start looking?
Majoko! Those belong to him and his mother!
GRRR
GURGLE
It's okay.
HEE HEE
There's plenty to share!

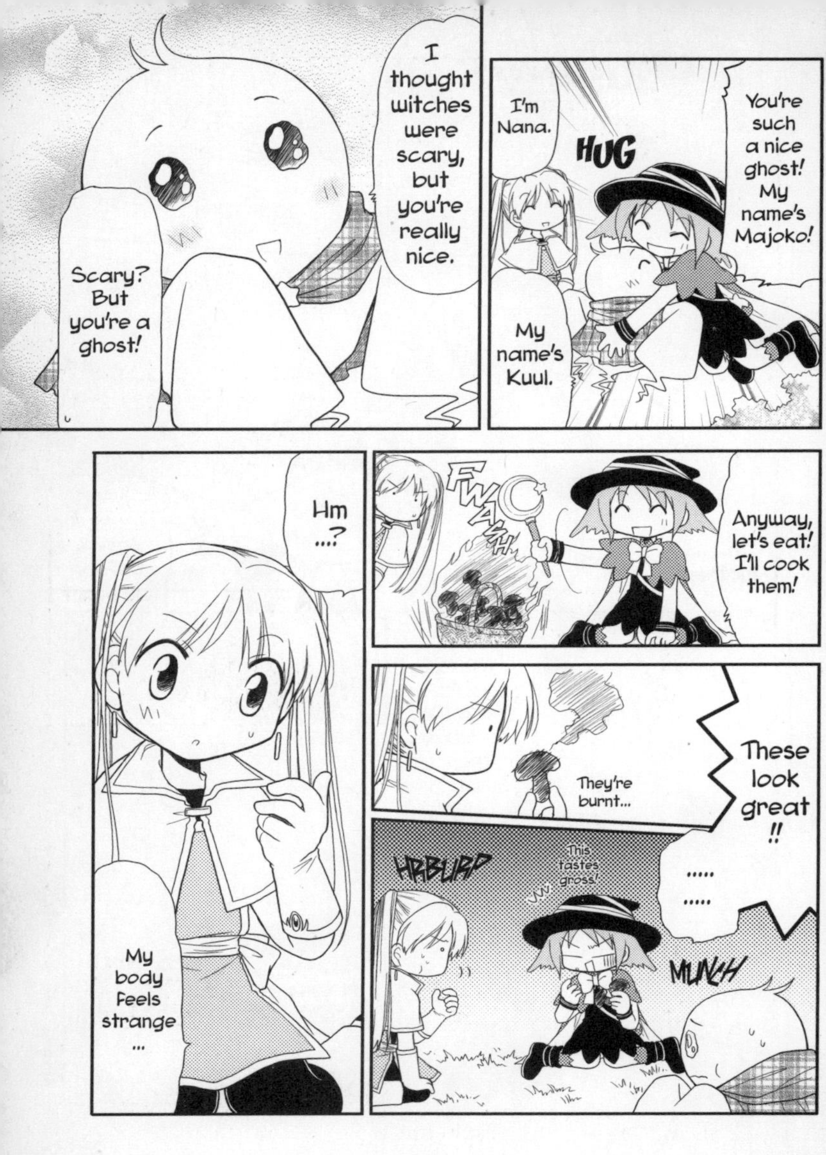
You're such a nice ghost! My name's Majoko!
HUG
I'm Nana.
My name's Kuul.
I thought witches were scary, but you're really nice.
Scary? But you're a ghost!
Anyway, let's eat! I'll cook them!
FWASH
These look great!!
They're burnt...
.....
.....
This tastes gross!
HRBURP
MUNCH
Hm ...?
My body feels strange ...

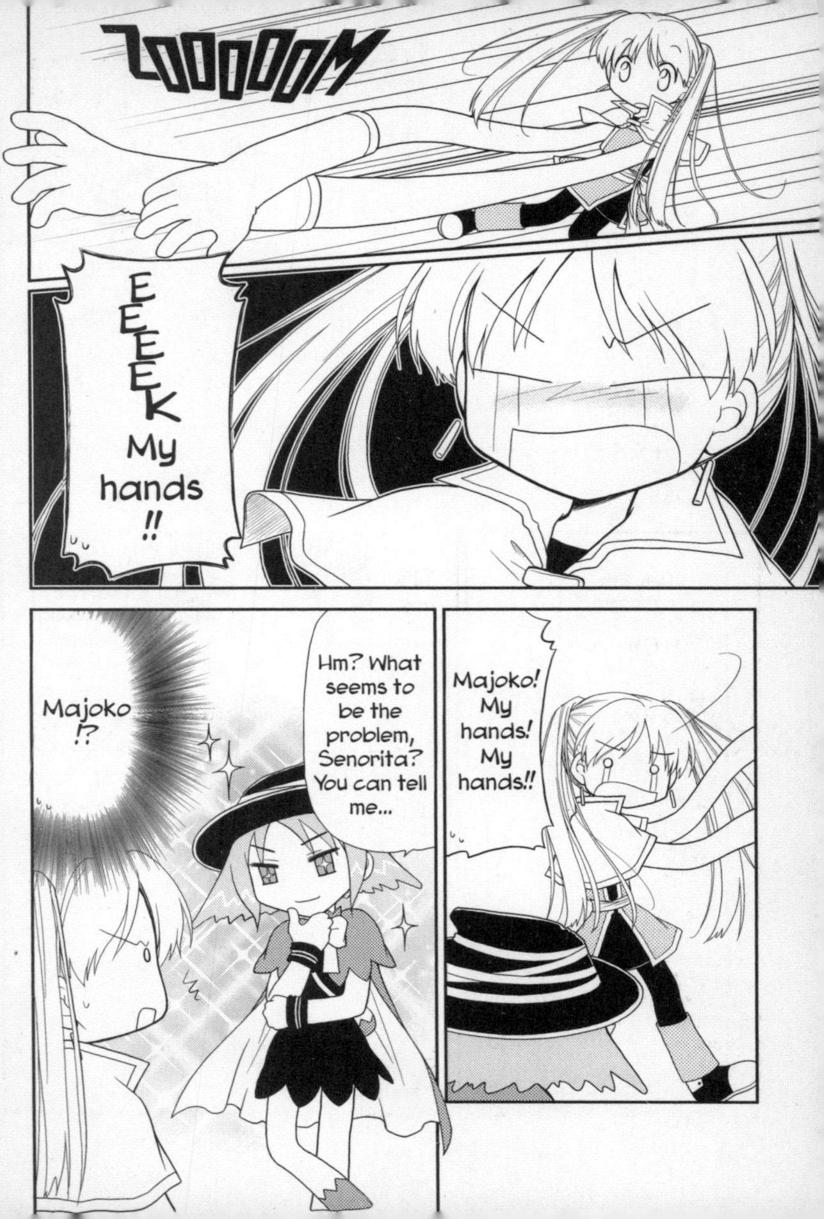
ZOOOOOOM
EEEEK My hands!!
Majoko! My hands! My hands!!
Hm? What seems to be the problem, Senorita? You can tell me...
Majoko!?

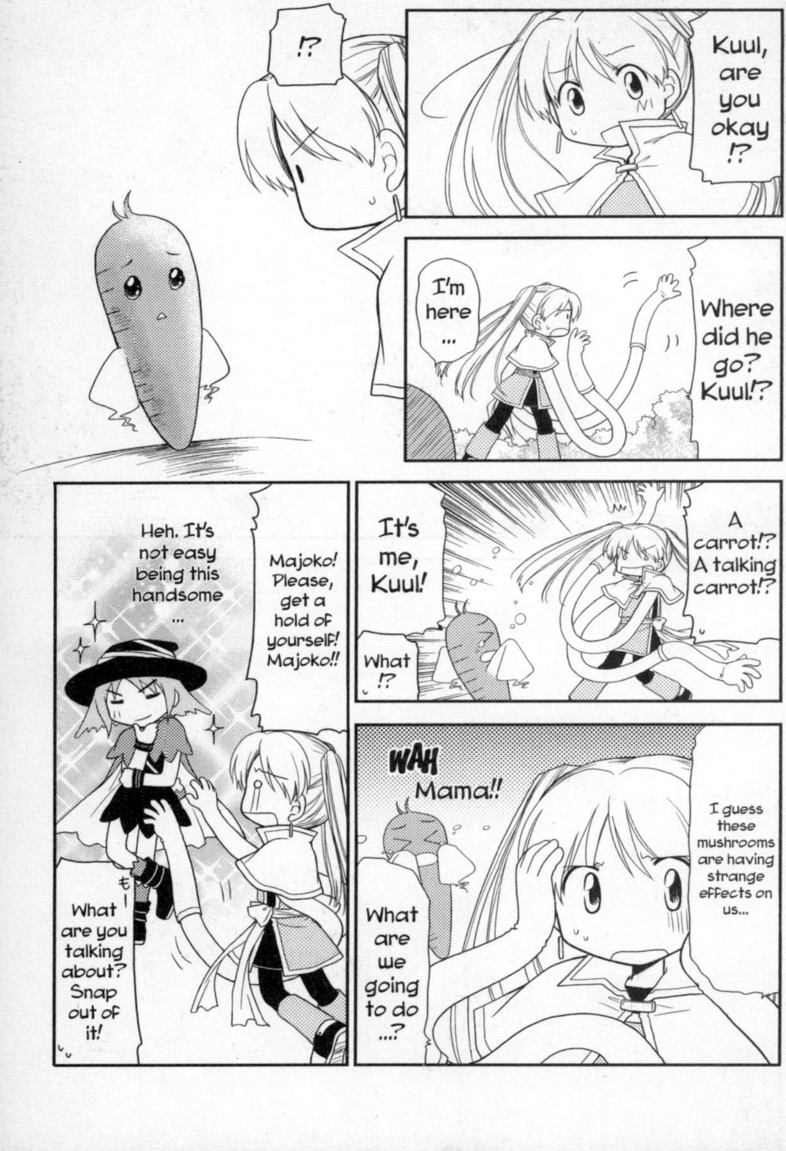
Kuul, are you okay!?
!?
Where did he go? Kuul!?
I'm here ...
A carrot!? A talking carrot!?
It's me, Kuul!
What !?
I guess these mushrooms are having strange effects on us...
WAH
Mama!!
What are we going to do ...?
Majoko! Please, get a hold of yourself! Majoko!!
Heh. It's not easy being this handsome ...
What are you talking about? Snap out of it!

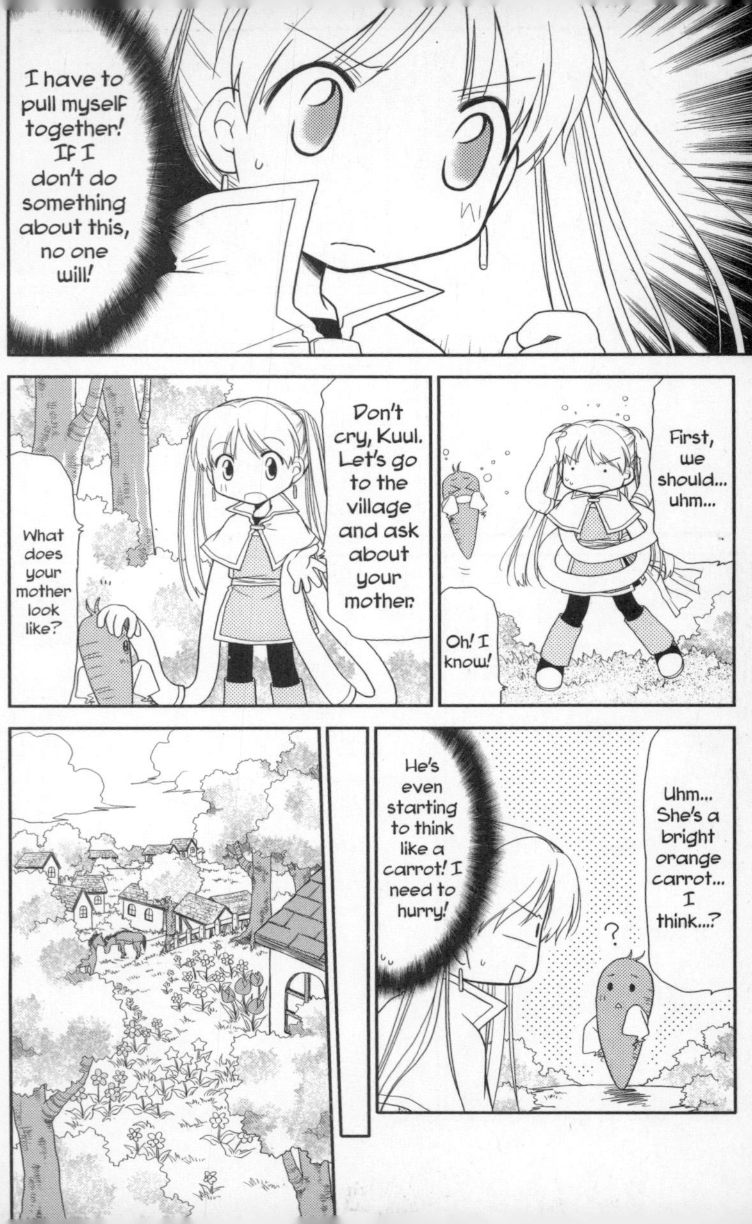
I have to pull myself together! If I don't do something about this, no one will!
First, we should... uhm...
Oh! I know!
Don't cry, Kuul. Let's go to the village and ask about your mother.
What does your mother look like?
...
Uhm... She's a bright orange carrot... I think...?
?
He's even starting to think like a carrot! I need to hurry!

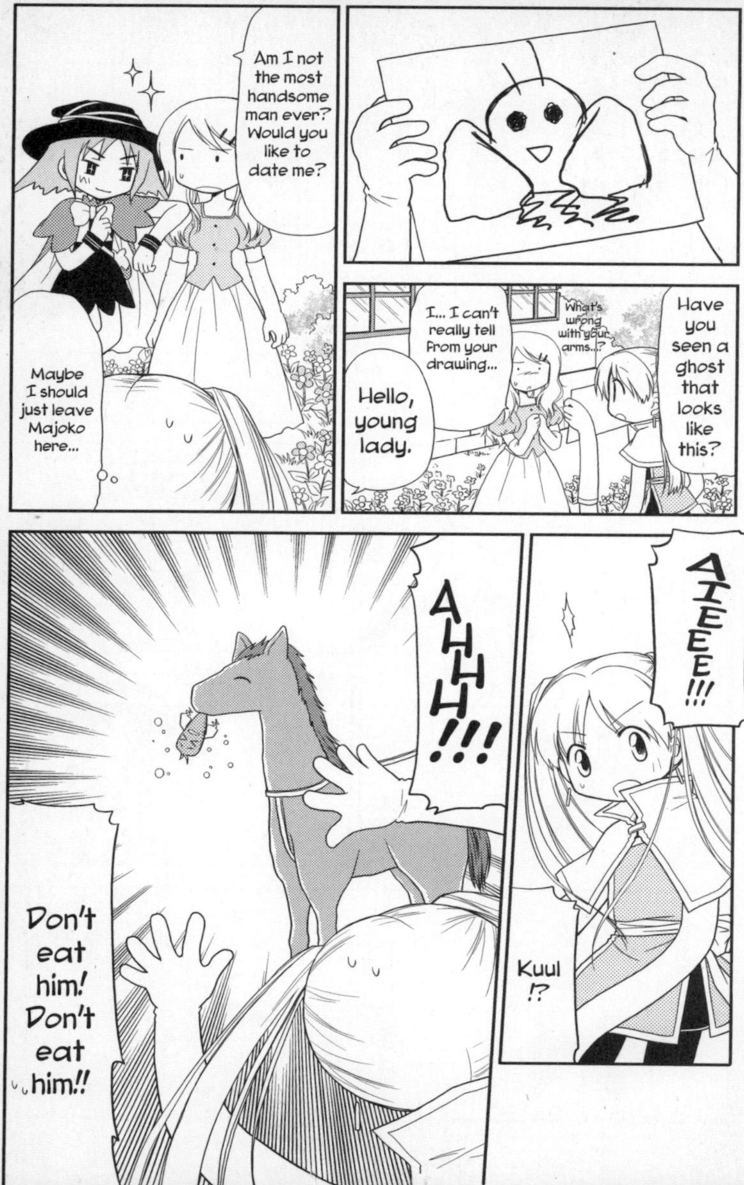

Have you seen a ghost that looks like this?
What's wrong with your arms...?
I... I can't really tell from your drawing...
Hello, young lady.
Am I not the most handsome man ever? Would you like to date me?
Maybe I should just leave Majoko here...
AIEEE!!!
Kuul !?
AHHHH!!!
Don't eat him! Don't eat him!!

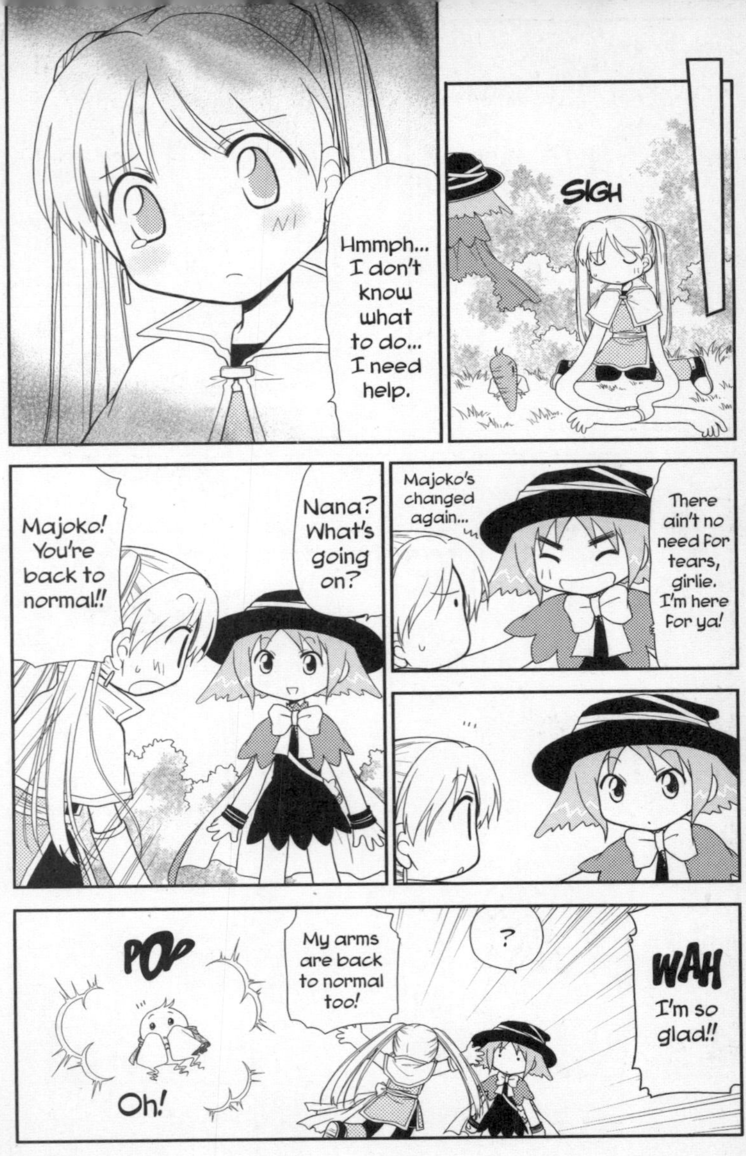
SIGH
Hmmph... I don't know what to do... I need help.
There ain't no need for tears, girlie. I'm here for ya!
Majoko's changed again...
Nana? What's going on?
Majoko! You're back to normal!!
WAH
I'm so glad!!
?
My arms are back to normal too!
POP
Oh!

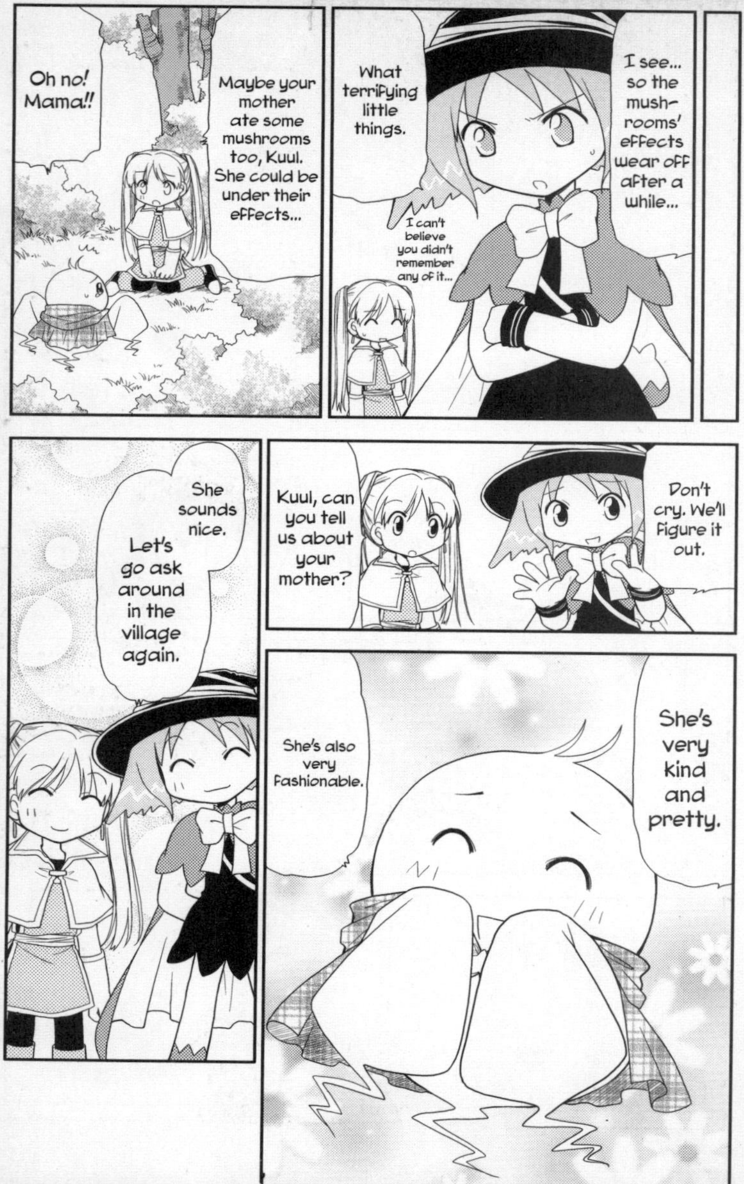
I see... so the mush-rooms' effects wear off after a while...
What terrifying little things.
I can't believe you didn't remember any of it...
Maybe your mother ate some mushrooms too, Kuul. She could be under their effects...
Oh no! Mama!!
Don't cry. We'll figure it out.
Kuul, can you tell us about your mother?
She's very kind and pretty.
She's also very fashionable.
She sounds nice.
Let's go ask around in the village again.

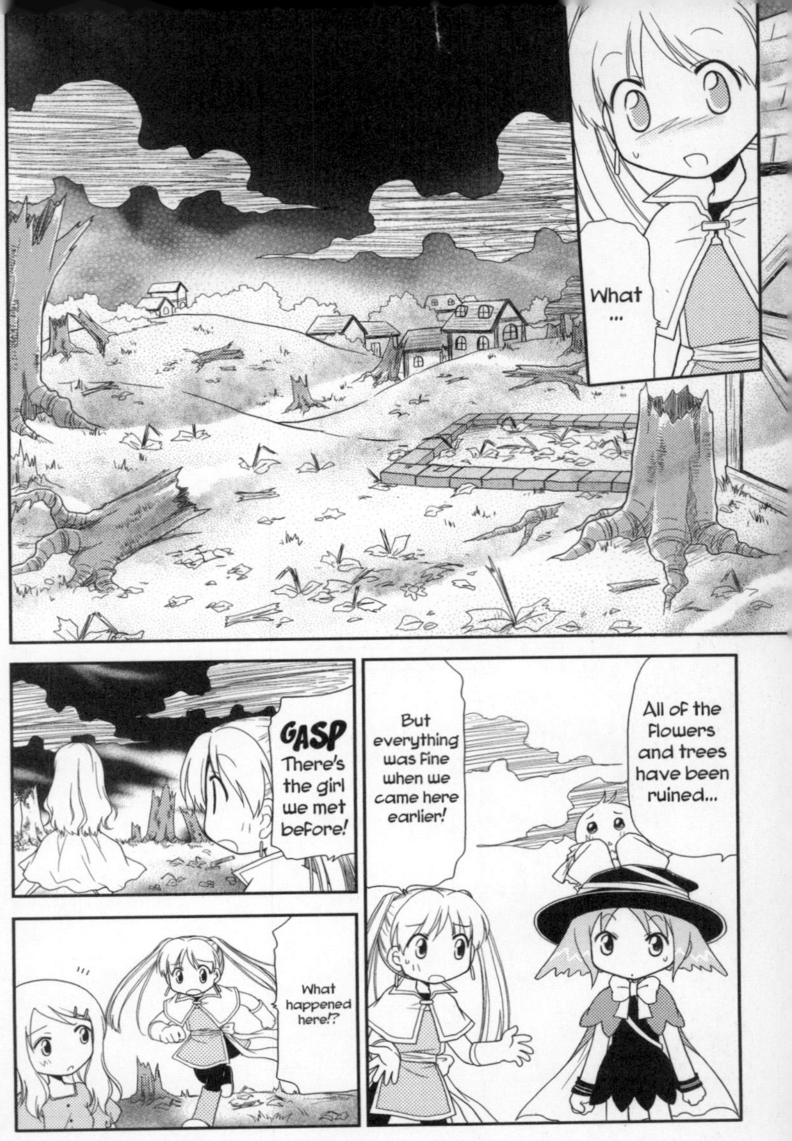
What ...
All of the flowers and trees have been ruined...
But everything was fine when we came here earlier!
GASP
There's the girl we met before!
What happened here!?

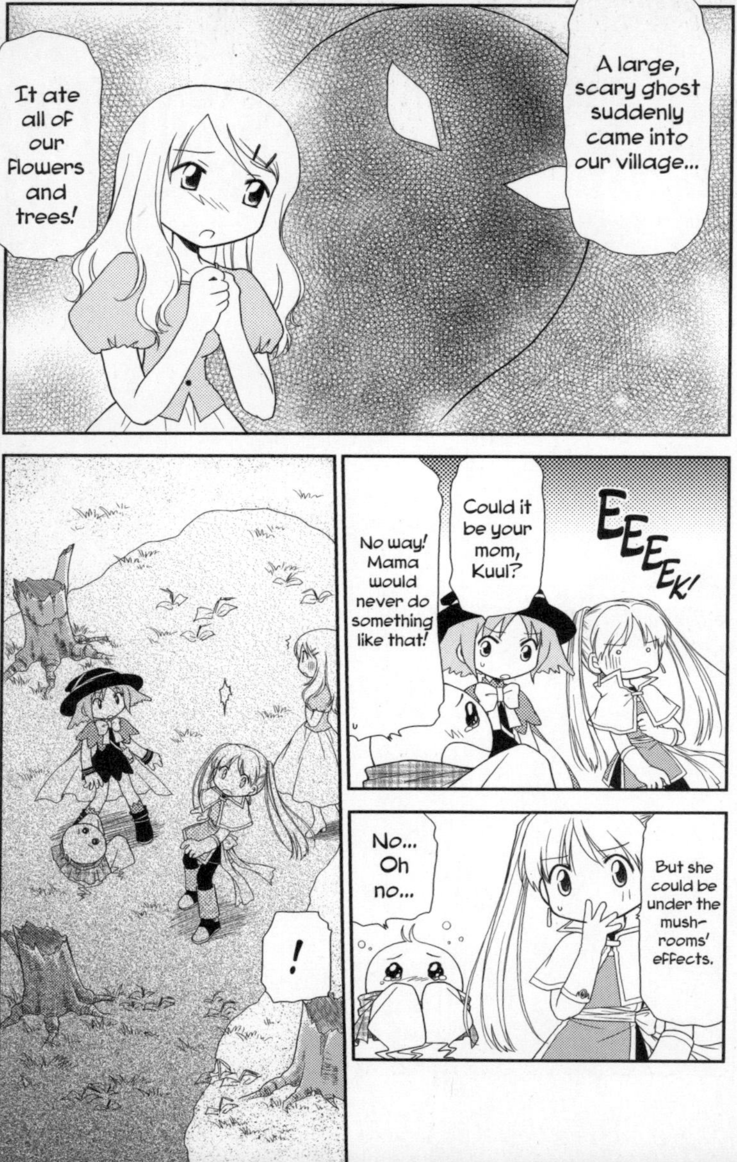
A large, scary ghost suddenly came into our village...
It ate all of our flowers and trees!
EEEEEK!
Could it be your mom, Kuul?
No way! Mama would never do something like that!
But she could be under the mush-rooms' effects.
No... Oh no...
!

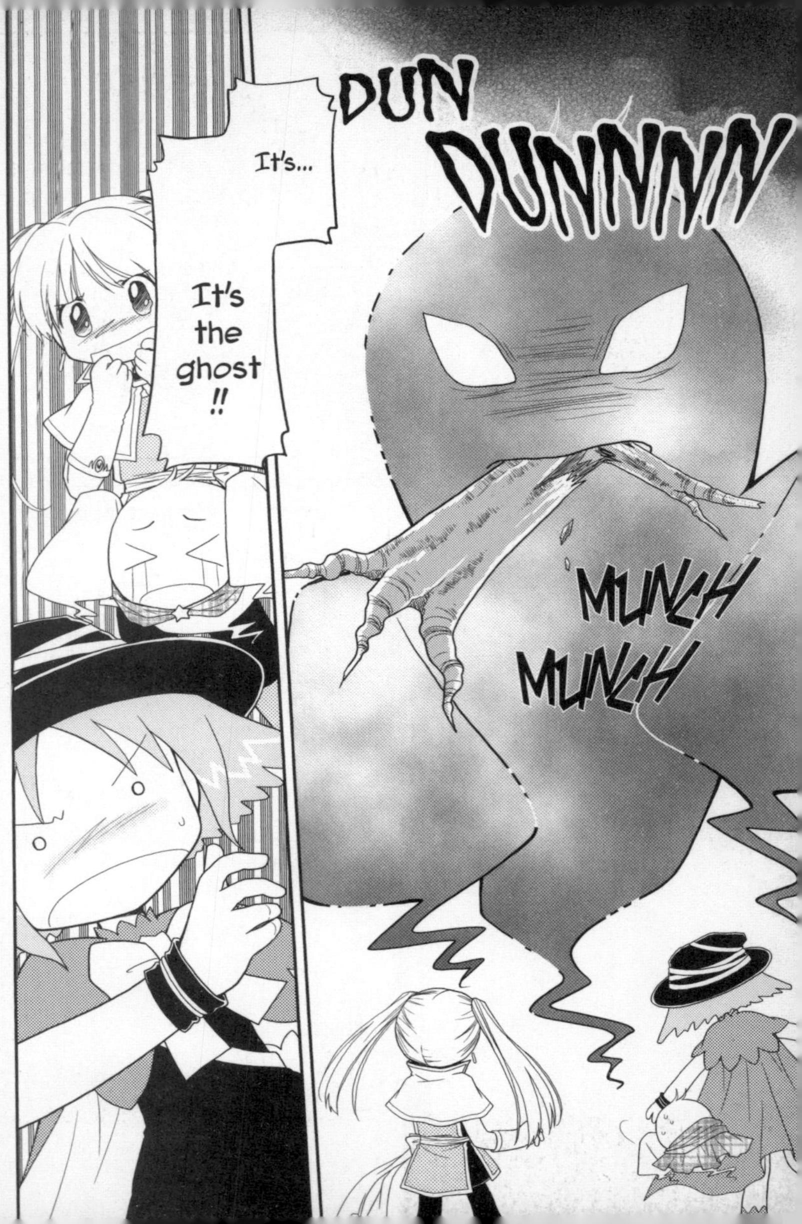
DUN DUNNNN
MUNCH MUNCH
It's...
It's the ghost !!

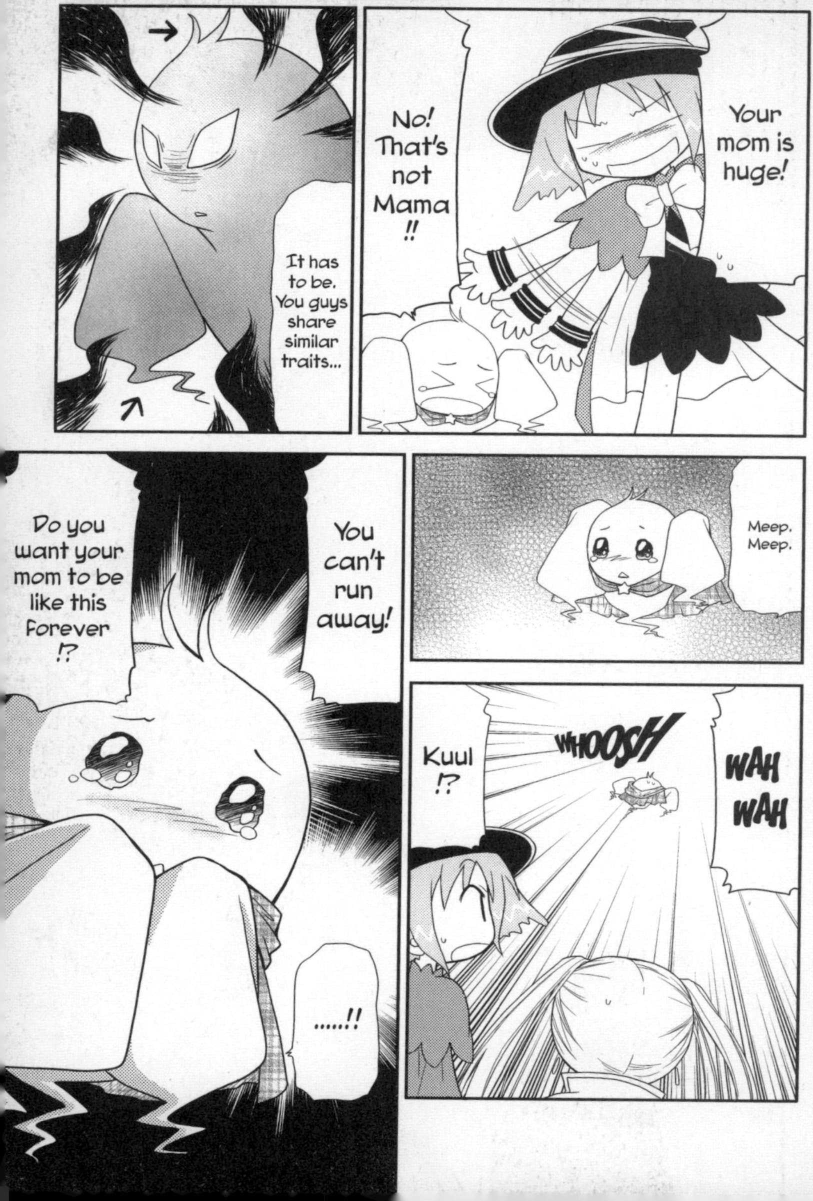
Your mom is huge!
No! That's not Mama !!
It has to be. You guys share similar traits...
Meep. Meep.
WAH WAH
WHOOSH
Kuul !?
You can't run away!
Do you want your mom to be like this forever !?
.....!!

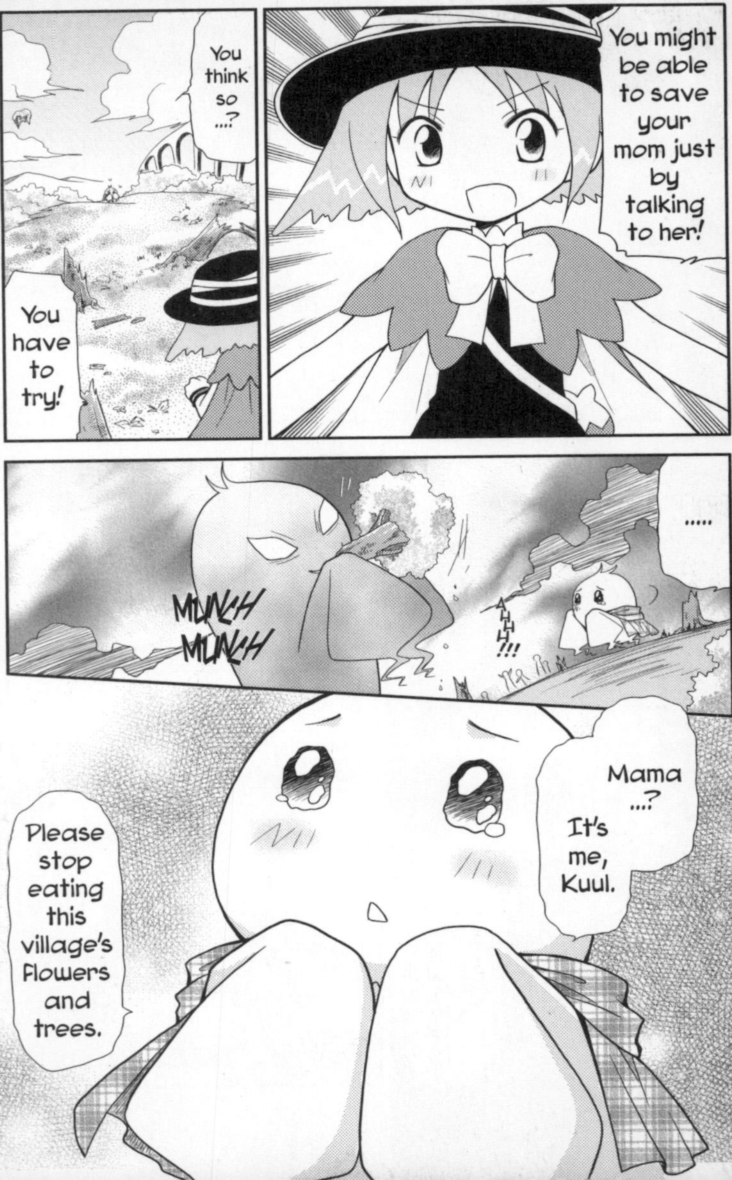
You might be able to save your mom just by talking to her!
You think so ...?
You have to try!
.....
AHHHH!!!
MUNCH MUNCH
Mama ...? It's me, Kuul.
Please stop eating this village's flowers and trees.

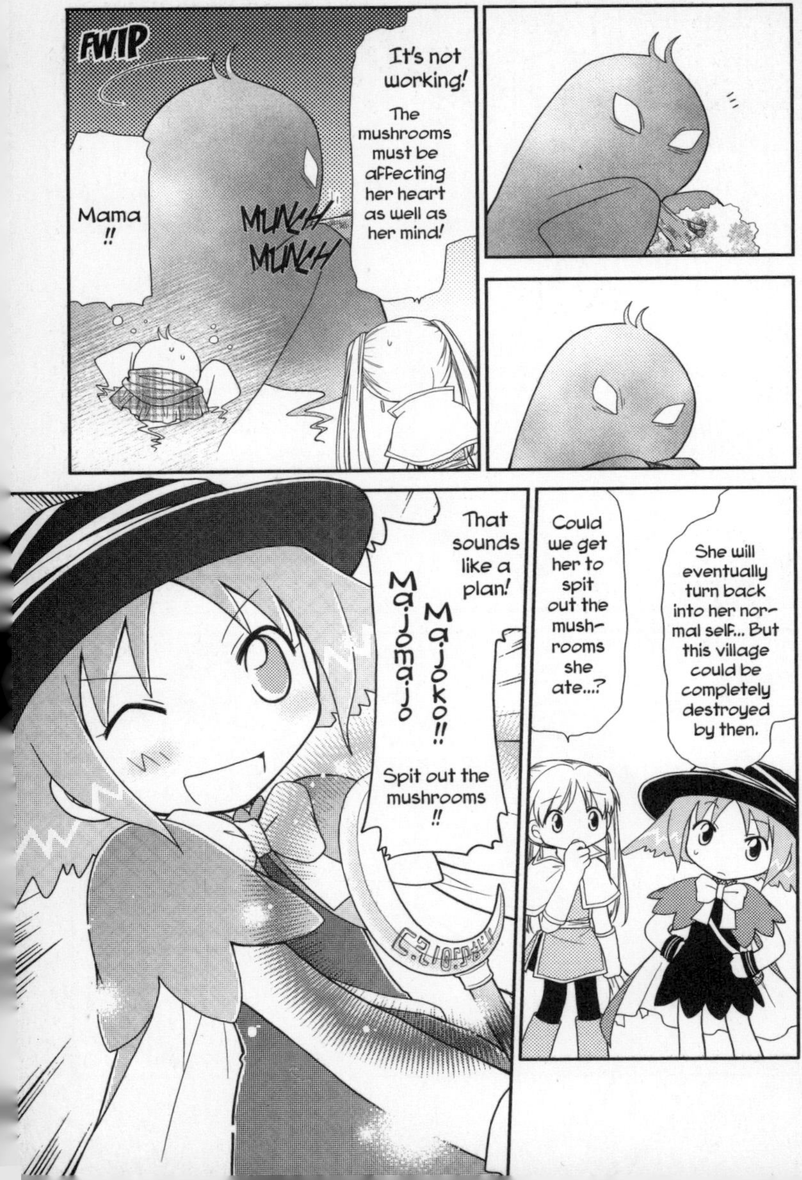
It's not working!
The mushrooms must be affecting her heart as well as her mind!
FWIP
MUNCH MUNCH
Mama!!
She will eventually turn back into her normal self... But this village could be completely destroyed by then.
Could we get her to spit out the mushrooms she ate...?
That sounds like a plan!
Majomajo Majoko!!
Spit out the mushrooms!!

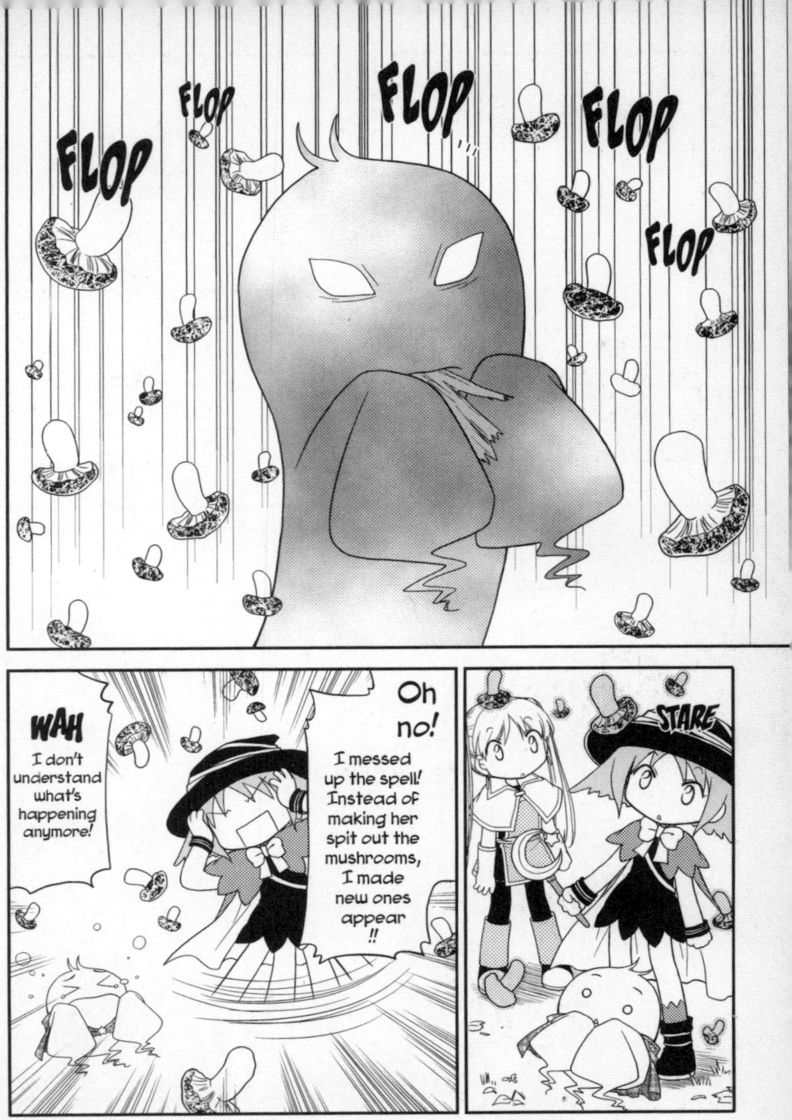
FLOP
FLOP
FLOP
FLOP
FLOP
STARE
Oh no!
I messed up the spell! Instead of making her spit out the mushrooms, I made new ones appear !!
WAH
I don't understand what's happening anymore!

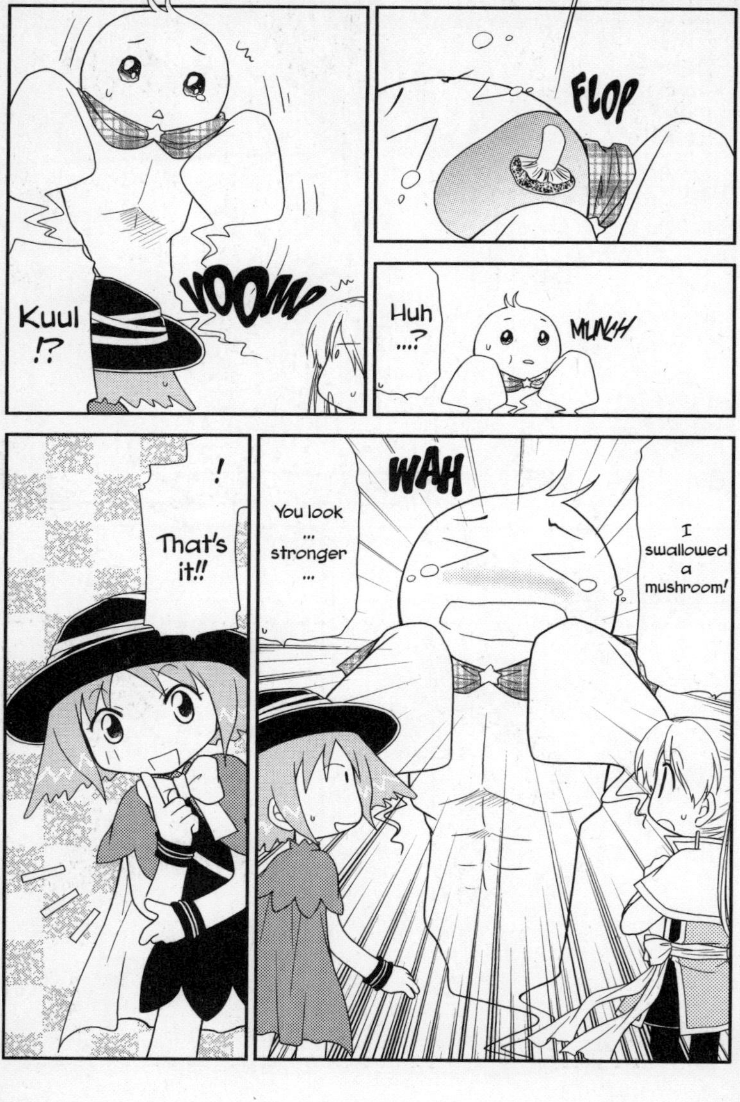
FLOP
Huh ...?
MUNCH
VOOMP
Kuul !?
WAH
I swallowed a mushroom!
You look ... stronger ...
!
That's it!!

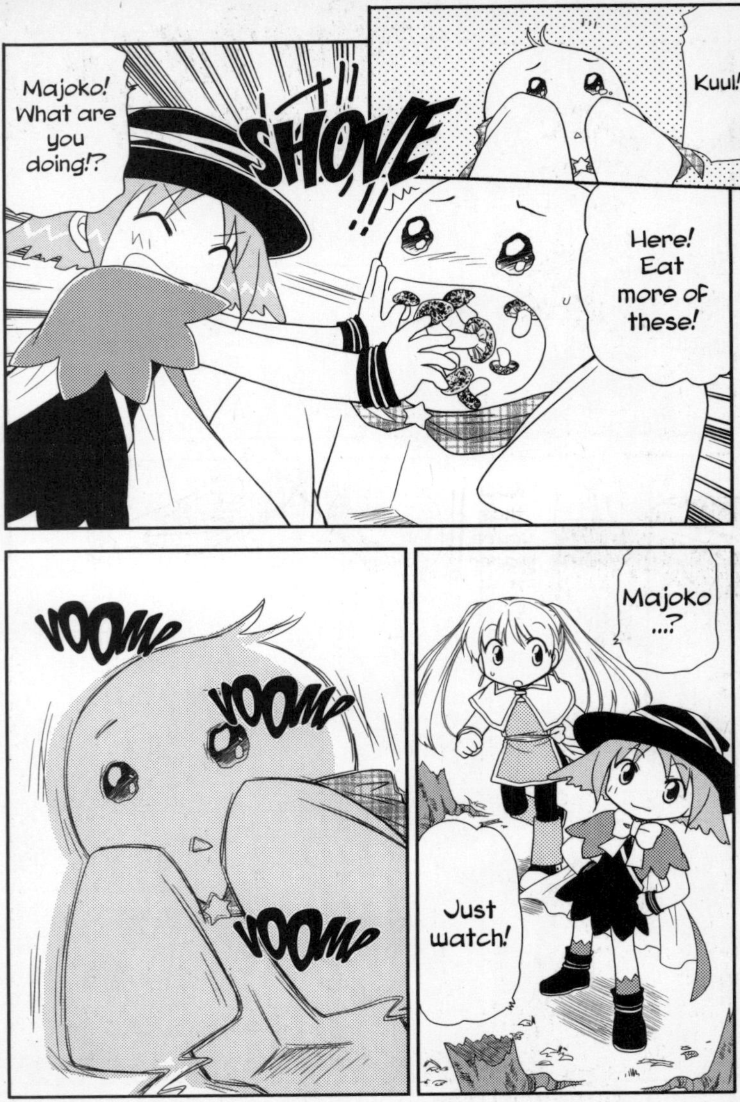
Kuul!
Here! Eat more of these!
SHOVE
Majoko! What are you doing!?
Majoko ...?
Just watch!
VOOM
VOOM
VOOM

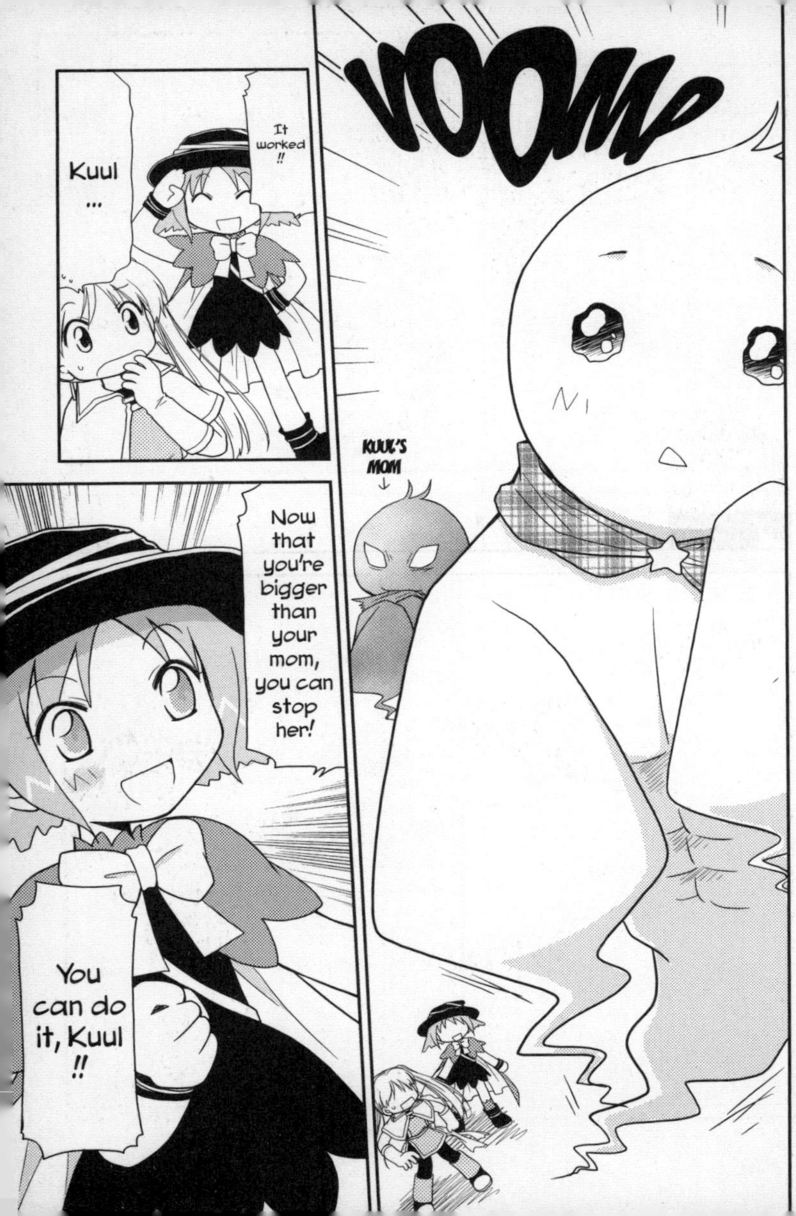
VOOM
KUUL'S MOM
It worked !!
Kuul ...
Now that you're bigger than your mom, you can stop her!
You can do it, Kuul !!

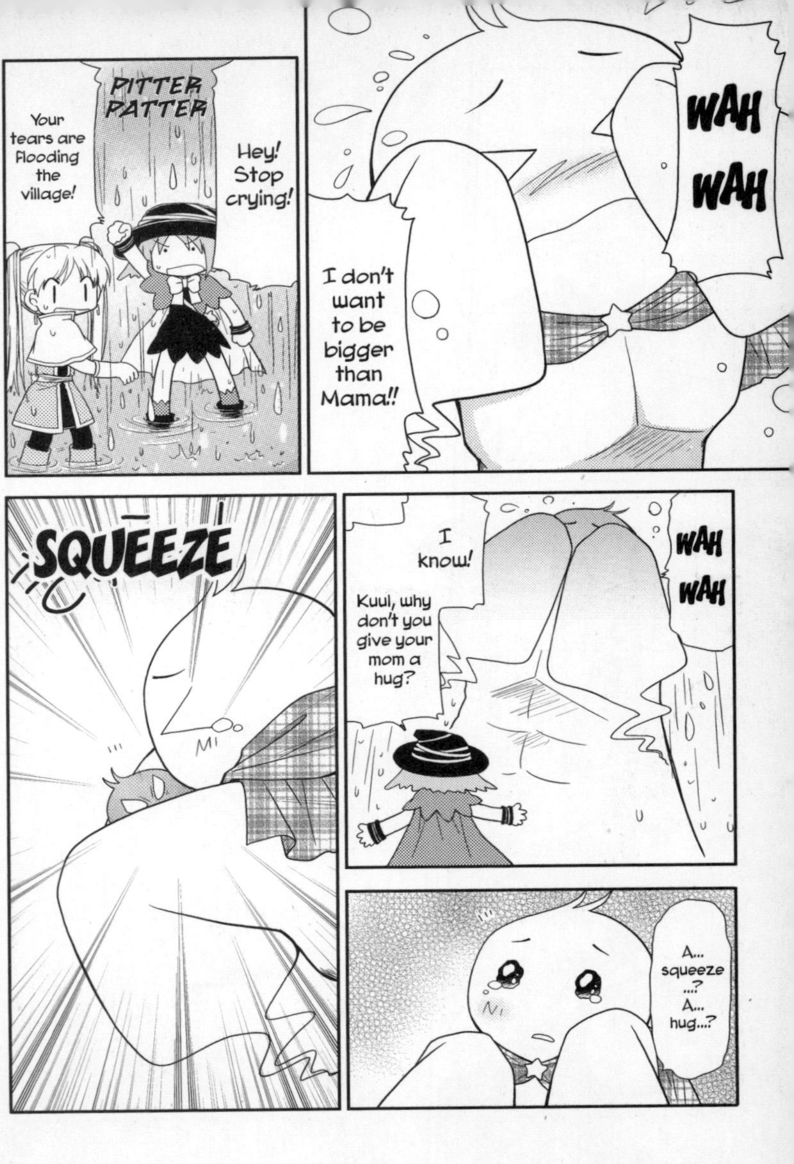
WAH
WAH
I don't want to be bigger than Mama!!
PITTER PATTER
Hey! Stop crying!
Your tears are flooding the village!
WAH
WAH
I know!
Kuul, why don't you give your mom a hug?
A... squeeze ...? A... hug...?
NI
SQUEEZE
MI

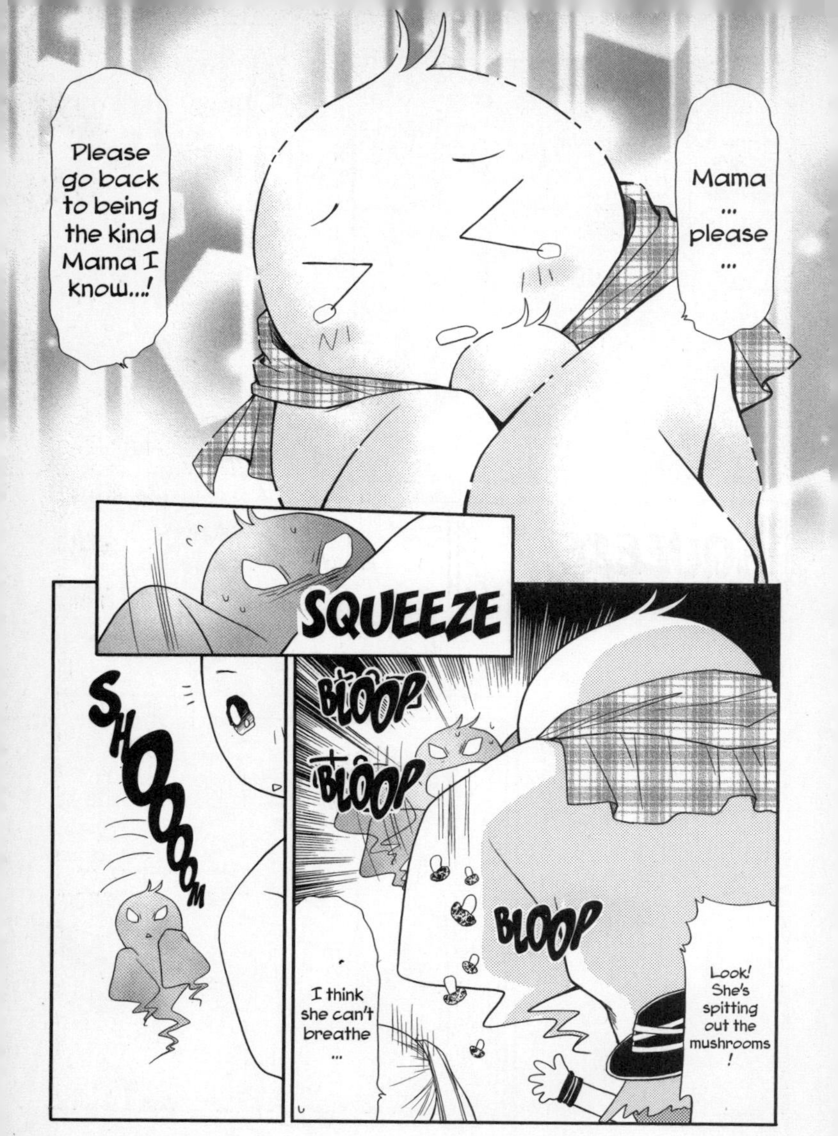
Mama ... please ...
Please go back to being the kind Mama I know...!
SQUEEZE
BLOOP
BLOOP
BLOOP
Look! She's spitting out the mushrooms!
I think she can't breathe ...
SHOOOOOM

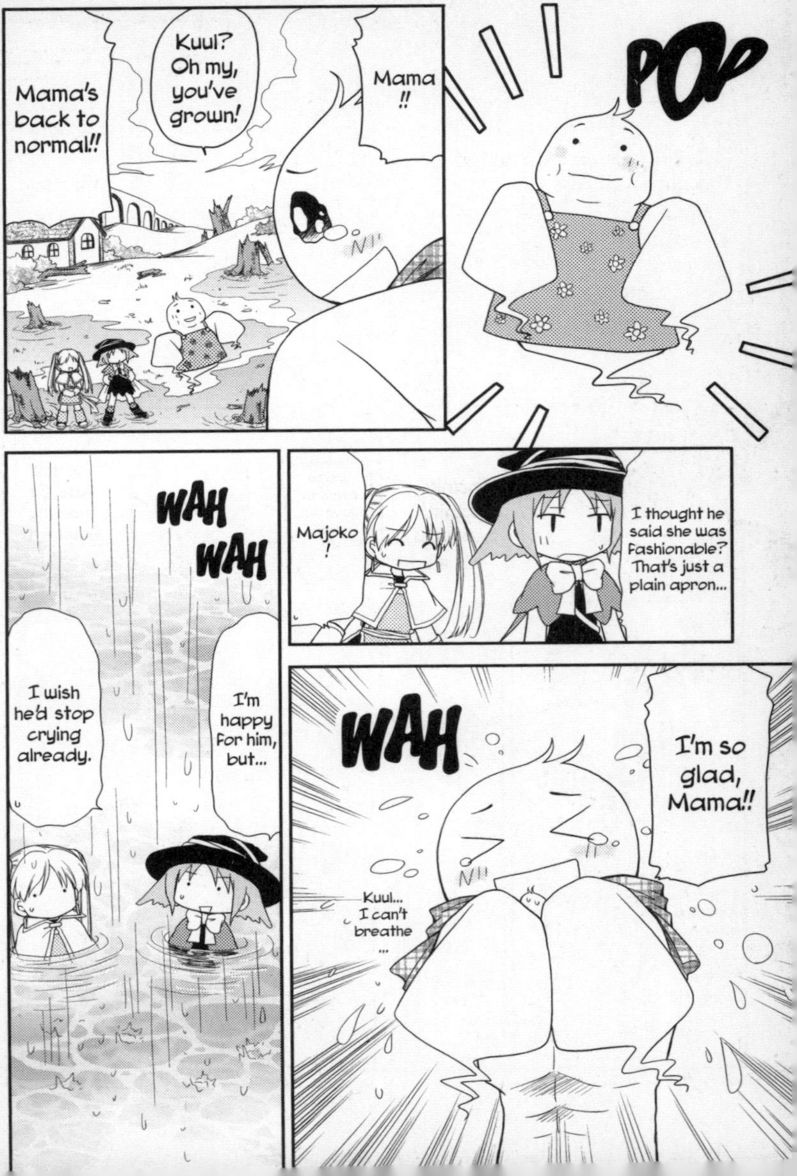
POP
Mama !!
Kuul? Oh my, you've grown!
Mama's back to normal!!
I thought he said she was fashionable? That's just a plain apron...
Majoko !
I'm so glad, Mama!!
WAH
Kuul... I can't breathe ...
WAH WAH
I'm happy for him, but...
I wish he'd stop crying already.

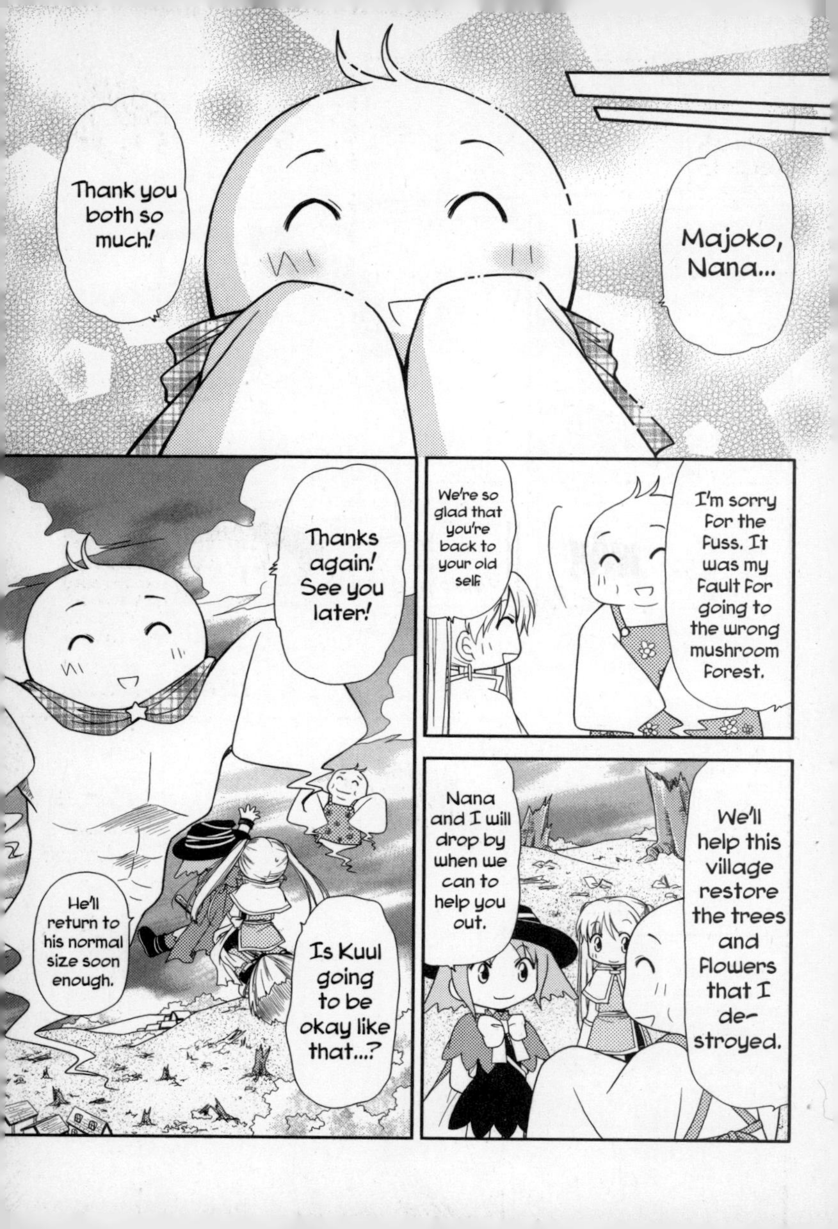
Majoko, Nana...
Thank you both so much!
I'm sorry for the fuss. It was my fault for going to the wrong mushroom forest.
We're so glad that you're back to your old self.
We'll help this village restore the trees and flowers that I de-stroyed.
Nana and I will drop by when we can to help you out.
Thanks again! See you later!
Is Kuul going to be okay like that...?
He'll return to his normal size soon enough.

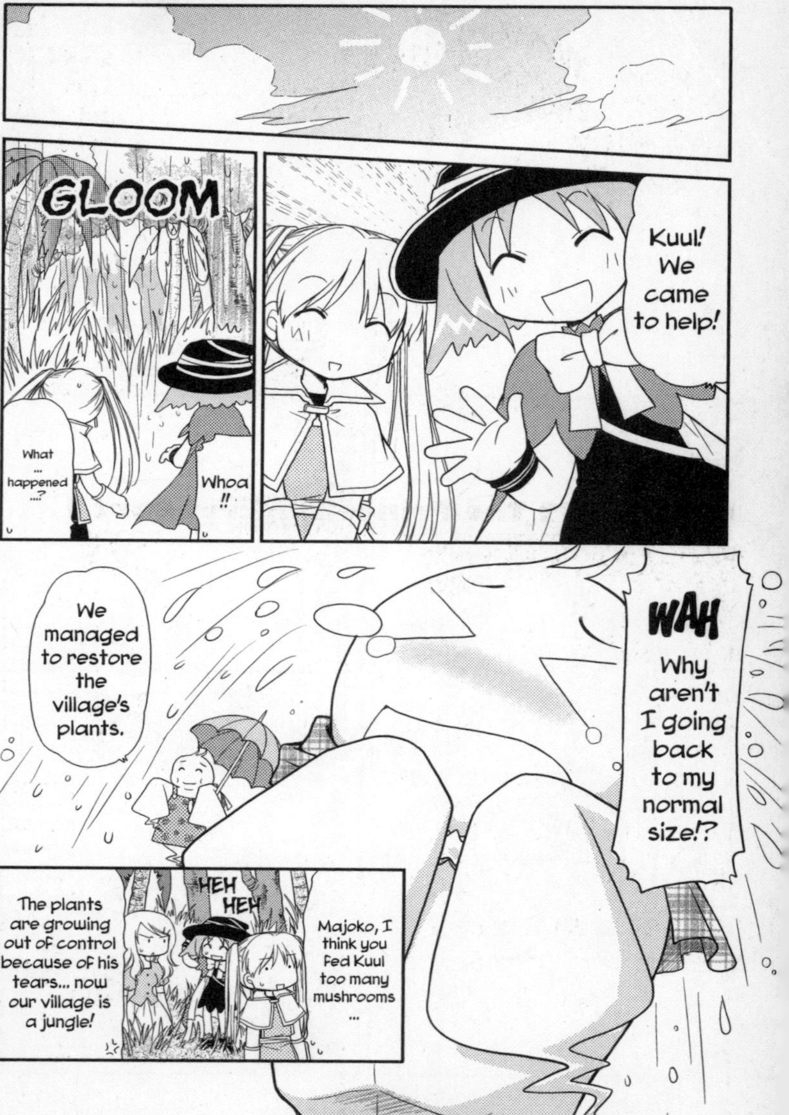
Kuul! We came to help!
GLOOM
Whoa!!
What ... happened ...?
WAH
Why aren't I going back to my normal size!?
We managed to restore the village's plants.
Majoko, I think you fed Kuul too many mushrooms ...
HEH HEH
The plants are growing out of control because of his tears... now our village is a jungle!

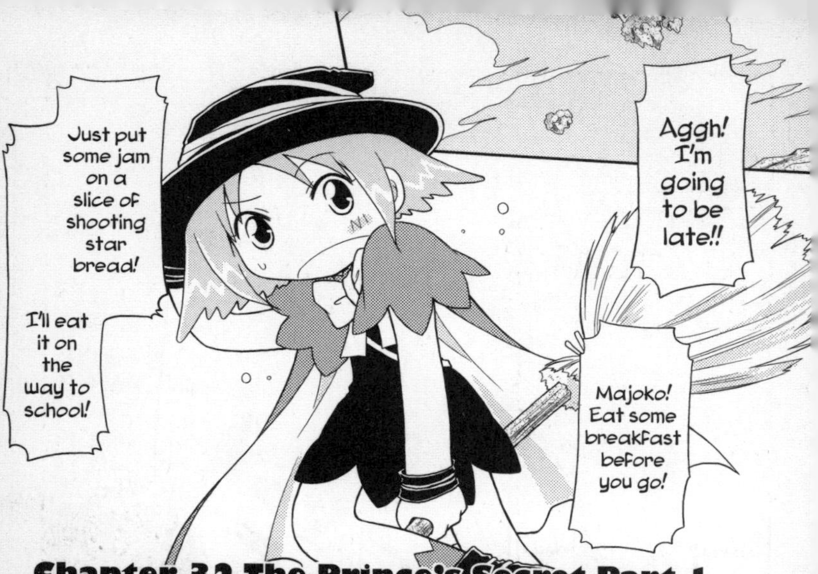
Aggh! I'm going to be late!!
Majoko! Eat some breakfast before you go!
Just put some jam on a slice of shooting star bread!
I'll eat it on the way to school!

Chapter 32 The Prince's Secret Part 1

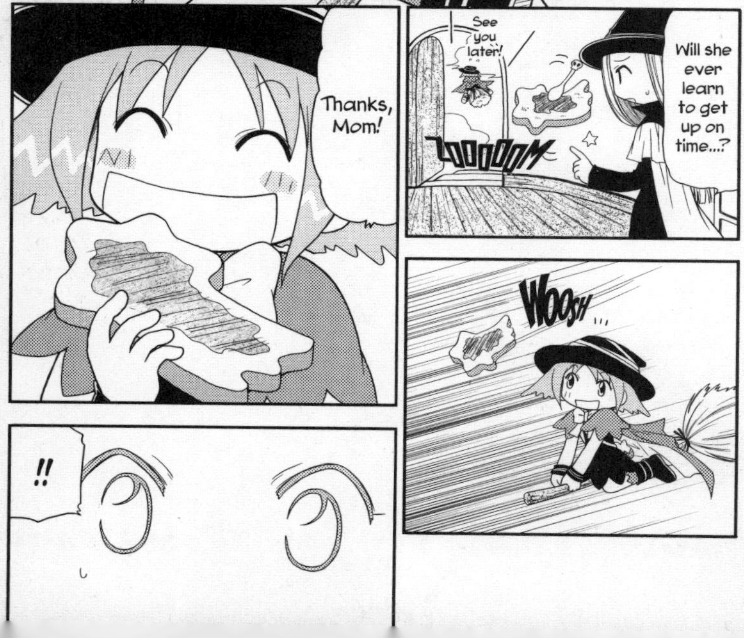
See you later!
ZOOOOOM
Will she ever learn to get up on time...?
Thanks, Mom!
WOOSH
!!

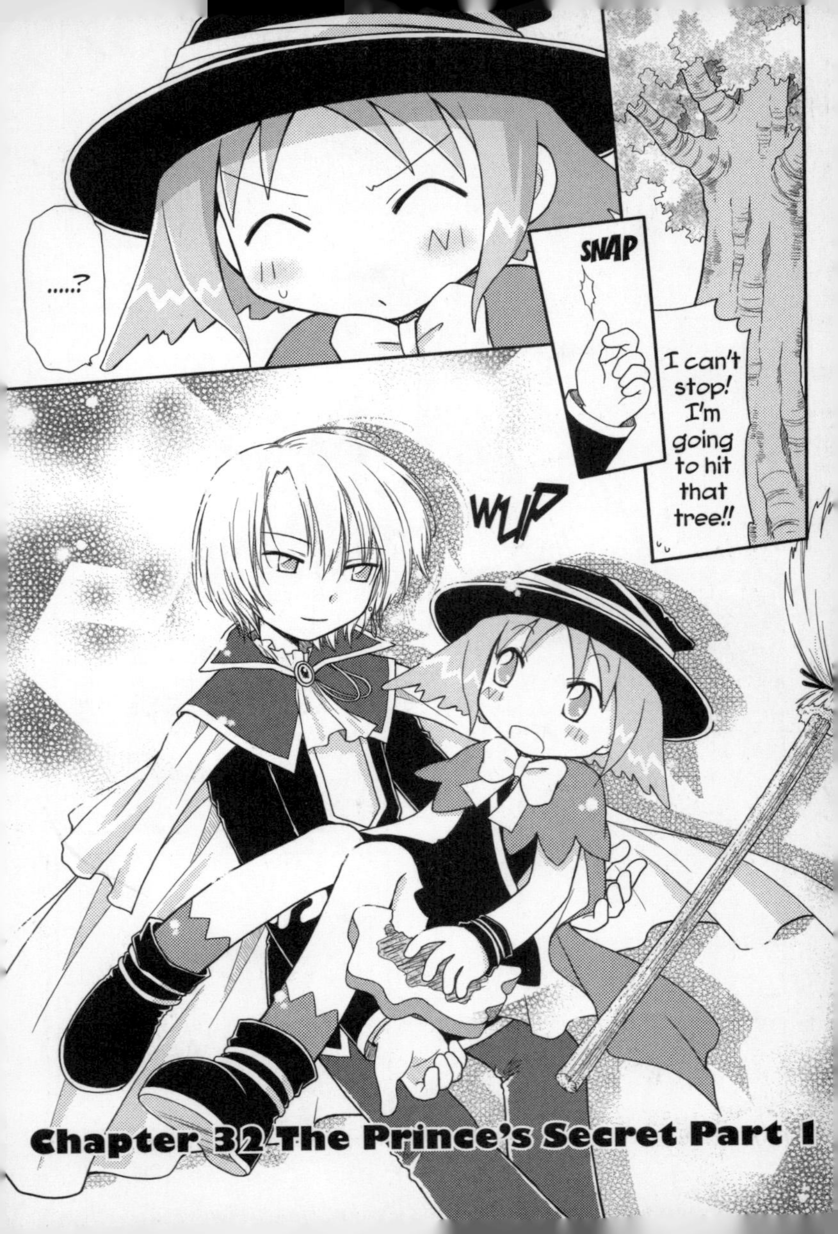
I can't stop! I'm going to hit that tree!!
SNAP
.....?
WUP
Chapter 32 The Prince's Secret Part 1

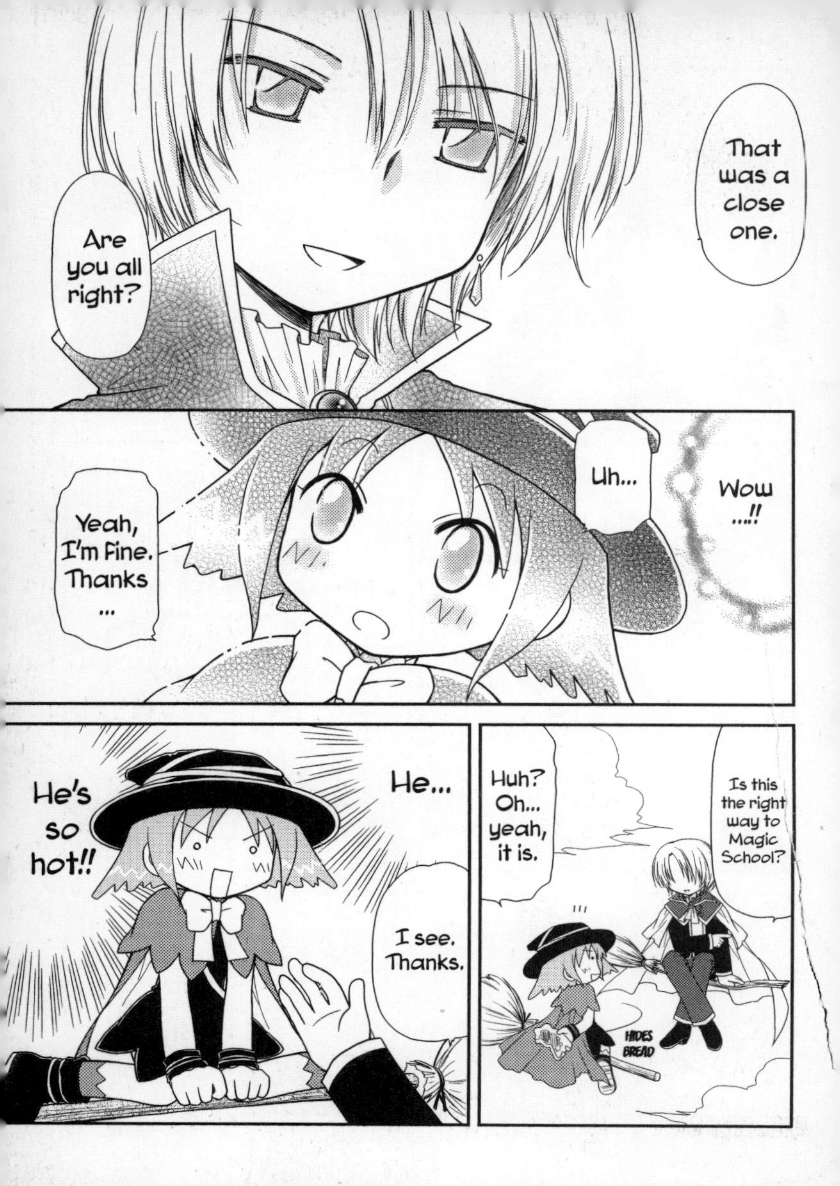
That was a close one.
Are you all right?
Wow ...!!
Uh...
Yeah, I'm fine. Thanks ...
Is this the right way to Magic School?
Huh? Oh... yeah, it is.
HIDES BREAD
He...
He's so hot!!
I see. Thanks.

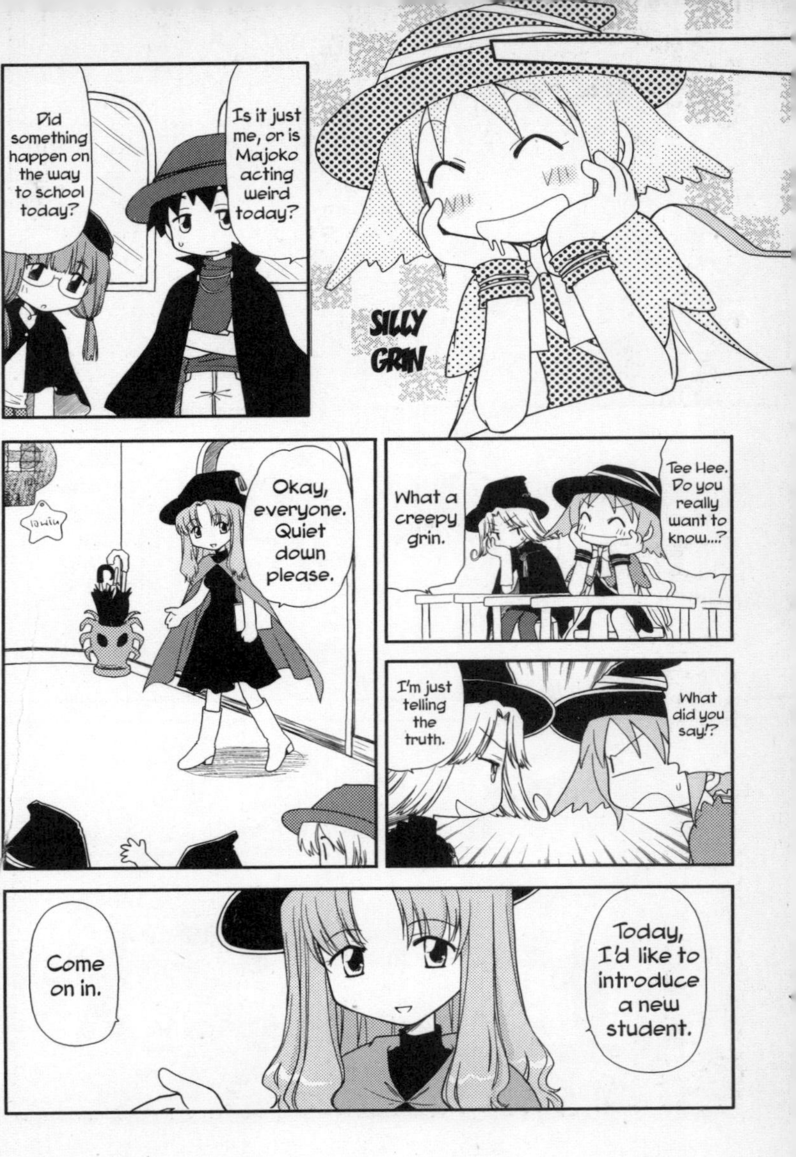
SILLY GRIN
Is it just me, or is Majoko acting weird today?
Did something happen on the way to school today?
Tee Hee. Do you really want to know...?
What a creepy grin.
What did you say!?
I'm just telling the truth.
Okay, everyone. Quiet down please.
Today, I'd like to introduce a new student.
Come on in.

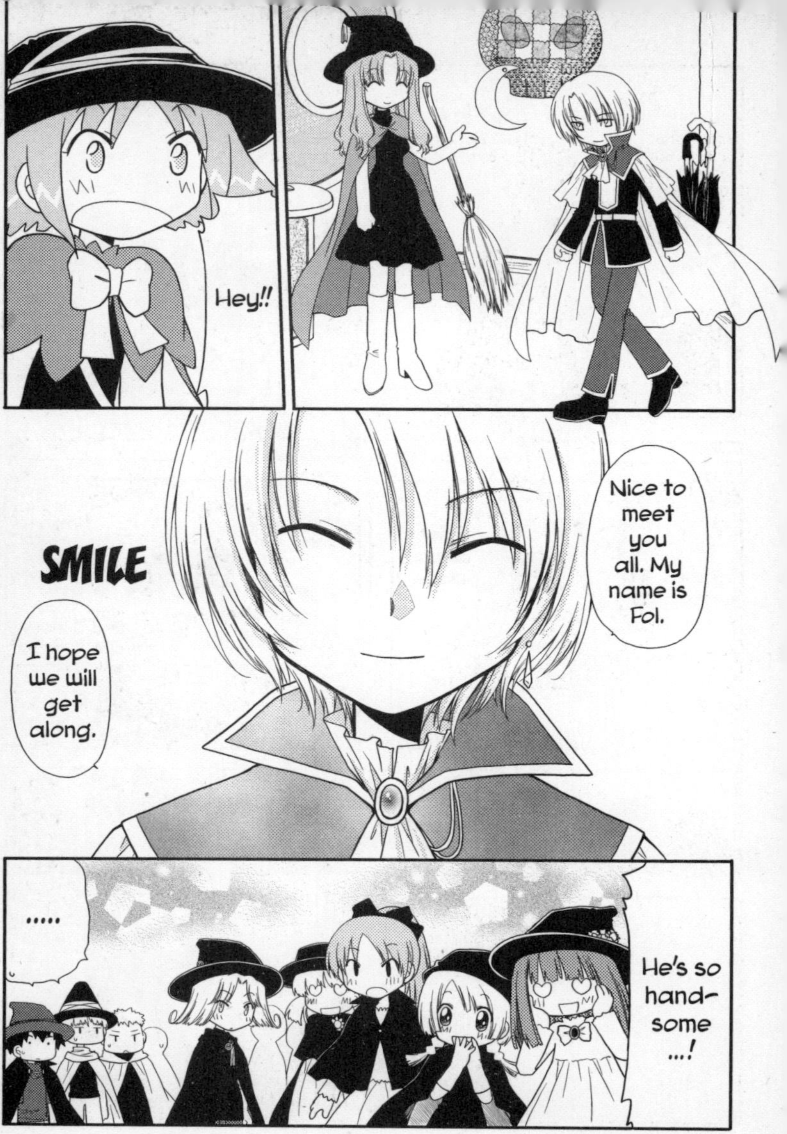
Hey!!
Nice to meet you all. My name is Fol.
SMILE
I hope we will get along.
He's so hand-some ...!
.....

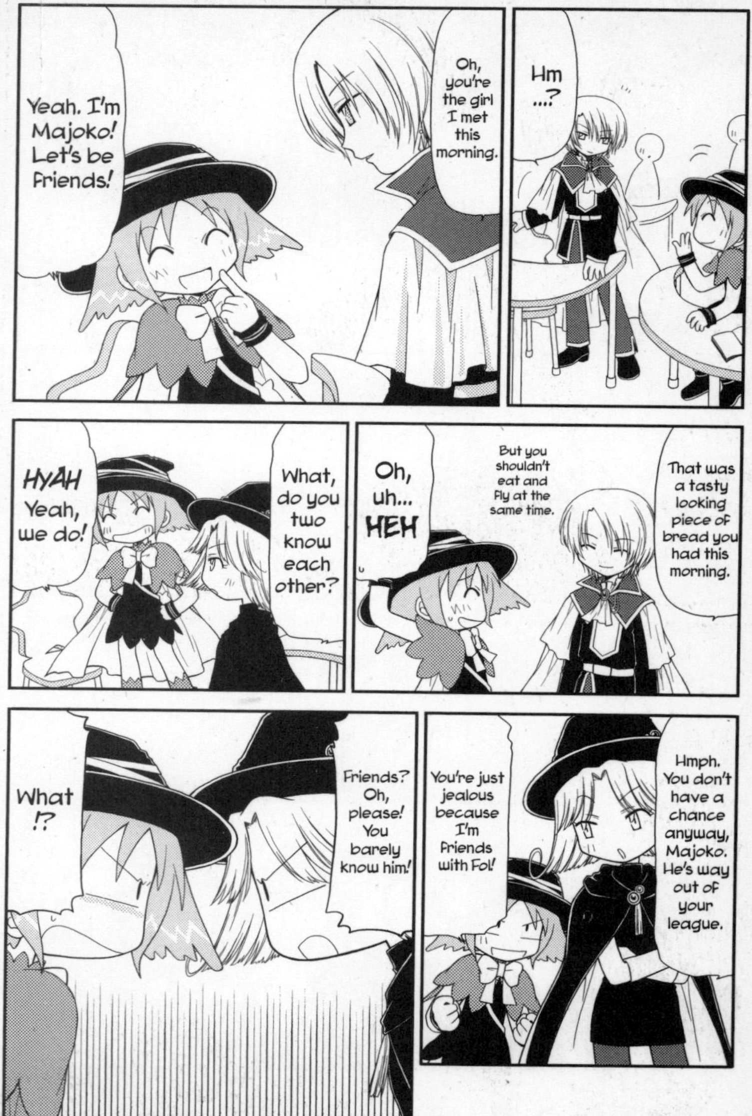
Hm ...?
Oh, you're the girl I met this morning.
Yeah. I'm Majoko! Let's be friends!
That was a tasty looking piece of bread you had this morning.
But you shouldn't eat and fly at the same time.
Oh, uh... HEH
What, do you two know each other?
HYAH Yeah, we do!
Hmph. You don't have a chance anyway, Majoko. He's way out of your league.
You're just jealous because I'm friends with Fol!
Friends? Oh, please! You barely know him!
What !?

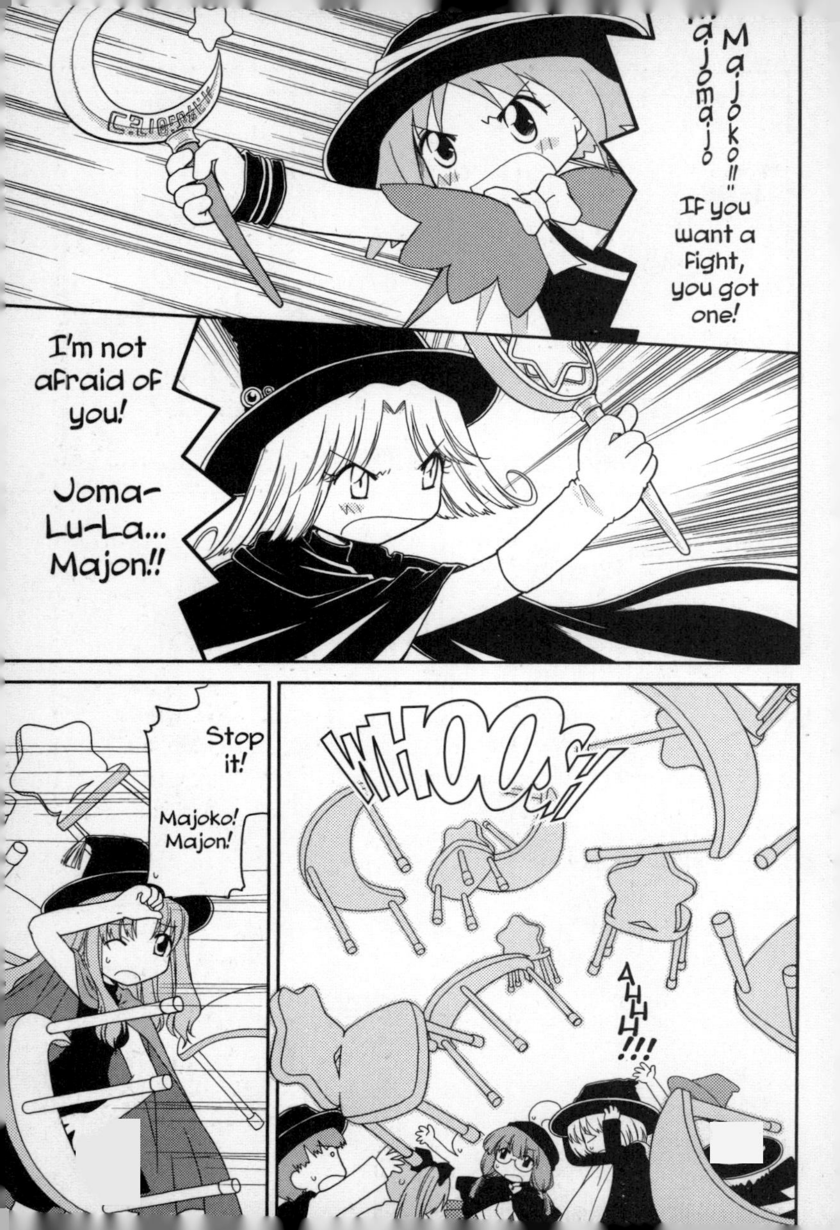
Majoko!!
ajomajo
If you want a fight, you got one!
I'm not afraid of you!
Joma-Lu-La... Majon!!
WHOOSH!
AHHH!!!
Stop it!
Majoko! Majon!

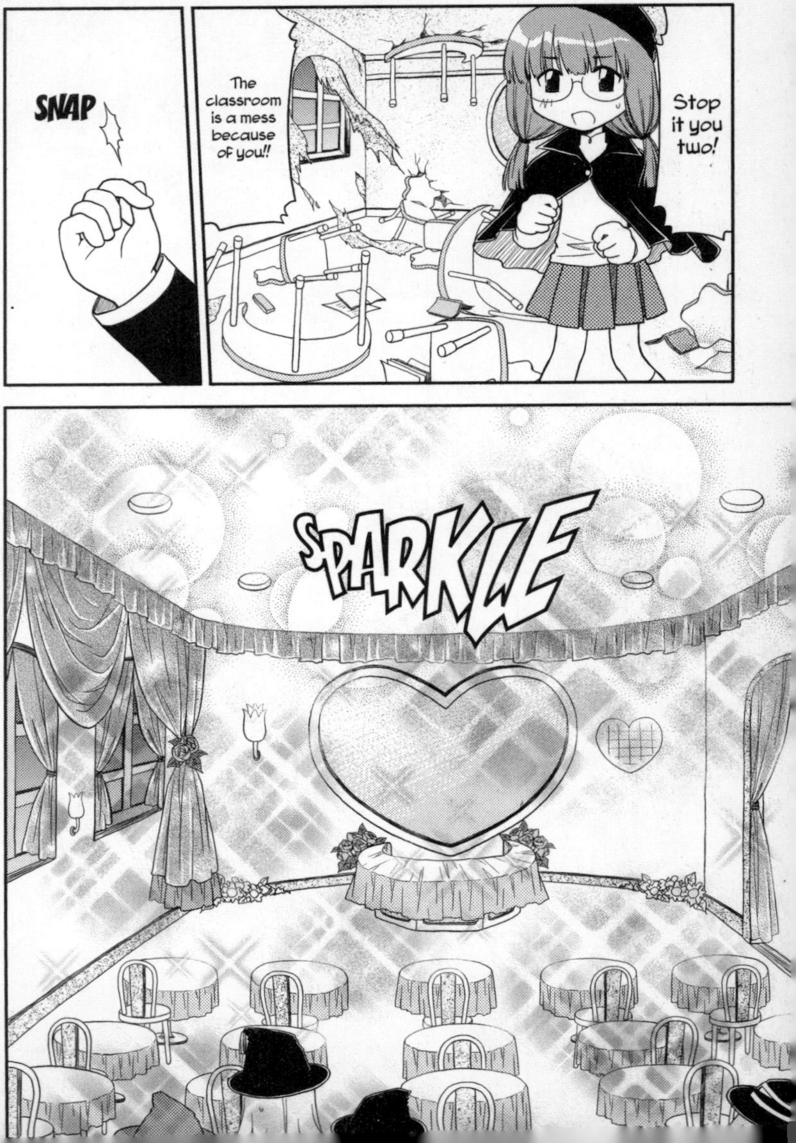
Stop it you two!
The classroom is a mess because of you!!
SNAP
SPARKLE

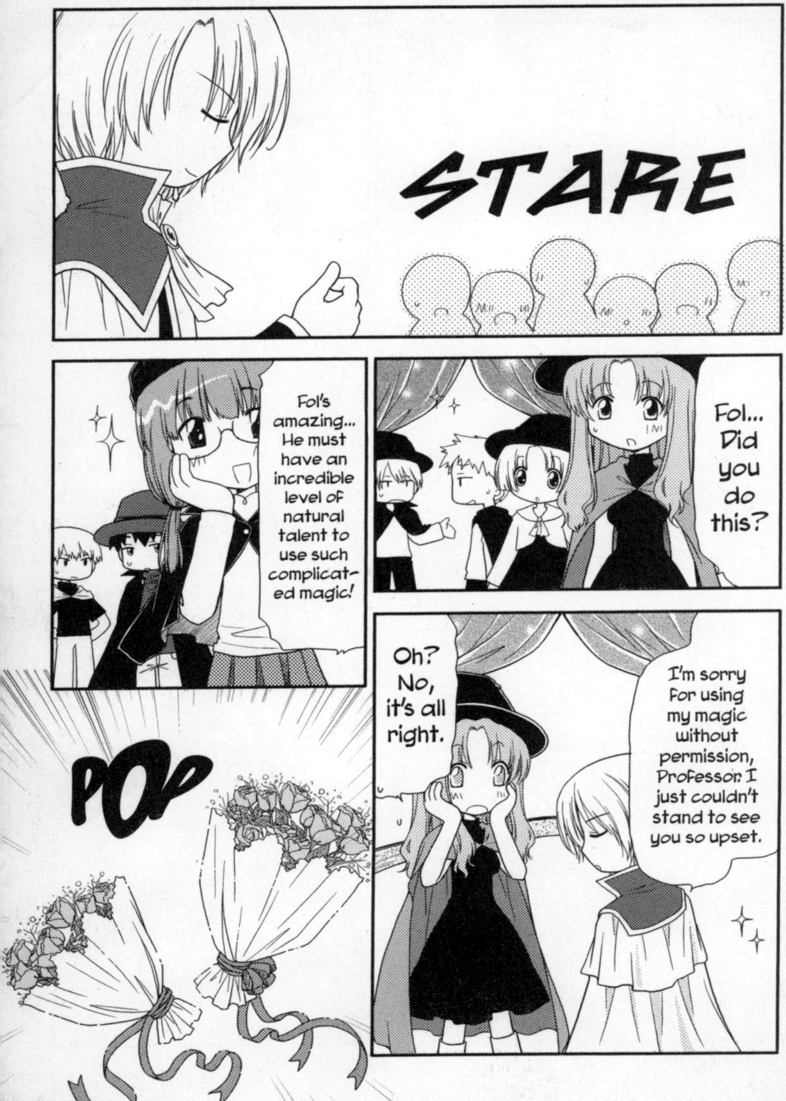
STARE
Fol... Did you do this?
Fol's amazing... He must have an incredible level of natural talent to use such complicated magic!
I'm sorry for using my magic without permission, Professor. I just couldn't stand to see you so upset.
Oh? No, it's all right.
POP

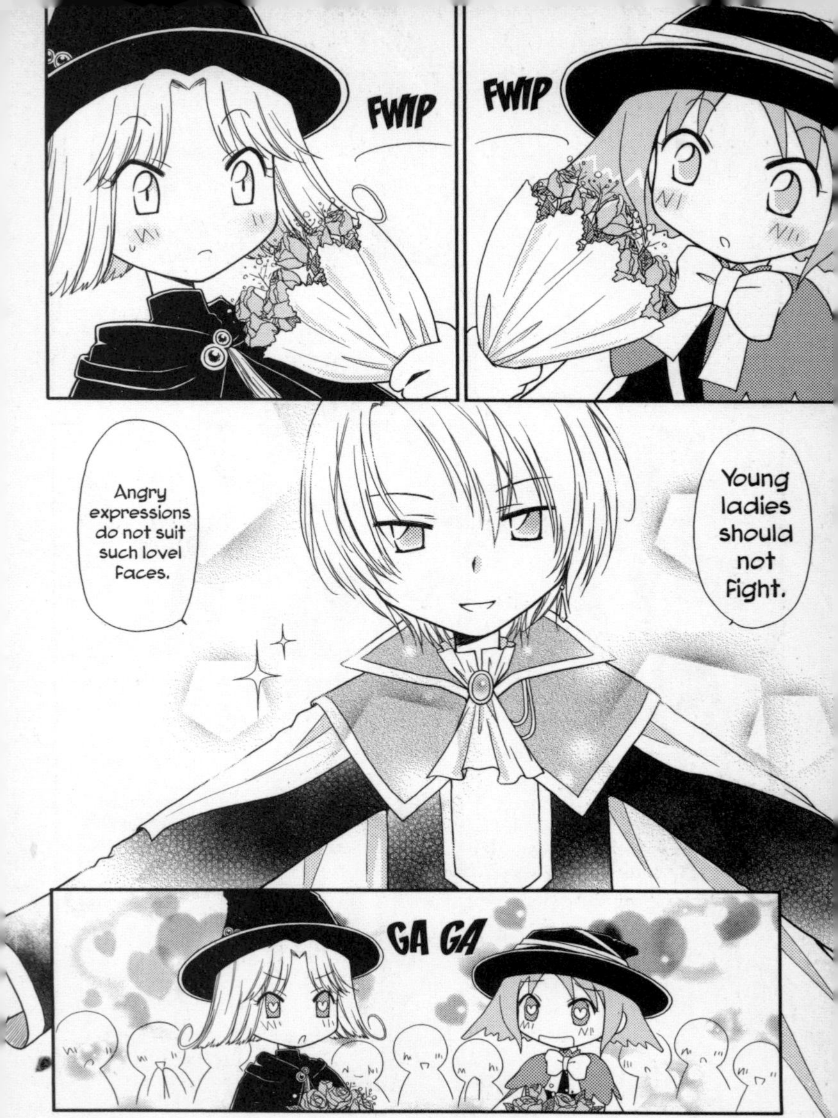
FWIP
FWIP
Young ladies should not fight.
Angry expressions do not suit such lovel faces.
GA GA

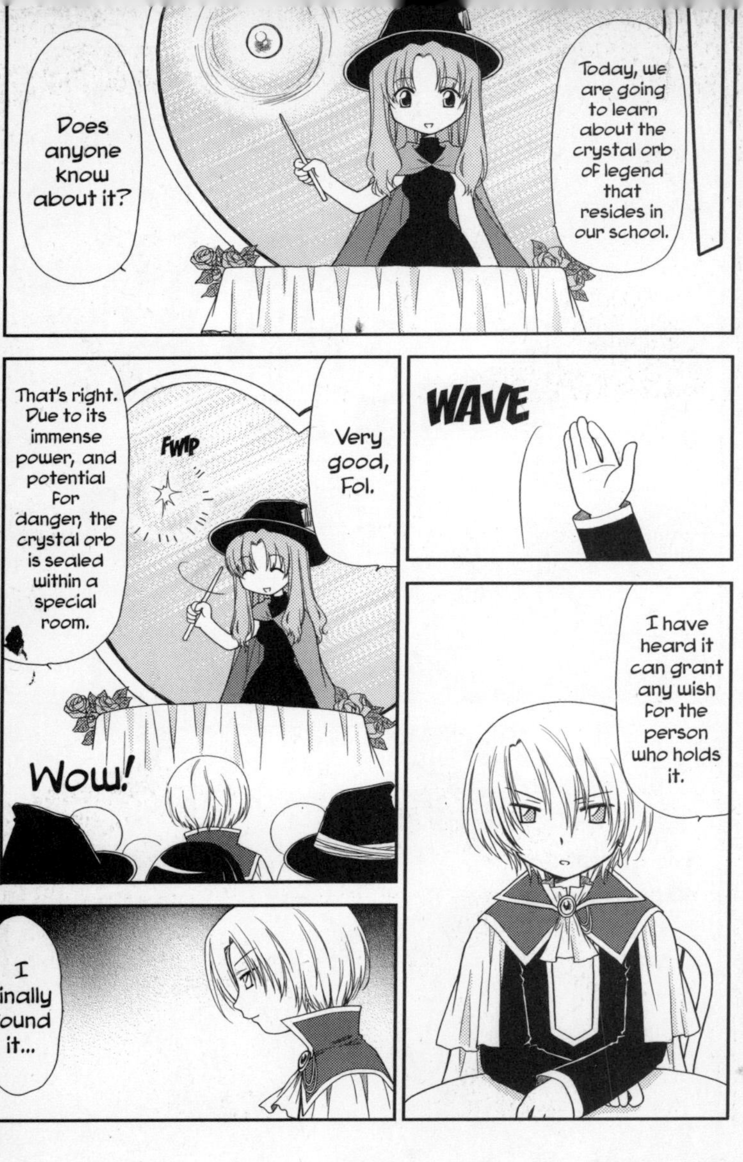
Today, we are going to learn about the crystal orb of legend that resides in our school.
Does anyone know about it?
WAVE
I have heard it can grant any wish for the person who holds it.
Very good, Fol.
FWIP
That's right. Due to its immense power, and potential for danger, the crystal orb is sealed within a special room.
Wow!
I finally found it...

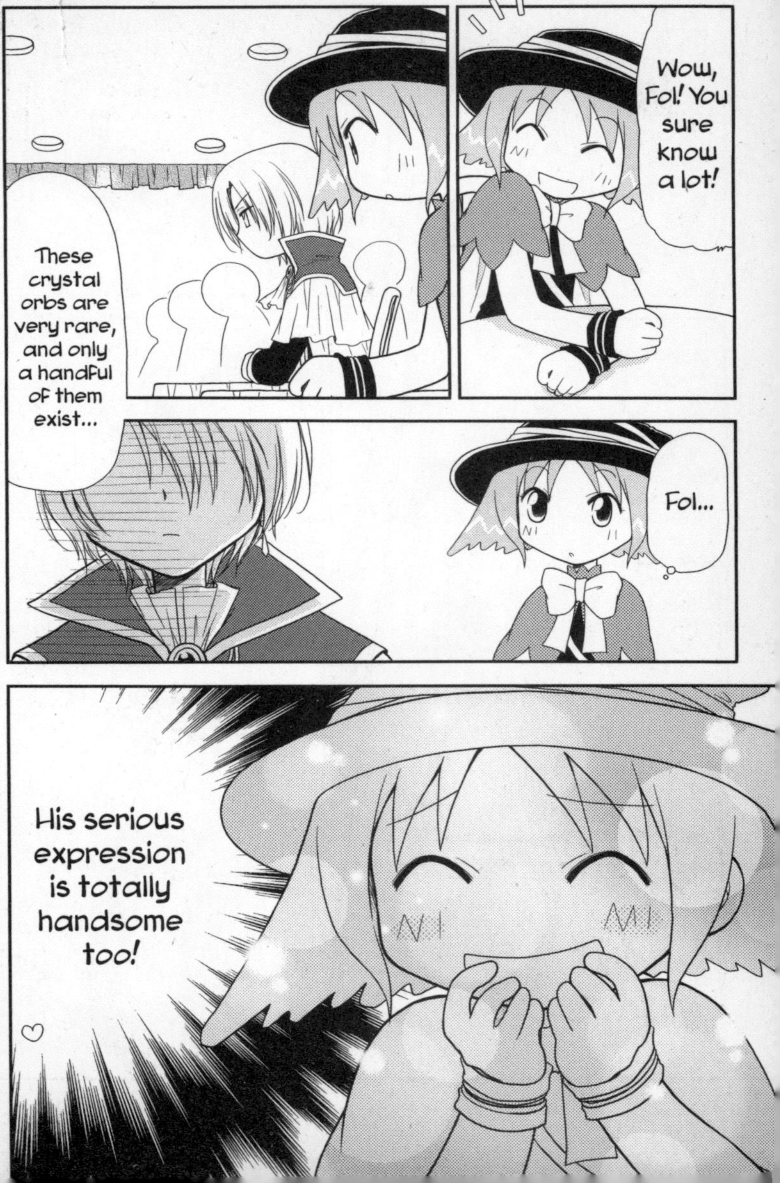
Wow, Fol! You sure know a lot!
These crystal orbs are very rare, and only a handful of them exist...
Fol...
His serious expression is totally handsome too!

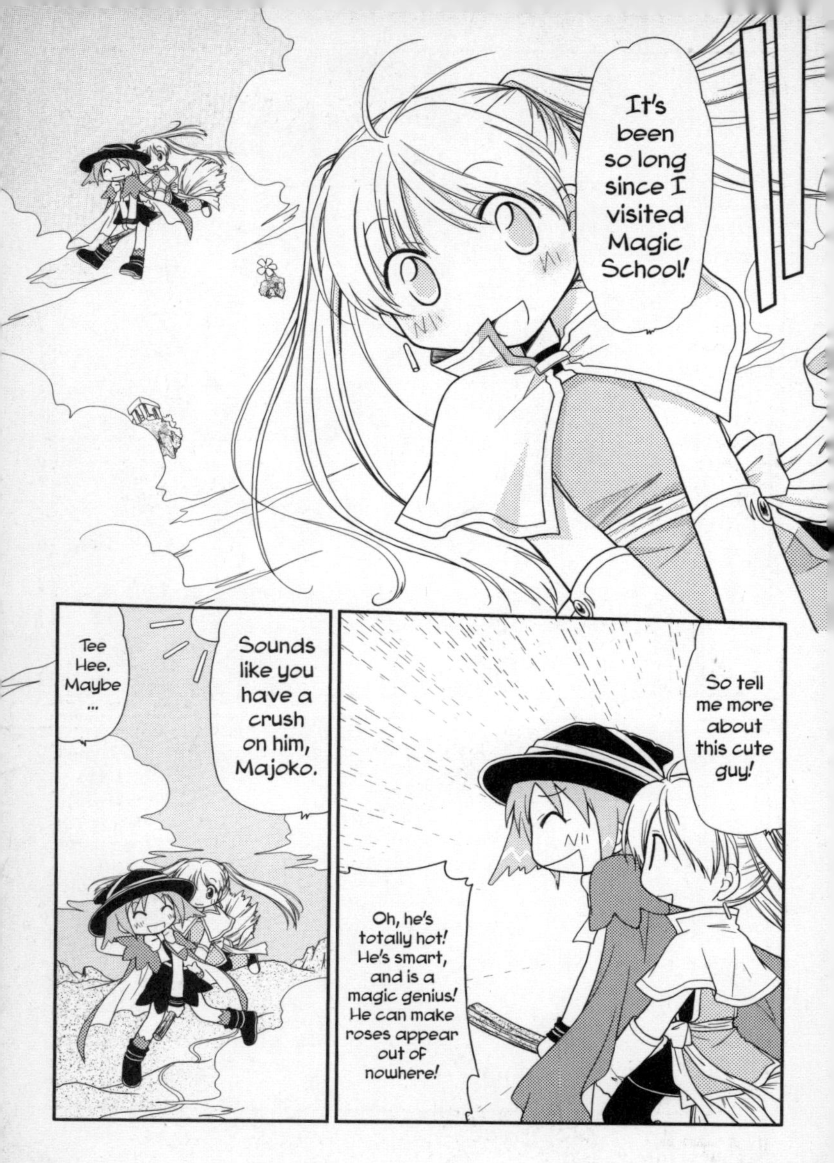
It's been so long since I visited Magic School!
So tell me more about this cute guy!
Oh, he's totally hot! He's smart, and is a magic genius! He can make roses appear out of nowhere!
Sounds like you have a crush on him, Majoko.
Tee Hee. Maybe ...

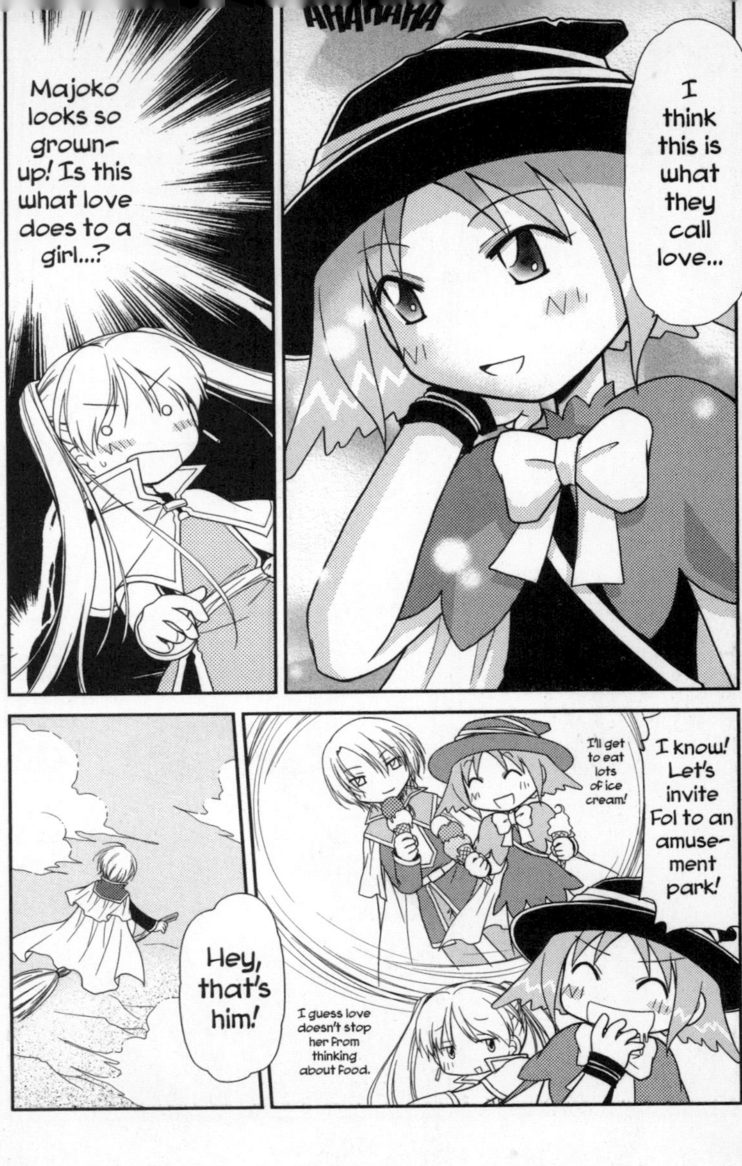
AHAHAHA
I think this is what they call love...
Majoko looks so grown-up! Is this what love does to a girl...?
I know! Let's invite Fol to an amusement park!
I'll get to eat lots of ice cream!
I guess love doesn't stop her from thinking about food.
Hey, that's him!

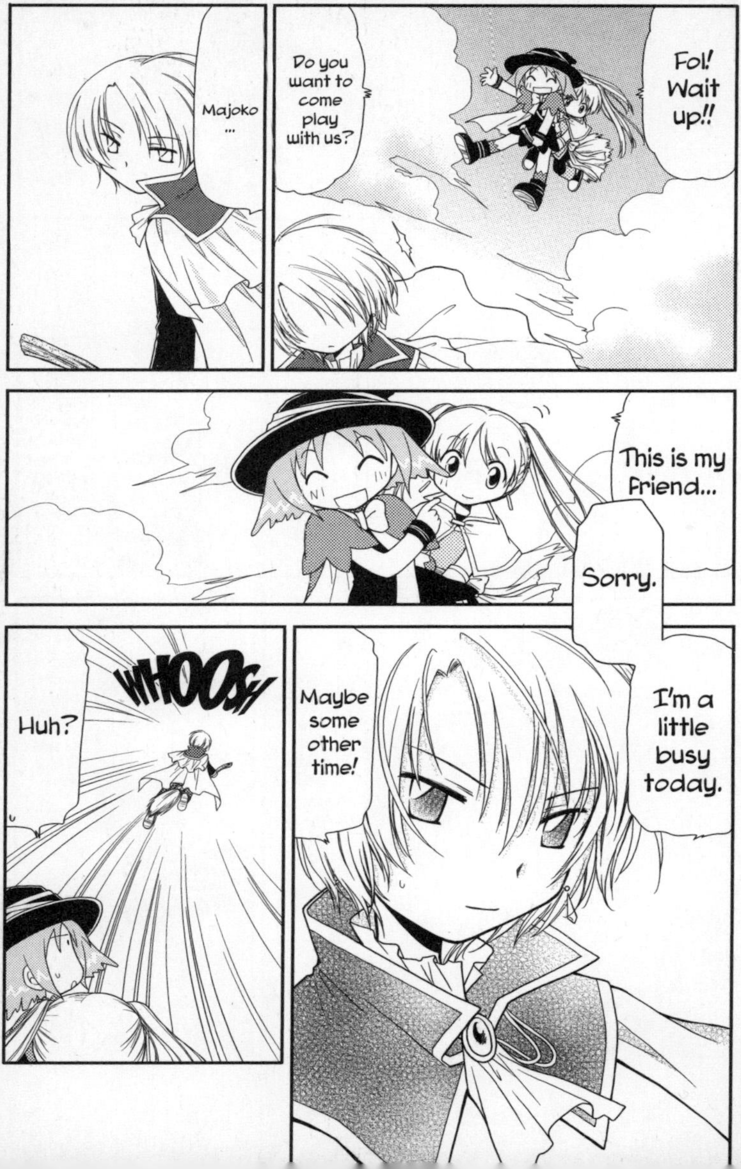
Fol! Wait up!!
Do you want to come play with us?
Majoko ...
This is my friend...
Sorry.
I'm a little busy today.
Maybe some other time!
WHOOSH
Huh?

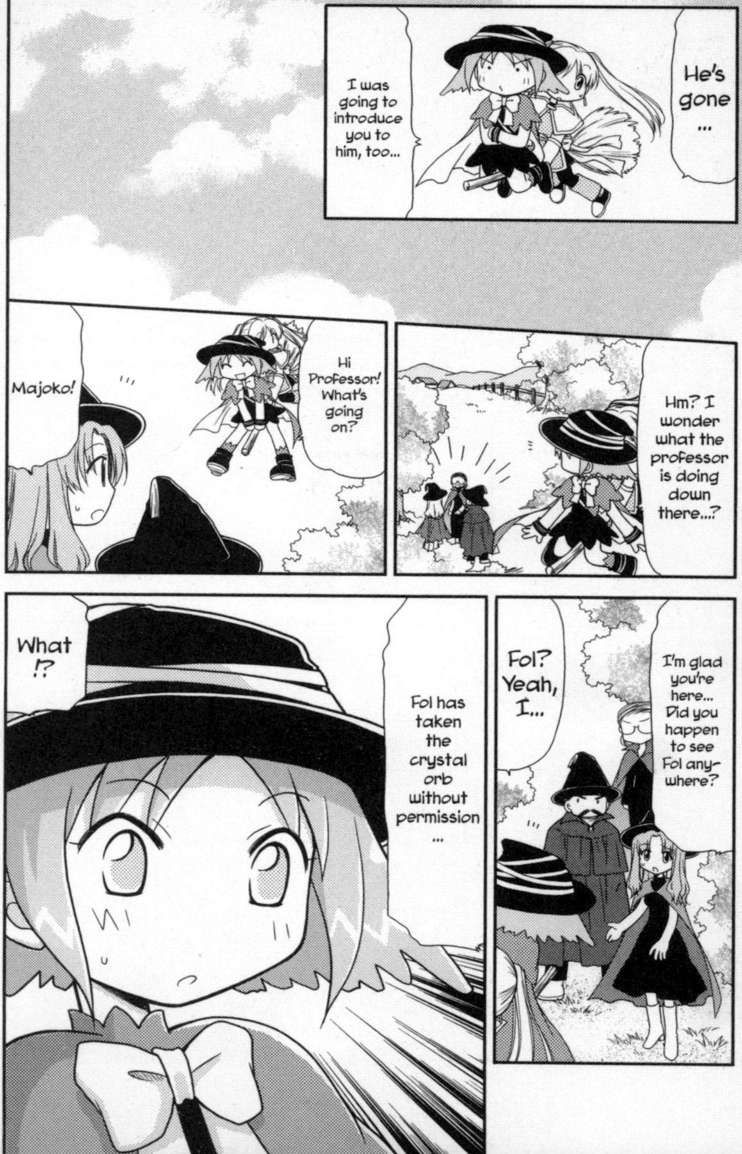
He's gone ...
I was going to introduce you to him, too...
Hm? I wonder what the professor is doing down there...?
Hi Professor! What's going on?
Majoko!
I'm glad you're here... Did you happen to see Fol anywhere?
Fol? Yeah, I...
Fol has taken the crystal orb without permission ...
What !?

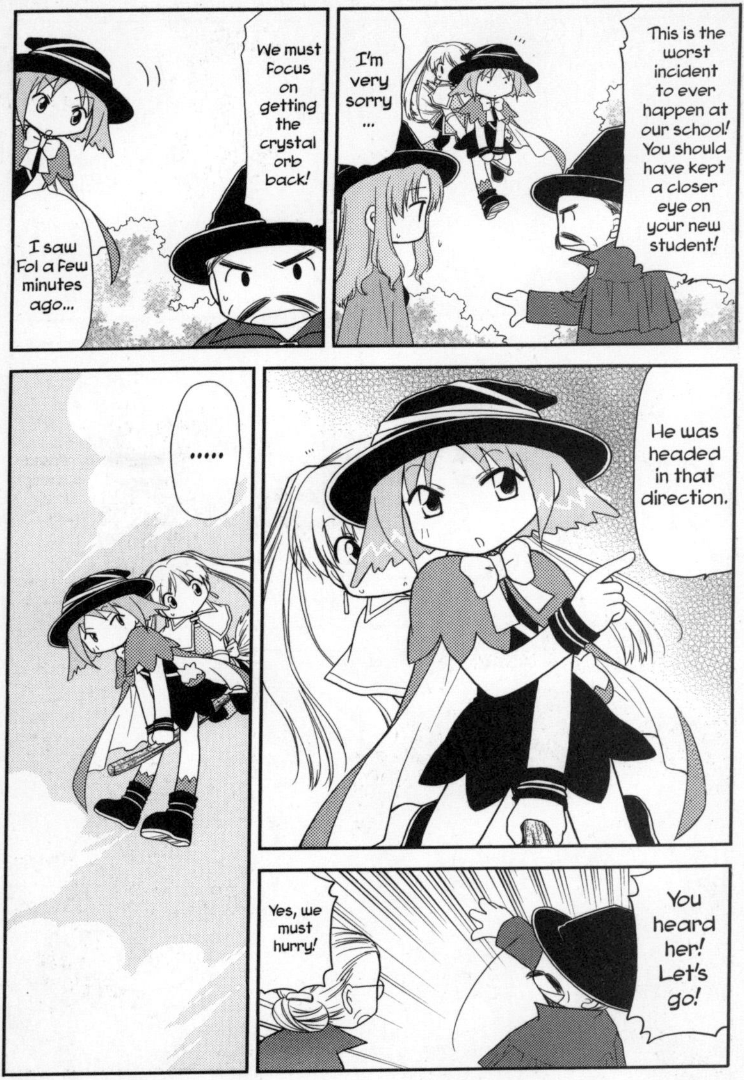
This is the worst incident to ever happen at our school! You should have kept a closer eye on your new student!
I'm very sorry ...
We must focus on getting the crystal orb back!
I saw Fol a few minutes ago...
He was headed in that direction.
You heard her! Let's go!
Yes, we must hurry!
......

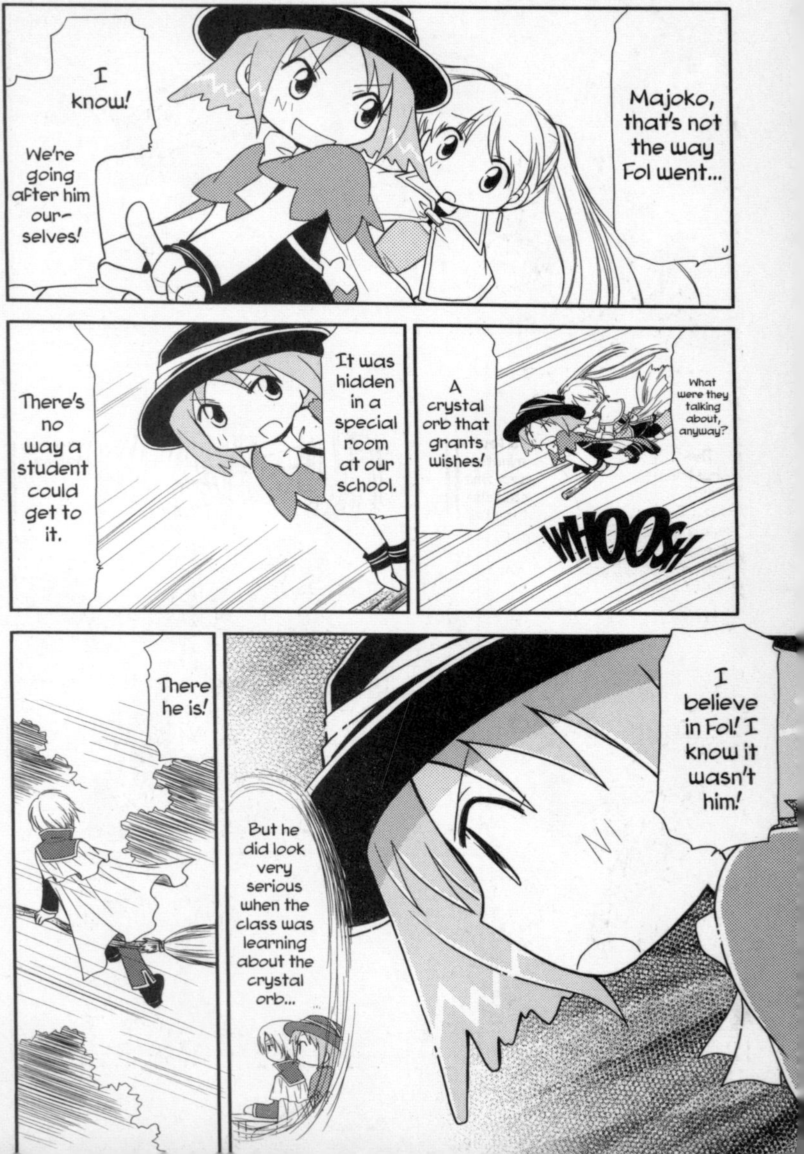

Majoko, that's not the way Fol went...
I know!
We're going after him ourselves!
What were they talking about, anyway?
A crystal orb that grants wishes!
WHOOSH
It was hidden in a special room at our school.
There's no way a student could get to it.
I believe in Fol! I know it wasn't him!
But he did look very serious when the class was learning about the crystal orb...
There he is!

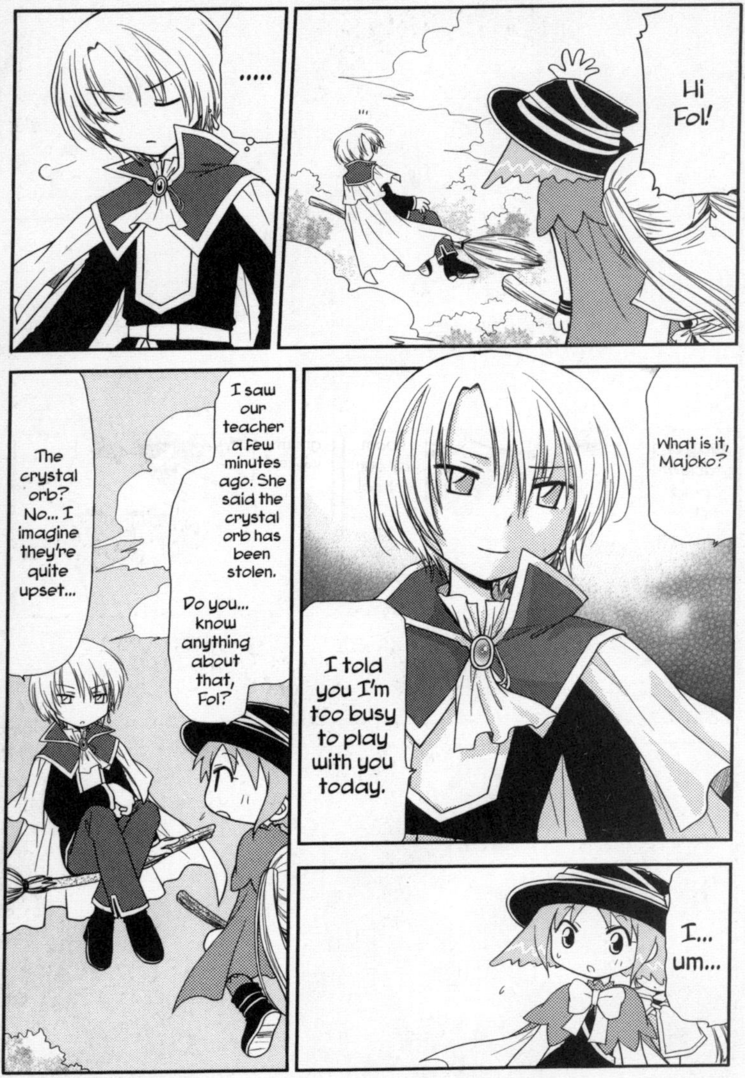
Hi Fol!
......
What is it, Majoko?
I told you I'm too busy to play with you today.
I... um...
I saw our teacher a few minutes ago. She said the crystal orb has been stolen.
Do you... know anything about that, Fol?
The crystal orb? No... I imagine they're quite upset...

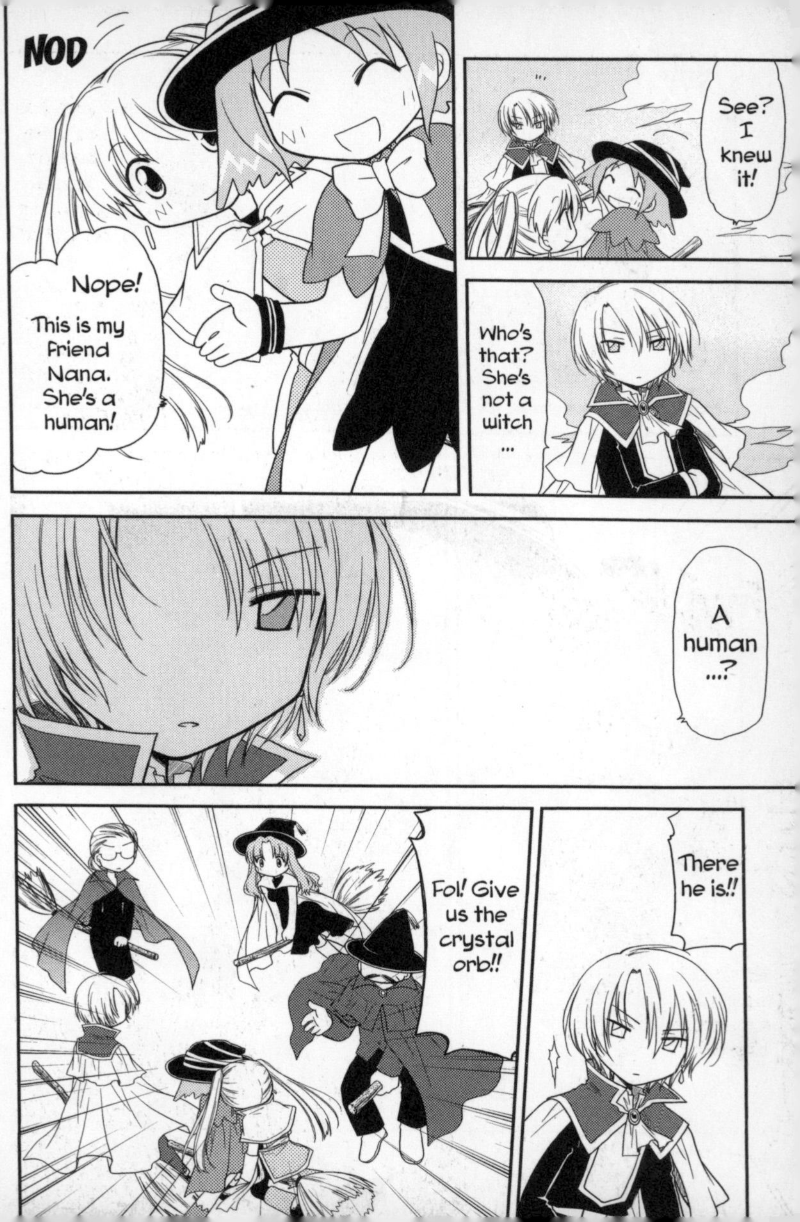

See? I knew it!
Who's that? She's not a witch ...
NOD
Nope!
This is my friend Nana. She's a human!
A human ...?
There he is!!
Fol! Give us the crystal orb!!

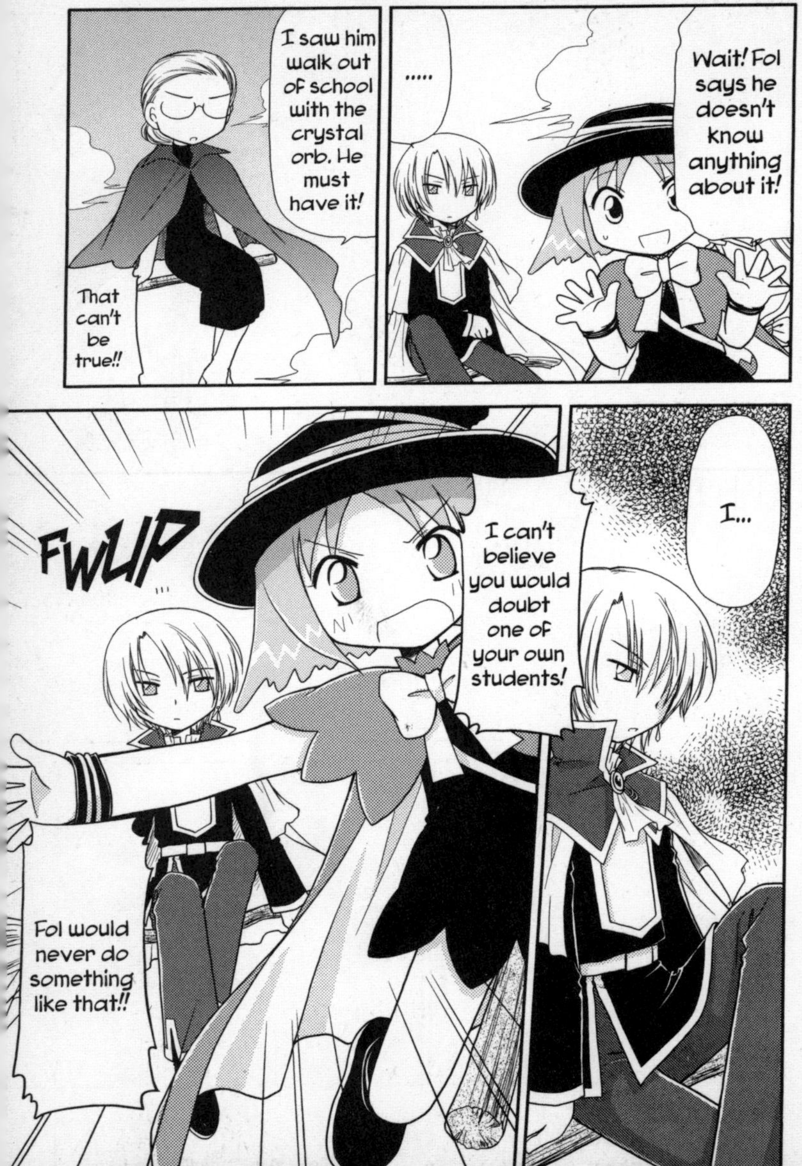
Wait! Fol says he doesn't know anything about it!
.....
I saw him walk out of school with the crystal orb. He must have it!
That can't be true!!
I...
I can't believe you would doubt one of your own students!
FWUP
Fol would never do something like that!!

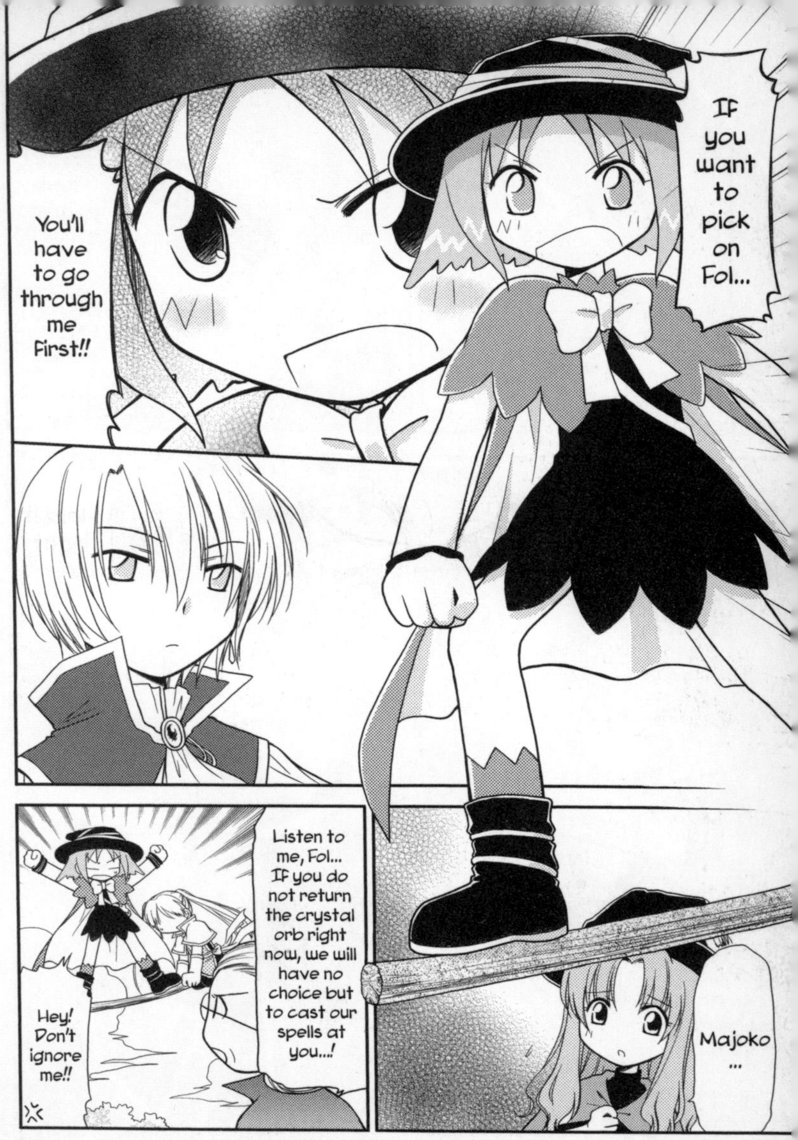
If you want to pick on Fol...
You'll have to go through me First!!
Majoko ...
Listen to me, Fol... If you do not return the crystal orb right now, we will have no choice but to cast our spells at you...!
Hey! Don't ignore me!!

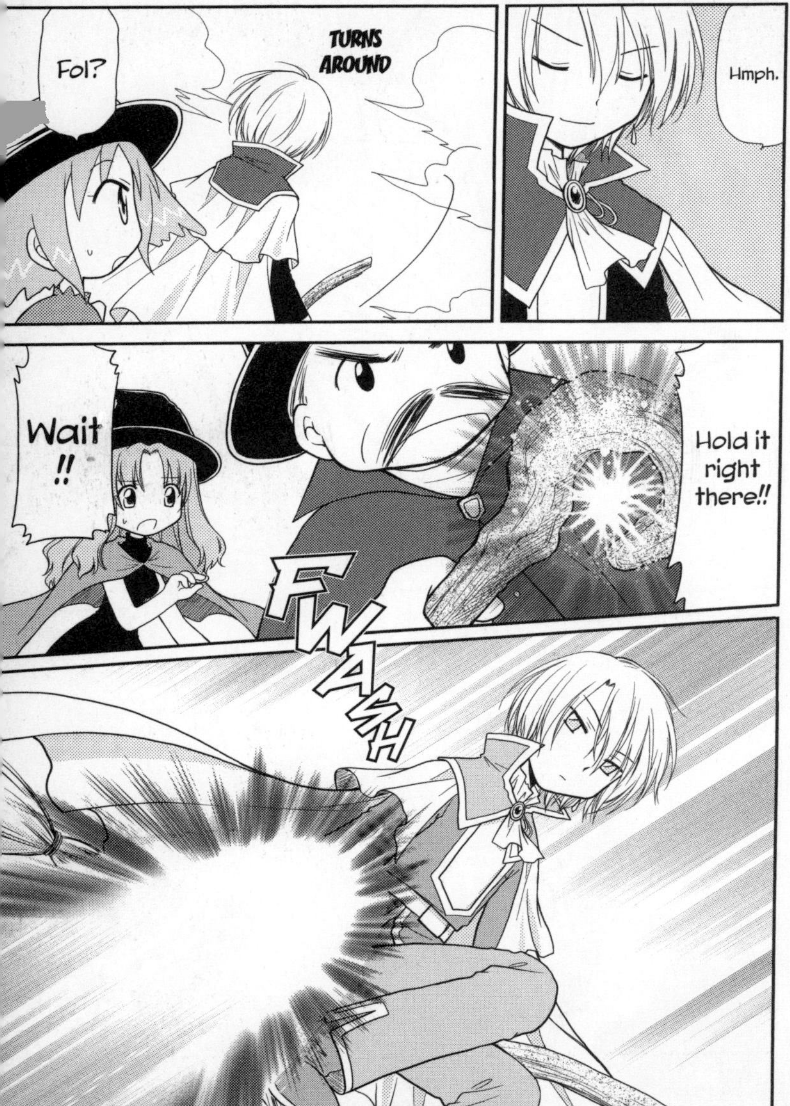
Hmph.
TURNS AROUND
Fol?
Hold it right there!!
Wait !!
FWASH

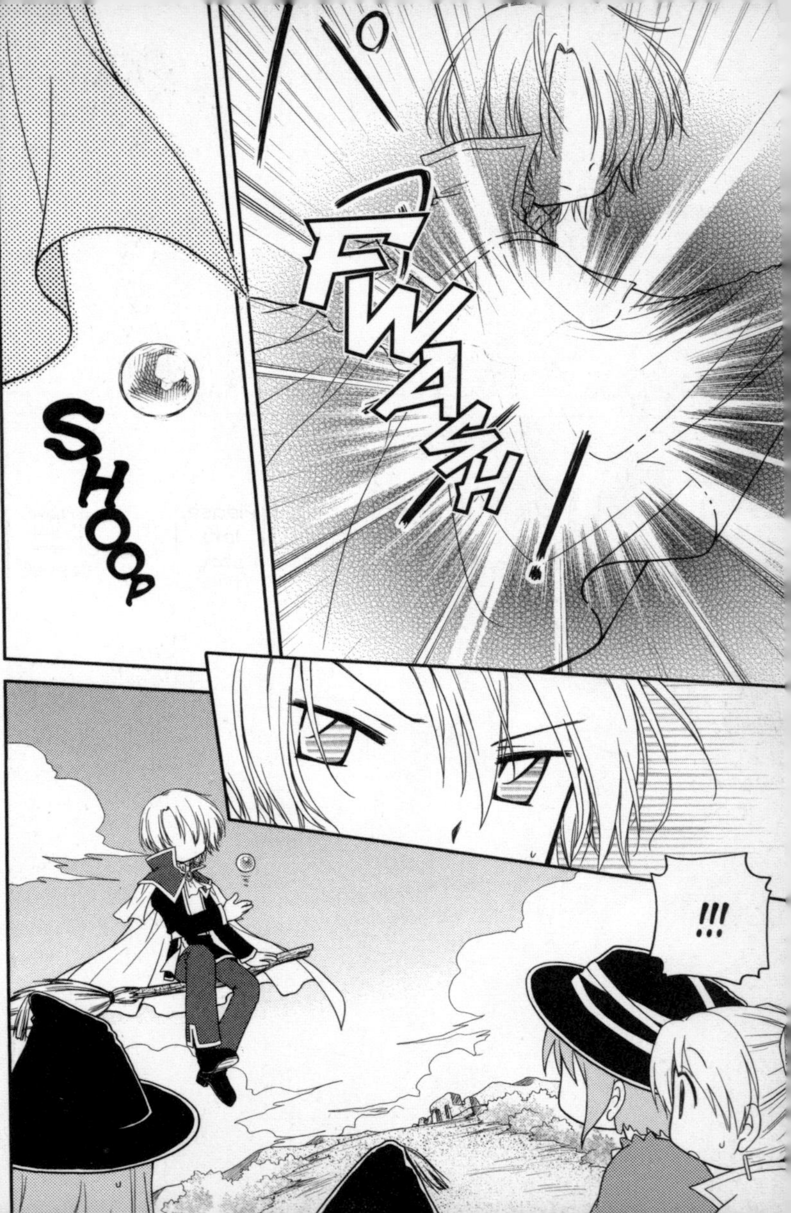
パ
FWASH!
SHOOP
!!!

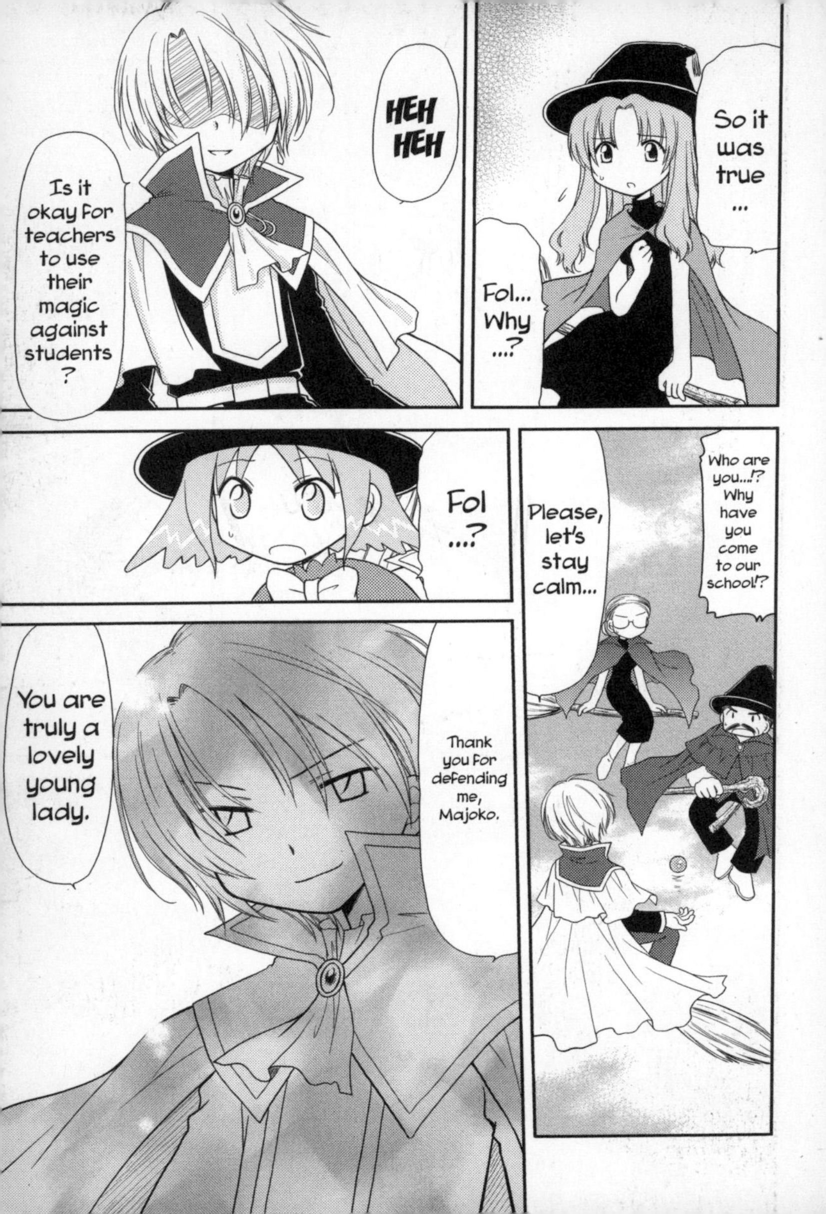
So it was true ...
Fol... Why ...?
HEH HEH
Is it okay for teachers to use their magic against students ?
Who are you...!? Why have you come to our school!?
Please, let's stay calm...
Fol ...?
Thank you for defending me, Majoko.
You are truly a lovely young lady.

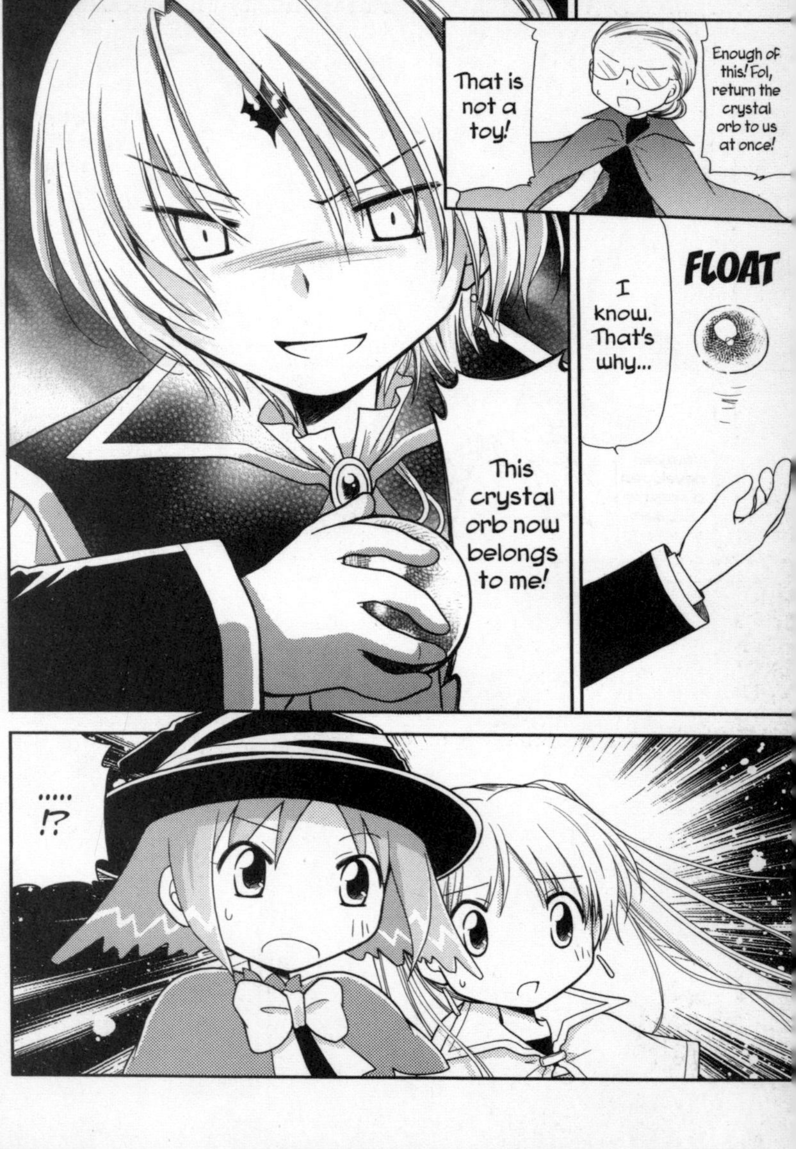
Enough of this! Fol, return the crystal orb to us at once!
That is not a toy!
I know. That's why...
FLOAT
This crystal orb now belongs to me!
......
!?

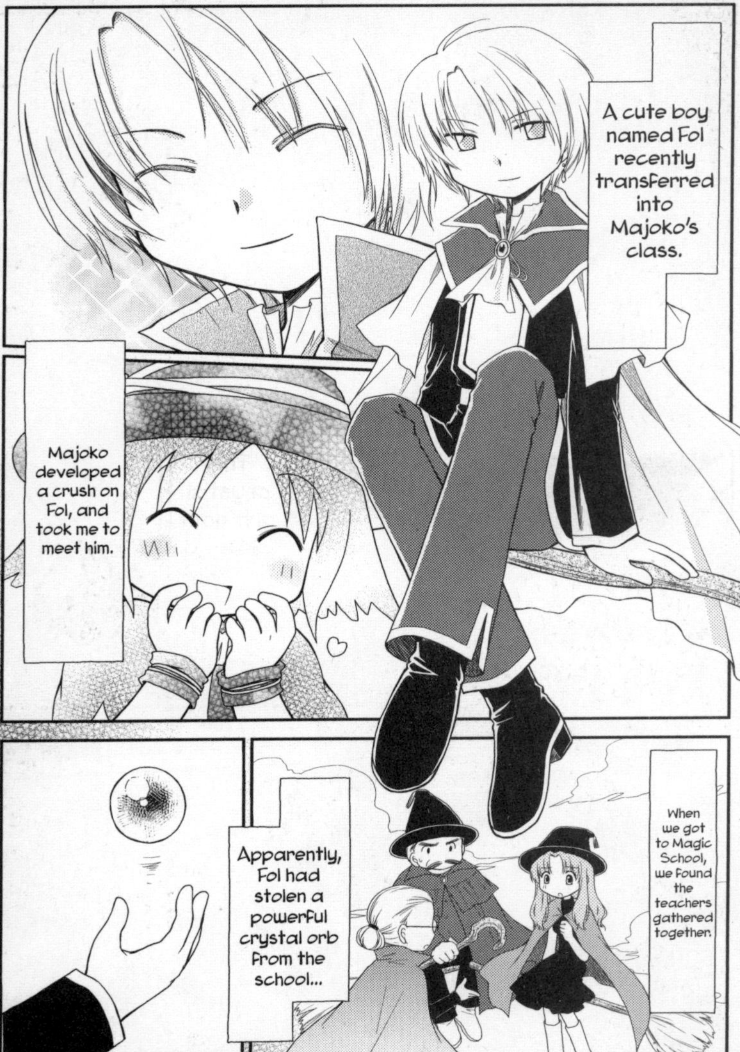
A cute boy named Fol recently transferred into Majoko's class.
Majoko developed a crush on Fol, and took me to meet him.
When we got to Magic School, we found the teachers gathered together.
Apparently, Fol had stolen a powerful crystal orb from the school...

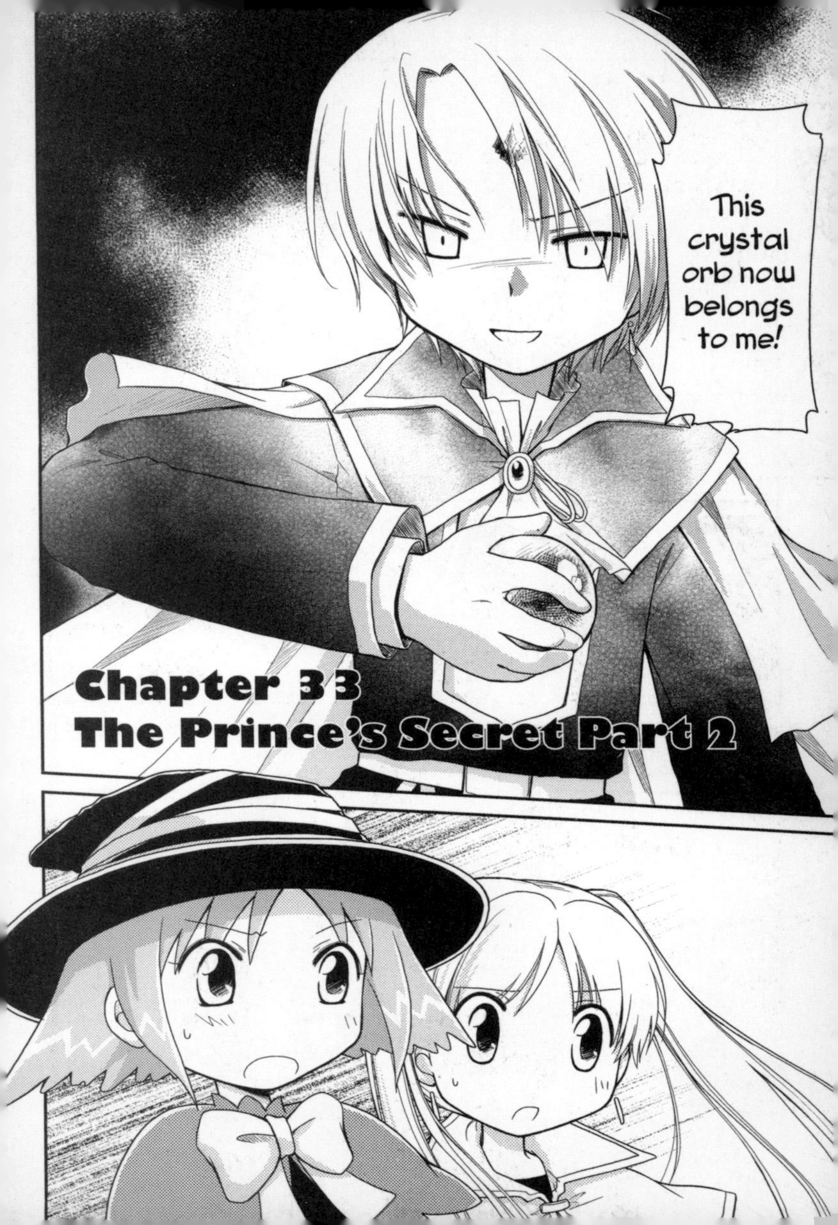
This crystal orb now belongs to me!
Chapter 33
The Prince's Secret Part 2

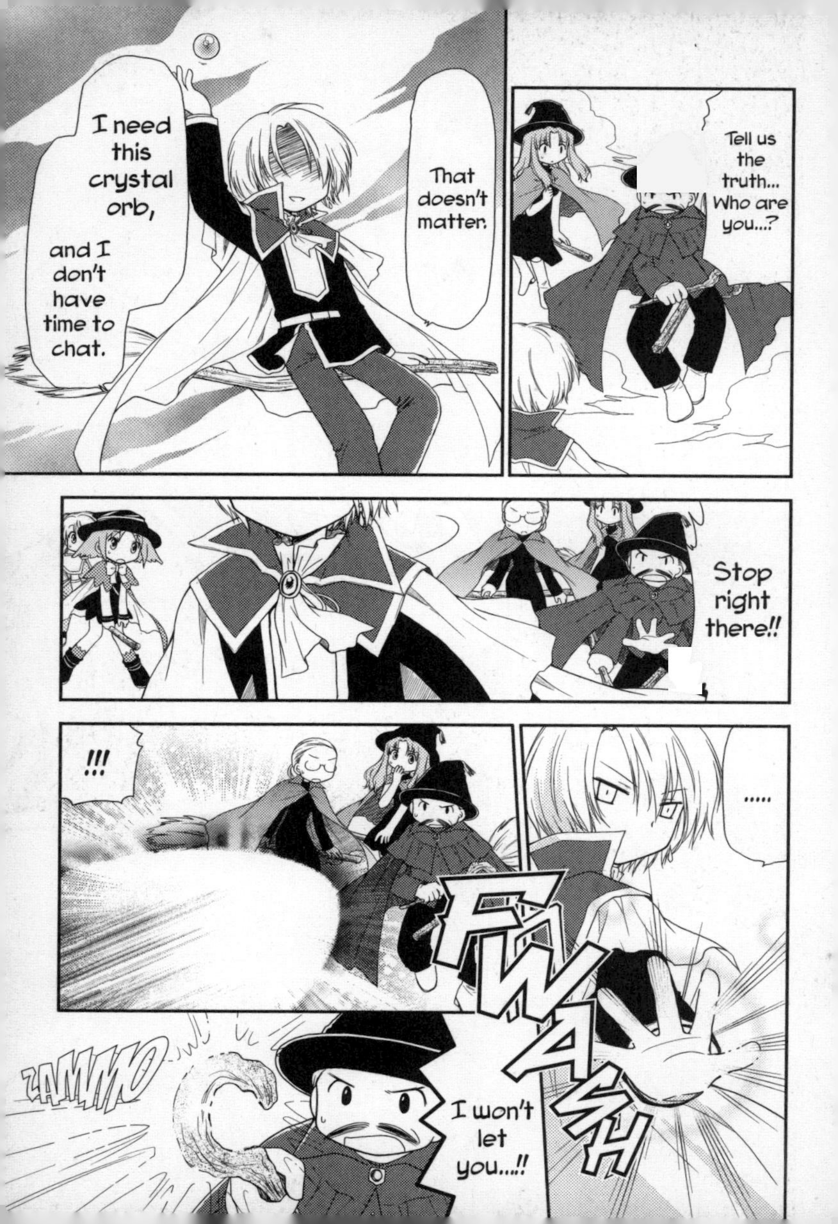
Tell us the truth... Who are you...?
That doesn't matter.
I need this crystal orb,
and I don't have time to chat.
Stop right there!!
.....
!!!
FWASH
I won't let you...!!

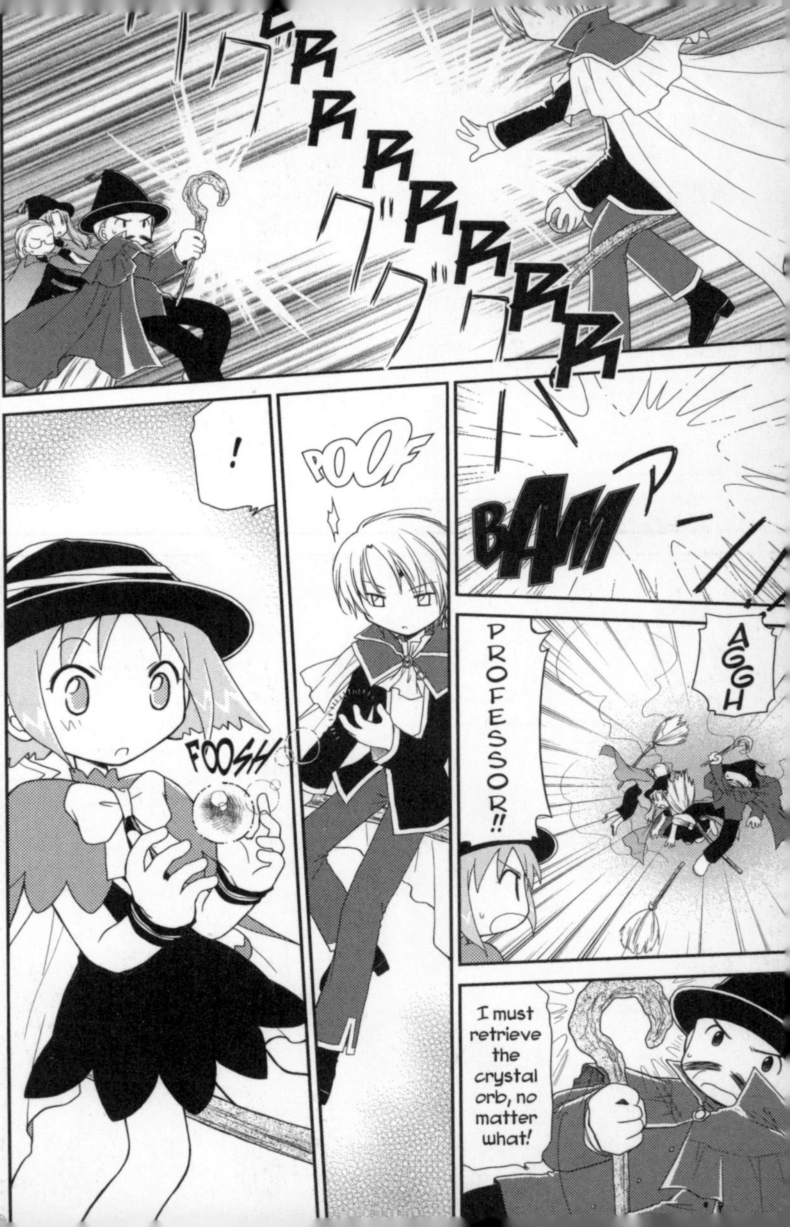
CRRRRRRR
BAM
AGGH
PROFESSOR!!
I must retrieve the crystal orb, no matter what!
POOF
!
FOOSH

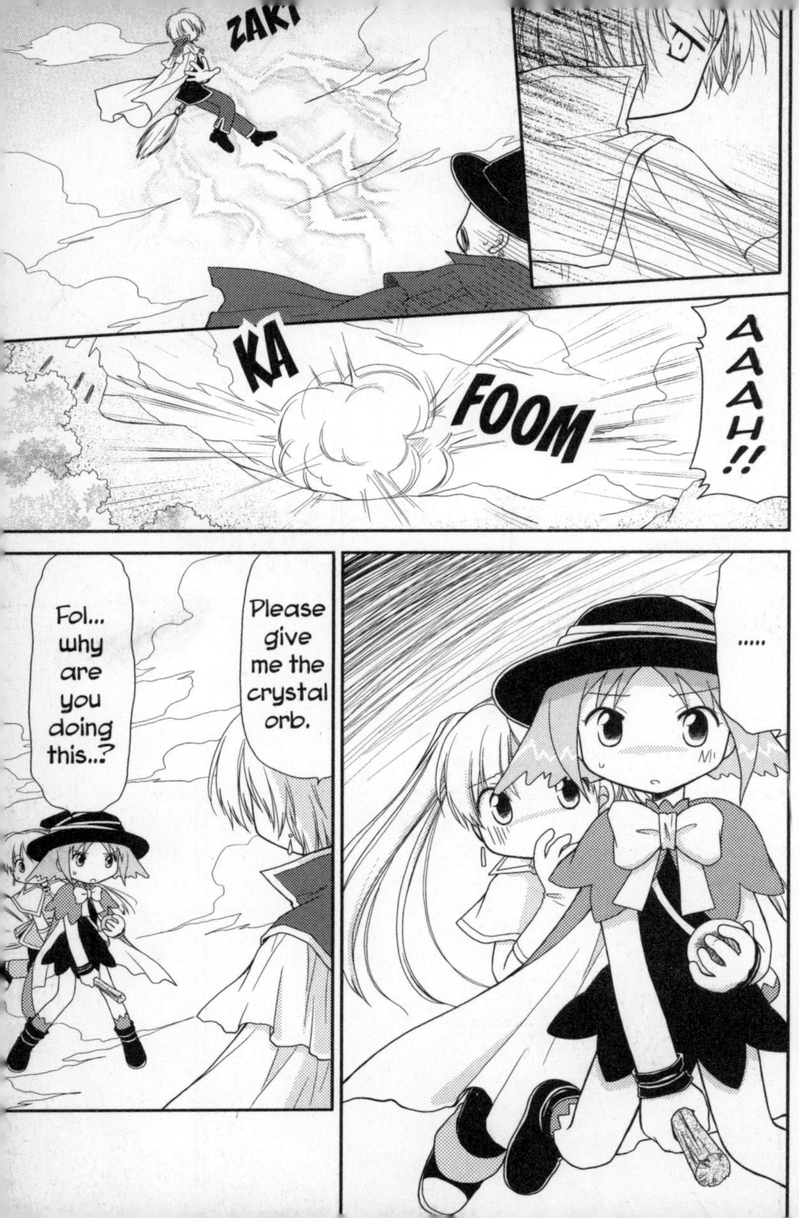
ZAKI
KA
FOOM
AAAAH!!
.....
Please give me the crystal orb.
Fol... why are you doing this..?

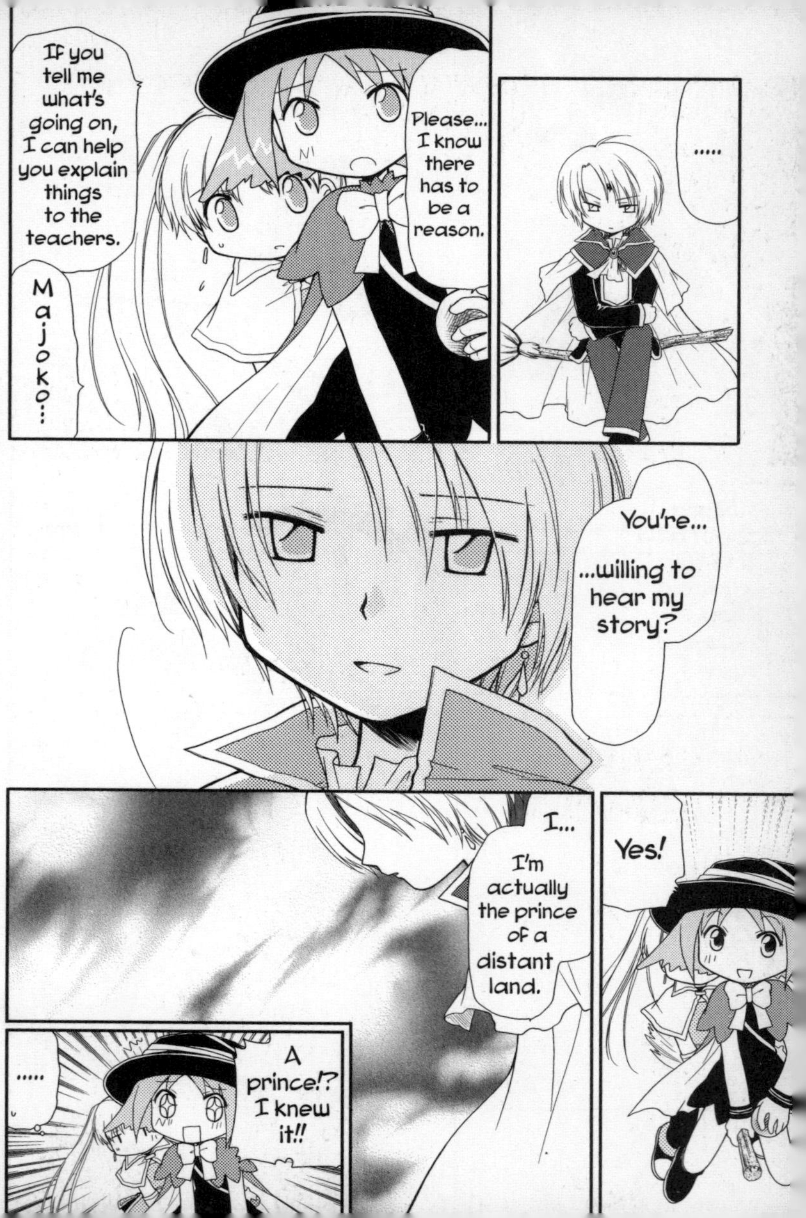
.....
Please... I know there has to be a reason.
If you tell me what's going on, I can help you explain things to the teachers.
Majoko...
You're...
...willing to hear my story?
Yes!
I...
I'm actually the prince of a distant land.
A prince!? I knew it!!
.....

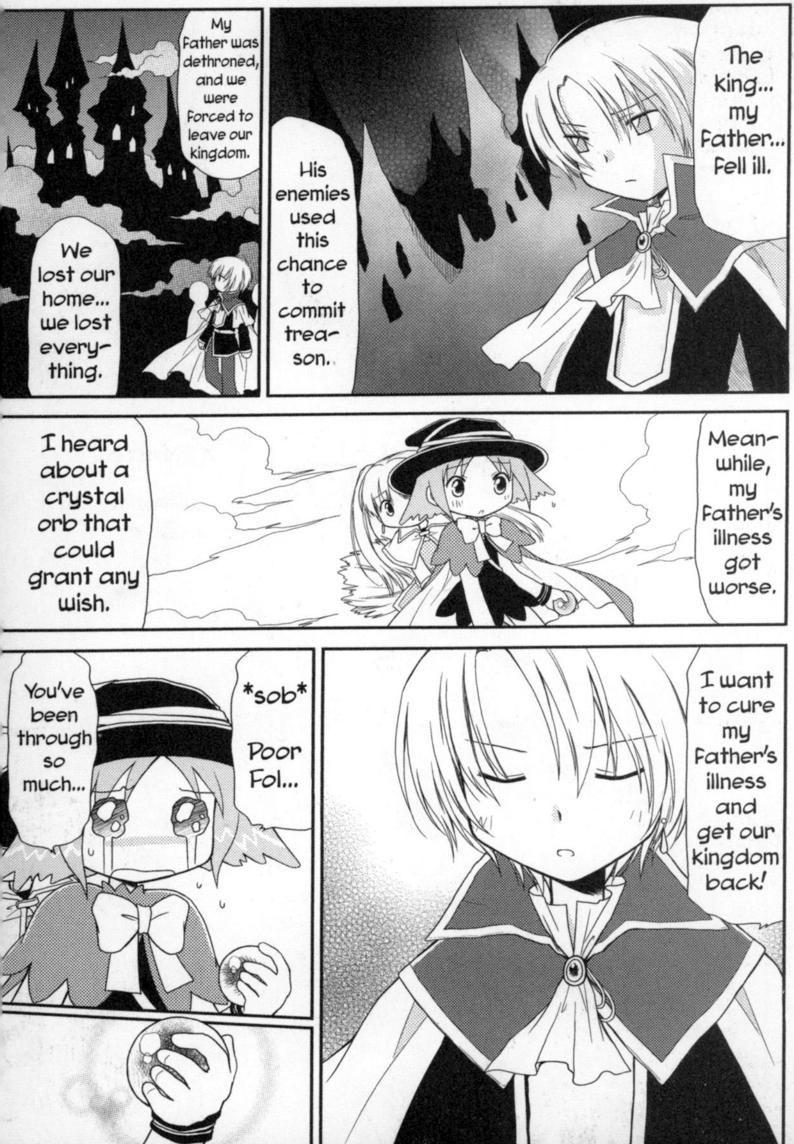
The king... my father... fell ill.
His enemies used this chance to commit trea-son.
My father was dethroned, and we were forced to leave our kingdom.
We lost our home... we lost every-thing.
Mean-while, my father's illness got worse.
I heard about a crystal orb that could grant any wish.
I want to cure my father's illness and get our kingdom back!
sob
Poor Fol...
You've been through so much...

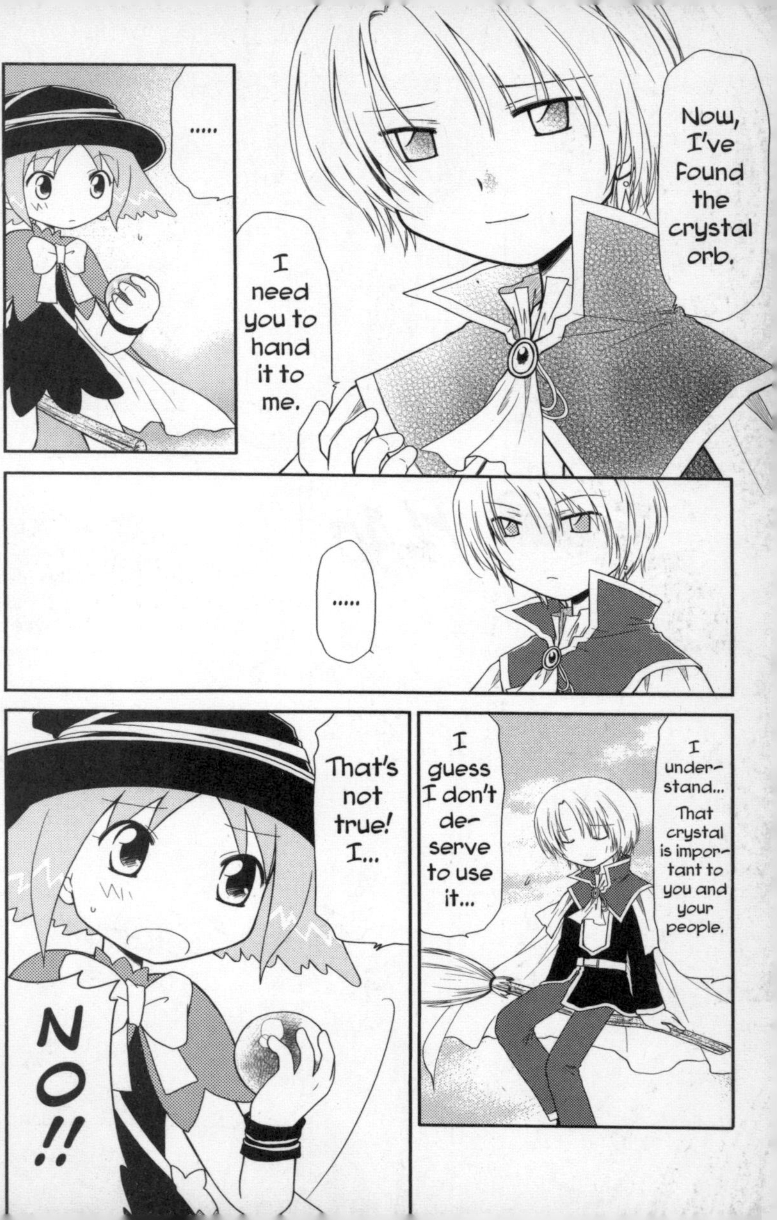
Now, I've found the crystal orb.
I need you to hand it to me.
.....
.....
I understand... That crystal is important to you and your people.
I guess I don't deserve to use it...
That's not true! I...
NO!!

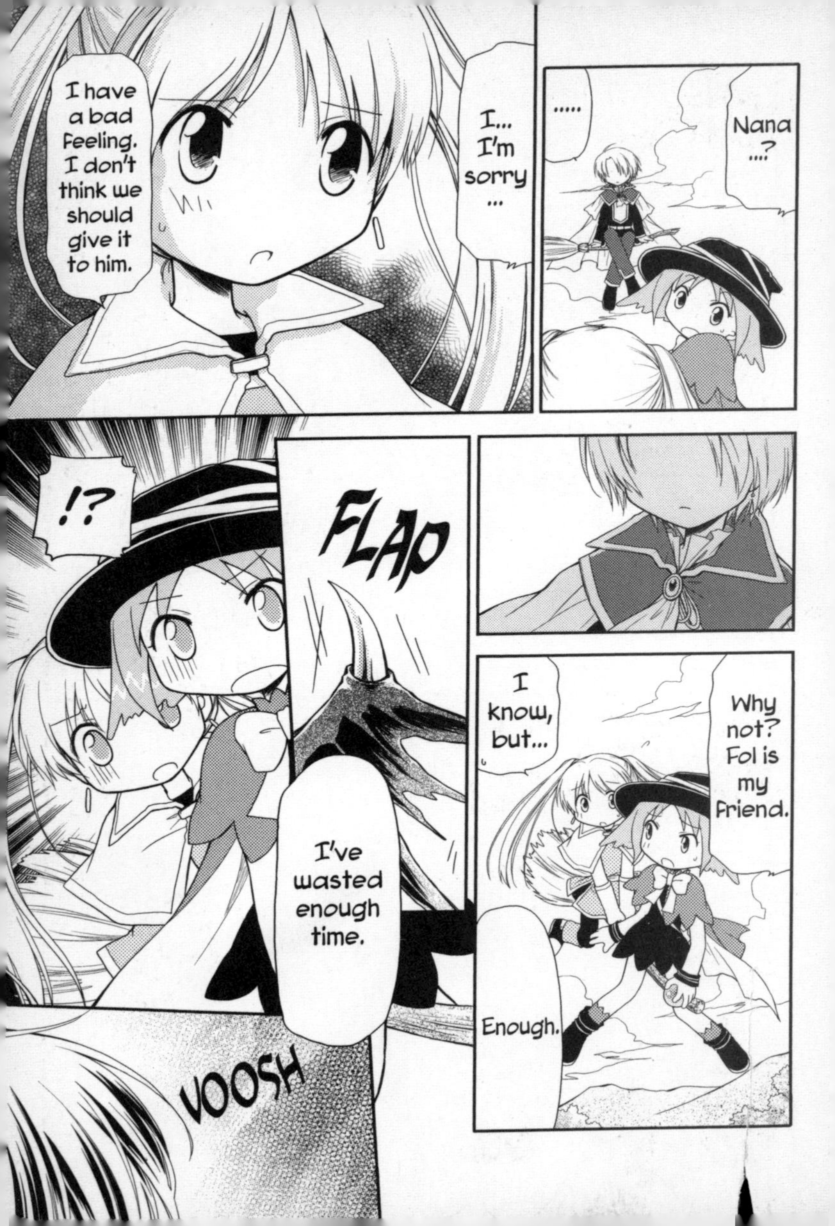
Nana ...?
.....
I... I'm sorry ...
I have a bad feeling. I don't think we should give it to him.
Why not? Fol is my friend.
I know, but...
Enough.
FLAP
I've wasted enough time.
!?
VOOSH

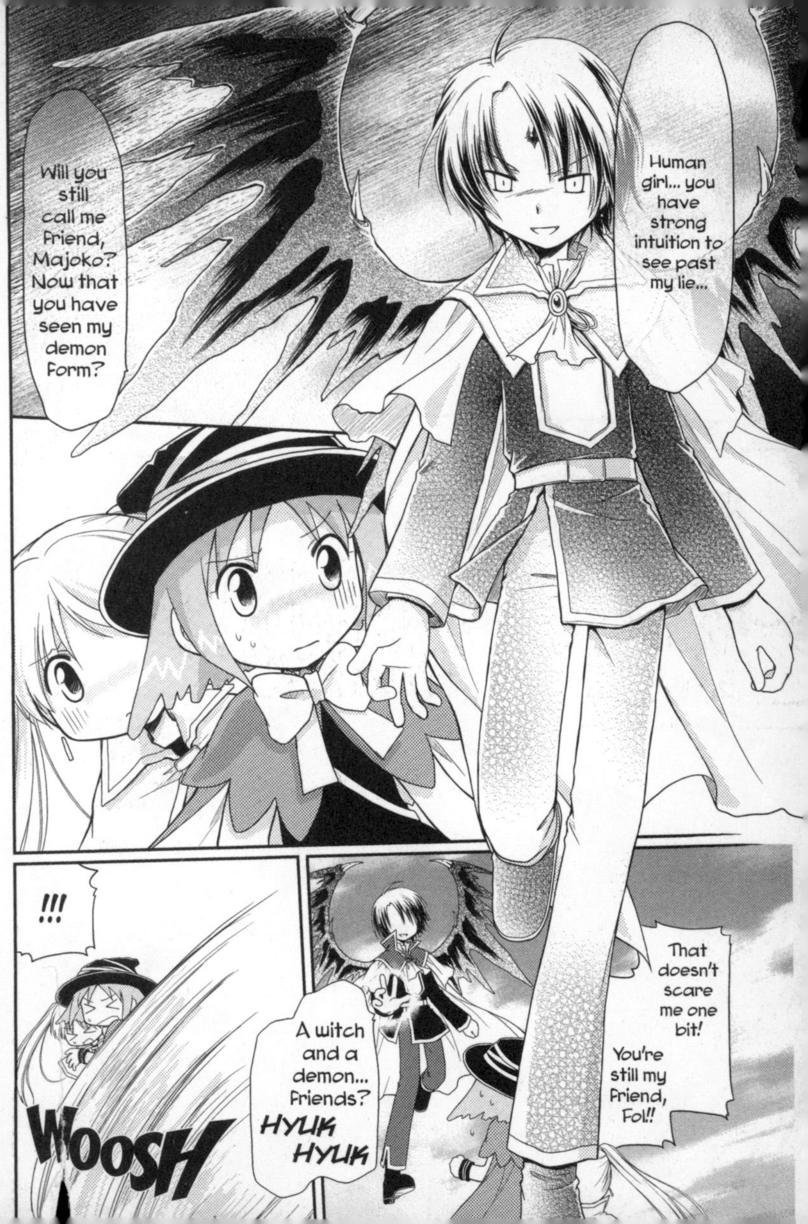
Human girl... you have strong intuition to see past my lie...
Will you still call me friend, Majoko? Now that you have seen my demon form?
That doesn't scare me one bit!
You're still my friend, Fol!!
A witch and a demon... friends?
HYUK HYUK
!!!
WOOSH

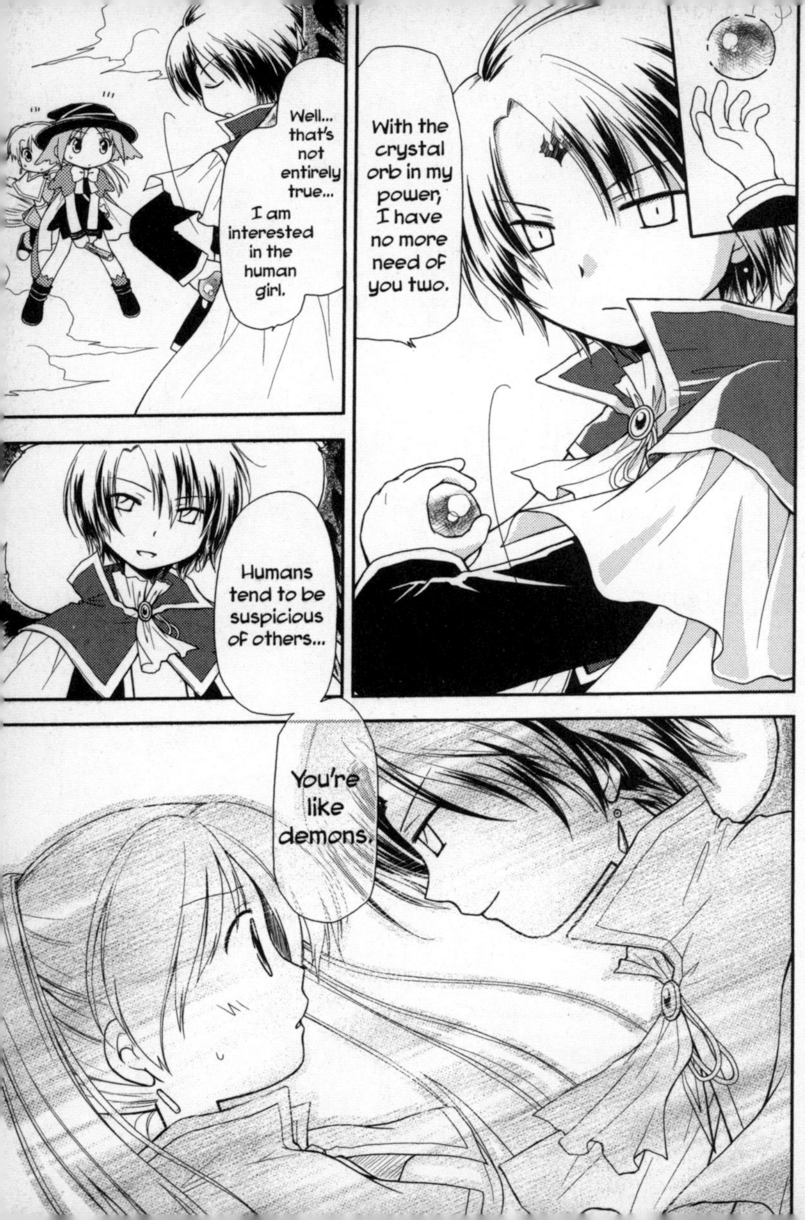
With the crystal orb in my power, I have no more need of you two.
Well... that's not entirely true...
I am interested in the human girl.
Humans tend to be suspicious of others...
You're like demons.

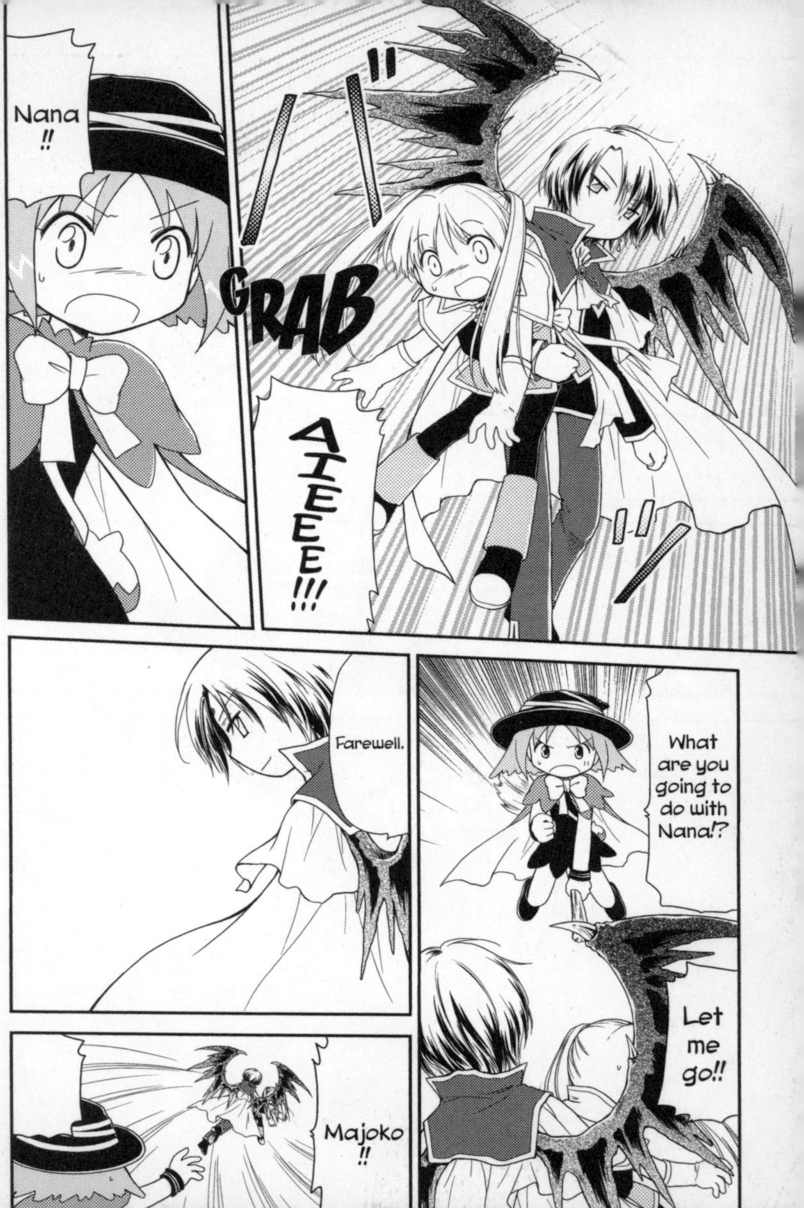
GRAB
AIEEEE!!!
Nana !!
What are you going to do with Nana!?
Farewell.
Let me go!!
Majoko !!

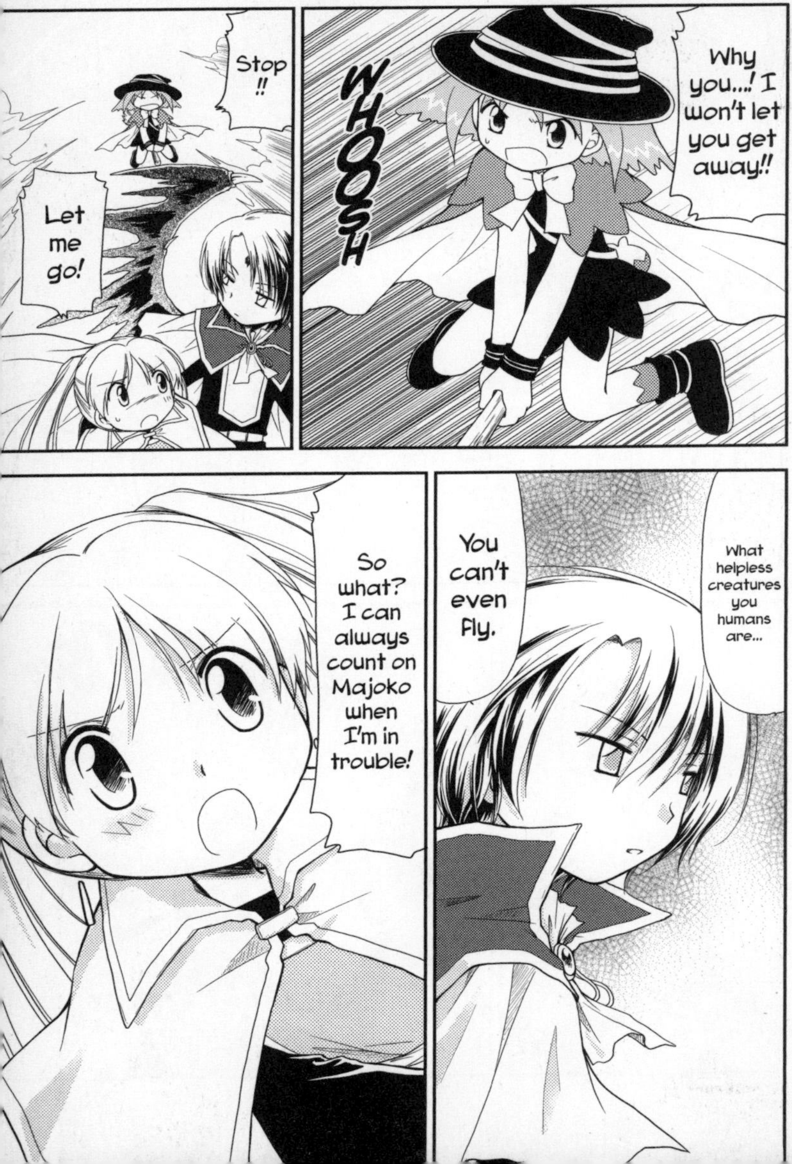
Why you...! I won't let you get away!!
WHOOSH
Stop!!
Let me go!
What helpless creatures you humans are...
You can't even fly.
So what? I can always count on Majoko when I'm in trouble!

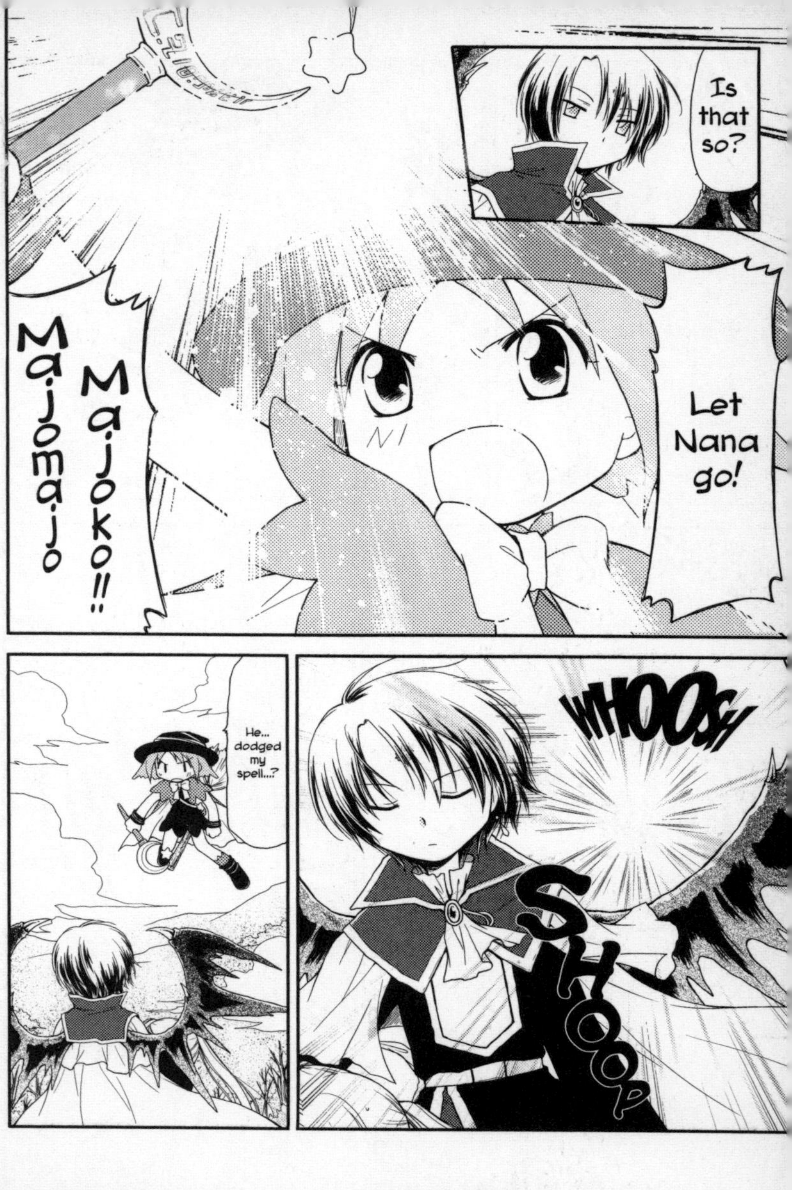

Is that so?
Let Nana go!
Majomajo
Majoko!!
WHOOSH
SHOOP
He... dodged my spell...?

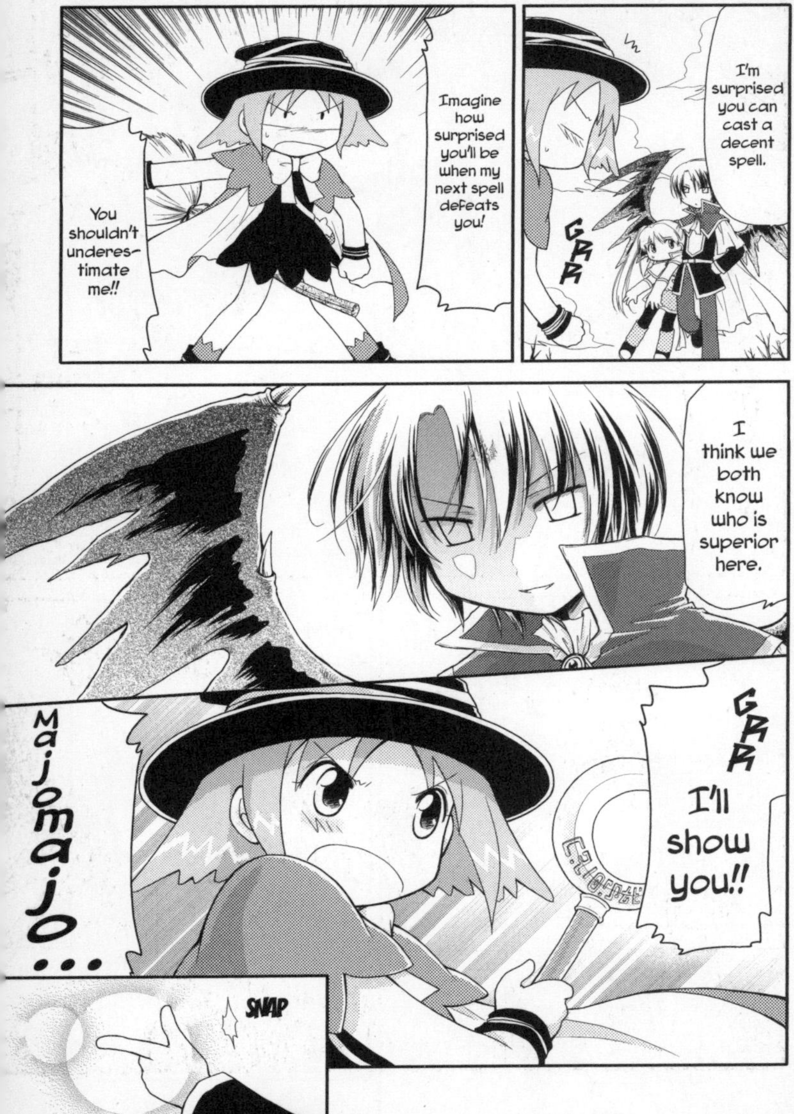
I'm surprised you can cast a decent spell.
GRR
Imagine how surprised you'll be when my next spell defeats you!
You shouldn't underes-timate me!!
I think we both know who is superior here.
GRR
I'll show you!!
Majomajo...
SNAP

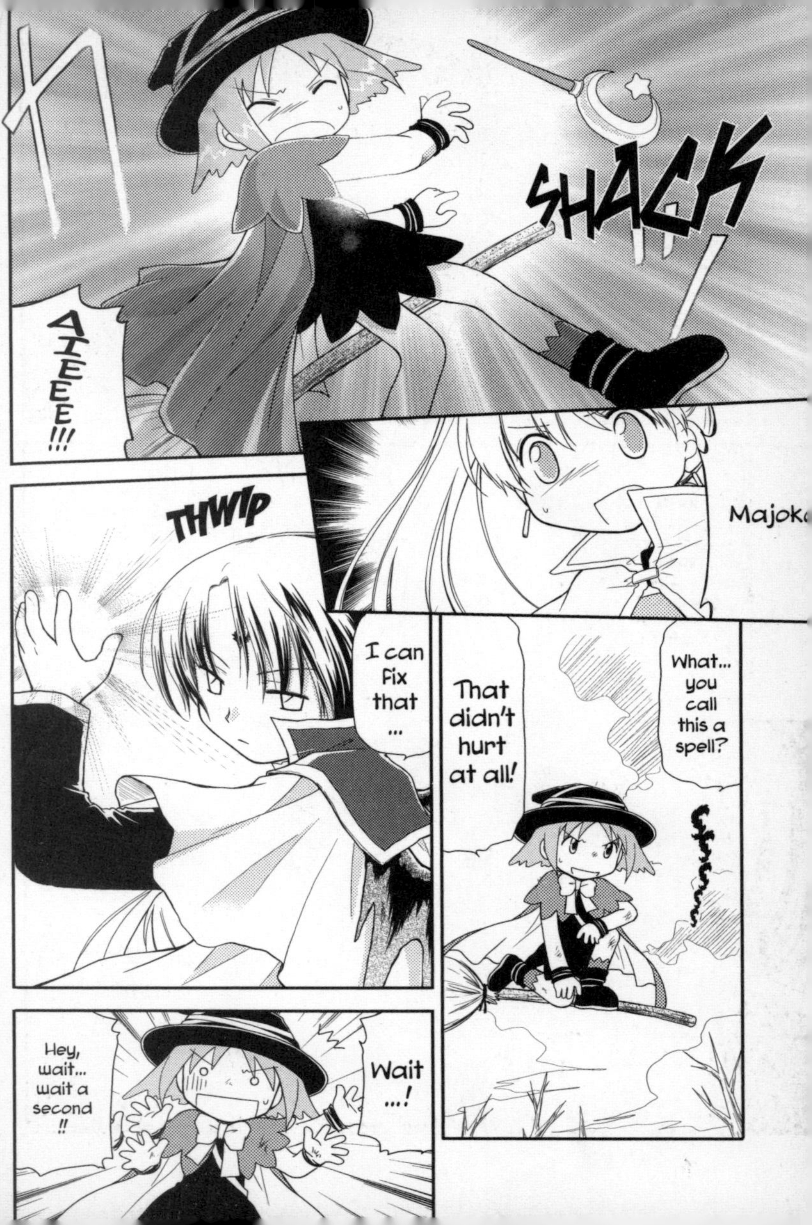
SHACK
AIEEE!!!
What... you call this a spell?
That didn't hurt at all!
THWIP
I can fix that ...
Wait ...!
Hey, wait... wait a second !!

Majoka

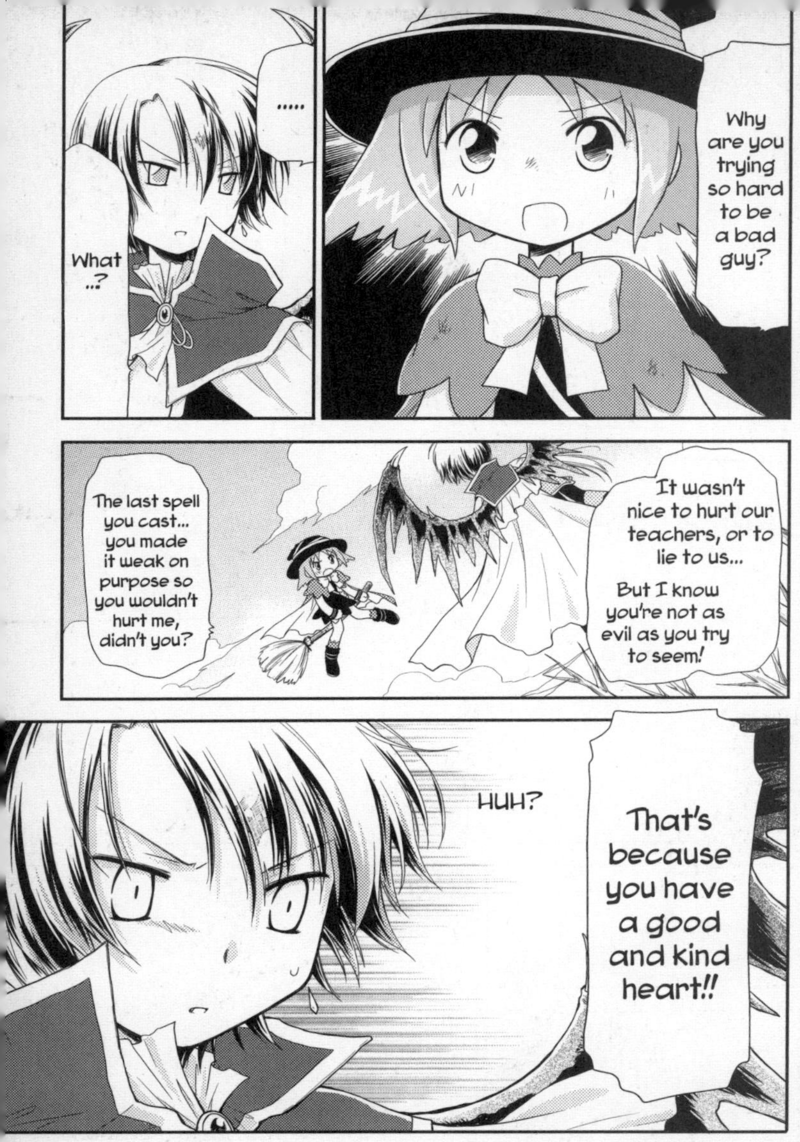
Why are you trying so hard to be a bad guy?
.....
What ...?
It wasn't nice to hurt our teachers, or to lie to us...
But I know you're not as evil as you try to seem!
The last spell you cast... you made it weak on purpose so you wouldn't hurt me, didn't you?
That's because you have a good and kind heart!!
HUH?

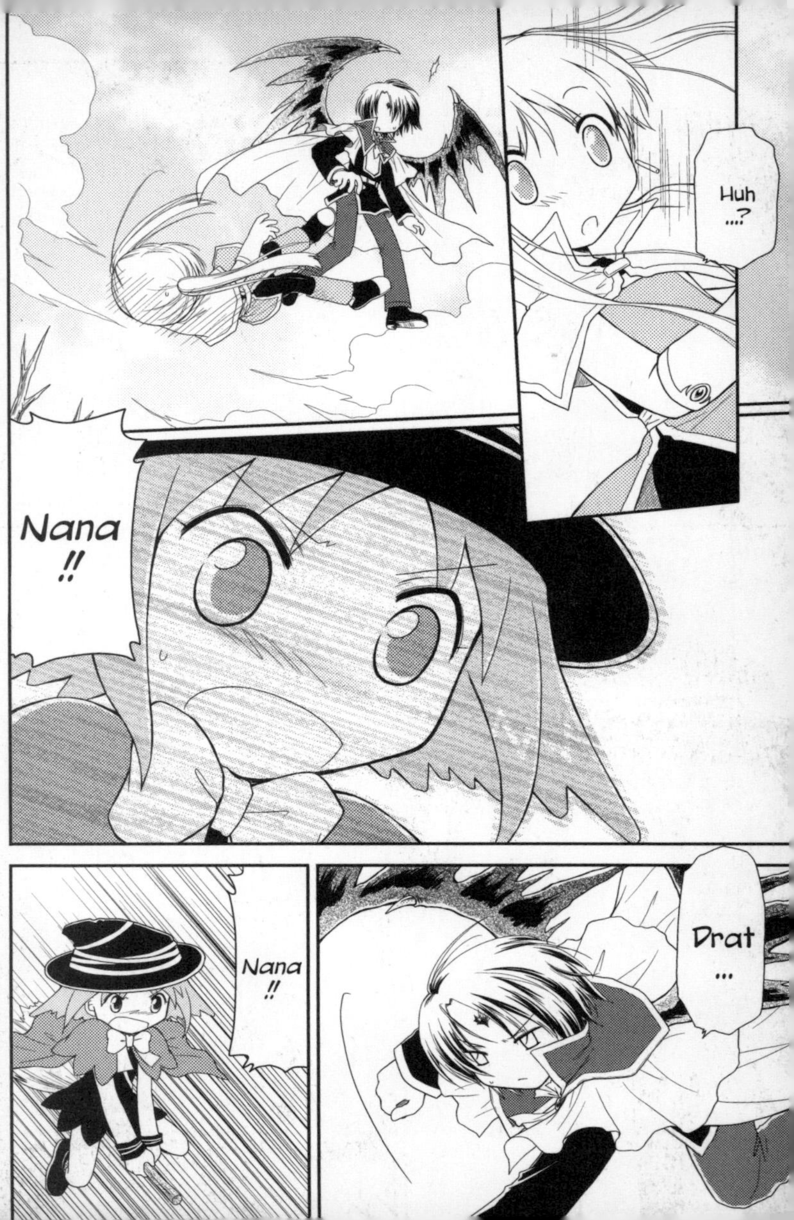
Huh ...?
Nana !!
Drat ...
Nana !!

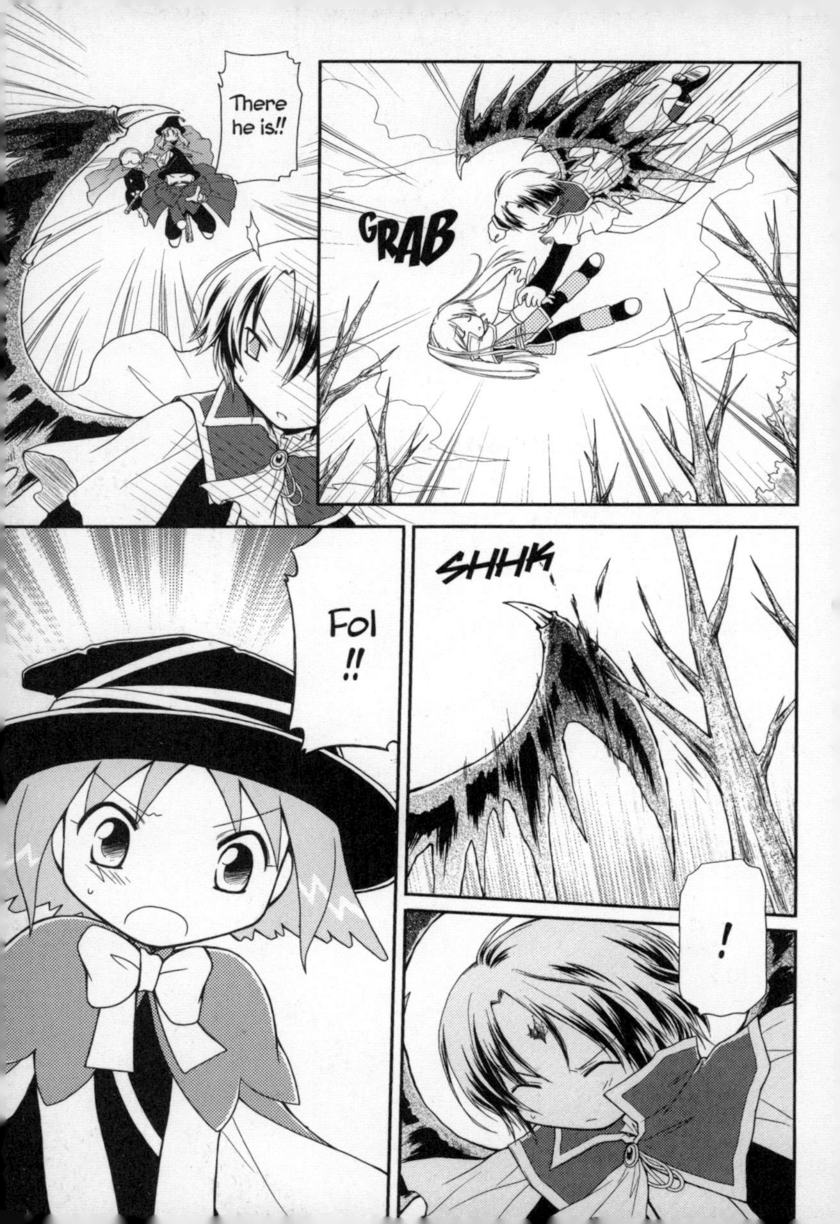
GRAB
There he is!!
SHHK
!
Fol !!

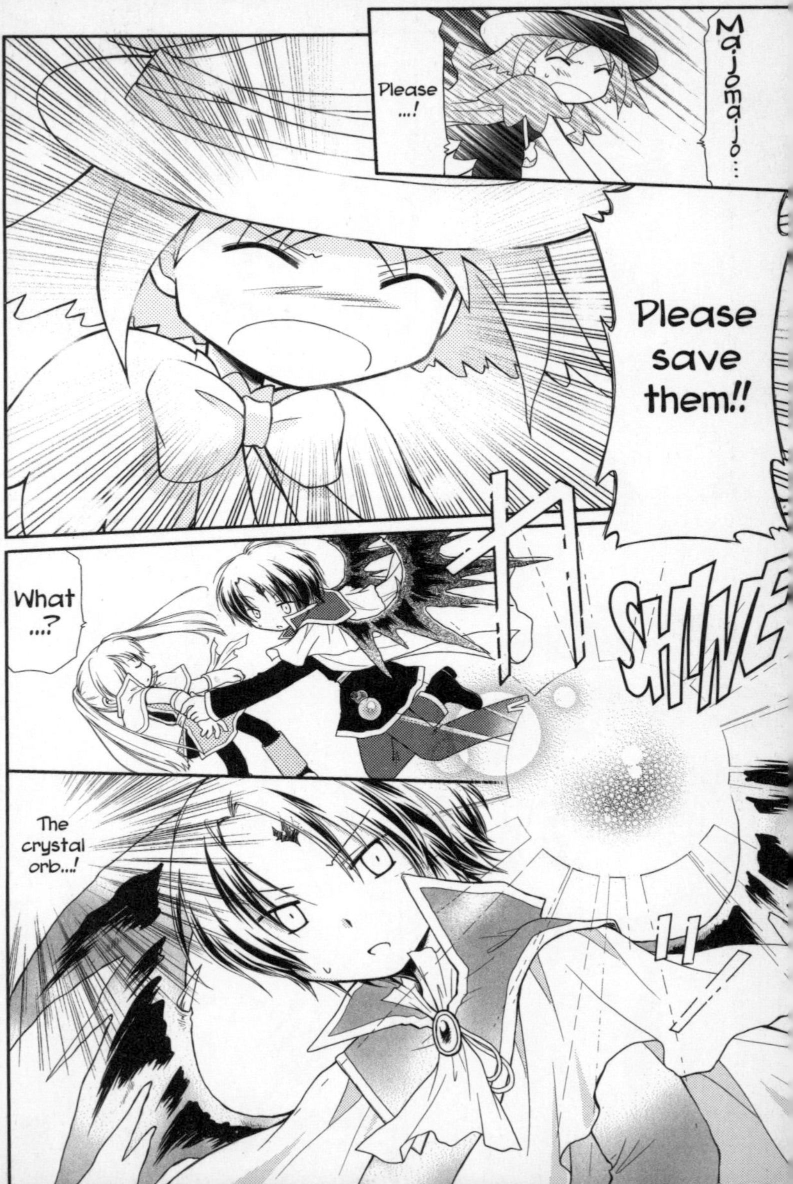
Majomajo...
Please ...!
Please save them!!
SHINE
What ...?
The crystal orb...!

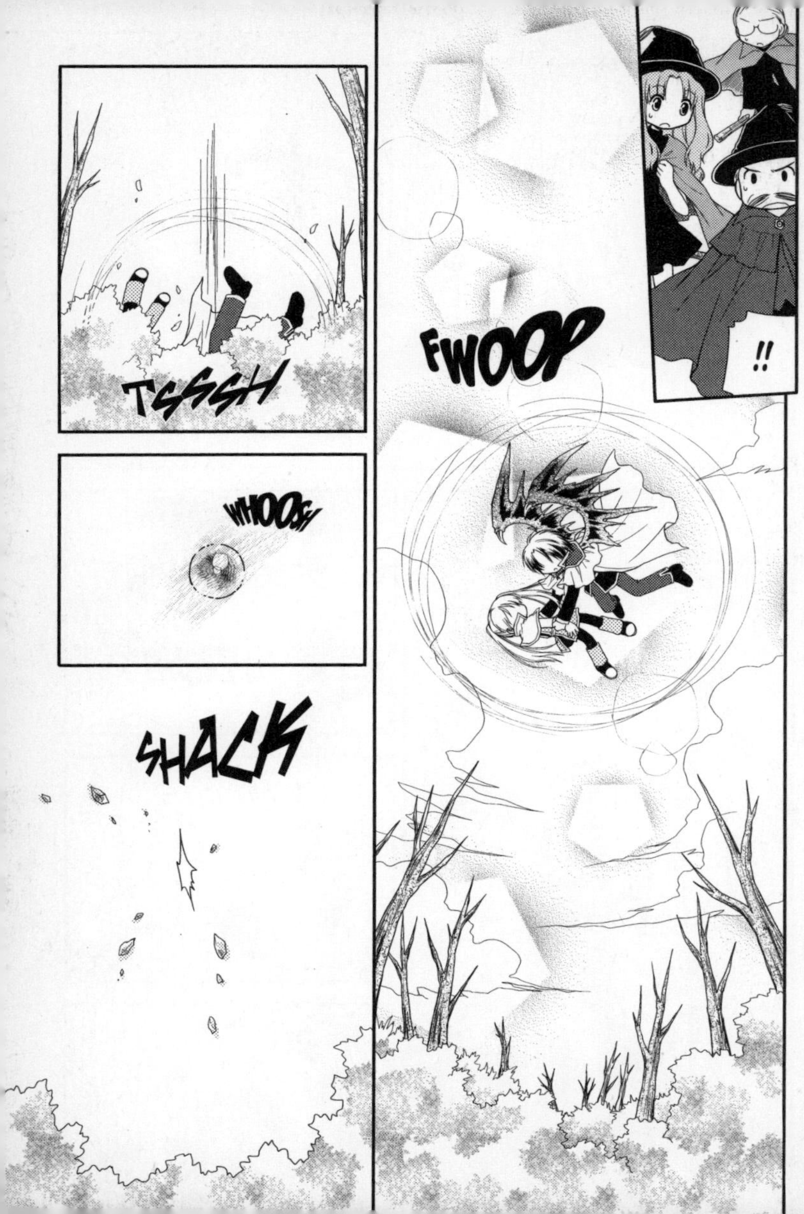
!!
FWOOP
TSSSH
WHOOSH
SHACK

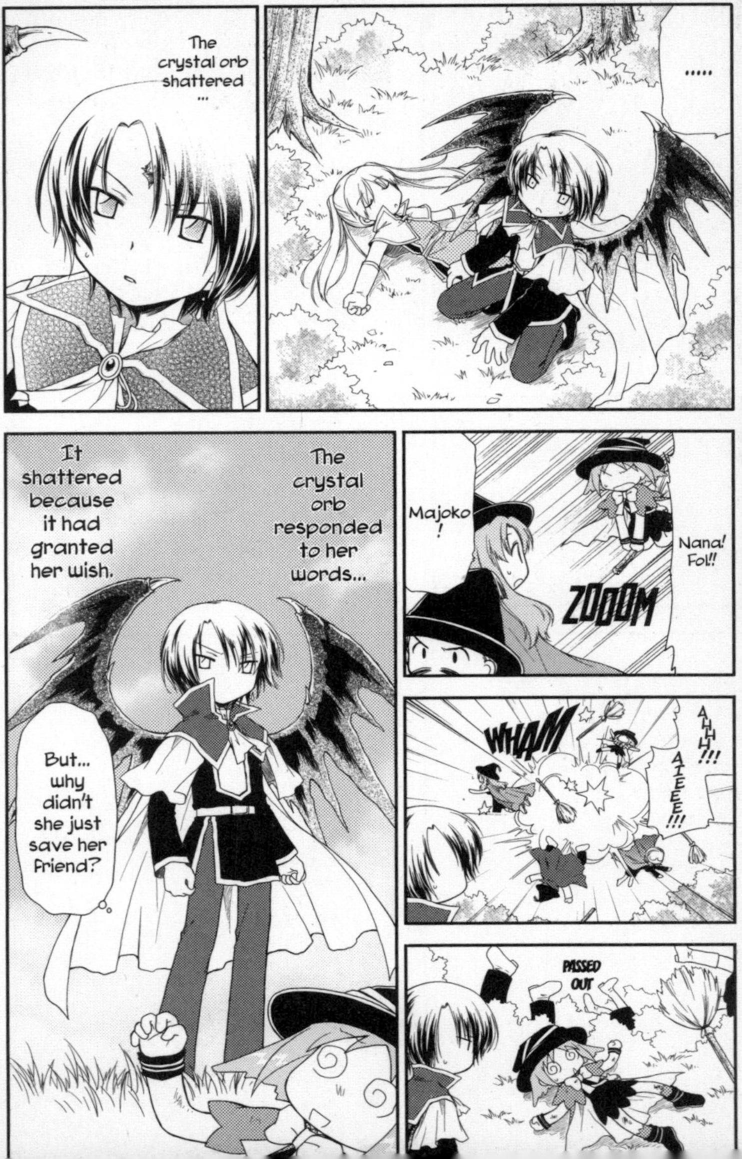
.....
The crystal orb shattered ...
Nana! Fol!!
Majoko!
ZOOOM
AHHH!!!
AIEEEE!!!
WHAM
PASSED OUT
The crystal orb responded to her words...
It shattered because it had granted her wish.
But... why didn't she just save her friend?

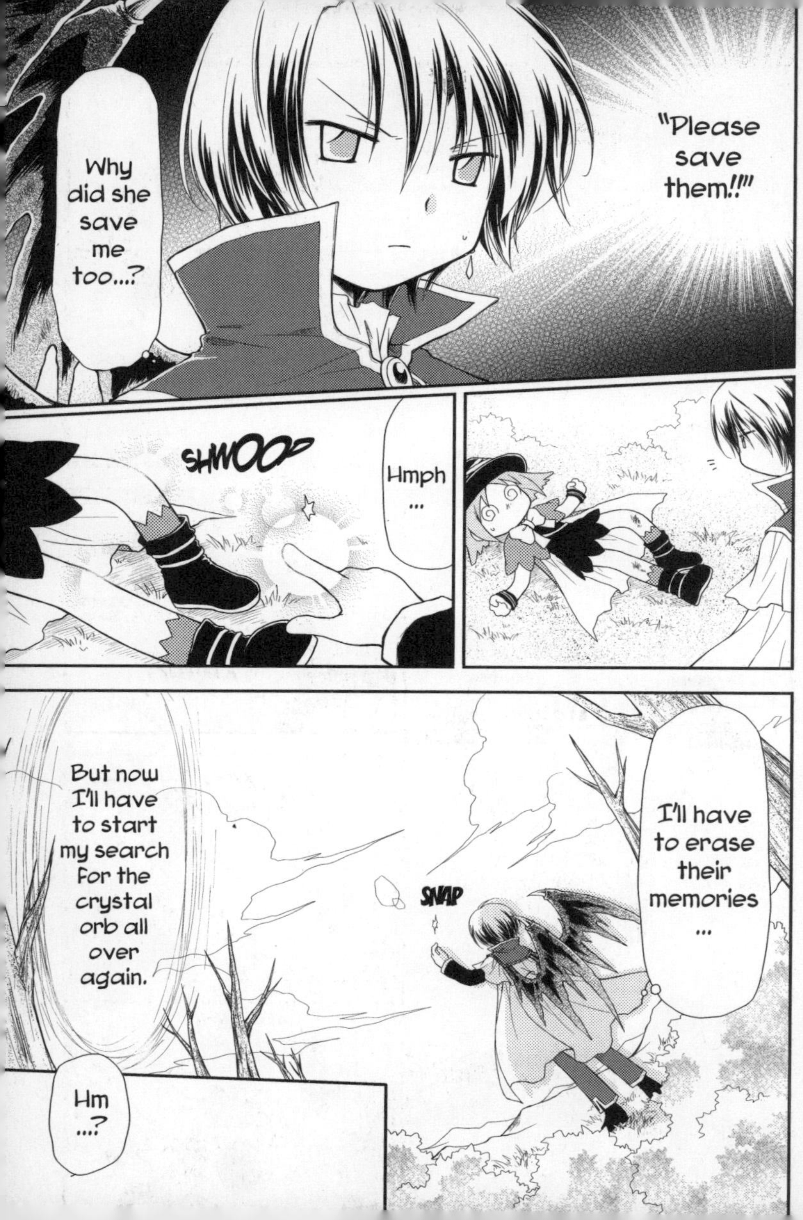
"Please save them!!"
Why did she save me too...?
Hmph ...
SHWOOP
I'll have to erase their memories ...
SNAP
But now I'll have to start my search for the crystal orb all over again.
Hm ...?

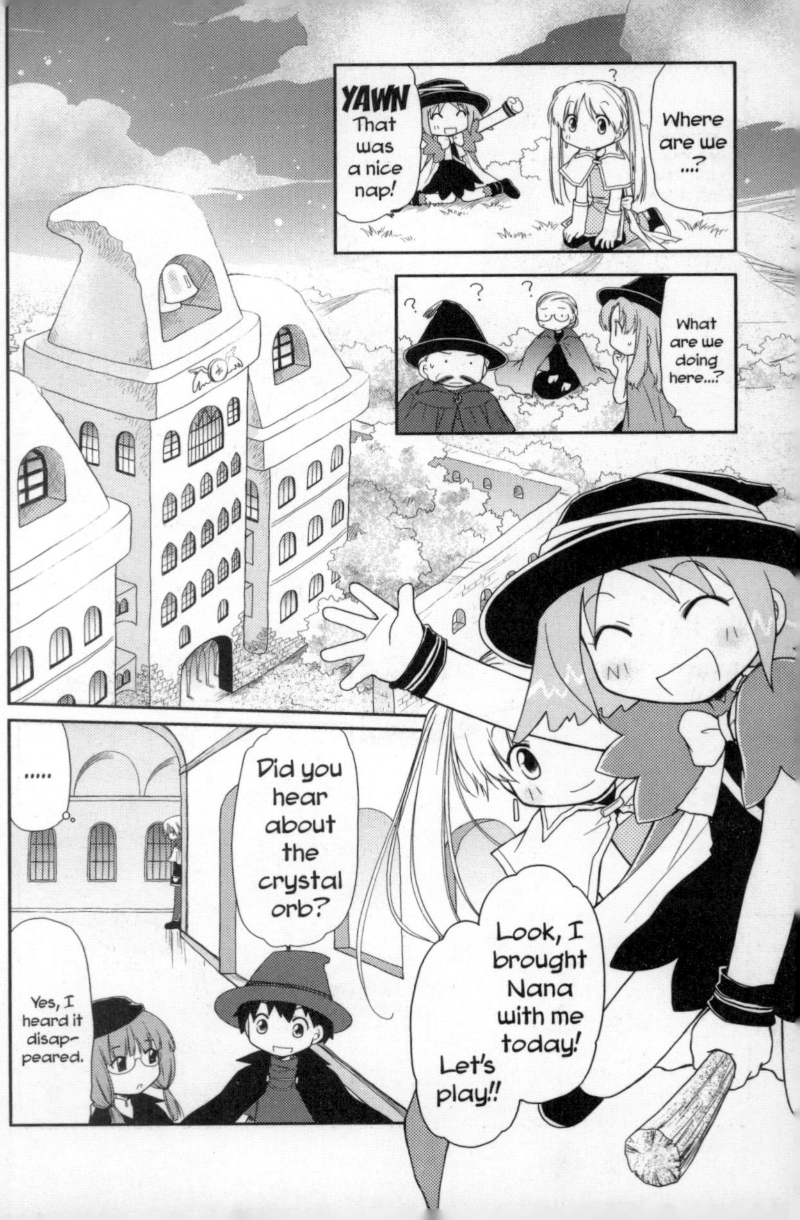
Where are we ...?
YAWN
That was a nice nap!
What are we doing here...?
Look, I brought Nana with me today!
Let's play!!
Did you hear about the crystal orb?
.....
Yes, I heard it disap-peared.

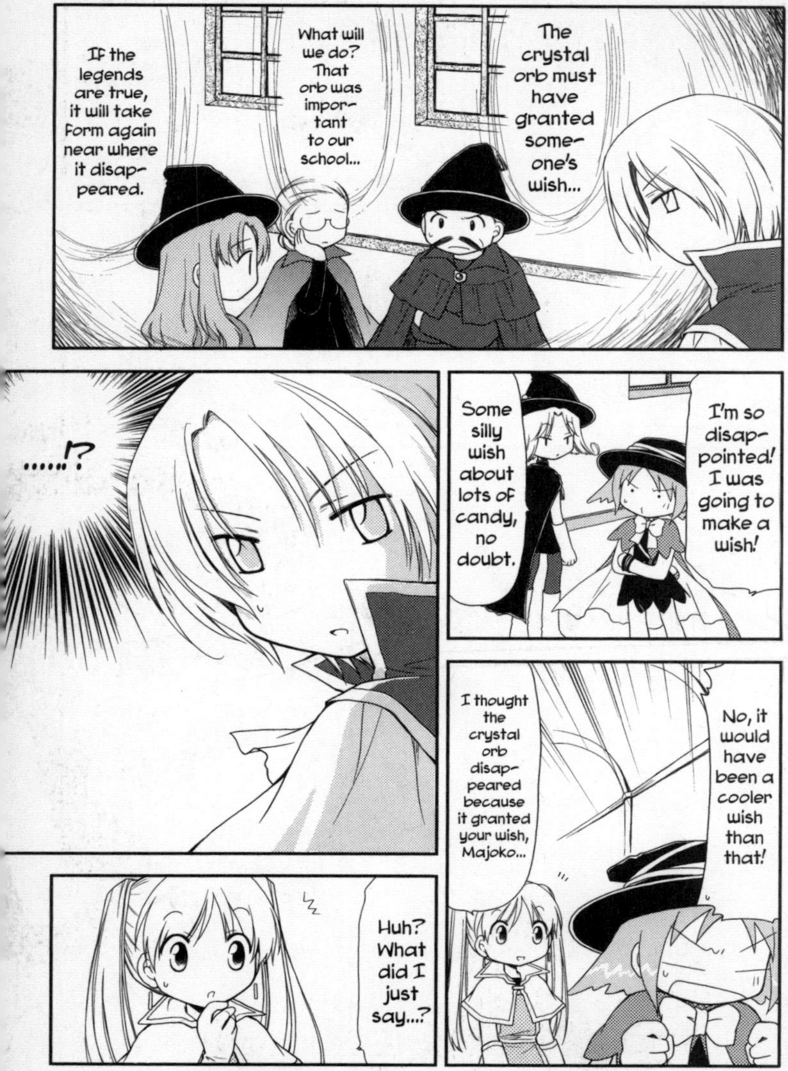
The crystal orb must have granted some-one's wish...
What will we do? That orb was impor-tant to our school...
If the legends are true, it will take form again near where it disap-peared.
I'm so disap-pointed! I was going to make a wish!
Some silly wish about lots of candy, no doubt.
......!?
No, it would have been a cooler wish than that!
I thought the crystal orb disap-peared because it granted your wish, Majoko...
Huh? What did I just say...?

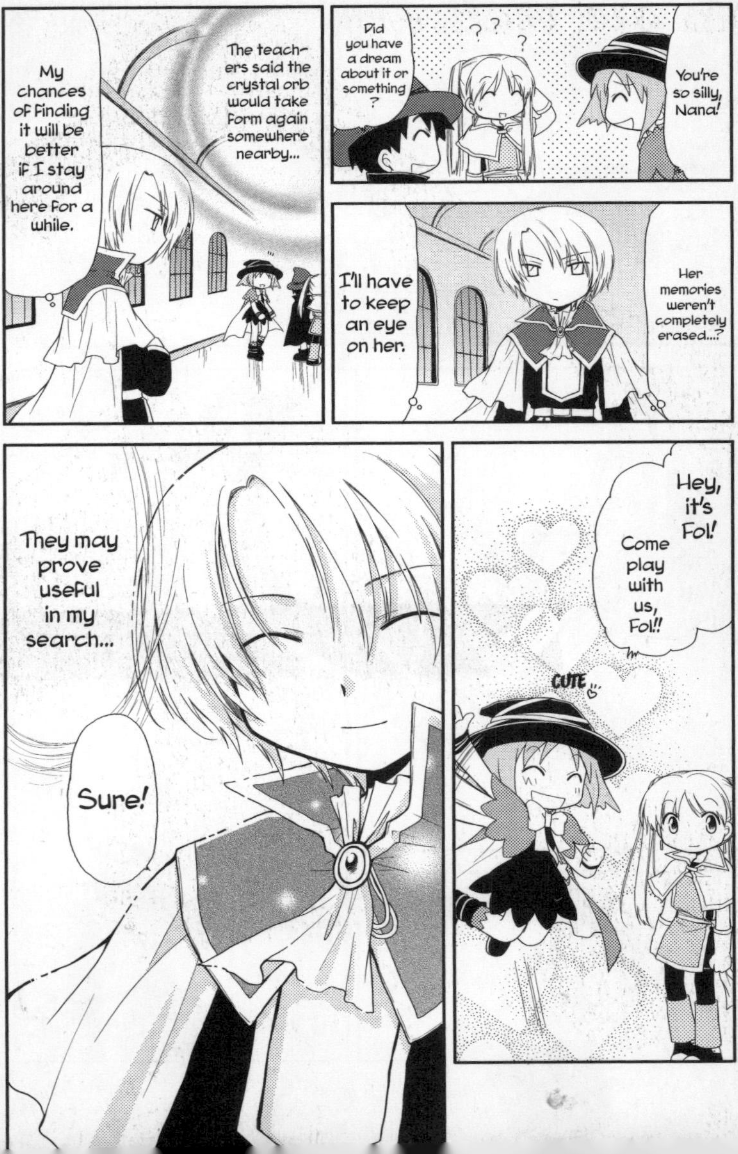
You're so silly, Nana!
Did you have a dream about it or something?
Her memories weren't completely erased...?
I'll have to keep an eye on her.
The teach-ers said the crystal orb would take form again somewhere nearby...
My chances of finding it will be better if I stay around here for a while.
Hey, it's Fol!
Come play with us, Fol!!
CUTE
They may prove useful in my search...
Sure!

Chapter 34
An Old Memory

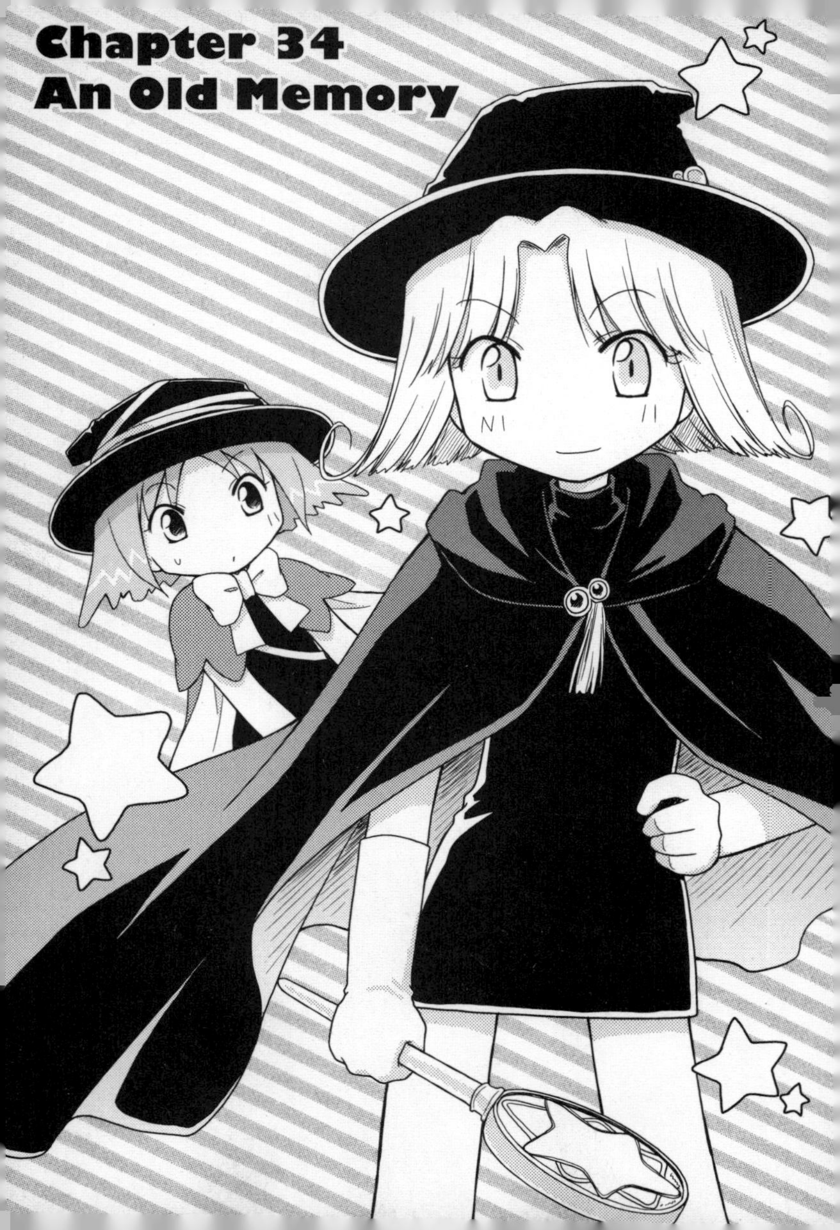

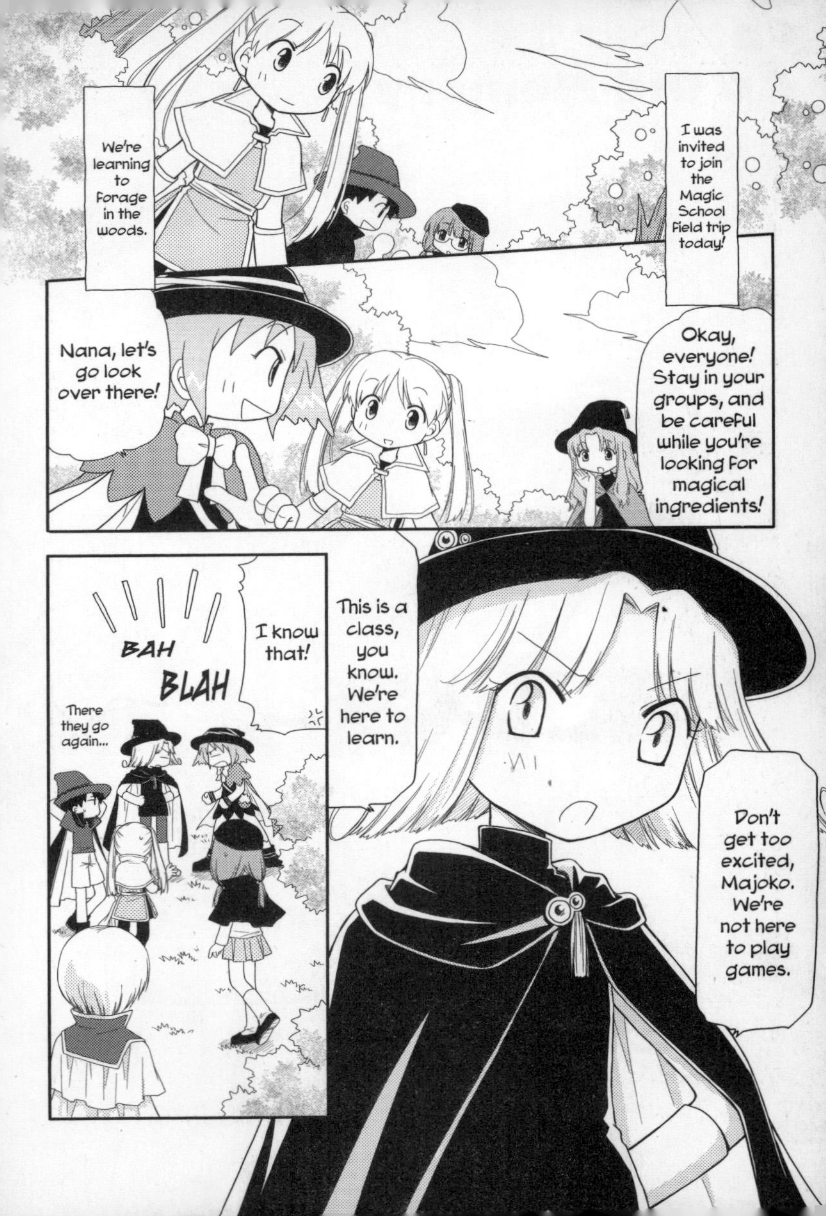
I was invited to join the Magic School field trip today!
We're learning to forage in the woods.
Okay, everyone! Stay in your groups, and be careful while you're looking for magical ingredients!
Nana, let's go look over there!
Don't get too excited, Majoko. We're not here to play games.
This is a class, you know. We're here to learn.
I know that!
BAH
BLAH
There they go again...

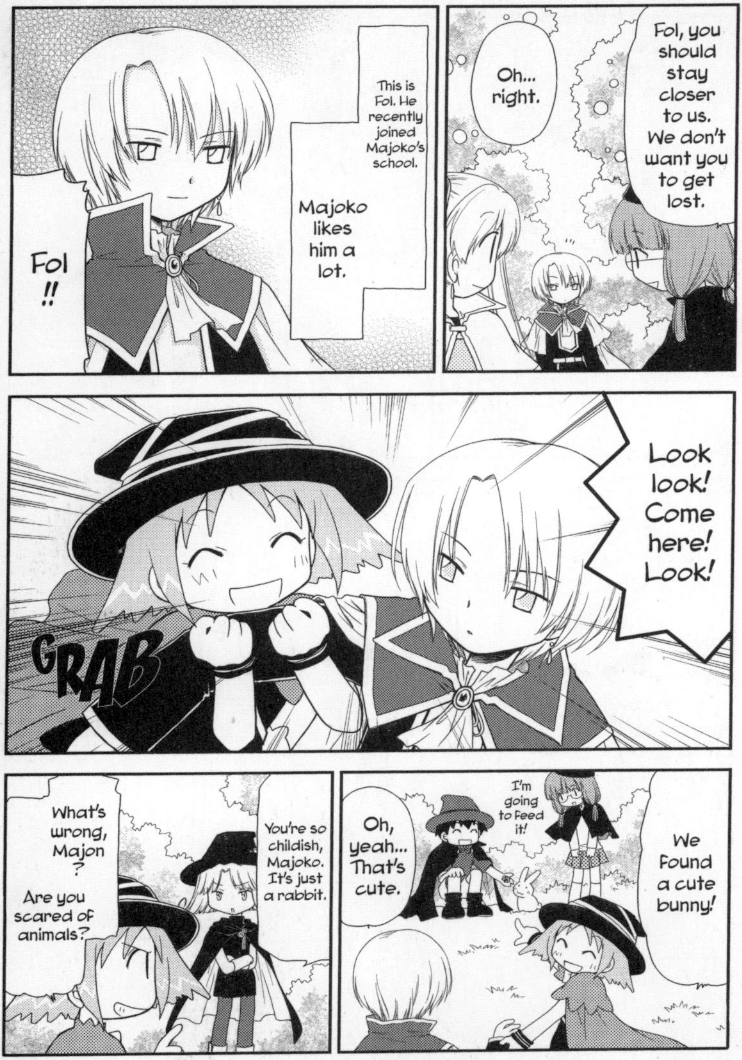
Fol, you should stay closer to us. We don't want you to get lost.
Oh... right.
This is Fol. He recently joined Majoko's school.
Majoko likes him a lot.
Fol !!
Look look! Come here! Look!
GRAB
We found a cute bunny!
I'm going to feed it!
Oh, yeah... That's cute.
You're so childish, Majoko. It's just a rabbit.
What's wrong, Majon ?
Are you scared of animals?

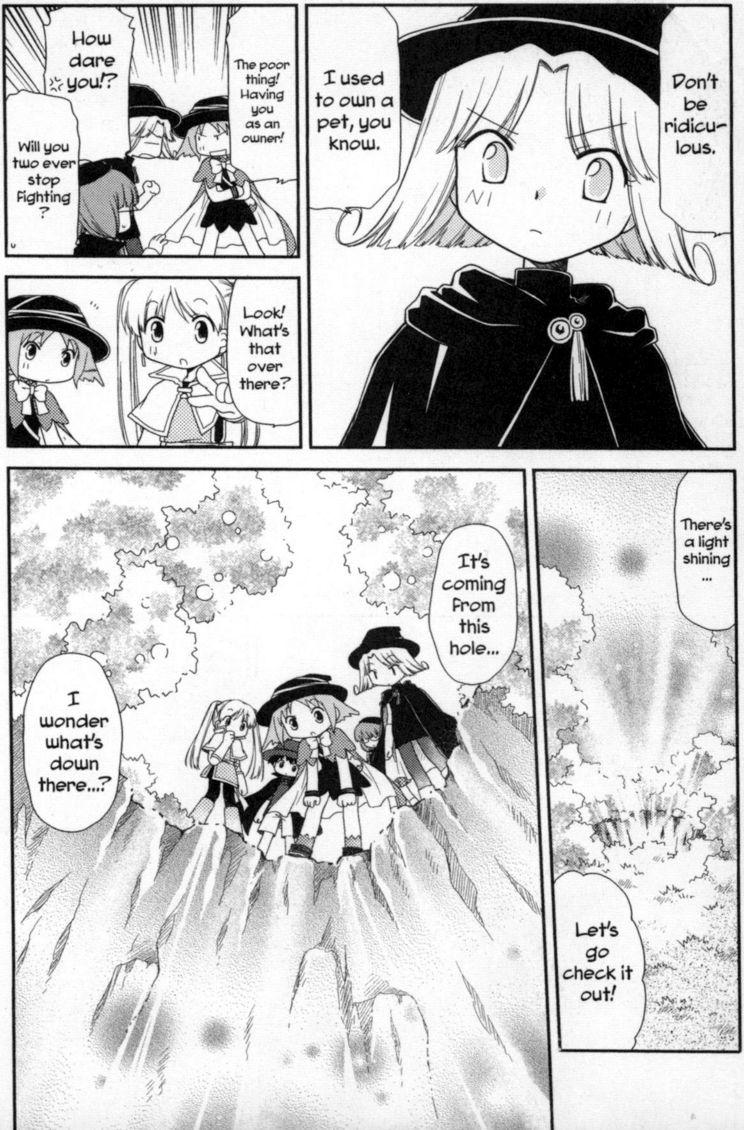
Don't be ridiculous.
I used to own a pet, you know.
The poor thing! Having you as an owner!
How dare you!?
Will you two ever stop fighting?
Look! What's that over there?
There's a light shining ...
Let's go check it out!
It's coming from this hole...
I wonder what's down there...?

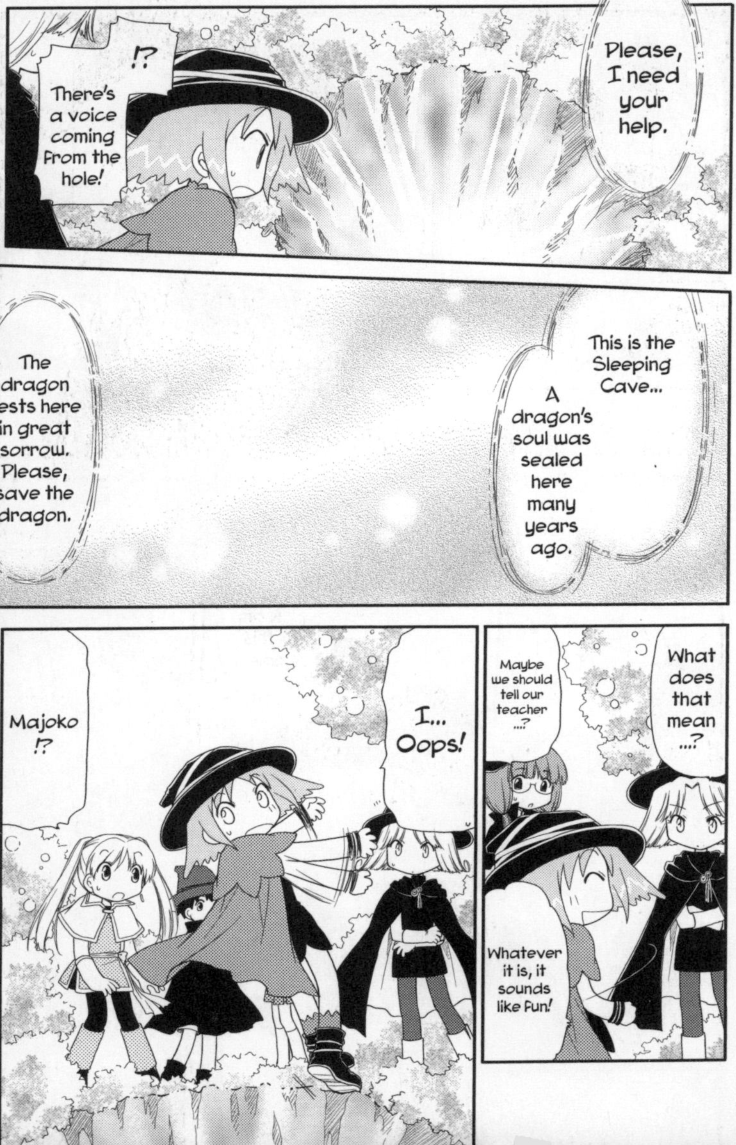
Please, I need your help.
!?
There's a voice coming from the hole!
This is the Sleeping Cave...
A dragon's soul was sealed here many years ago.
The dragon rests here in great sorrow. Please, save the dragon.
What does that mean ...?
Maybe we should tell our teacher ...?
Whatever it is, it sounds like fun!
I... Oops!
Majoko !?

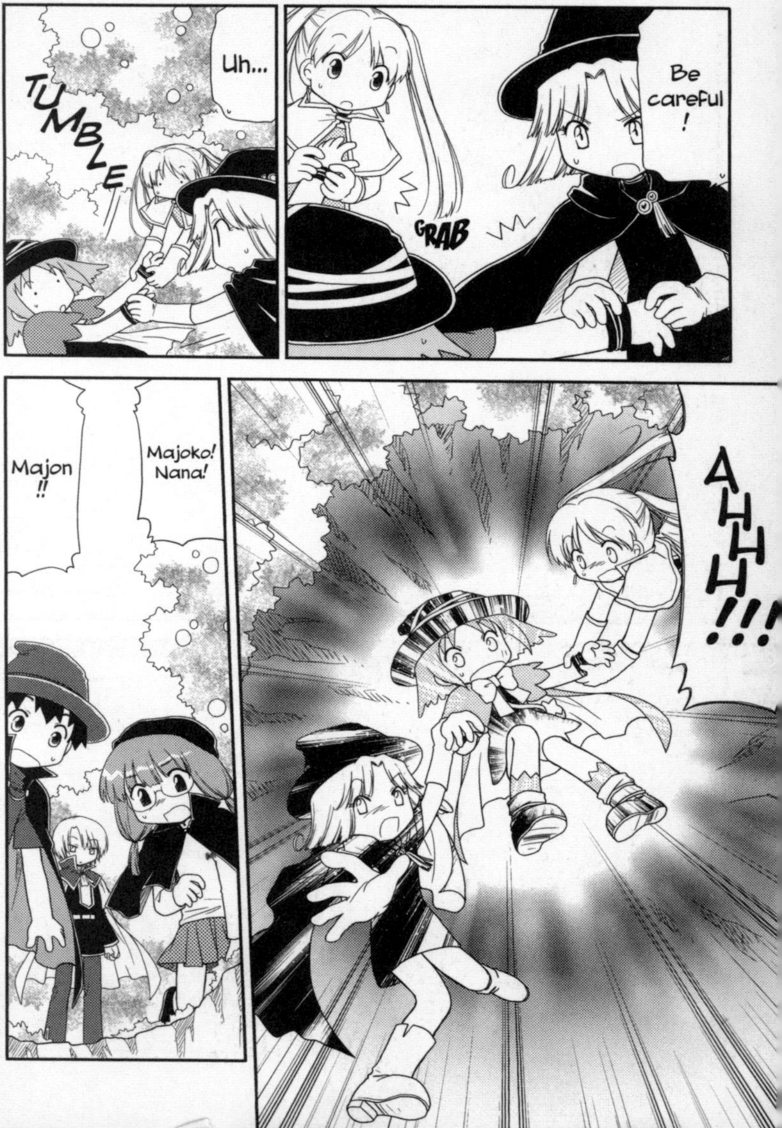
Be careful!
GRAB
Uh...
TUMBLE
AHHHH!!!
Majoko! Nana!
Majon!!

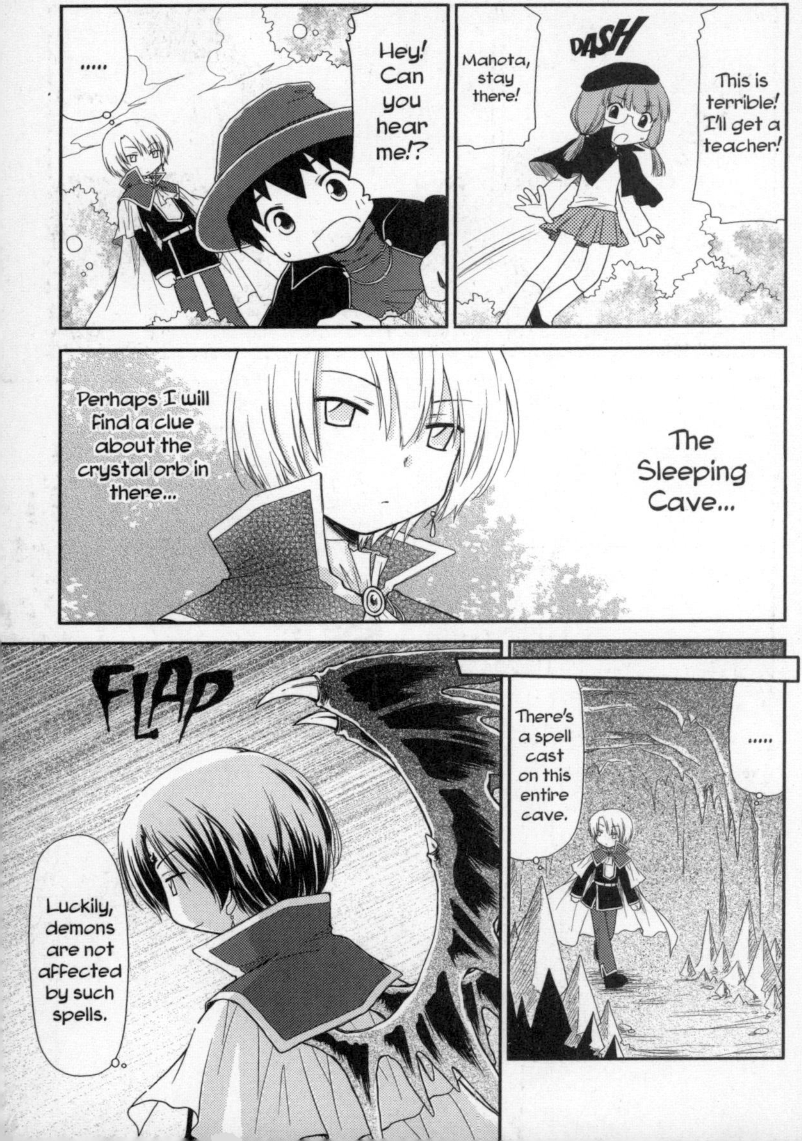
This is terrible! I'll get a teacher!
DASH
Mahota, stay there!
Hey! Can you hear me!?
.....
The Sleeping Cave...
Perhaps I will find a clue about the crystal orb in there...
.....
There's a spell cast on this entire cave.
FLAP
Luckily, demons are not affected by such spells.

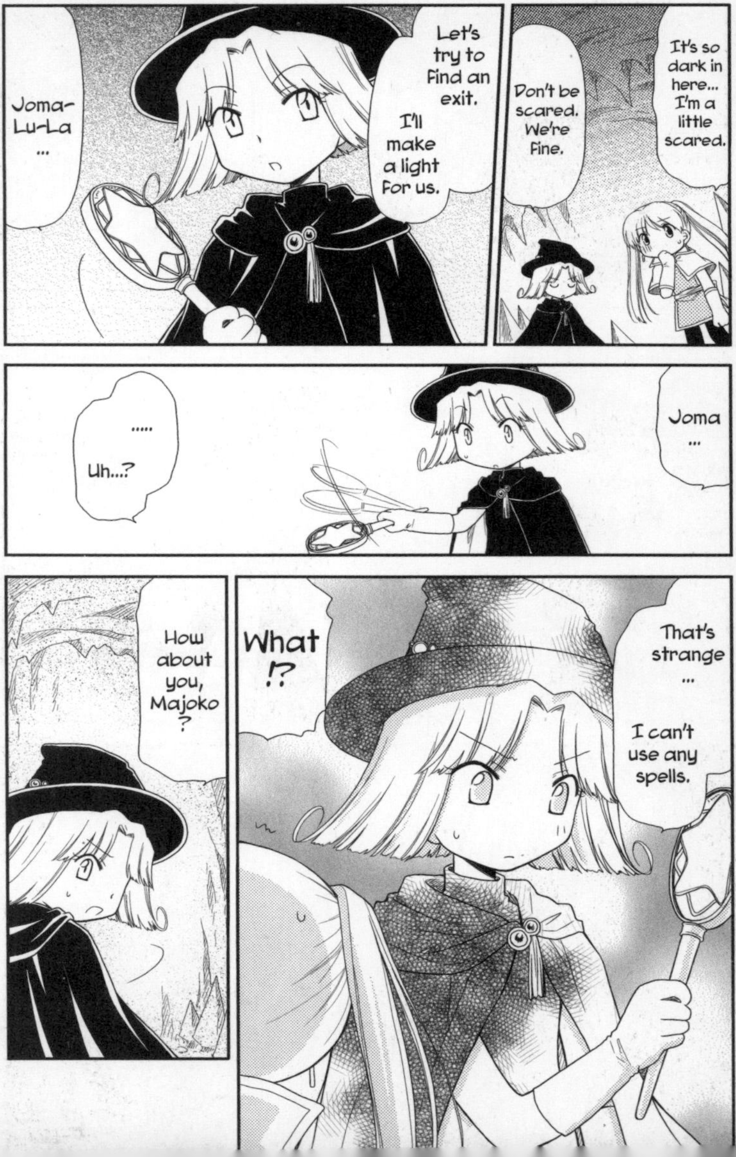
It's so dark in here... I'm a little scared.
Don't be scared. We're fine.
Let's try to find an exit.
I'll make a light for us.
Joma-Lu-La ...
Joma ...
.....
Uh...?
That's strange ...
I can't use any spells.
What !?
How about you, Majoko ?

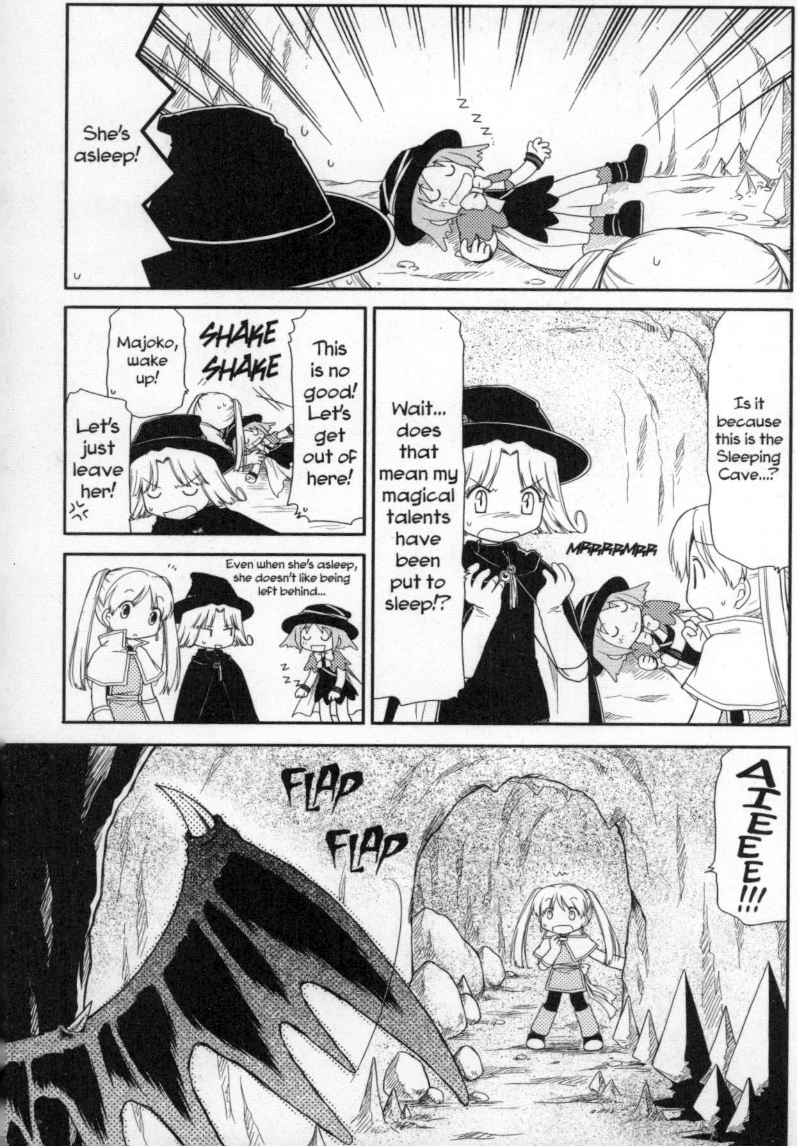
Z Z Z
She's asleep!
Is it because this is the Sleeping Cave...?
Wait... does that mean my magical talents have been put to sleep!?
MRRRRMRR
This is no good! Let's get out of here!
SHAKE SHAKE
Majoko, wake up!
Let's just leave her!
Even when she's asleep, she doesn't like being left behind...
Z Z Z
AIEEE!!!
FLAP
FLAP

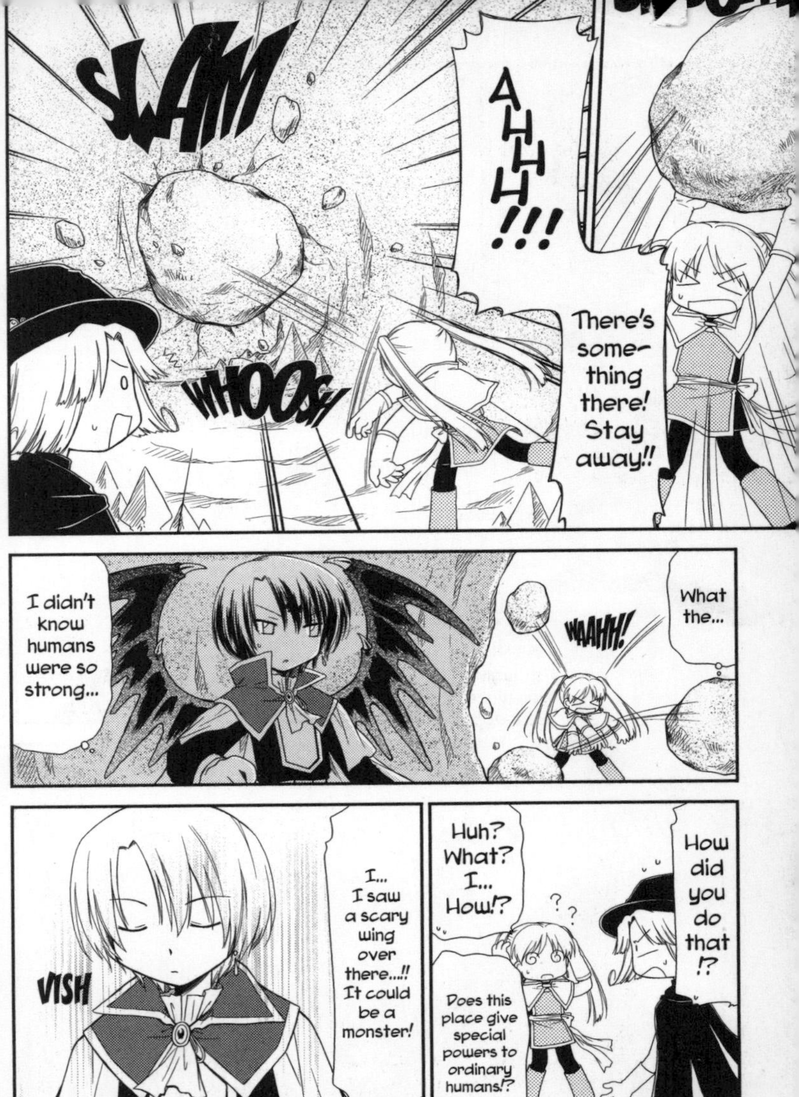
AHHHH!!!
There's some-thing there! Stay away!!
SLAM
WHOOSH
What the...
WAAHH!
I didn't know humans were so strong...
How did you do that!?
Huh? What? I... How!?
Does this place give special powers to ordinary humans!?
I... I saw a scary wing over there...!! It could be a monster!
VISH

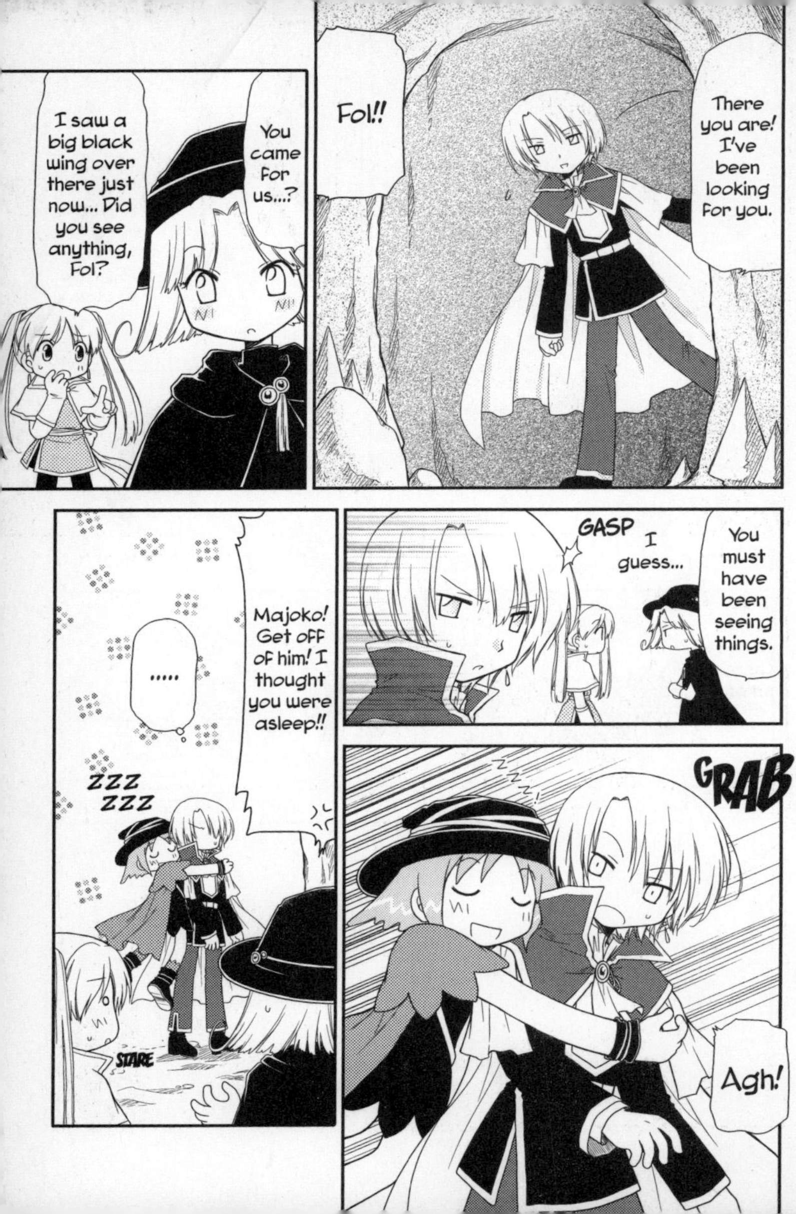

There you are! I've been looking for you.
Fol!!
You came for us...?
I saw a big black wing over there just now... Did you see anything, Fol?
You must have been seeing things.
I guess...
GASP
GRAB
Agh!
Majoko! Get off of him! I thought you were asleep!!
.....
ZZZ ZZZ
STARE

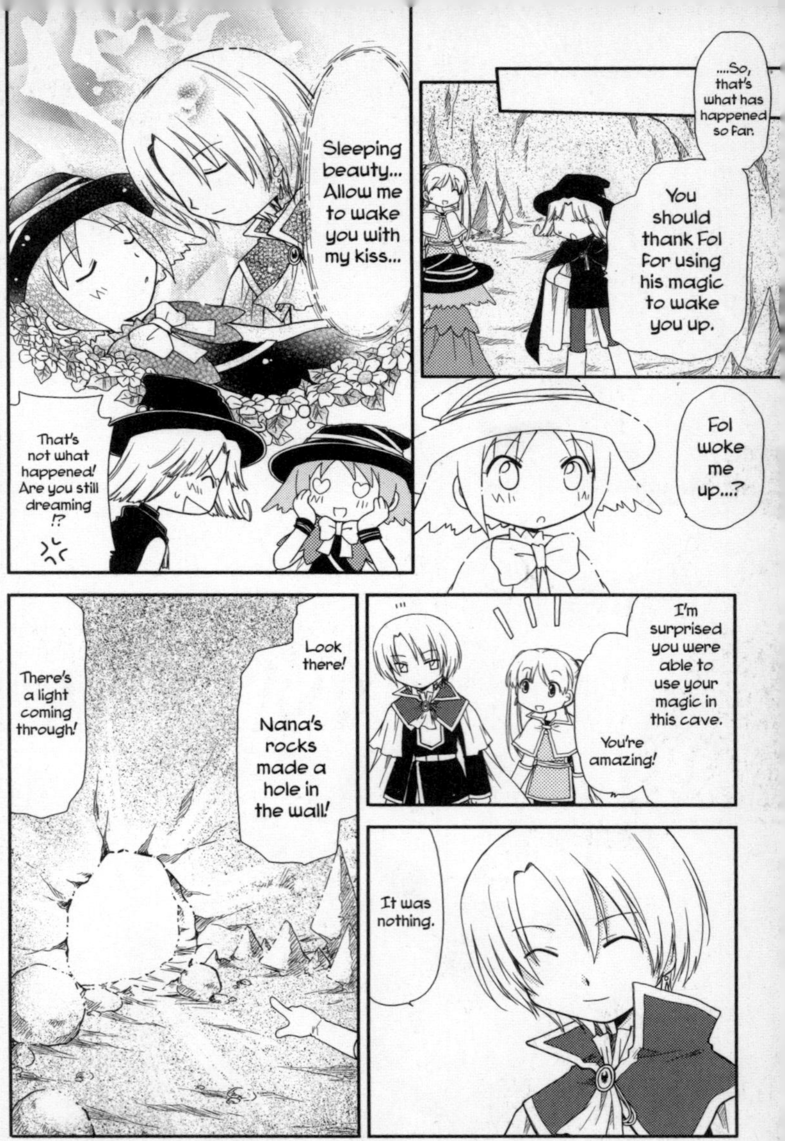
....So, that's what has happened so far.
You should thank Fol for using his magic to wake you up.
Fol woke me up...?
Sleeping beauty... Allow me to wake you with my kiss...
That's not what happened! Are you still dreaming!?
I'm surprised you were able to use your magic in this cave.
You're amazing!
It was nothing.
Look there!
Nana's rocks made a hole in the wall!
There's a light coming through!

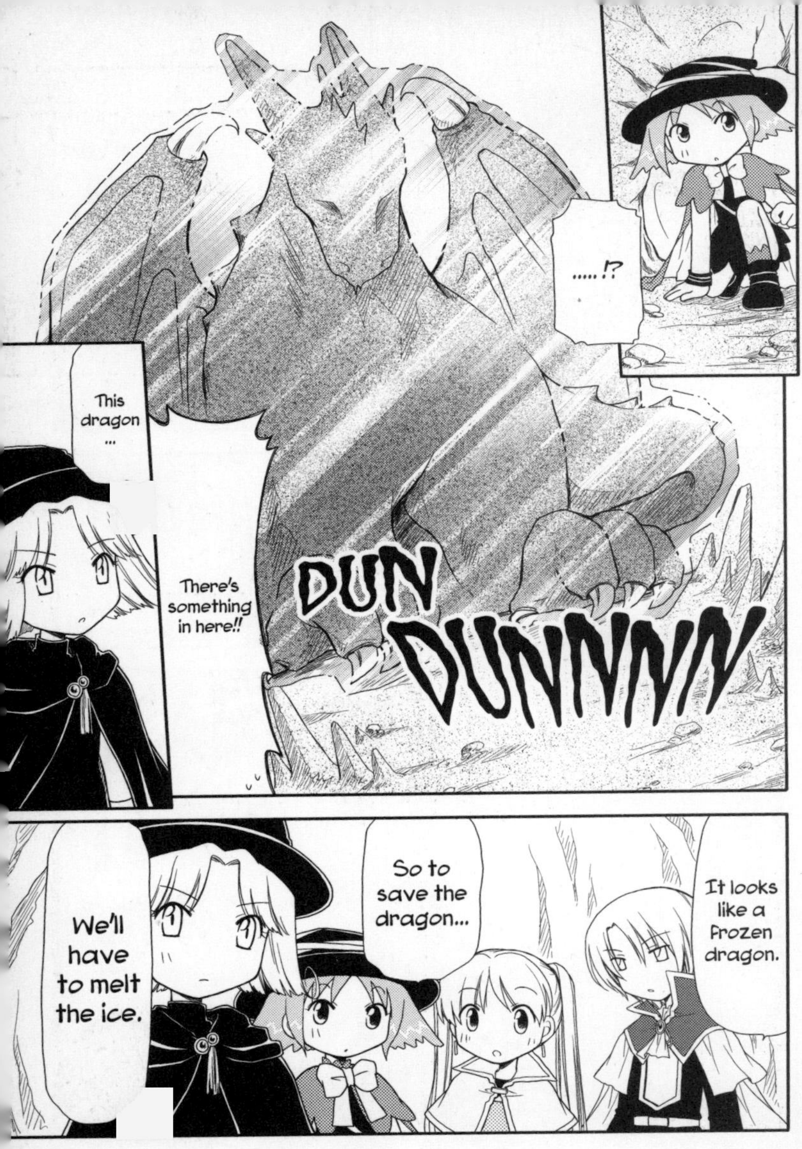
......!?
DUN
DUNNNN
This dragon ...
There's something in here!!
It looks like a frozen dragon.
So to save the dragon...
We'll have to melt the ice.

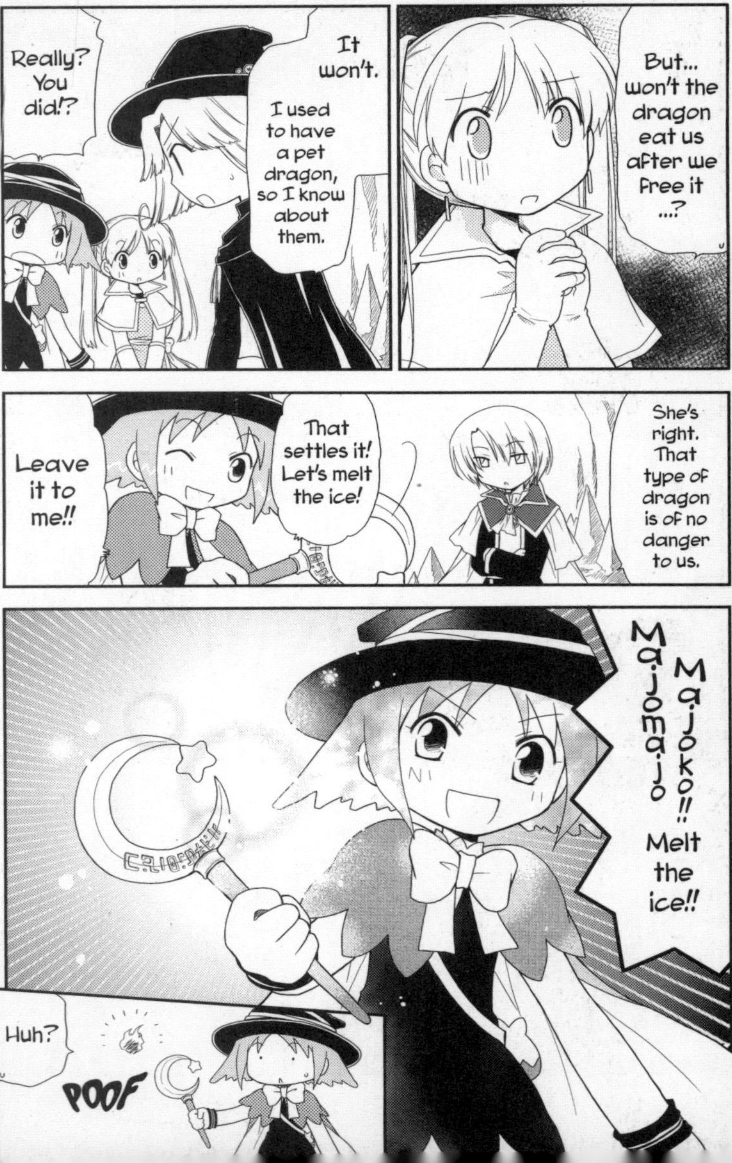
But... won't the dragon eat us after we free it ...?
It won't.
I used to have a pet dragon, so I know about them.
Really? You did!?
She's right. That type of dragon is of no danger to us.
That settles it! Let's melt the ice!
Leave it to me!!
Majomajo Majoko!!
Melt the ice!!
Huh?
POOF

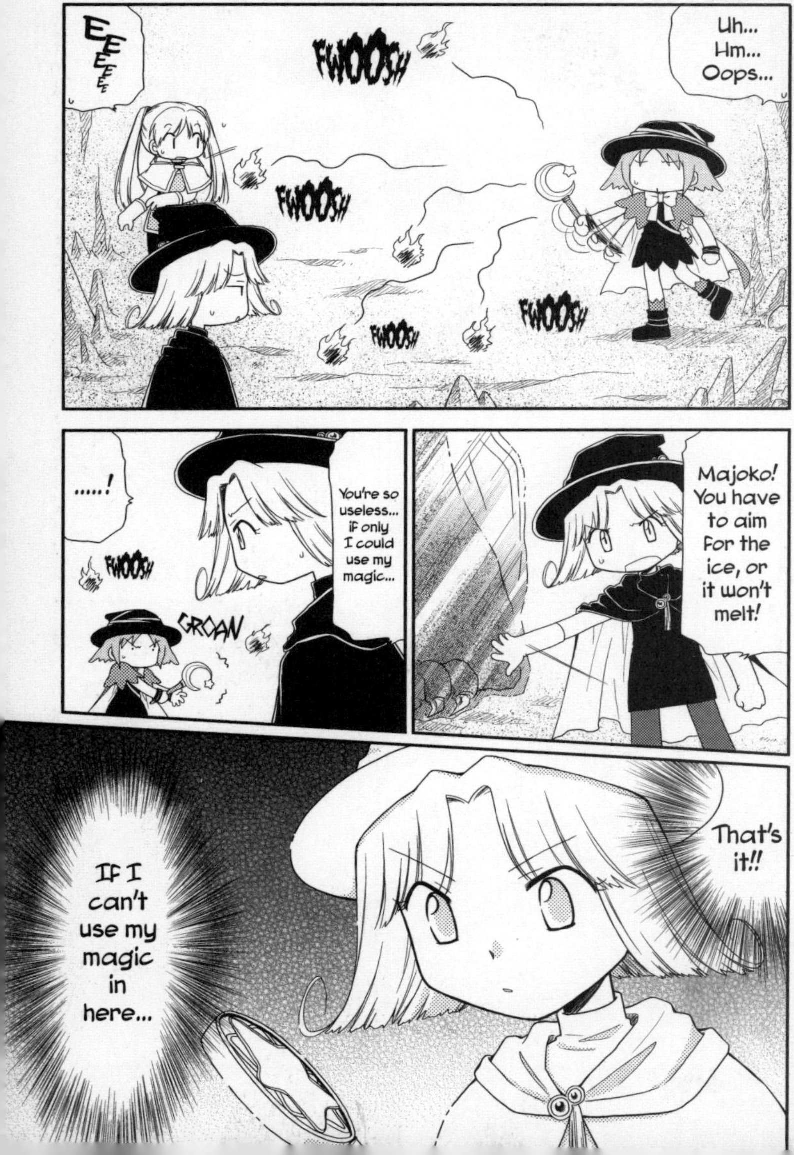
Uh... Hm... Oops...
FWOOSH
EEEEEEE
FWOOSH
FWOOSH
FWOOSH
FWOOSH
Majoko! You have to aim for the ice, or it won't melt!
You're so useless... if only I could use my magic...
.....!
FWOOSH
GROAN
That's it!!
If I can't use my magic in here...

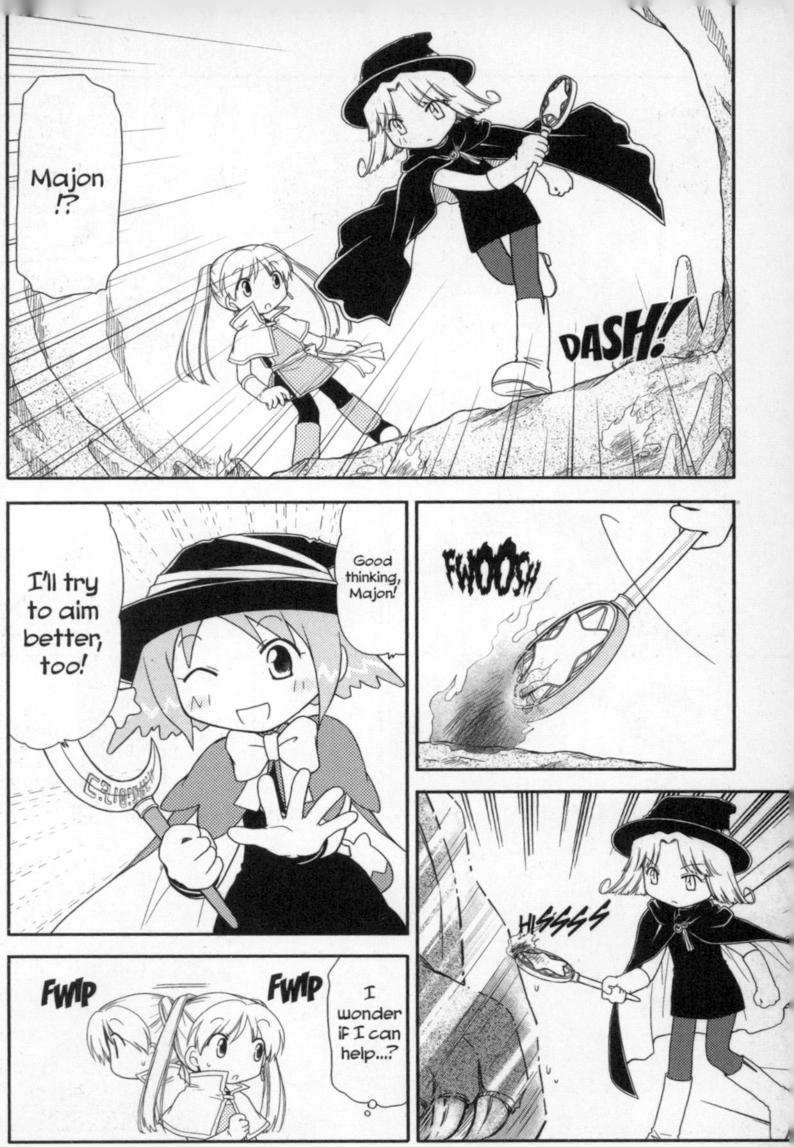
Majon !?
DASH!
FWOOSH
HISSSS
Good thinking, Majon!
I'll try to aim better, too!
I wonder if I can help...?
FWIP
FWIP

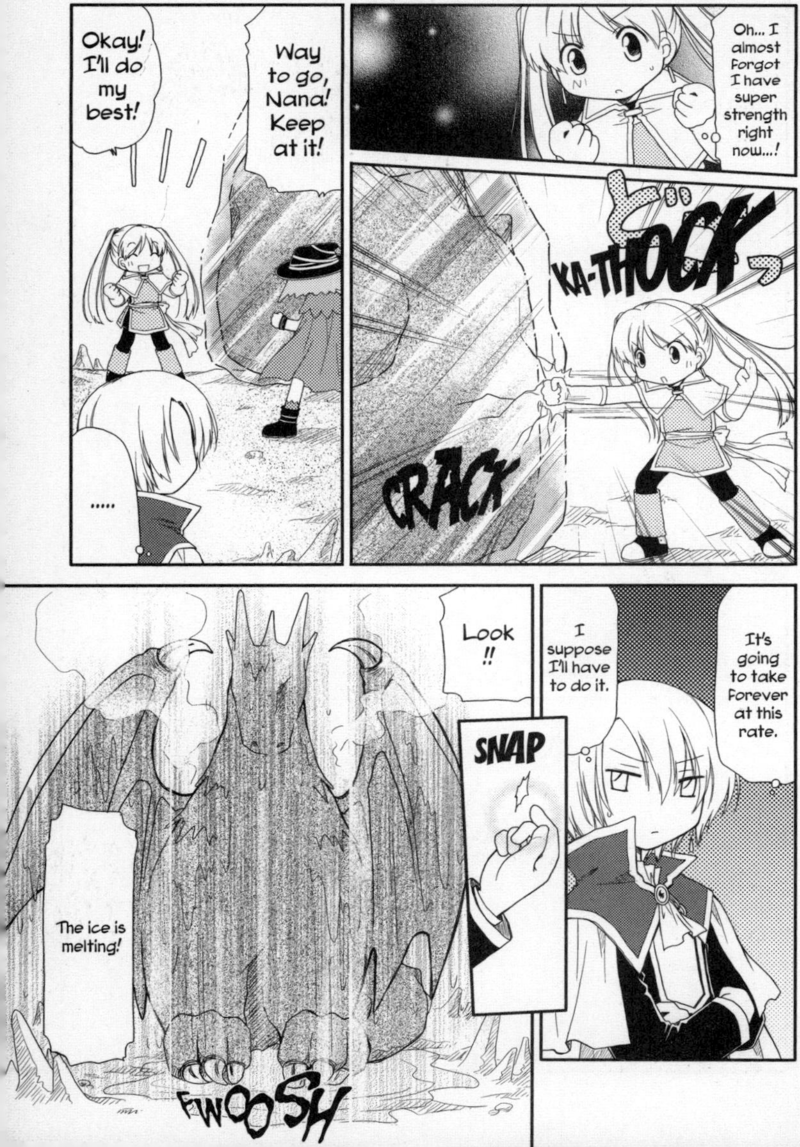
Oh... I almost forgot I have super strength right now...!
KA-THOCK
CRACK
Way to go, Nana! Keep at it!
Okay! I'll do my best!
......
It's going to take forever at this rate.
I suppose I'll have to do it.
SNAP
Look!!
The ice is melting!
FWOOSH

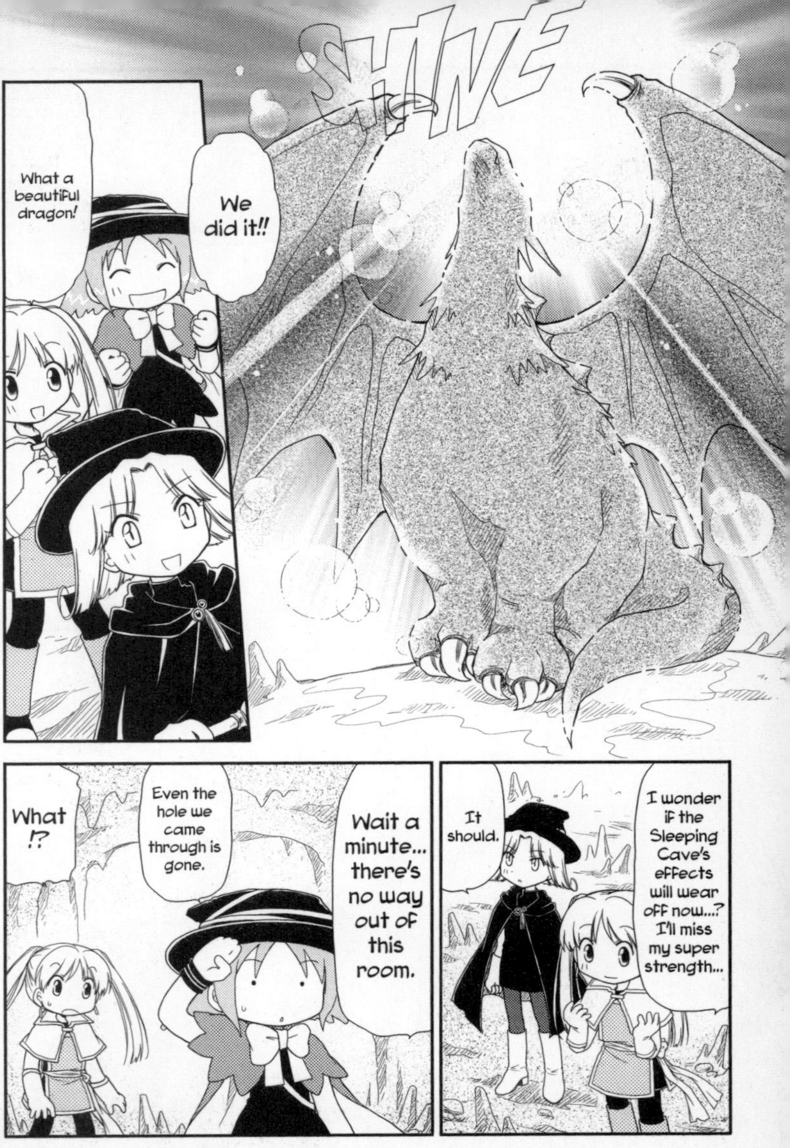
SHINE
We did it!!
What a beautiful dragon!
I wonder if the Sleeping Cave's effects will wear off now...? I'll miss my super strength...
It should.
Wait a minute... there's no way out of this room.
Even the hole we came through is gone.
What!?

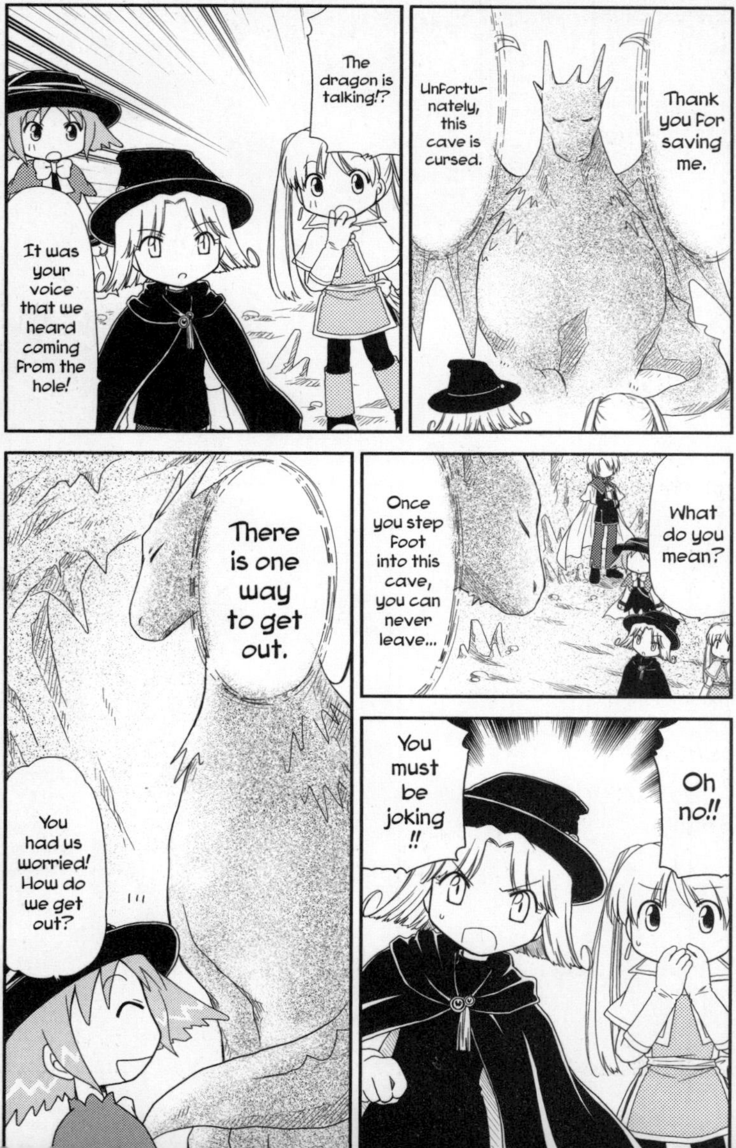
Thank you for saving me.
Unfortunately, this cave is cursed.
The dragon is talking!?
It was your voice that we heard coming from the hole!
What do you mean?
Once you step foot into this cave, you can never leave...
Oh no!!
You must be joking!!
There is one way to get out.
You had us worried! How do we get out?

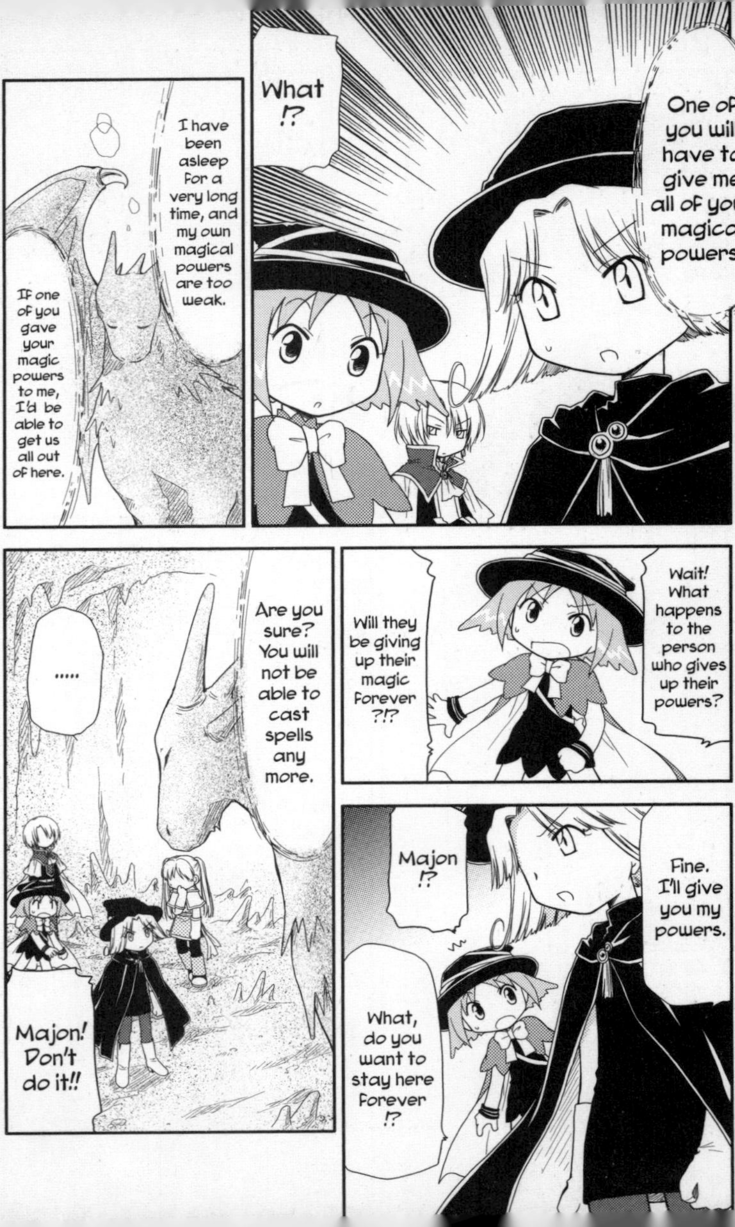
One of you will have to give me all of your magical powers.
What !?
I have been asleep for a very long time, and my own magical powers are too weak.
If one of you gave your magic powers to me, I'd be able to get us all out of here.
Wait! What happens to the person who gives up their powers?
Will they be giving up their magic forever ?!?
Fine. I'll give you my powers.
Majon !?
What, do you want to stay here forever !?
Are you sure? You will not be able to cast spells any more.
.....
Majon! Don't do it!!

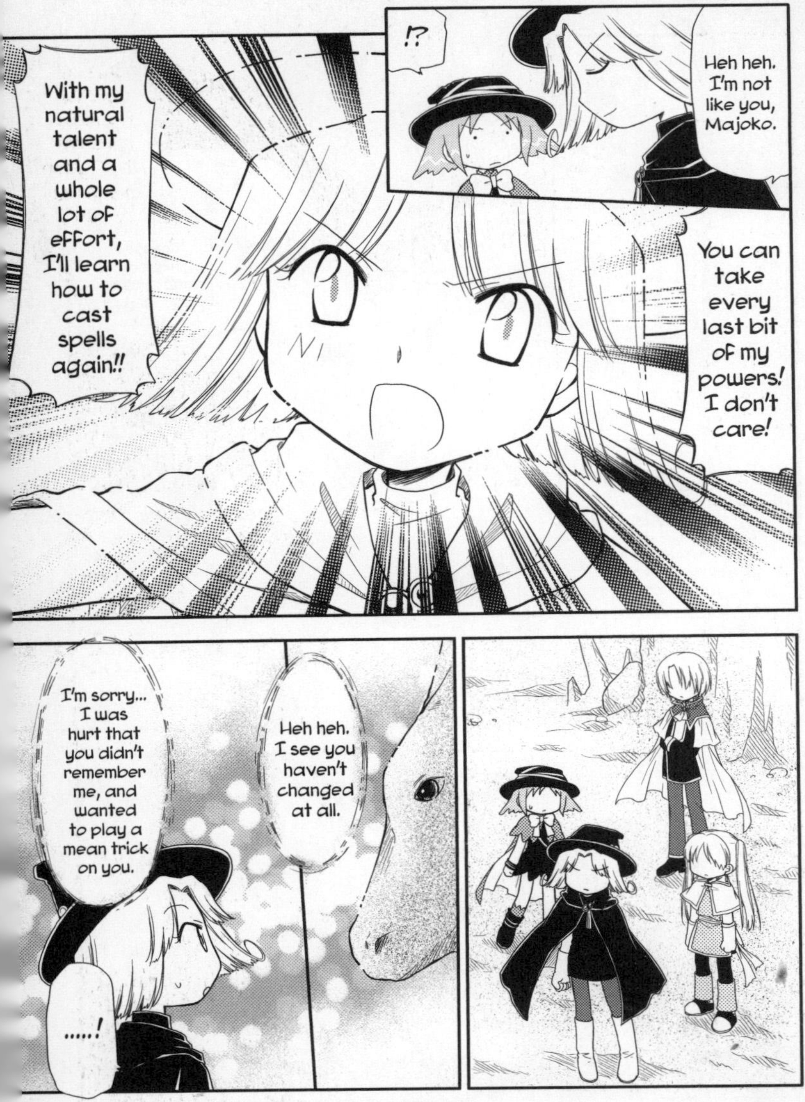
Heh heh. I'm not like you, Majoko.
!?
You can take every last bit of my powers! I don't care!
With my natural talent and a whole lot of effort, I'll learn how to cast spells again!!
Heh heh. I see you haven't changed at all.
I'm sorry... I was hurt that you didn't remember me, and wanted to play a mean trick on you.
.....!

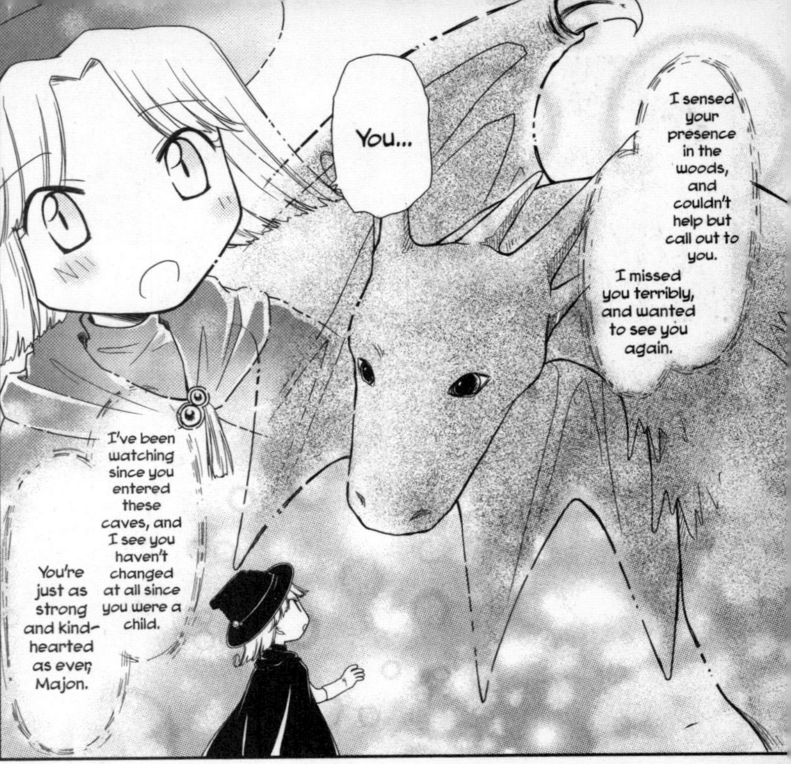
I sensed your presence in the woods, and couldn't help but call out to you.
I missed you terribly, and wanted to see you again.
You...
I've been watching since you entered these caves, and I see you haven't changed at all since you were a child.
You're just as strong and kind-hearted as ever, Majon.

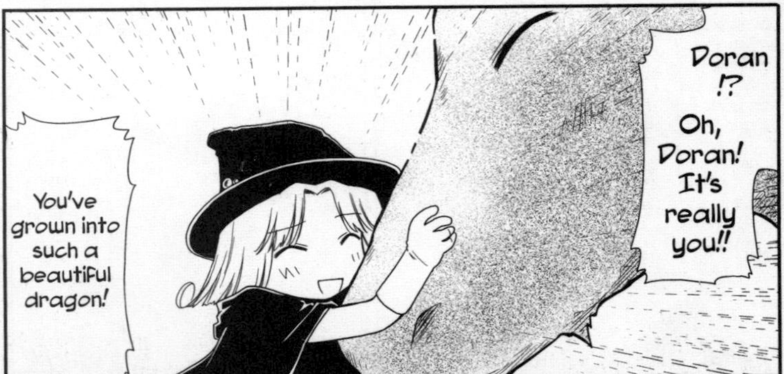
Doran!?
Oh, Doran! It's really you!!
You've grown into such a beautiful dragon!

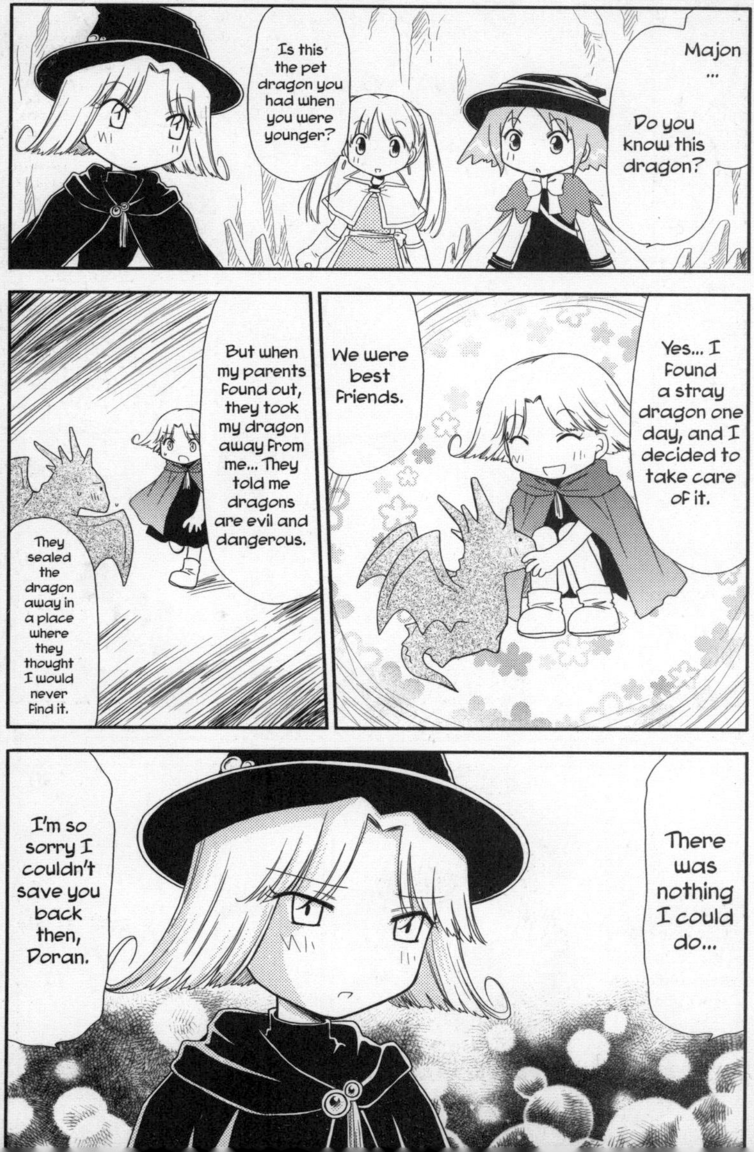
Majon ... Do you know this dragon?
Is this the pet dragon you had when you were younger?
Yes... I found a stray dragon one day, and I decided to take care of it.
We were best friends.
But when my parents found out, they took my dragon away from me... They told me dragons are evil and dangerous.
They sealed the dragon away in a place where they thought I would never find it.
There was nothing I could do...
I'm so sorry I couldn't save you back then, Doran.

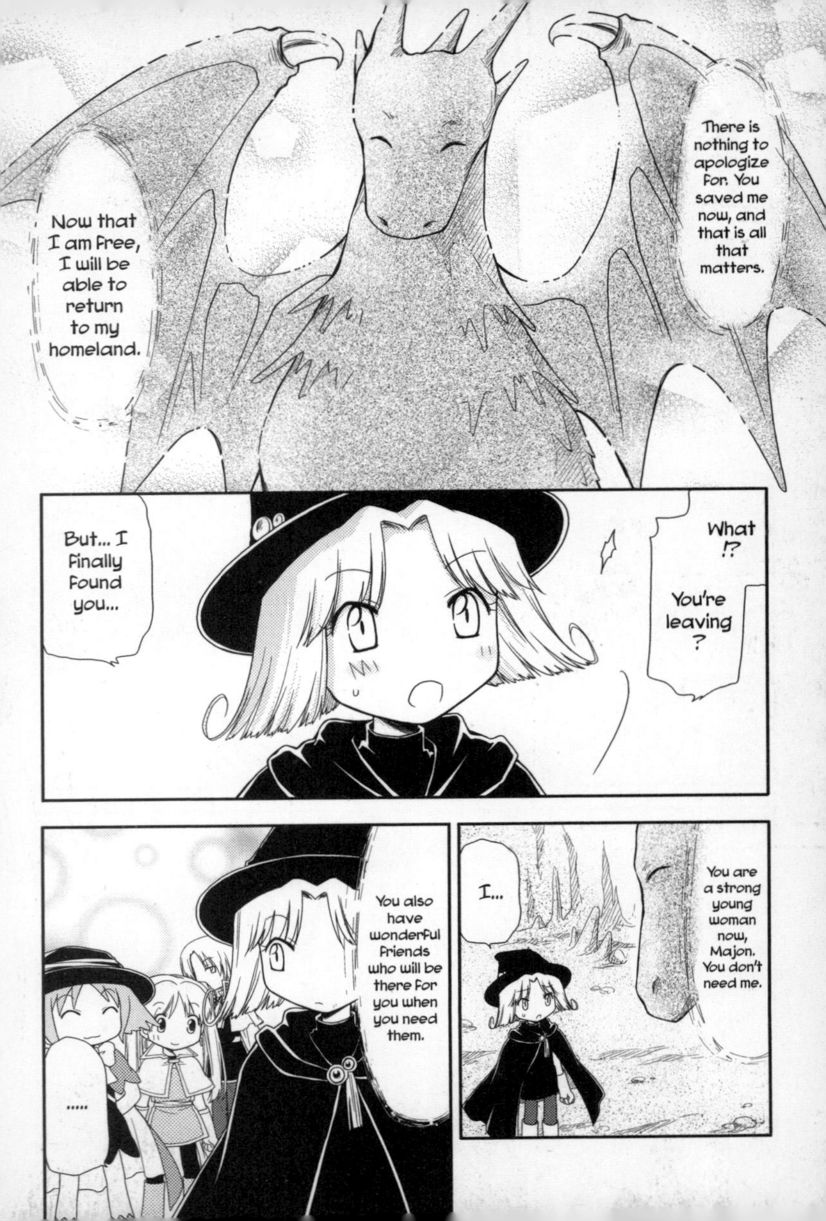
There is nothing to apologize for. You saved me now, and that is all that matters.
Now that I am free, I will be able to return to my homeland.
What!? You're leaving?
But... I finally found you...
You are a strong young woman now, Majon. You don't need me.
I...
You also have wonderful friends who will be there for you when you need them.
.....

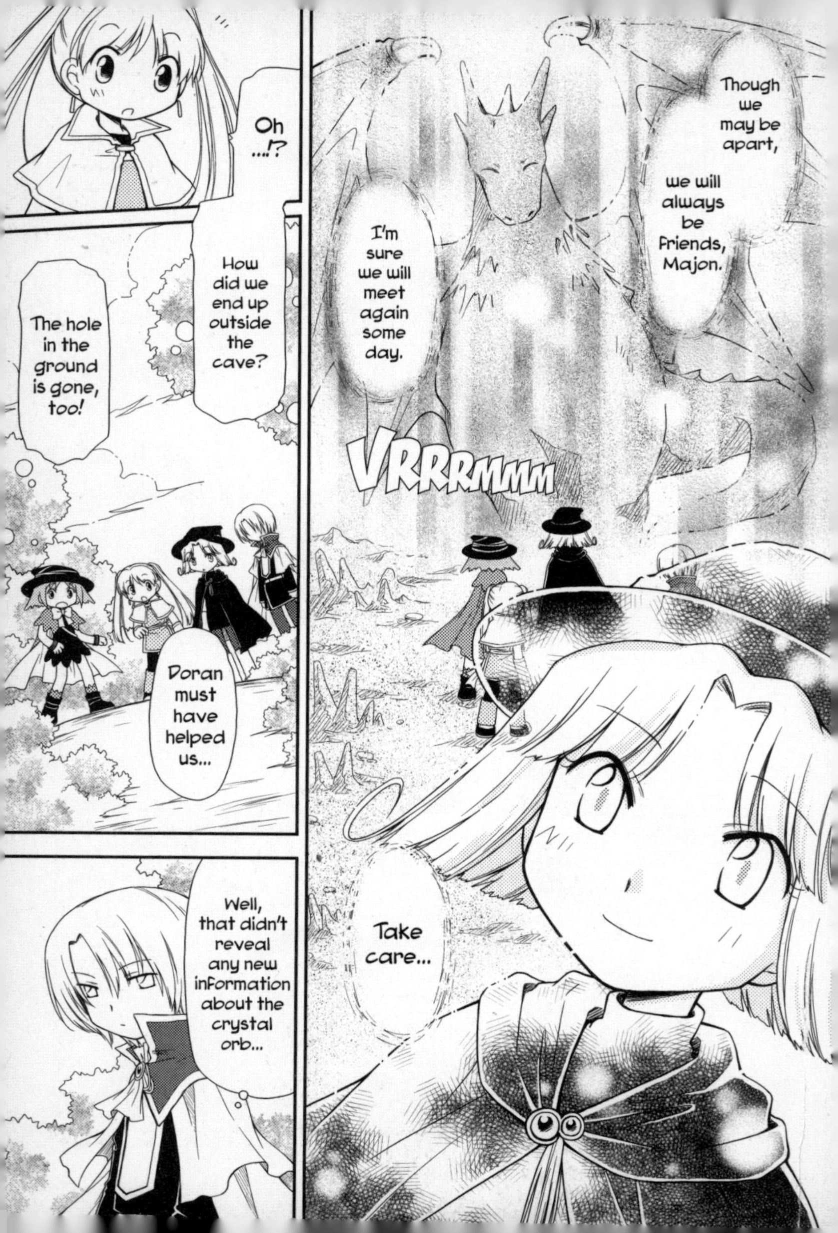
Though we may be apart,
we will always be friends, Majon.
I'm sure we will meet again some day.
VRRRMMMM
Take care...
Oh ...!?
How did we end up outside the cave?
The hole in the ground is gone, too!
Doran must have helped us...
Well, that didn't reveal any new information about the crystal orb...

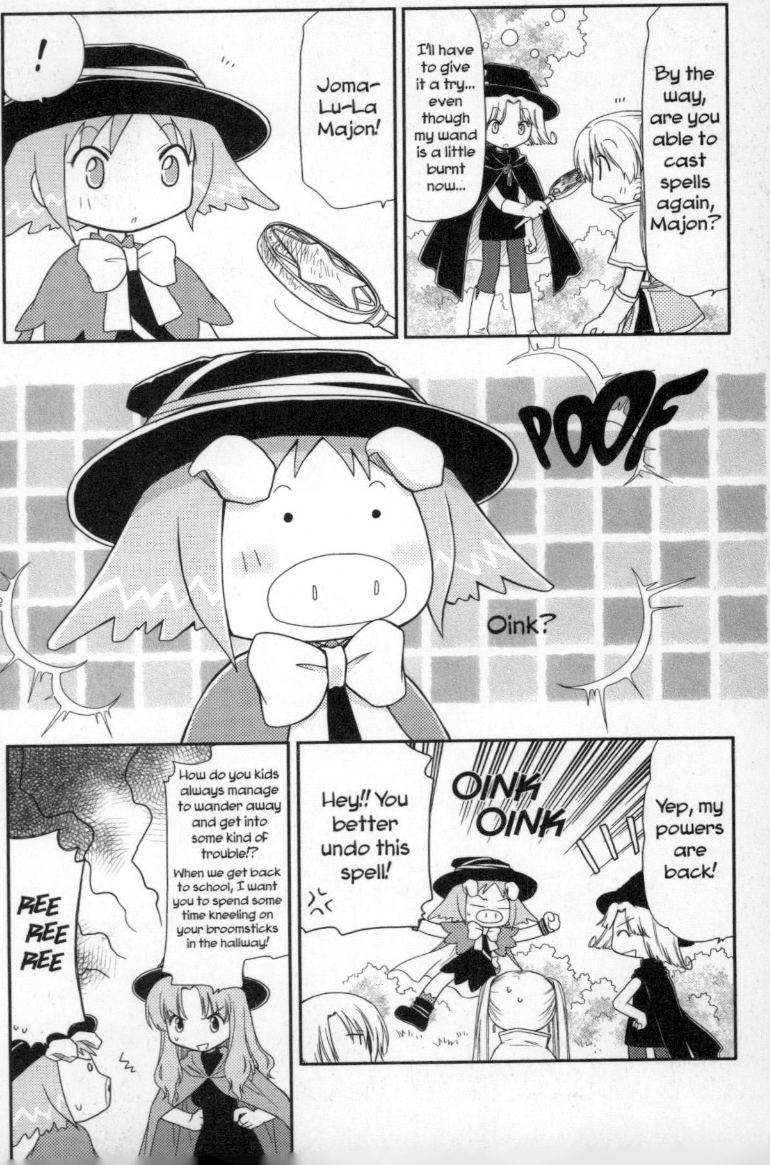
By the way, are you able to cast spells again, Majon?
I'll have to give it a try... even though my wand is a little burnt now...
Joma-Lu-La Majon!
!
POOF
Oink?
Yep, my powers are back!
OINK OINK
Hey!! You better undo this spell!
How do you kids always manage to wander away and get into some kind of trouble!?
When we get back to school, I want you to spend some time kneeling on your broomsticks in the hallway!
REE REE REE

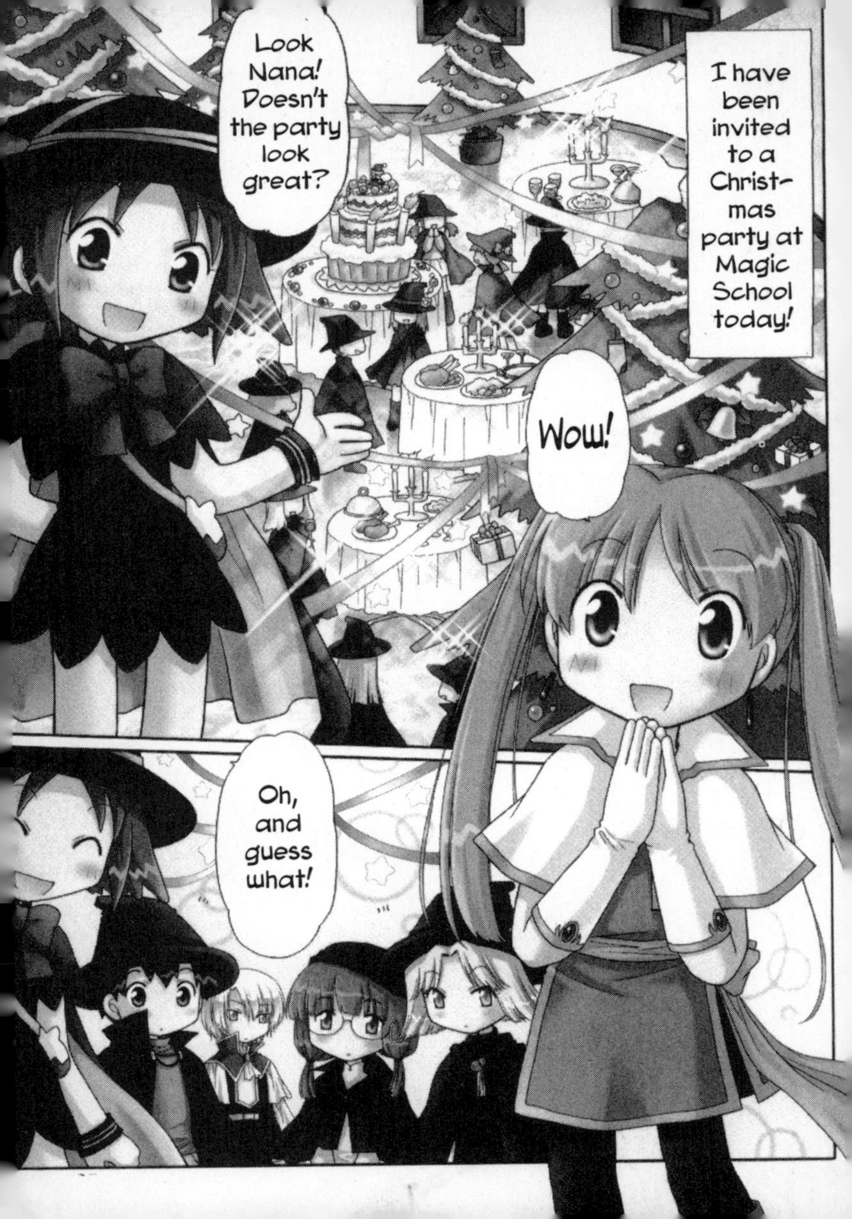
I have been invited to a Christmas party at Magic School today!
Look Nana! Doesn't the party look great?
Wow!
Oh, and guess what!

Chapter 35
The Magic of Happiness

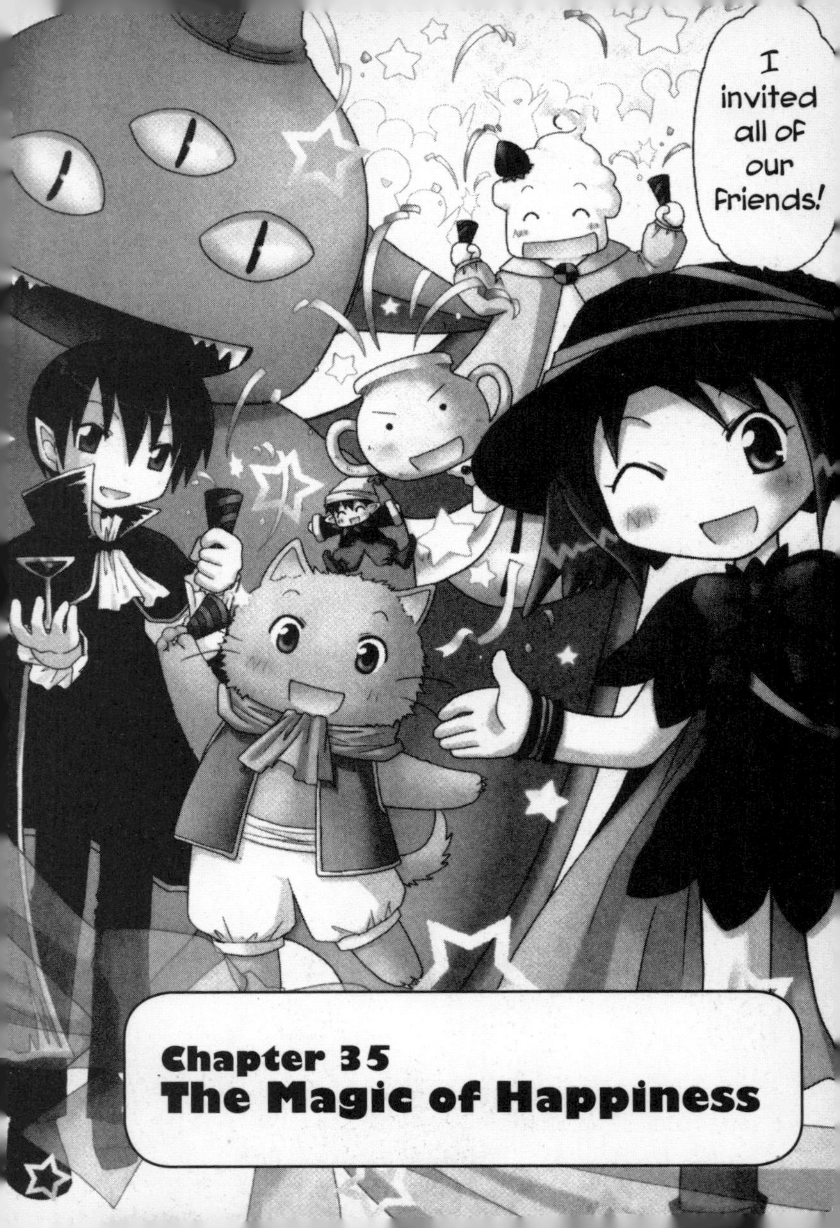
I invited all of our friends!

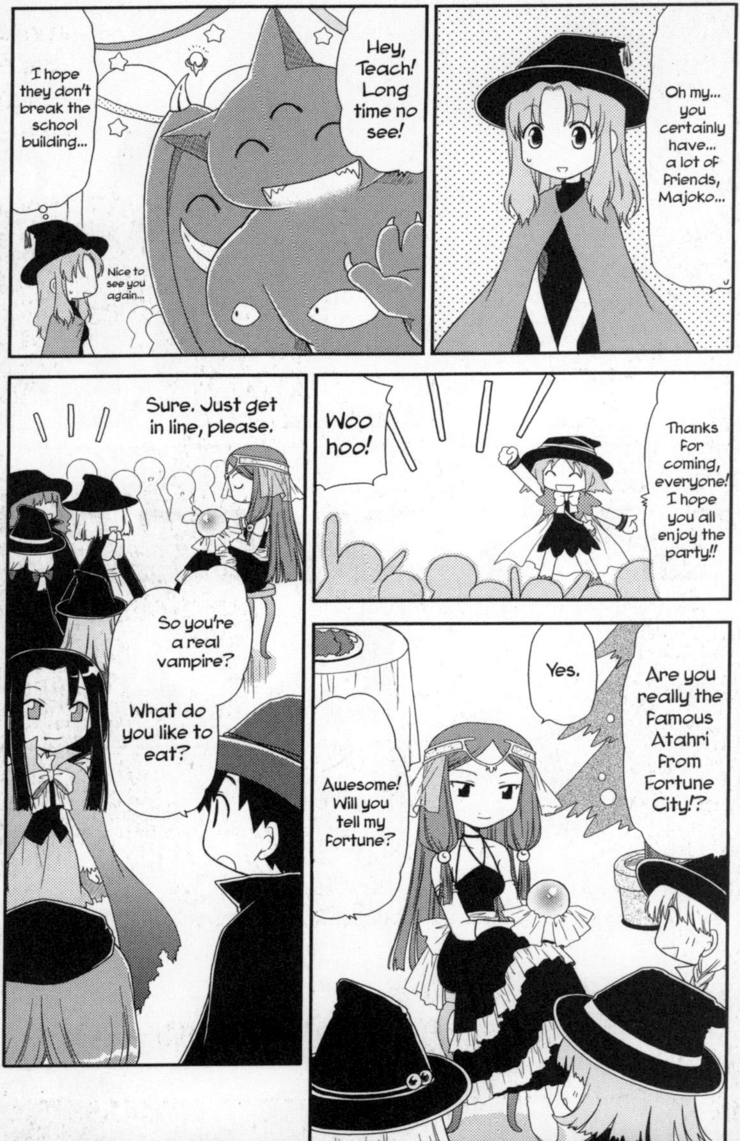
Oh my... you certainly have... a lot of friends, Majoko...
Hey, Teach! Long time no see!
I hope they don't break the school building...
Nice to see you again...
Thanks for coming, everyone! I hope you all enjoy the party!!
Woo hoo!
Are you really the famous Atahri from Fortune City!?
Yes.
Awesome! Will you tell my fortune?
Sure. Just get in line, please.
So you're a real vampire?
What do you like to eat?

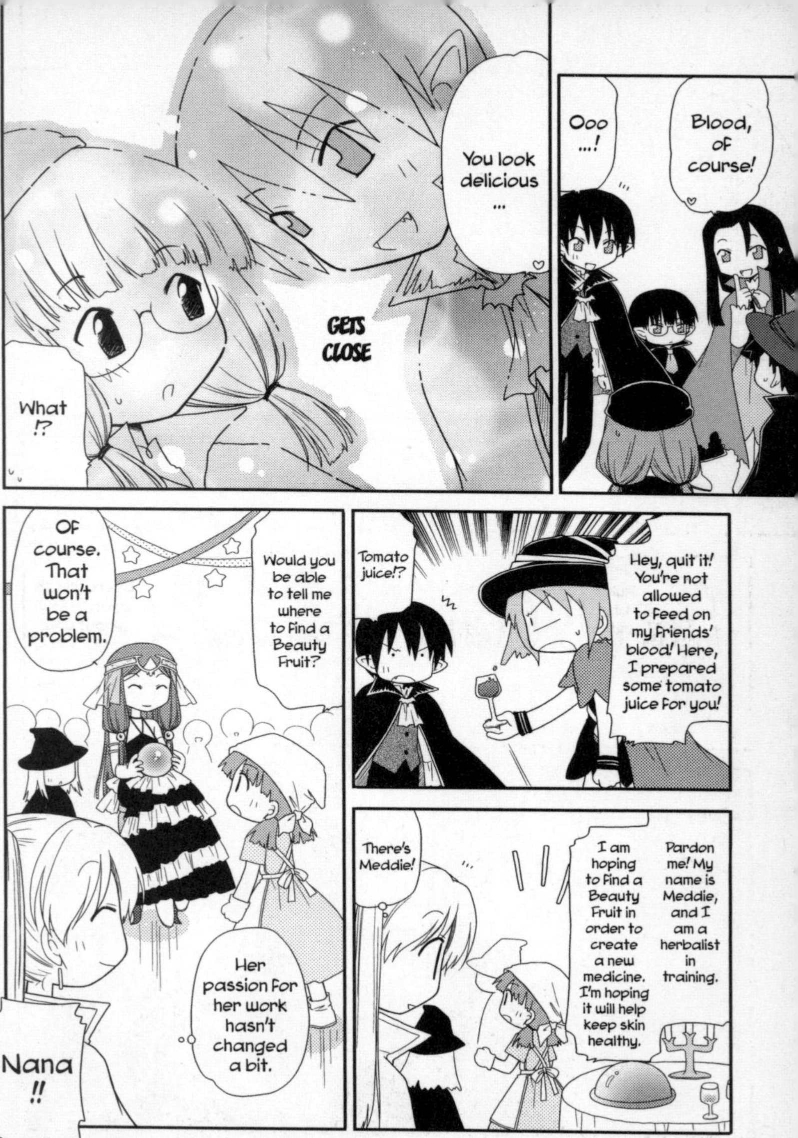
Blood, of course!
Ooo ...!
You look delicious ...
GETS CLOSE
What !?
Hey, quit it! You're not allowed to feed on my friends' blood! Here, I prepared some tomato juice for you!
Tomato juice!?
Pardon me! My name is Meddie, and I am a herbalist in training.
I am hoping to find a Beauty Fruit in order to create a new medicine. I'm hoping it will help keep skin healthy.
There's Meddie!
Would you be able to tell me where to find a Beauty Fruit?
Of course. That won't be a problem.
Her passion for her work hasn't changed a bit.
Nana !!

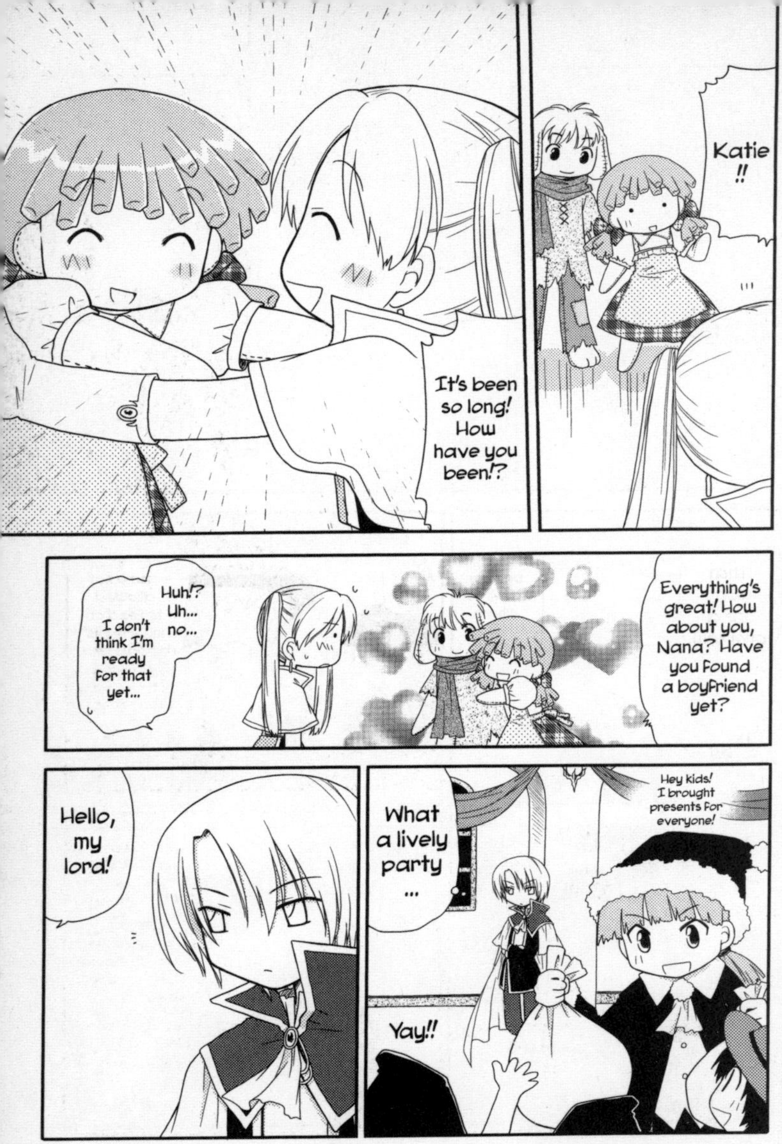
Katie!!
It's been so long! How have you been!?
Everything's great! How about you, Nana? Have you found a boyfriend yet?
Huh!? Uh... no...
I don't think I'm ready for that yet...
Hey kids! I brought presents for everyone!
What a lively party...
Yay!!
Hello, my lord!

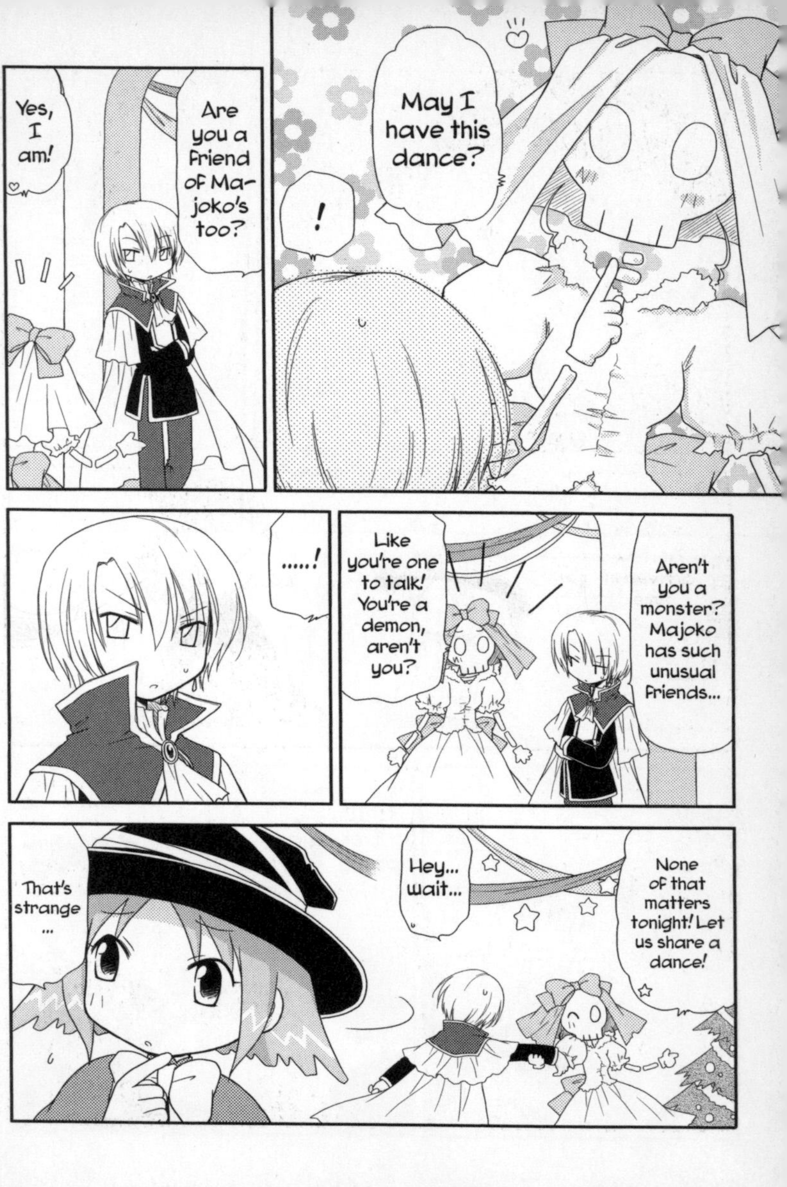
May I have this dance?
!
Are you a friend of Ma-joko's too?
Yes, I am!
Aren't you a monster? Majoko has such unusual friends...
Like you're one to talk! You're a demon, aren't you?
......!
None of that matters tonight! Let us share a dance!
Hey... wait...
That's strange ...

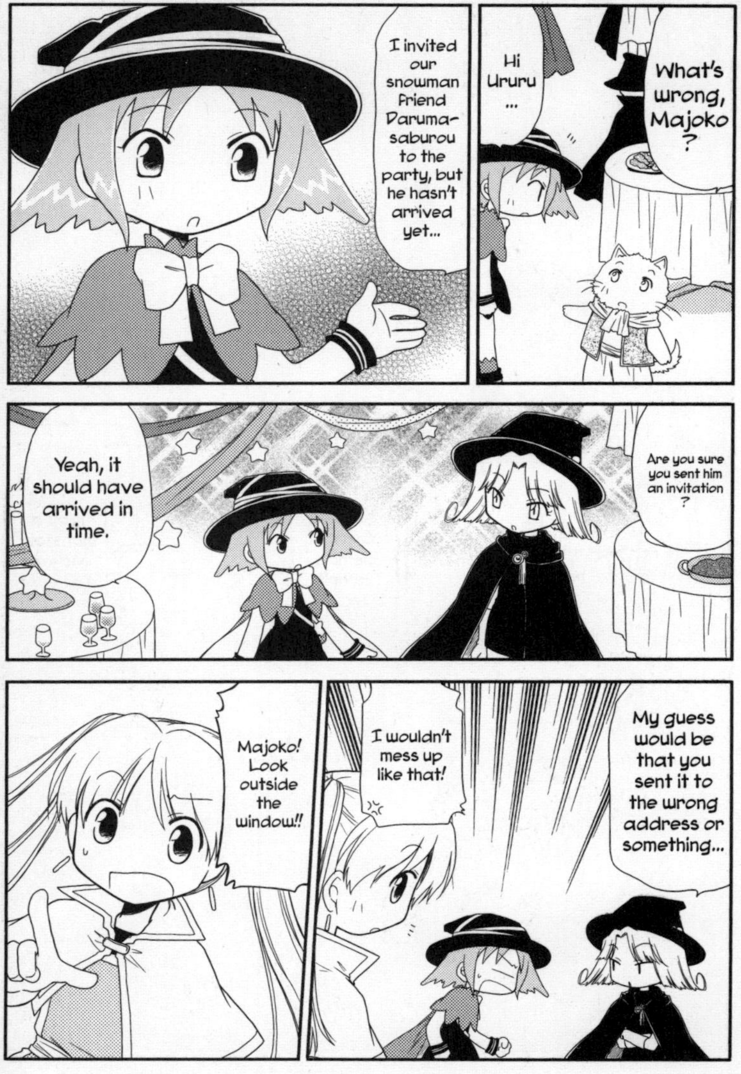
What's wrong, Majoko?
Hi Ururu ...
I invited our snowman friend Daruma-saburou to the party, but he hasn't arrived yet...
Are you sure you sent him an invitation?
Yeah, it should have arrived in time.
My guess would be that you sent it to the wrong address or something...
I wouldn't mess up like that!
Majoko! Look outside the window!!

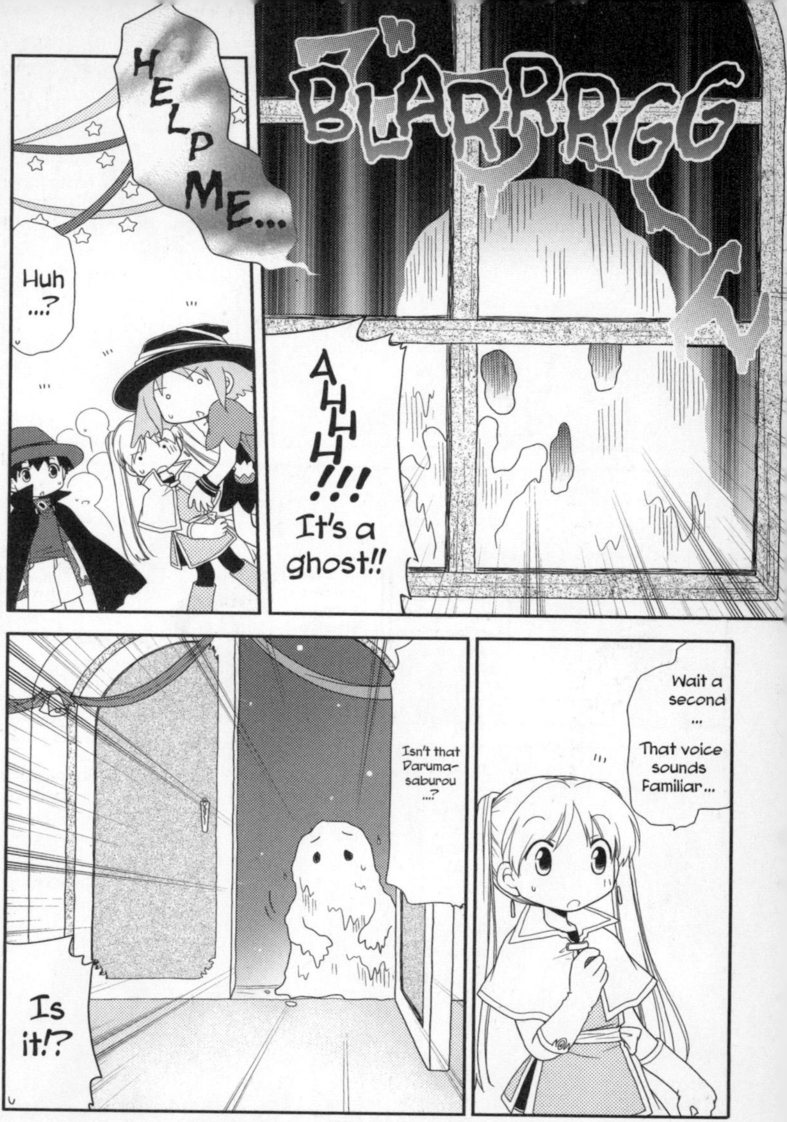
BLARRRGG
HELP ME...
AHHHH!!! It's a ghost!!
Huh ...?
Wait a second ...
That voice sounds familiar...
Isn't that Daruma-saburou ...?
Is it!?

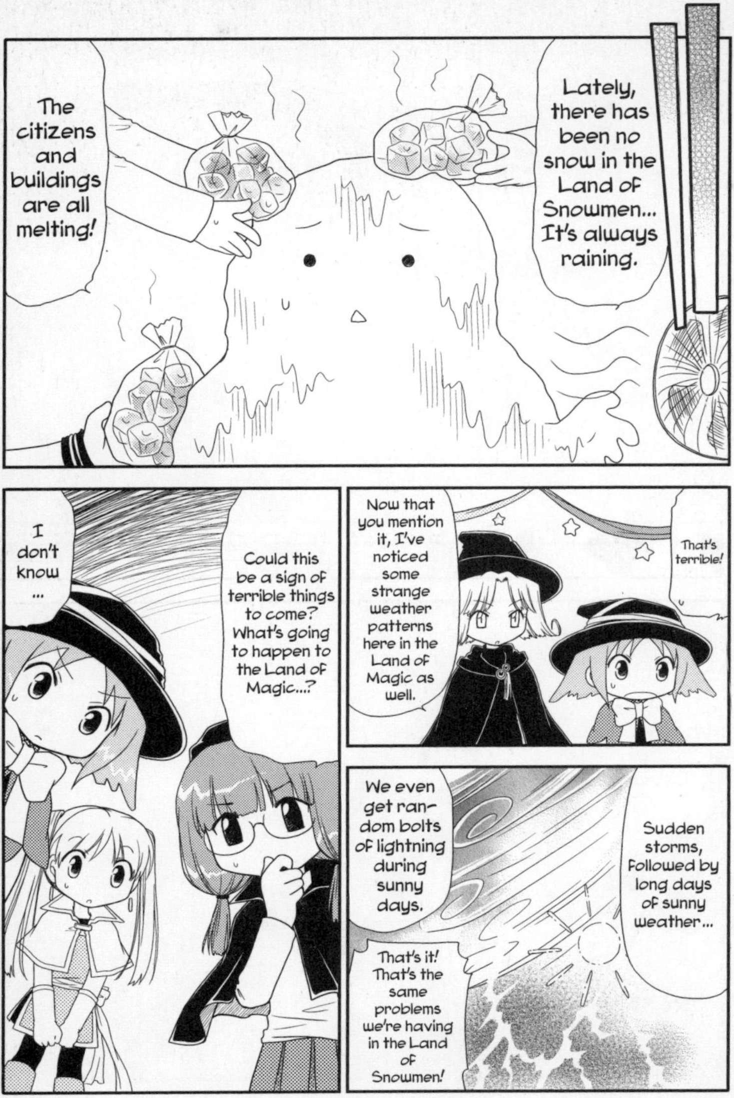
Lately, there has been no snow in the Land of Snowmen... It's always raining.
The citizens and buildings are all melting!
That's terrible!
Now that you mention it, I've noticed some strange weather patterns here in the Land of Magic as well.
Sudden storms, followed by long days of sunny weather...
We even get ran-dom bolts of lightning during sunny days.
That's it! That's the same problems we're having in the Land of Snowmen!
Could this be a sign of terrible things to come? What's going to happen to the Land of Magic...?
I don't know ...

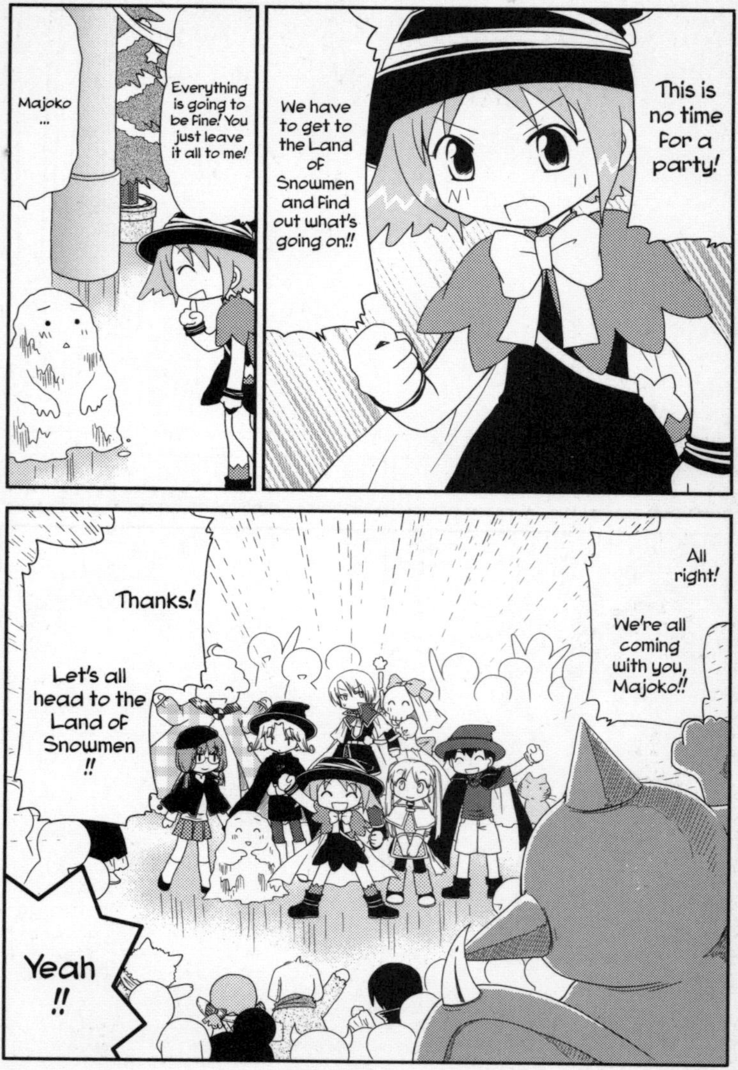
This is no time for a party!
We have to get to the Land of Snowmen and find out what's going on!!
Everything is going to be fine! You just leave it all to me!
Majoko ...
All right!
We're all coming with you, Majoko!!
Thanks!
Let's all head to the Land of Snowmen !!
Yeah !!

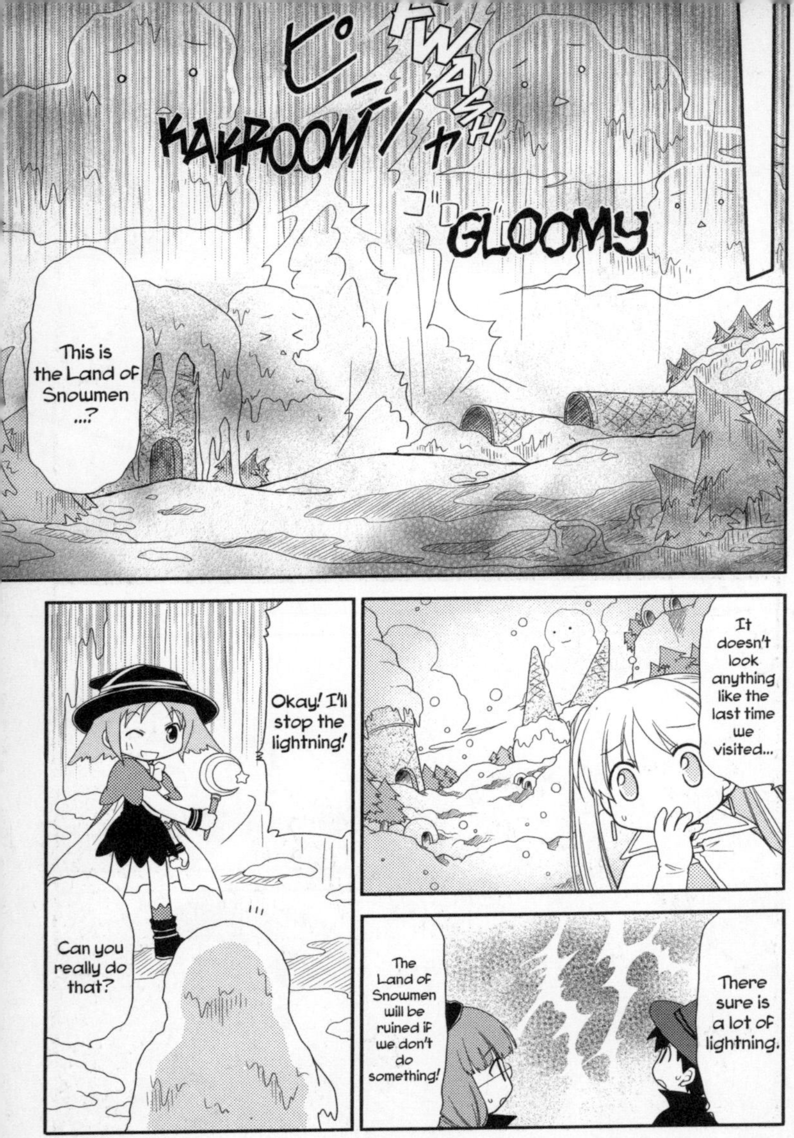
ピ
FWASH
KAKROOM
ゴロ
GLOOMY
This is the Land of Snowmen ...?
It doesn't look anything like the last time we visited...
There sure is a lot of lightning.
The Land of Snowmen will be ruined if we don't do something!
Okay! I'll stop the lightning!
Can you really do that?

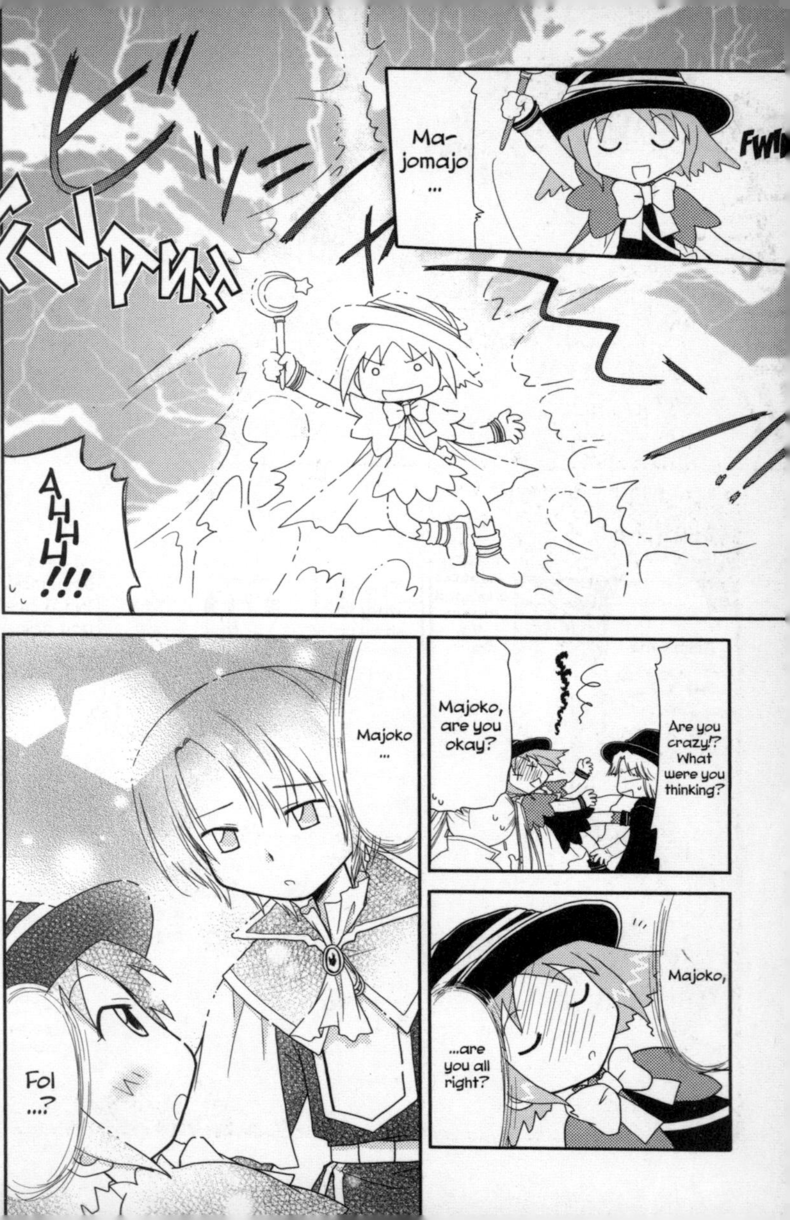
Ma-jomajo ...
FWI
FWASH
AHHHH!!!
Are you crazy!? What were you thinking?
Majoko, are you okay?
Majoko,
...are you all right?
Majoko ...
Fol ...?

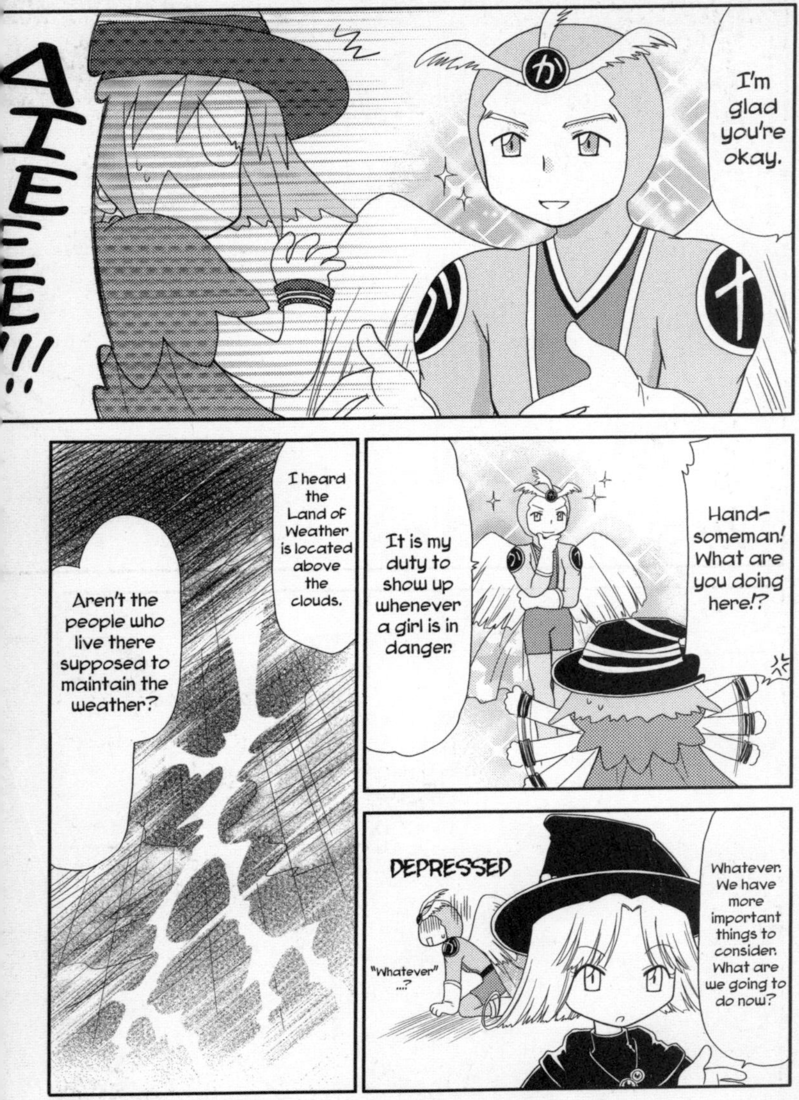
I'm glad you're okay.
AIEEEE!!
Hand-someman! What are you doing here!?
It is my duty to show up whenever a girl is in danger.
Whatever. We have more important things to consider. What are we going to do now?
DEPRESSED
"Whatever" ...?
I heard the Land of Weather is located above the clouds.
Aren't the people who live there supposed to maintain the weather?

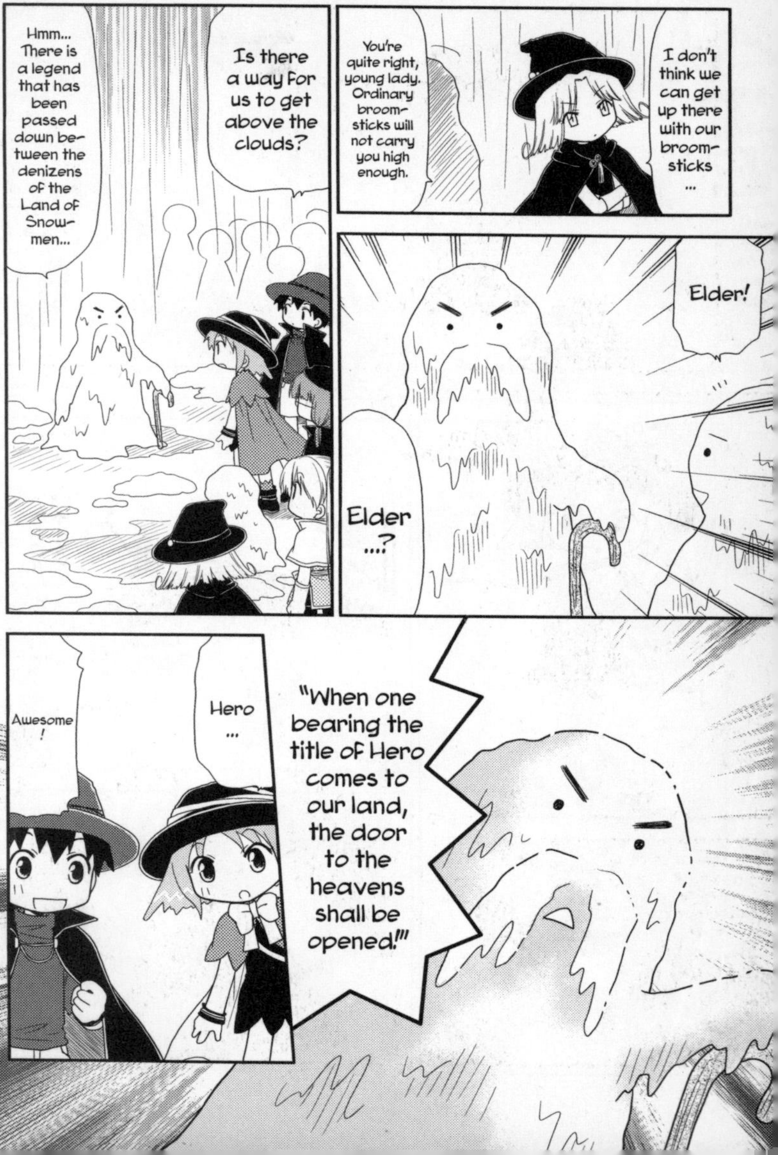
I don't think we can get up there with our broom-sticks ...
You're quite right, young lady. Ordinary broom-sticks will not carry you high enough.
Elder!
Elder ...?
Is there a way for us to get above the clouds?
Hmm... There is a legend that has been passed down be-tween the denizens of the Land of Snow-men...
"When one bearing the title of Hero comes to our land, the door to the heavens shall be opened!"
Hero ...
Awesome !

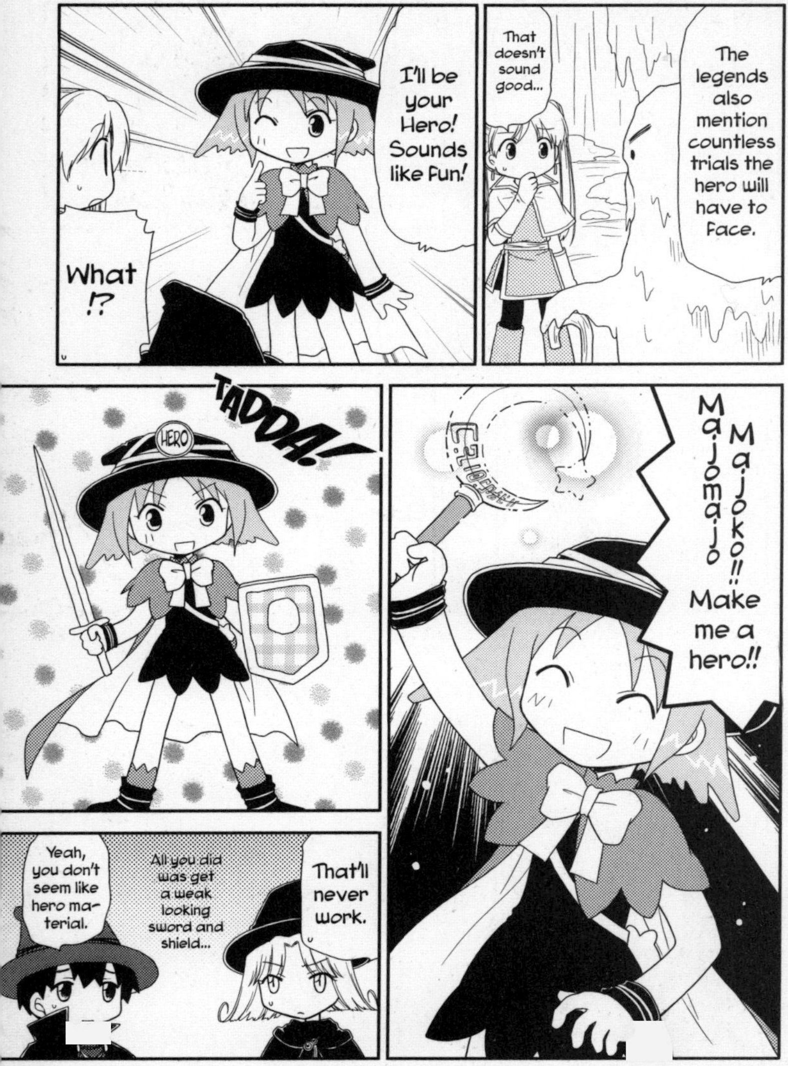
The legends also mention countless trials the hero will have to face.
That doesn't sound good...
I'll be your Hero! Sounds like fun!
What!?
Majomajo Majoko!! Make me a hero!!
TADDA!
HERO
That'll never work.
All you did was get a weak looking sword and shield...
Yeah, you don't seem like hero material.

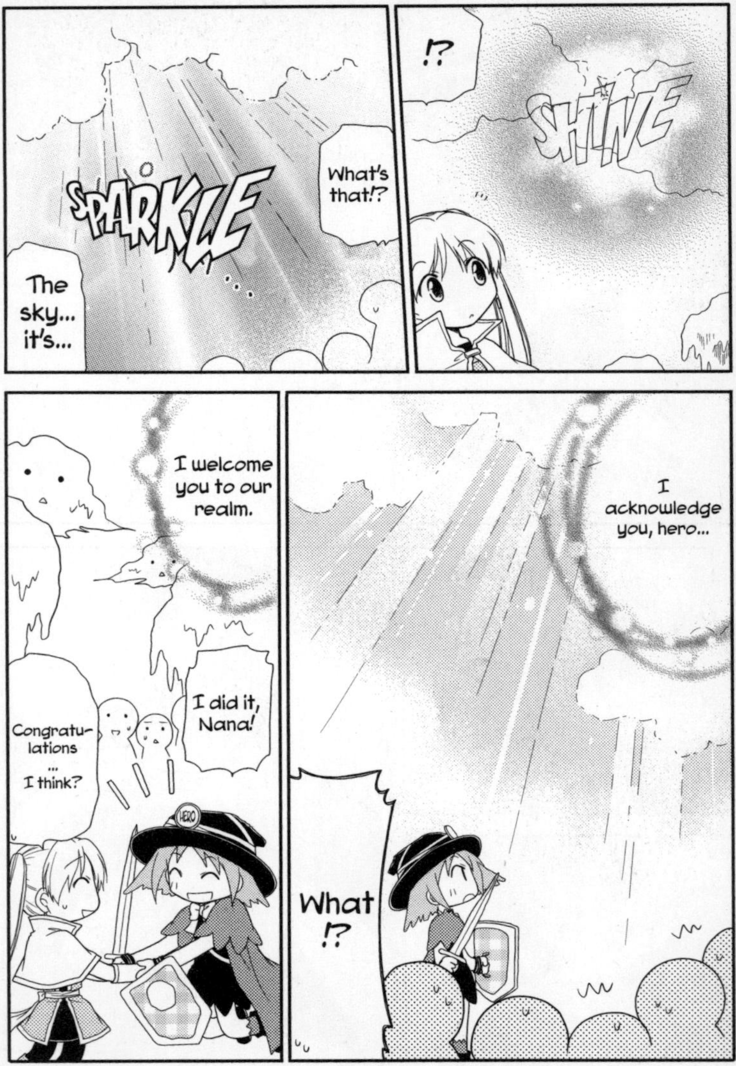
!?
SHINE
What's that!?
SPARKLE
The sky... it's...
I acknowledge you, hero...
What!?
I welcome you to our realm.
I did it, Nana!
Congratulations... I think?

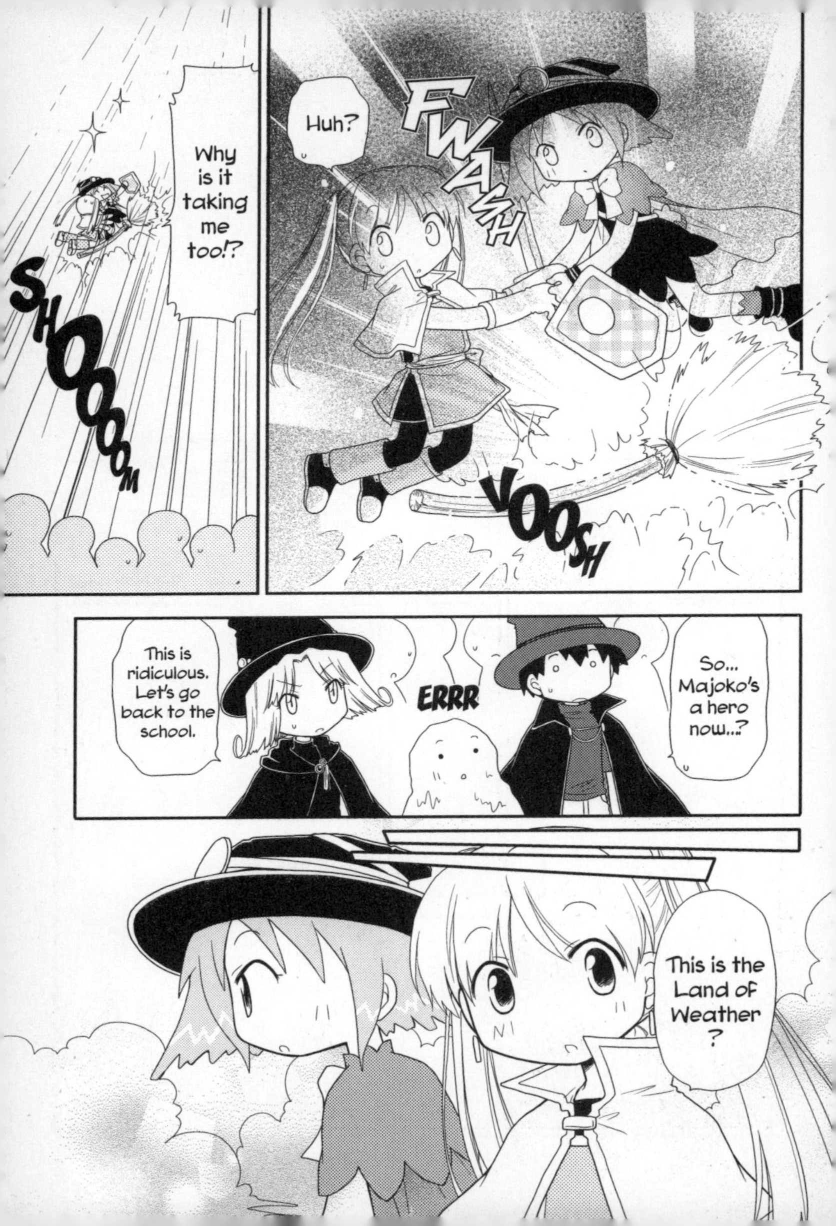
Huh?
FWASH
VOOSH
Why is it taking me too!?
SHOOOOOM
So... Majoko's a hero now..?
ERRR
This is ridiculous. Let's go back to the school.
This is the Land of Weather?

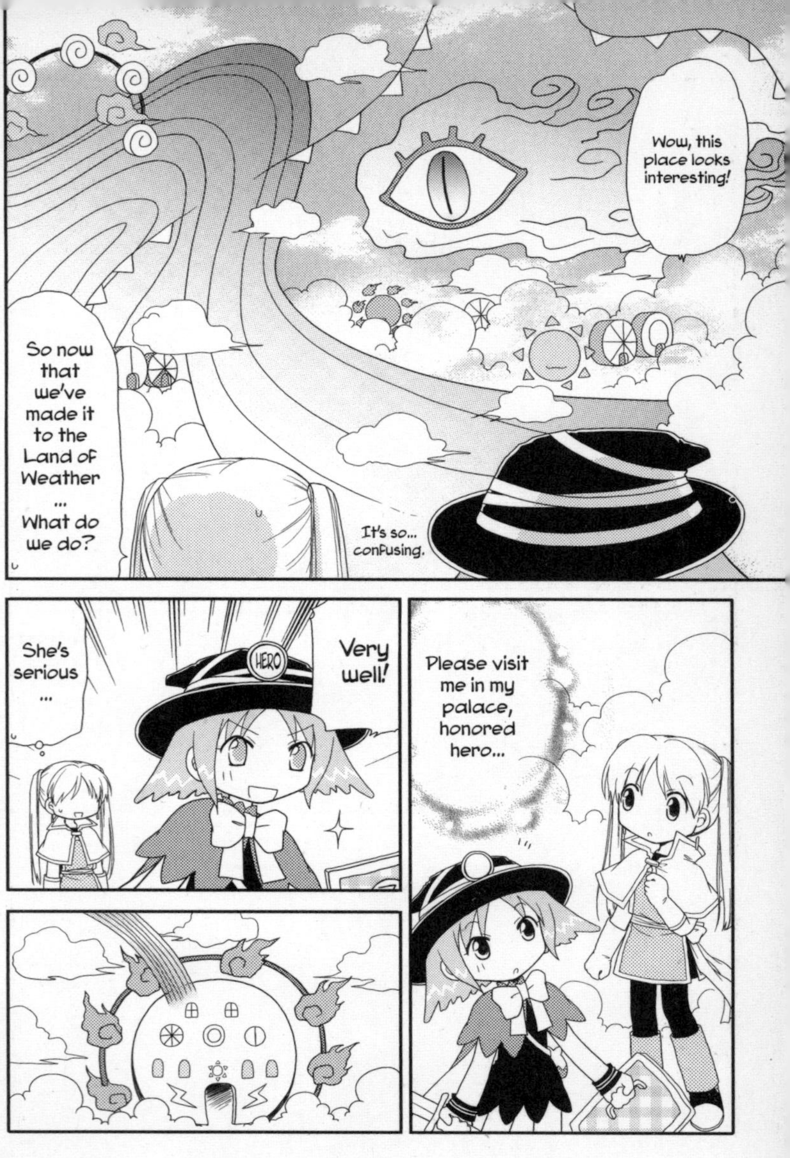
Wow, this place looks interesting!
So now that we've made it to the Land of Weather ... What do we do?
It's so... confusing.
Please visit me in my palace, honored hero...
Very well!
HERO
She's serious ...

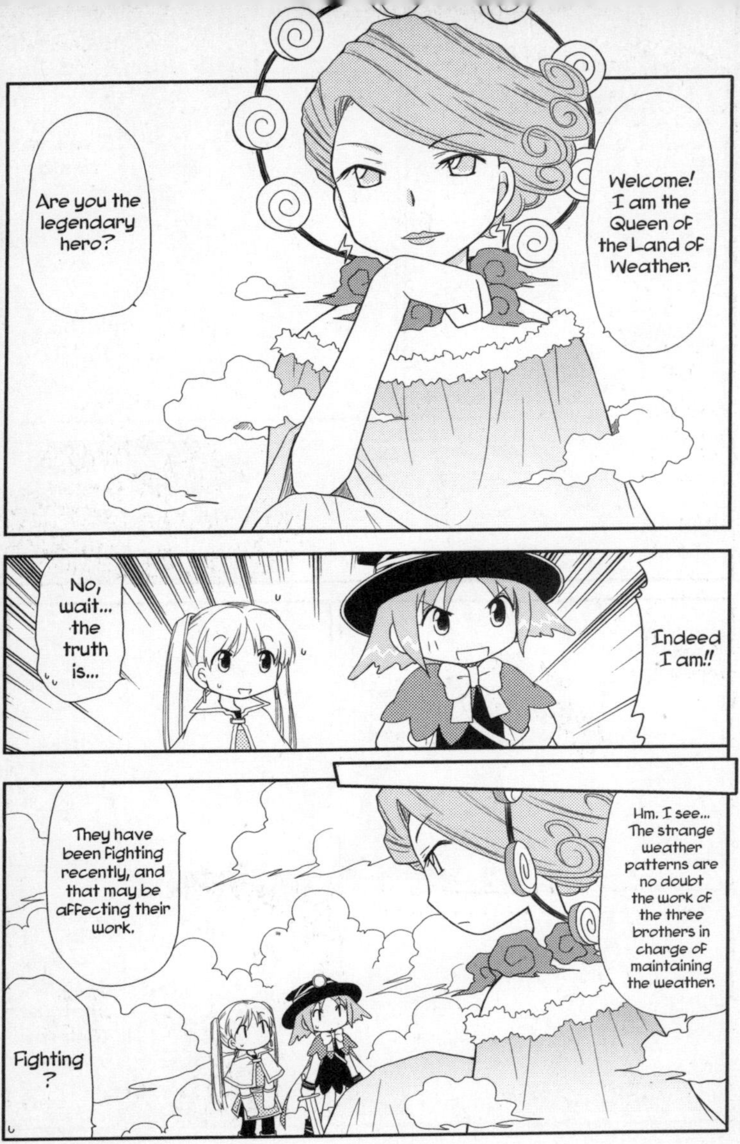
Welcome! I am the Queen of the Land of Weather.
Are you the legendary hero?
Indeed I am!!
No, wait... the truth is...
Hm. I see... The strange weather patterns are no doubt the work of the three brothers in charge of maintaining the weather.
They have been fighting recently, and that may be affecting their work.
Fighting?

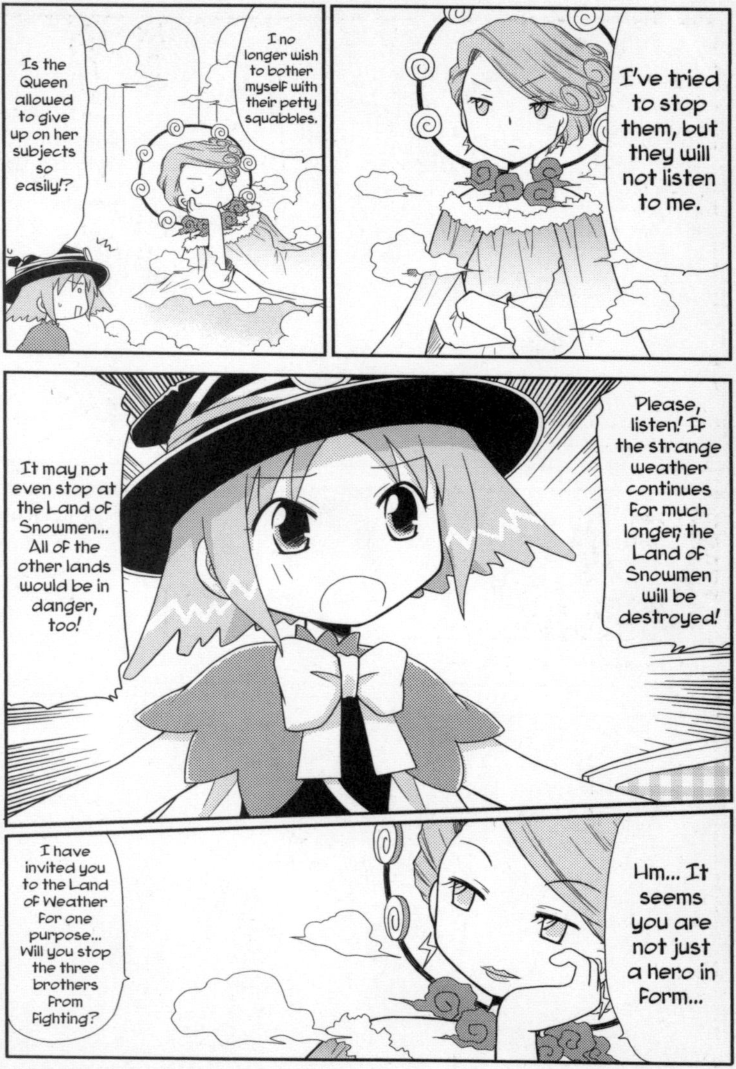
I've tried to stop them, but they will not listen to me.
I no longer wish to bother myself with their petty squabbles.
Is the Queen allowed to give up on her subjects so easily!?
Please, listen! If the strange weather continues for much longer, the Land of Snowmen will be destroyed!
It may not even stop at the Land of Snowmen... All of the other lands would be in danger, too!
Hm... It seems you are not just a hero in form...
I have invited you to the Land of Weather for one purpose... Will you stop the three brothers from fighting?

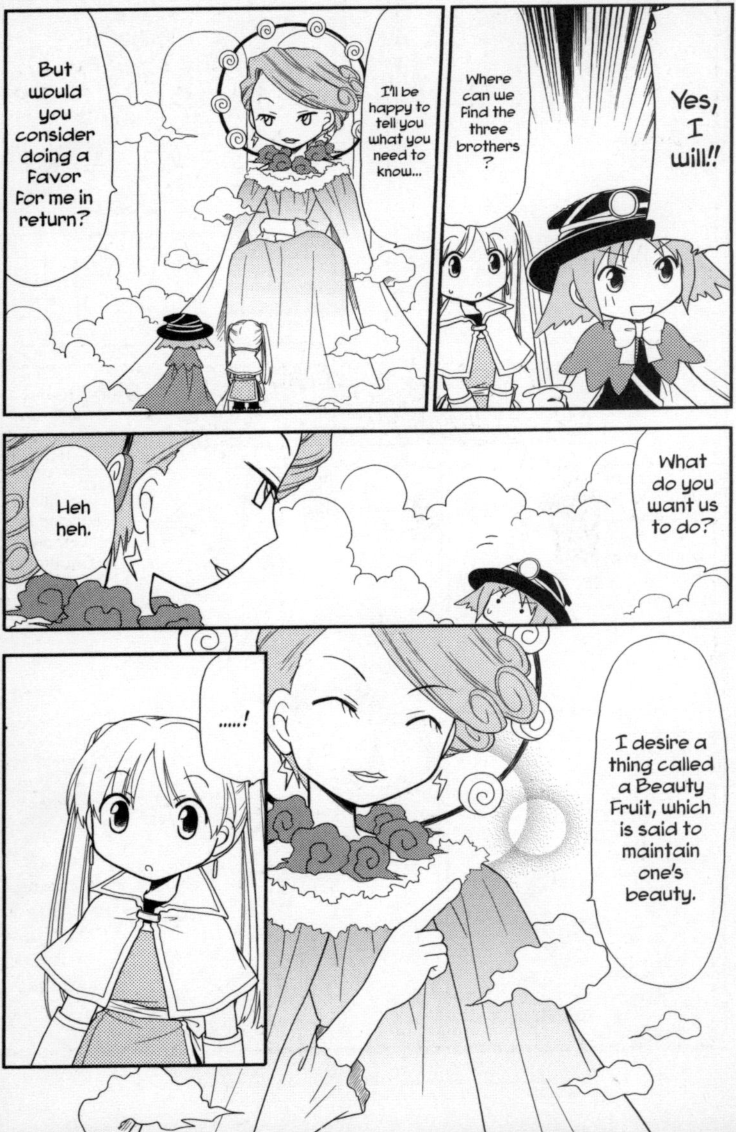
Yes, I will!!
Where can we find the three brothers?
I'll be happy to tell you what you need to know...
But would you consider doing a favor for me in return?
What do you want us to do?
Heh heh.
I desire a thing called a Beauty Fruit, which is said to maintain one's beauty.
......!

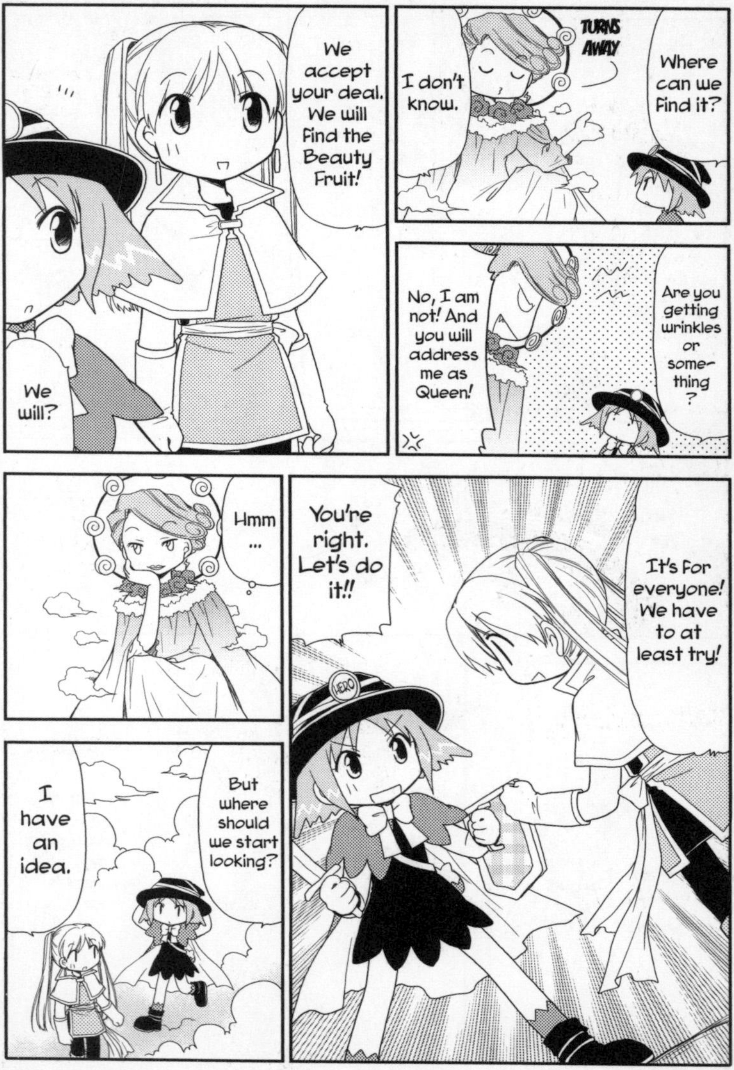
Where can we find it?
TURNS AWAY
I don't know.
Are you getting wrinkles or some-thing?
No, I am not! And you will address me as Queen!
We accept your deal. We will find the Beauty Fruit!
We will?
It's for everyone! We have to at least try!
You're right. Let's do it!!
Hmm ...
But where should we start looking?
I have an idea.

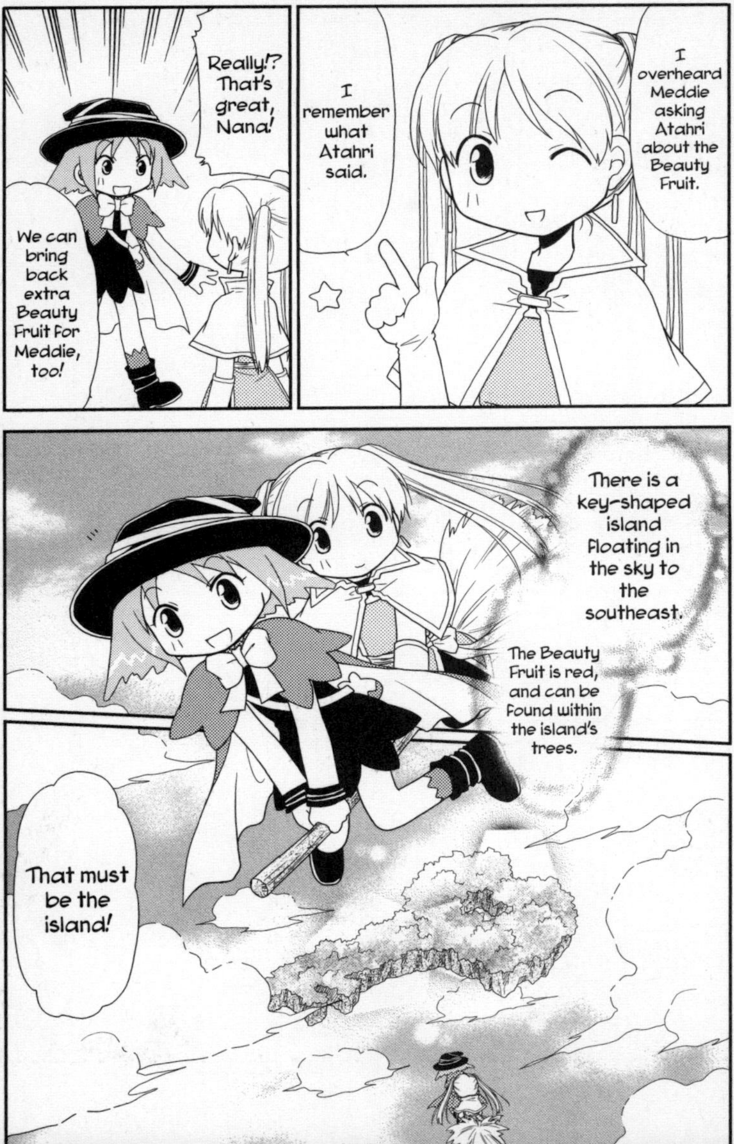
I overheard Meddie asking Atahri about the Beauty Fruit.
I remember what Atahri said.
Really!? That's great, Nana!
We can bring back extra Beauty Fruit for Meddie, too!
There is a key-shaped island floating in the sky to the southeast.
The Beauty Fruit is red, and can be found within the island's trees.
That must be the island!

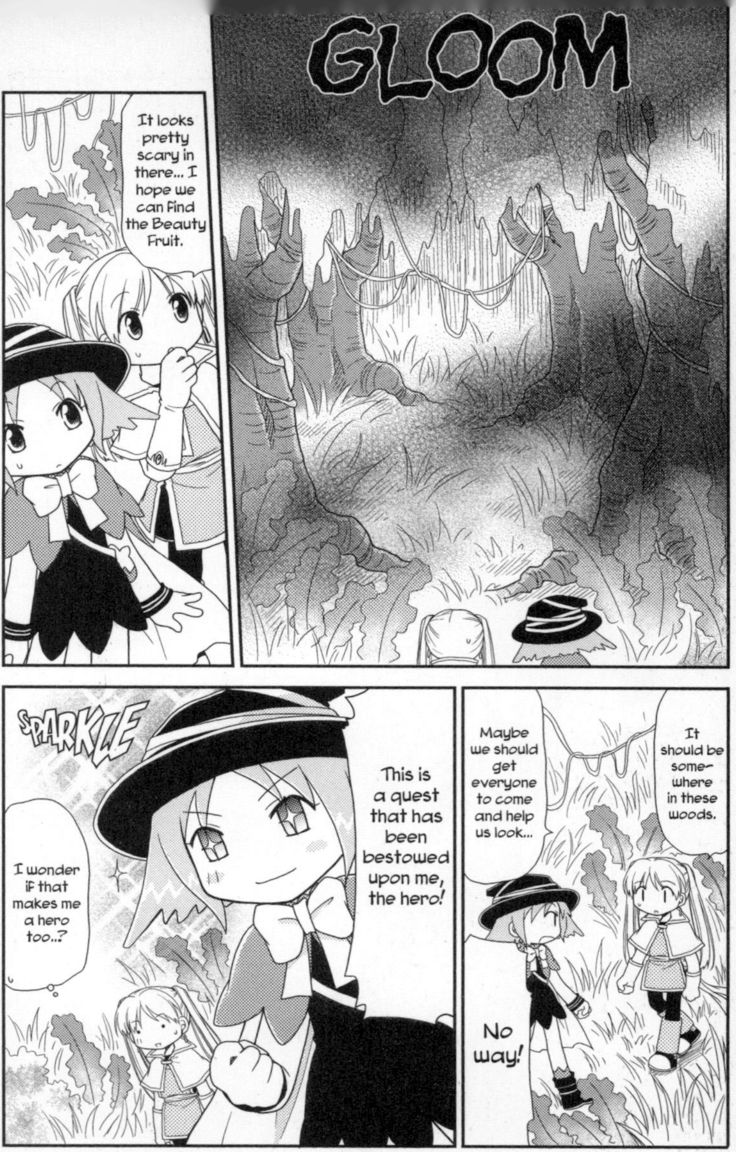
GLOOM
It looks pretty scary in there... I hope we can find the Beauty Fruit.
It should be some-where in these woods.
Maybe we should get everyone to come and help us look...
No way!
SPARKLE
This is a quest that has been bestowed upon me, the hero!
I wonder if that makes me a hero too..?

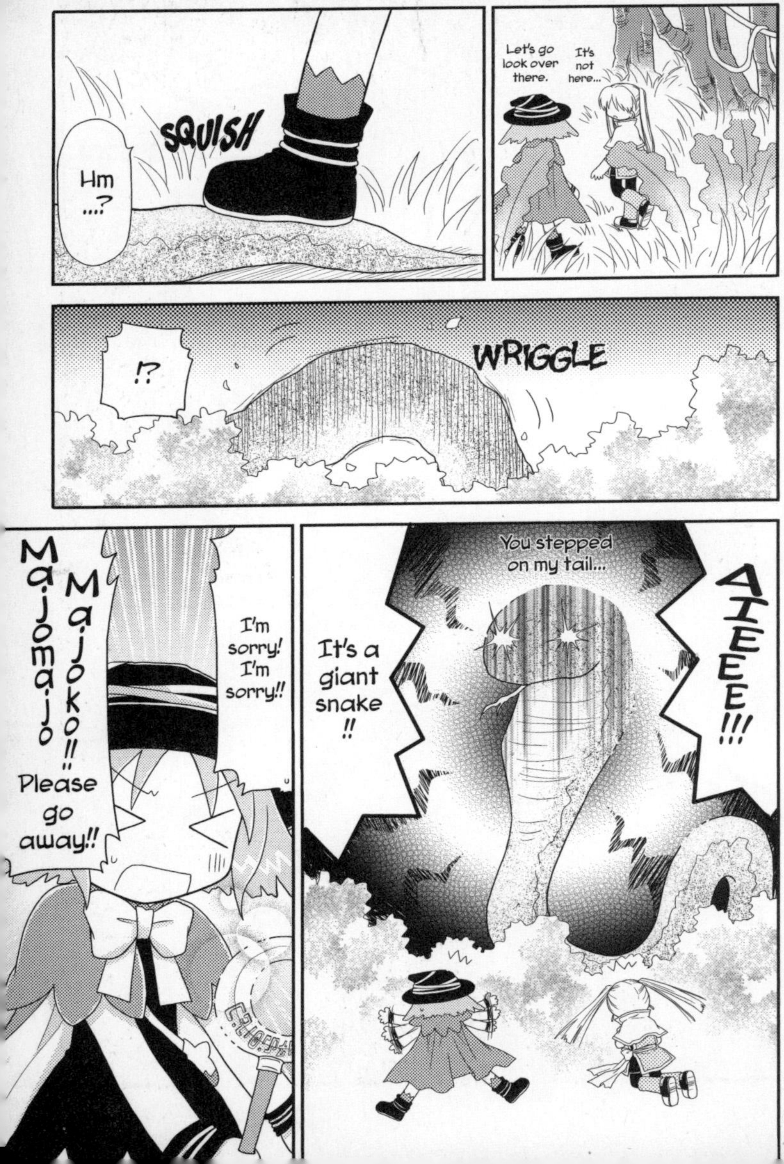
It's not here...
Let's go look over there.
SQUISH
Hm ...?
WRIGGLE
!?
You stepped on my tail...
AIEEEE!!!
It's a giant snake!!
I'm sorry! I'm sorry!!
Majoko!!
Majomajo
Please go away!!

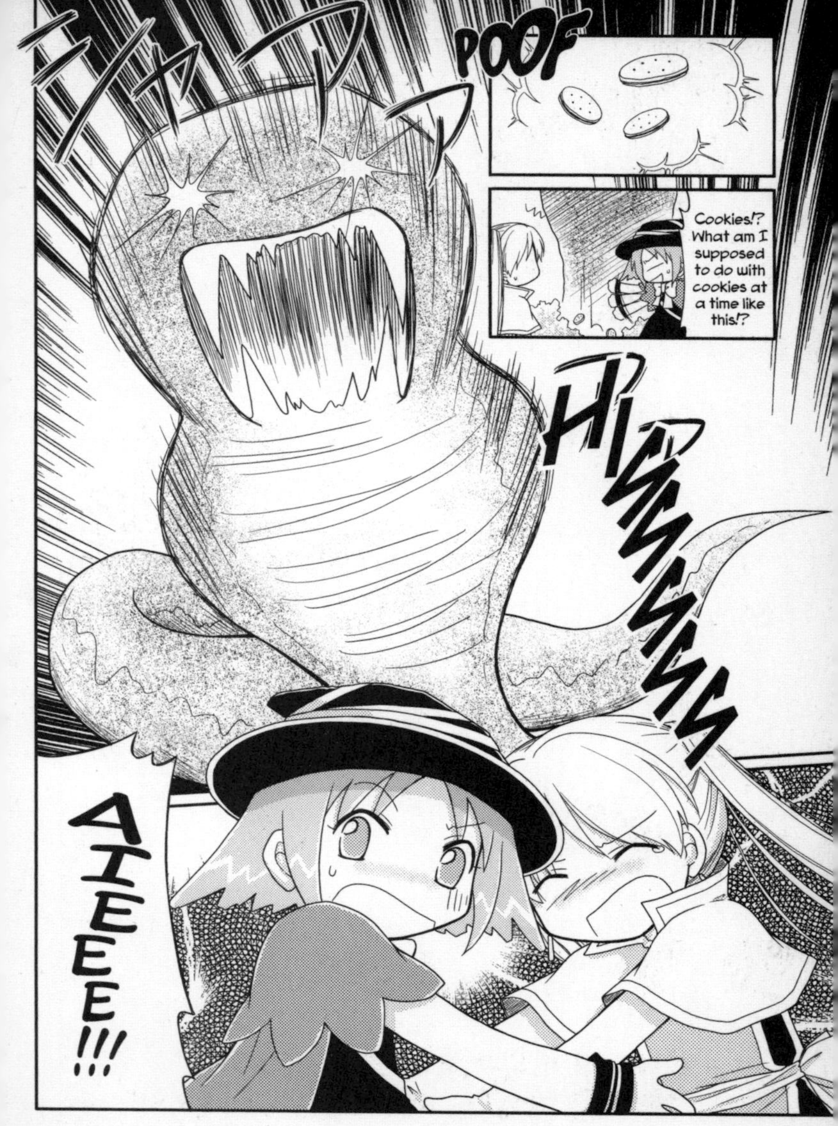
POOF
Cookies!? What am I supposed to do with cookies at a time like this!?
HISSSSS
AIEEE!!!

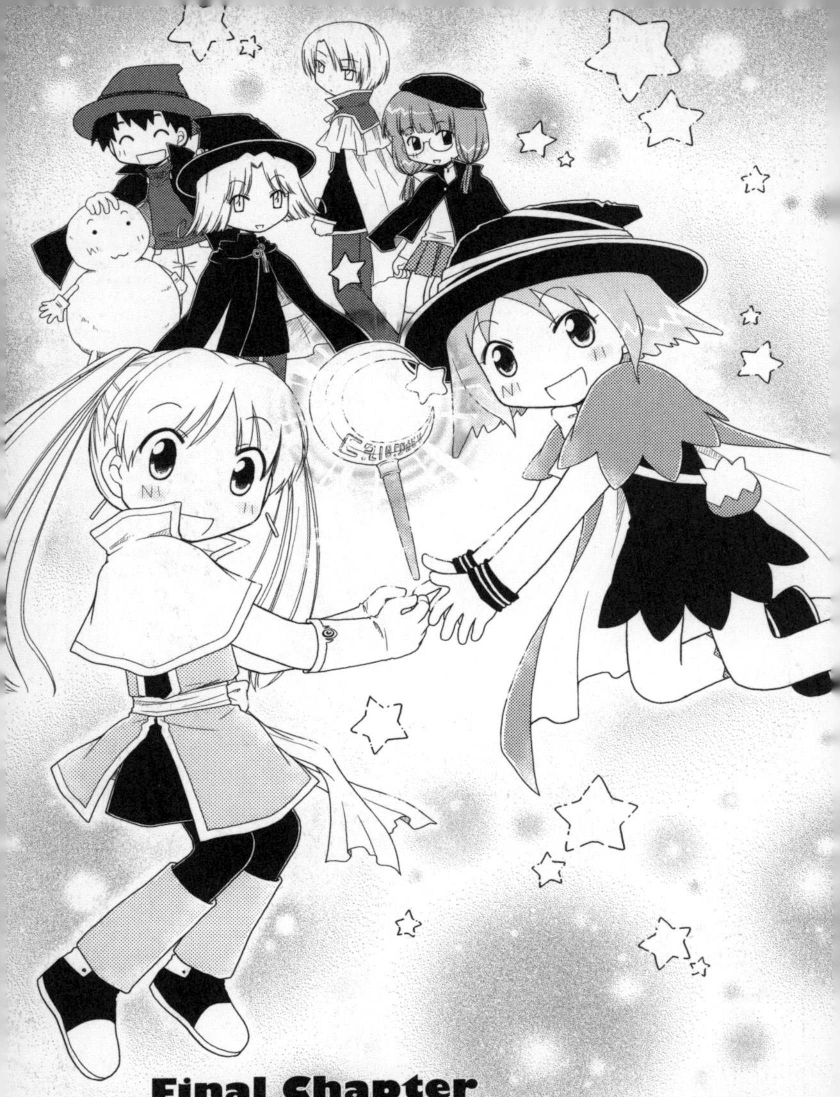

Final Chapter
The Magic of Happiness

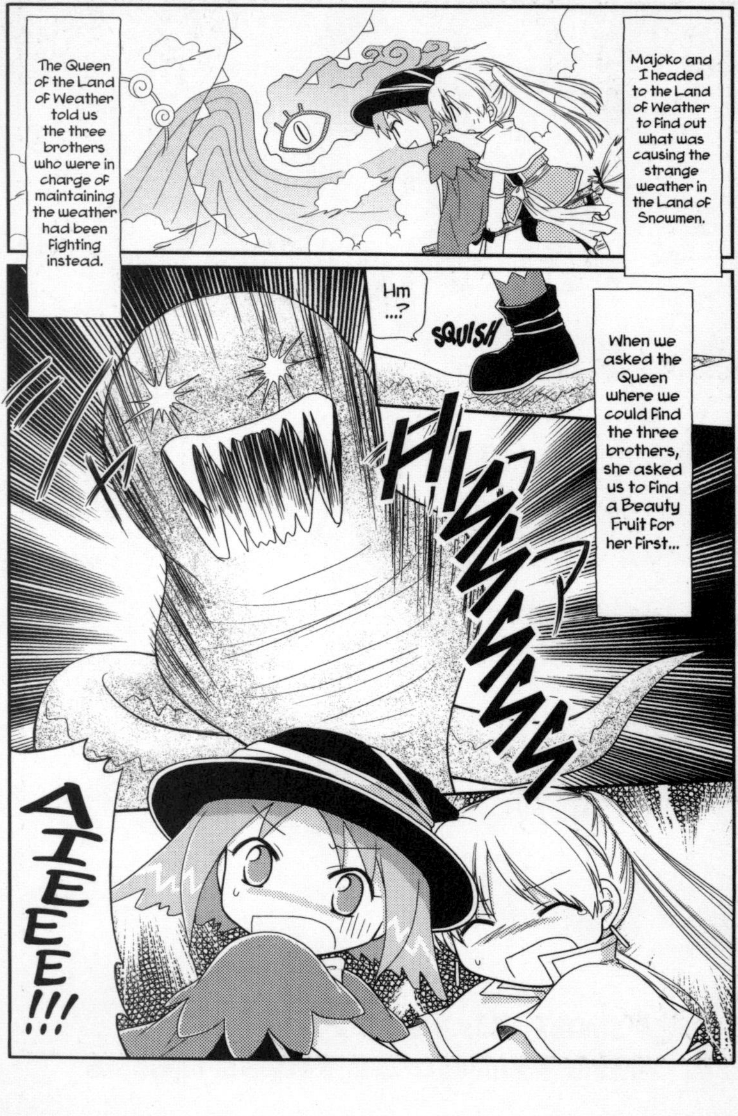
Majoko and I headed to the Land of Weather to find out what was causing the strange weather in the Land of Snowmen.
The Queen of the Land of Weather told us the three brothers who were in charge of maintaining the weather had been fighting instead.
When we asked the Queen where we could find the three brothers, she asked us to find a Beauty Fruit for her first...
Hm ...?
SQUISH
AIEEEE!!!

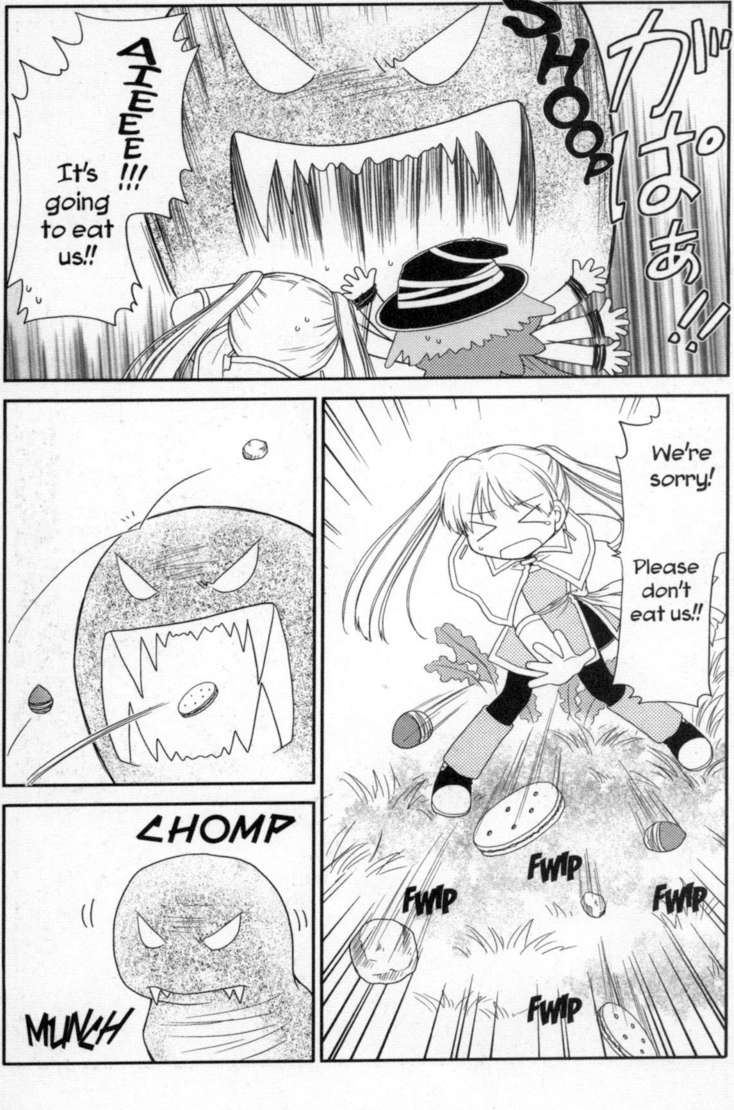
がぱぁ!!
SHOOP
AIEEEE!!!
It's going to eat us!!
We're sorry!
Please don't eat us!!
FWIP
FWIP
FWIP
FWIP
CHOMP
MUNCH

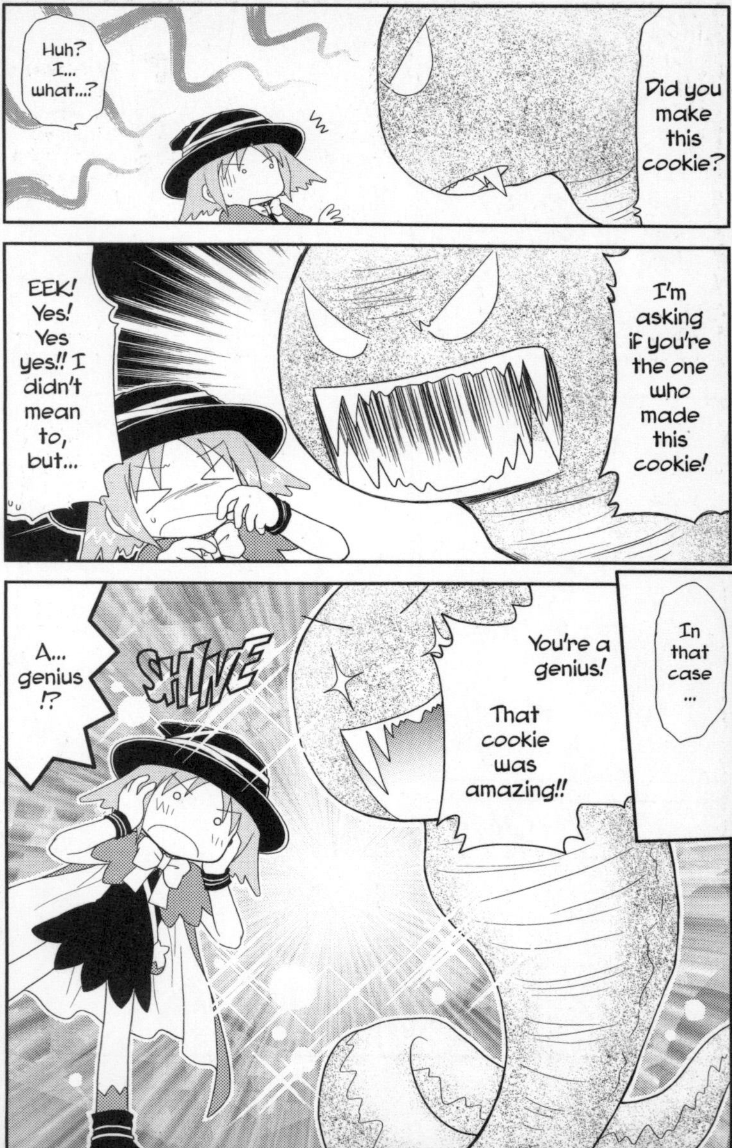
Did you make this cookie?
Huh? I... what...?
I'm asking if you're the one who made this cookie!
EEK! Yes! Yes yes!! I didn't mean to, but...
In that case ...
You're a genius!
That cookie was amazing!!
SHINE
A... genius!?

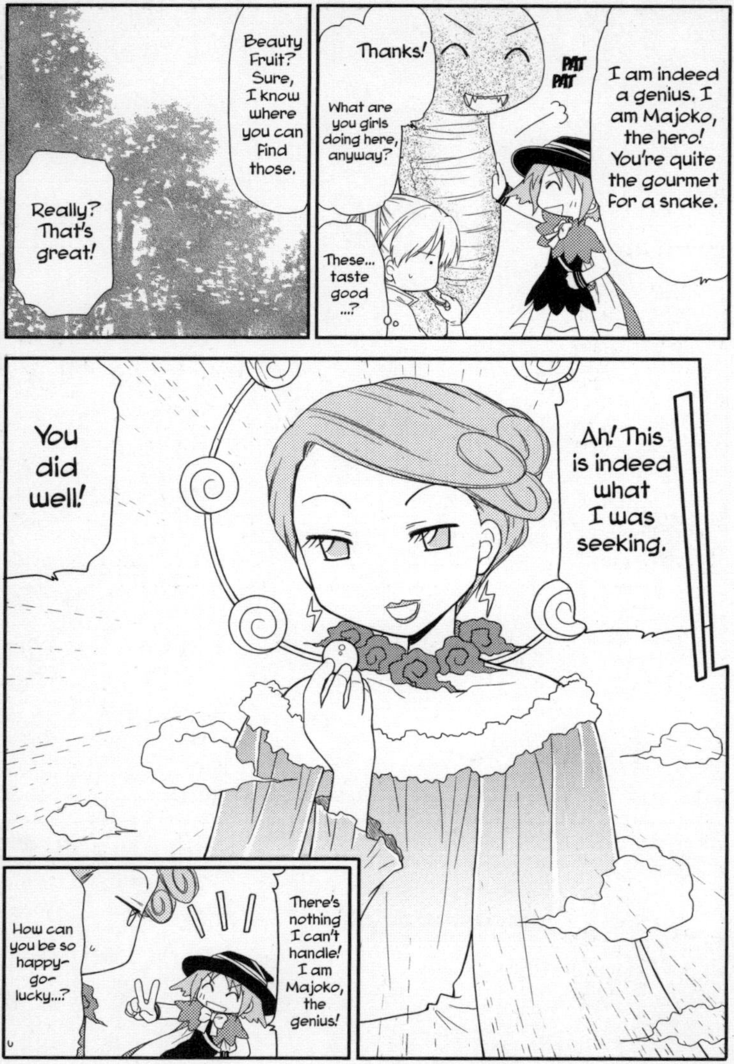
I am indeed a genius. I am Majoko, the hero! You're quite the gourmet for a snake.
PAT PAT
Thanks!
What are you girls doing here, anyway?
These... taste good ...?
Beauty Fruit? Sure, I know where you can find those.
Really? That's great!
Ah! This is indeed what I was seeking.
You did well!
There's nothing I can't handle! I am Majoko, the genius!
How can you be so happy-go-lucky...?

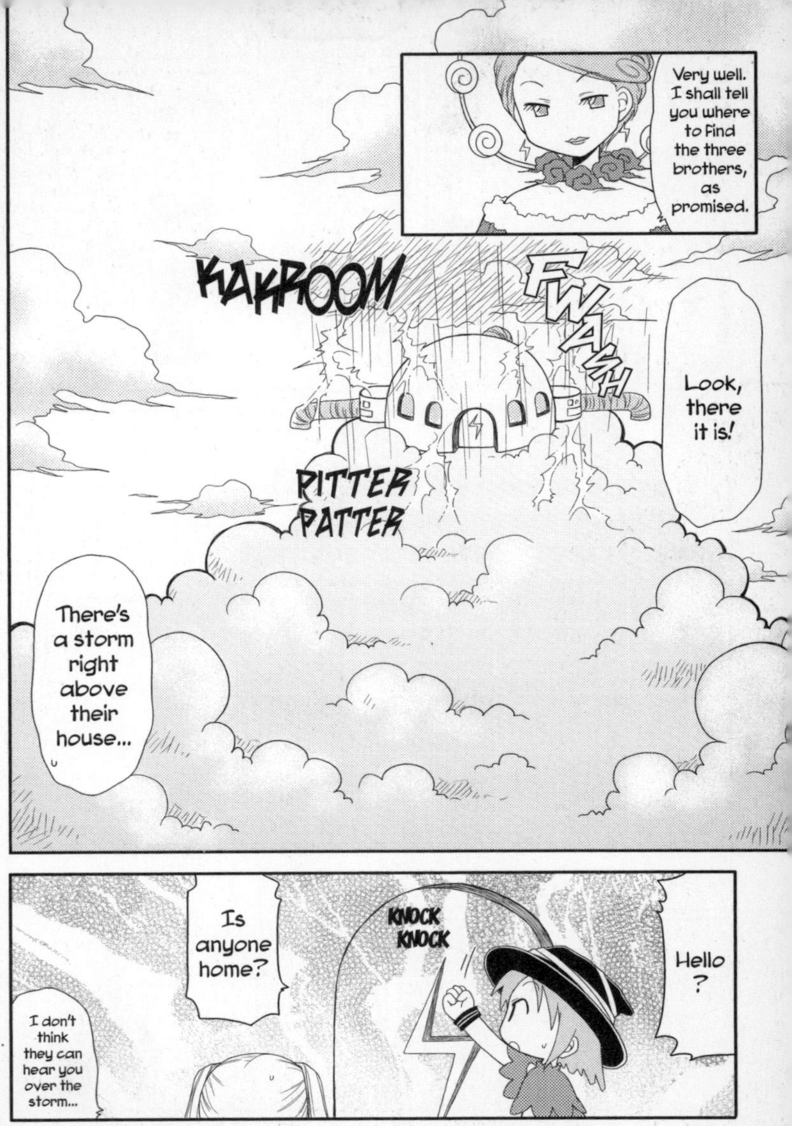
Very well. I shall tell you where to find the three brothers, as promised.
FWASH
KAKROOM
Look, there it is!
PITTER PATTER
There's a storm right above their house...
Hello?
KNOCK KNOCK
Is anyone home?
I don't think they can hear you over the storm...

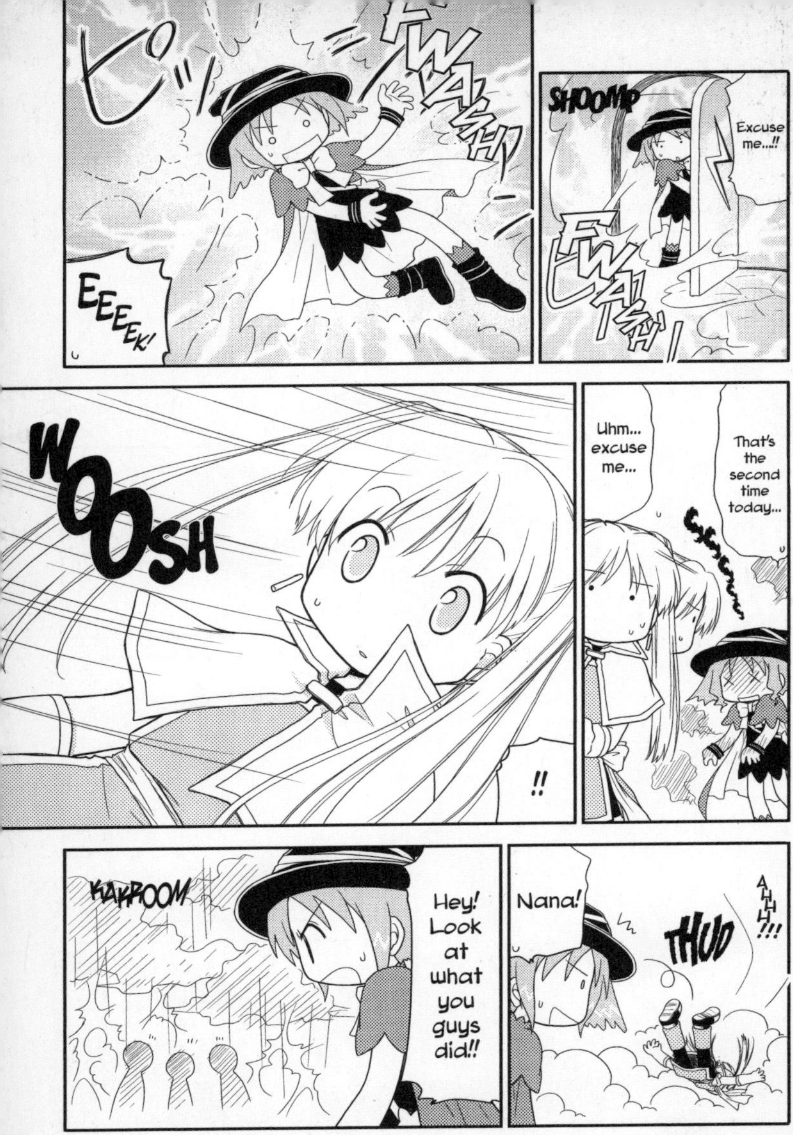
SHOOMP
Excuse me...!!
FWASH
ピッ
FWASH
EEEEK!
That's the second time today...
Uhm... excuse me...
WOOSH
!!
Nana!
THUD
AHHHH!!!
Hey! Look at what you guys did!!
KAKROOM

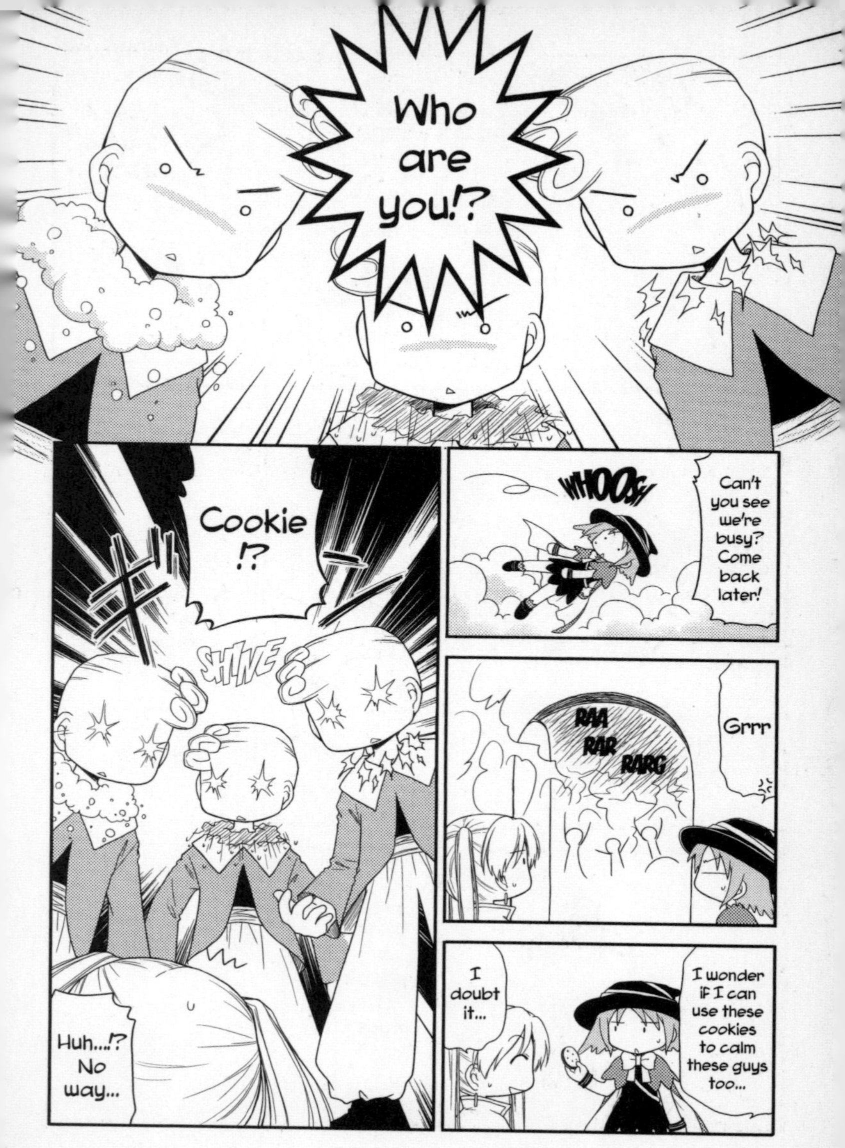
Who are you!?
WHOOSH
Can't you see we're busy? Come back later!
RAA RAR RARG
Grrr
I wonder if I can use these cookies to calm these guys too...
I doubt it...
Cookie!?
SHINE
Huh...!? No way...

This all started because you ate my cookie!
It's your fault for leaving it lying around!!
STARE
I was saving it for when I was done working! Do you know how much work it is to keep the snow going!?
You guys have it easy! Rain and lightning only need to occur once in a while.
I'm a lightning specialist! A specialist! That's pretty demanding work too!
FWASH
Hey, rain isn't easy either!!
They're fighting over a cookie? How childish...
Hmm ...

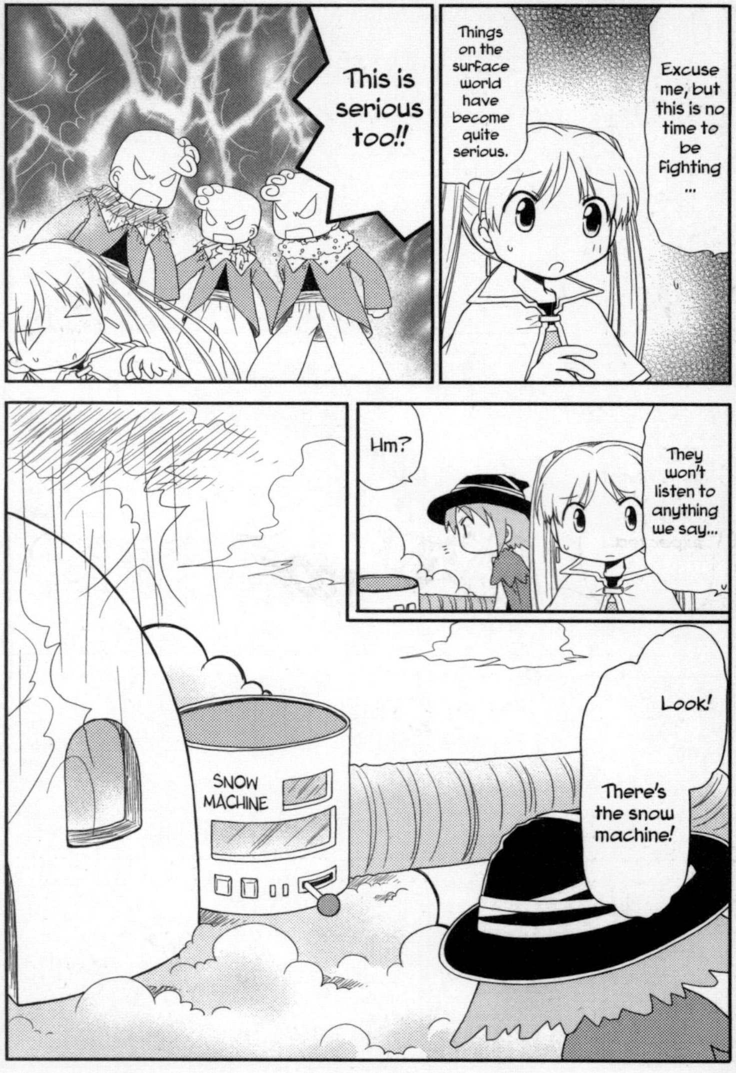
Excuse me, but this is no time to be fighting ...
Things on the surface world have become quite serious.
This is serious too!!
They won't listen to anything we say...
Hm?
Look!
There's the snow machine!
SNOW MACHINE

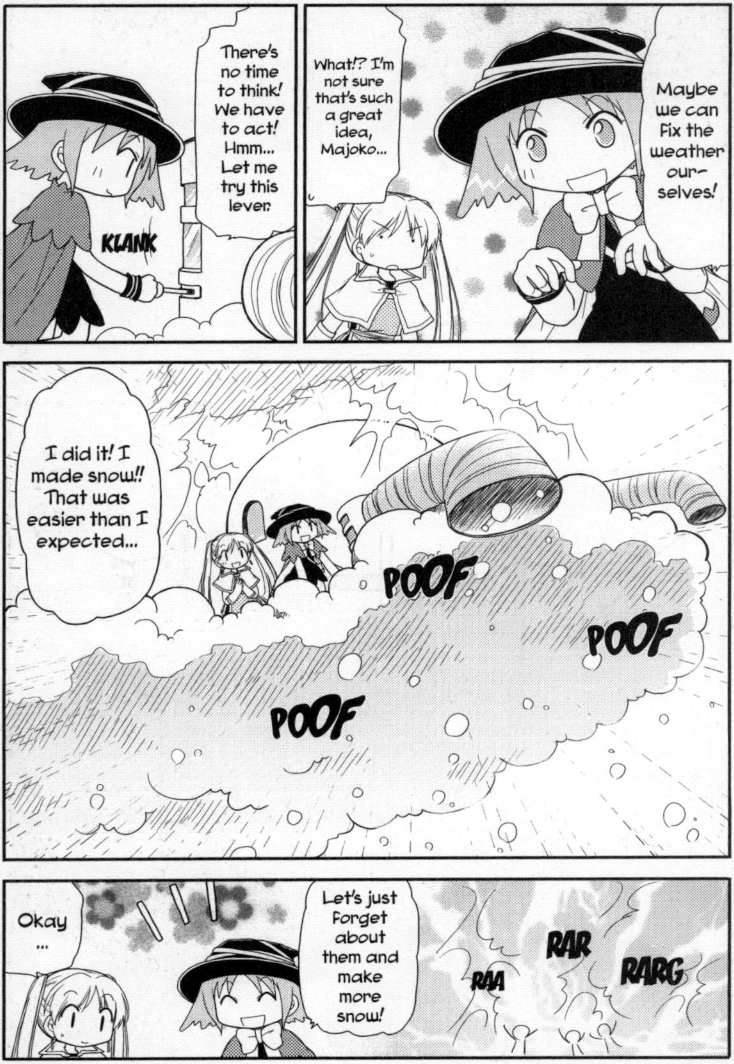
Maybe we can Fix the weather our-selves!
What!? I'm not sure that's such a great idea, Majoko...
There's no time to think! We have to act! Hmm... Let me try this lever.
KLANK
I did it! I made snow!! That was easier than I expected...
POOF
POOF
POOF
RAR
RARG
RAA
Let's just forget about them and make more snow!
Okay ...

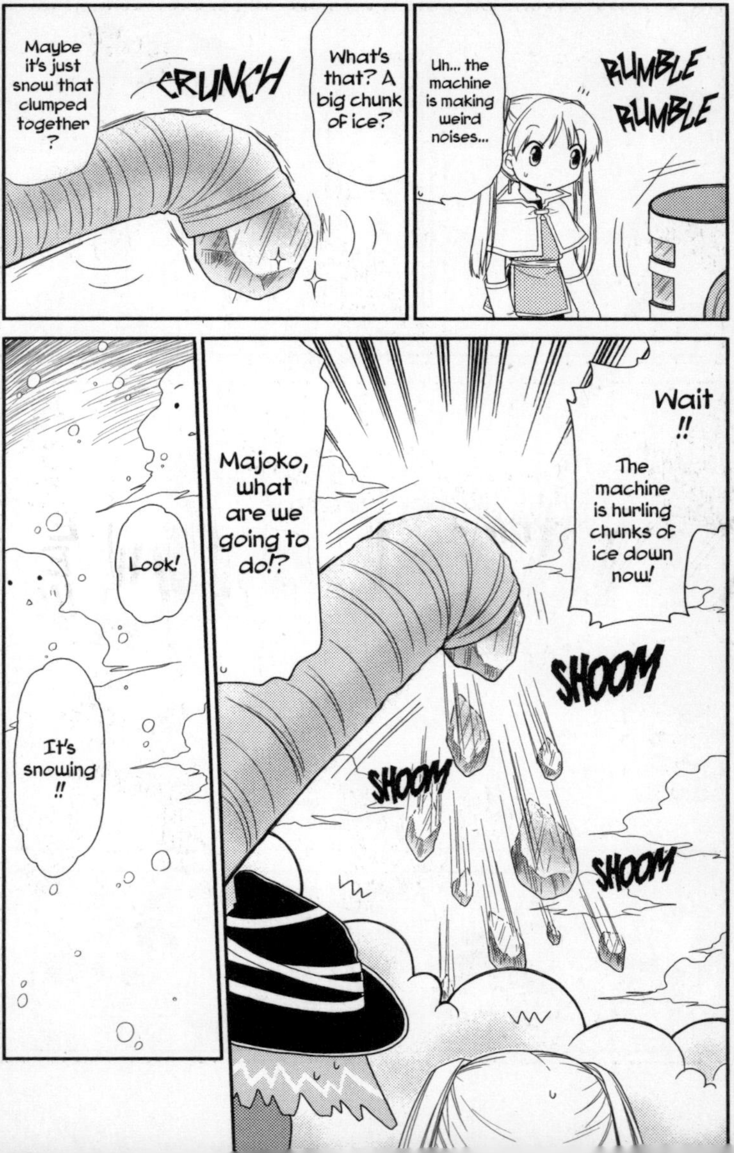
Uh... the machine is making weird noises...
RUMBLE RUMBLE
What's that? A big chunk of ice?
CRUNCH
Maybe it's just snow that clumped together?
Wait!!
The machine is hurling chunks of ice down now!
Majoko, what are we going to do!?
SHOOM
SHOOM
SHOOM
Look!
It's snowing!!

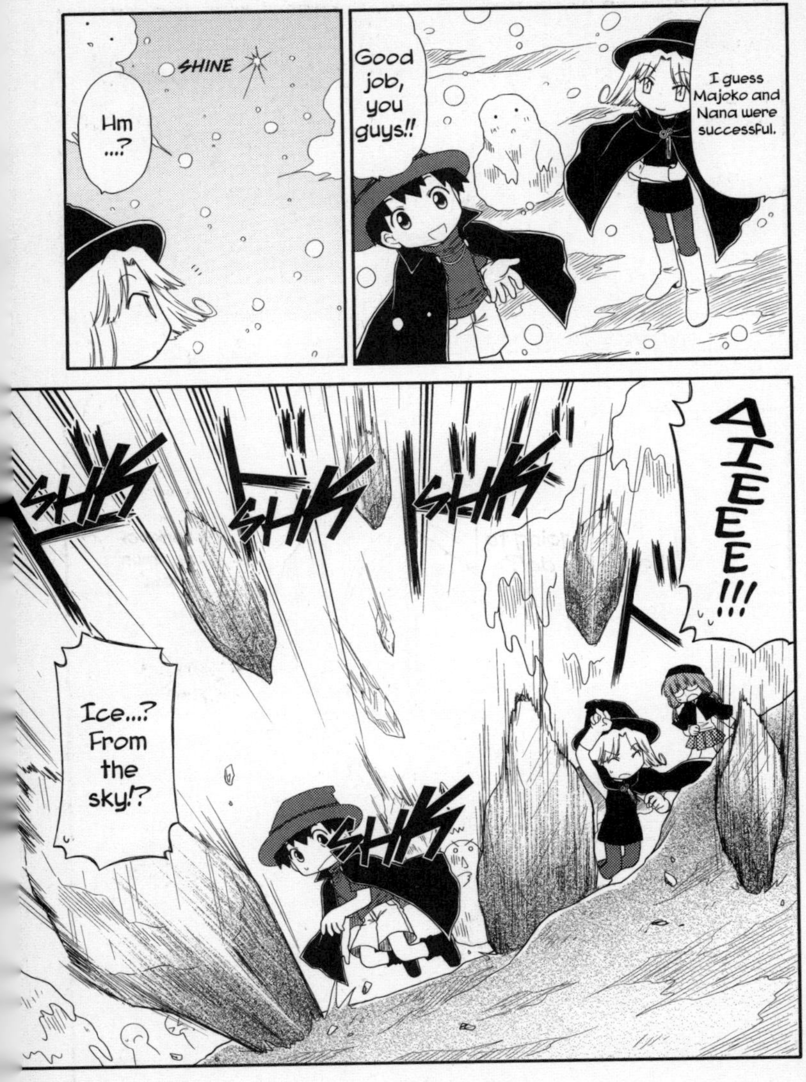
I guess Majoko and Nana were successful.
Good job, you guys!!
SHINE
Hm ...?
AIEEEE!!!
SHIK
SHIK
SHIK
Ice...? From the sky!?
SHIK

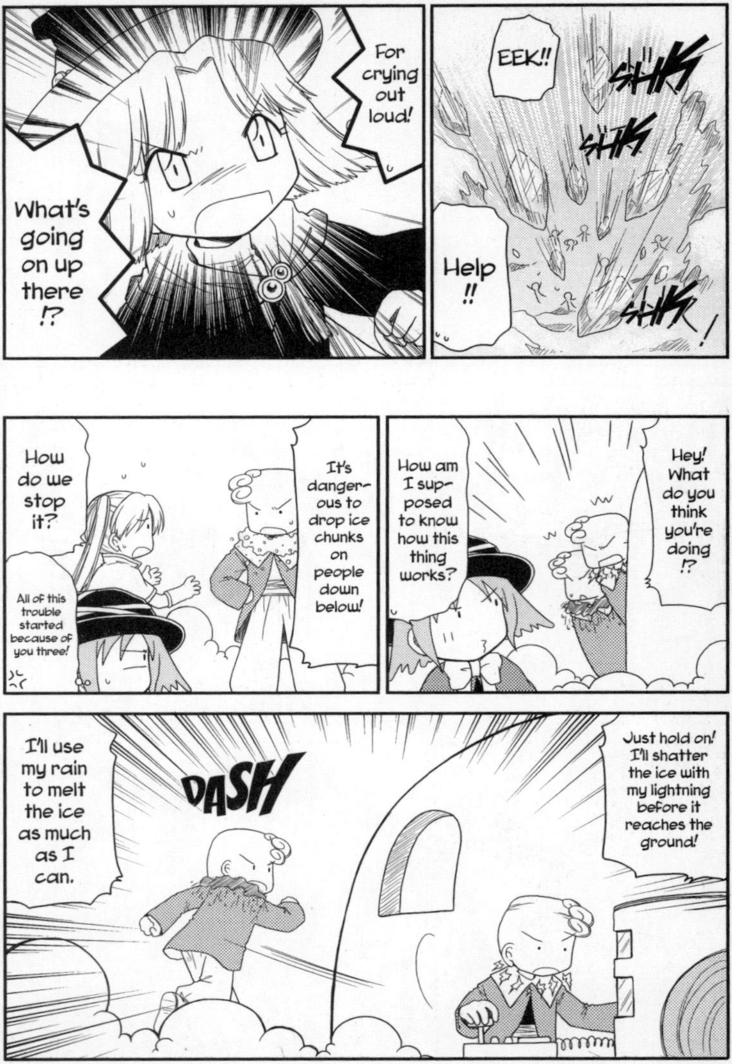
EEK!!
SHIK
SHIK
Help!!
SHIK
For crying out loud!
What's going on up there!?
Hey! What do you think you're doing!?
How am I supposed to know how this thing works?
It's dangerous to drop ice chunks on people down below!
How do we stop it?
All of this trouble started because of you three!
Just hold on! I'll shatter the ice with my lightning before it reaches the ground!
DASH
I'll use my rain to melt the ice as much as I can.

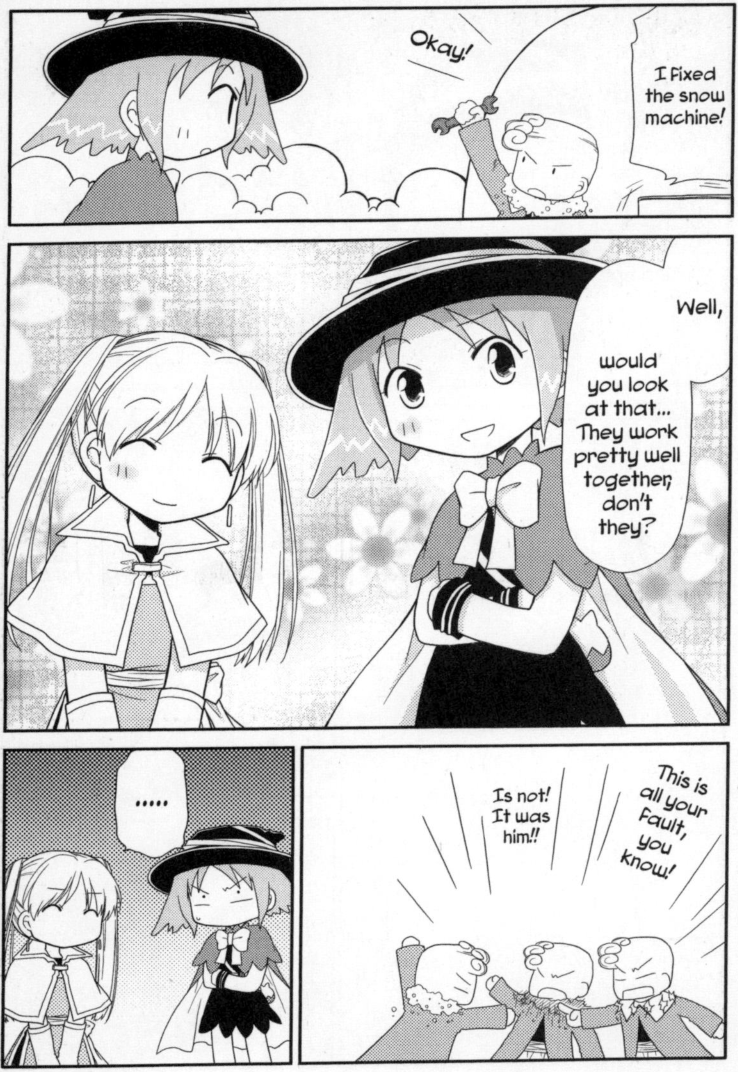
Okay!
I fixed the snow machine!
Well,
would you look at that... They work pretty well together, don't they?
This is all your fault, you know!
Is not! It was him!!
......

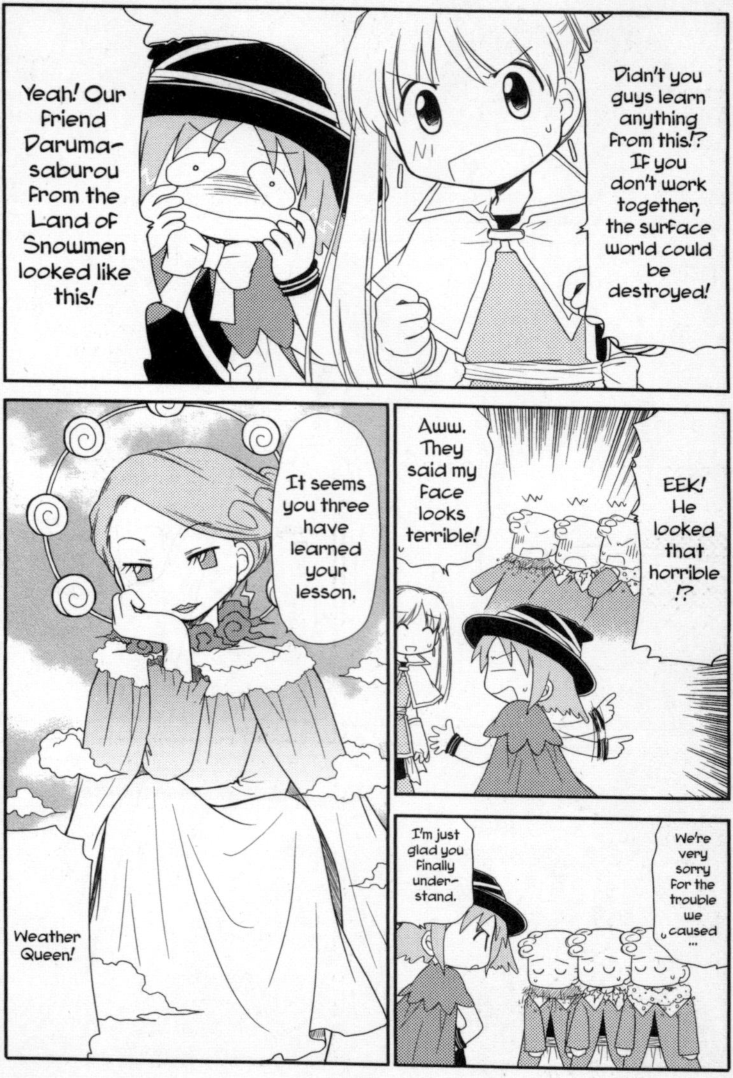
Didn't you guys learn anything from this!? If you don't work together, the surface world could be destroyed!
Yeah! Our friend Daruma-saburou from the Land of Snowmen looked like this!
EEK! He looked that horrible!?
Aww. They said my face looks terrible!
We're very sorry for the trouble we caused ...
I'm just glad you finally understand.
It seems you three have learned your lesson.
Weather Queen!

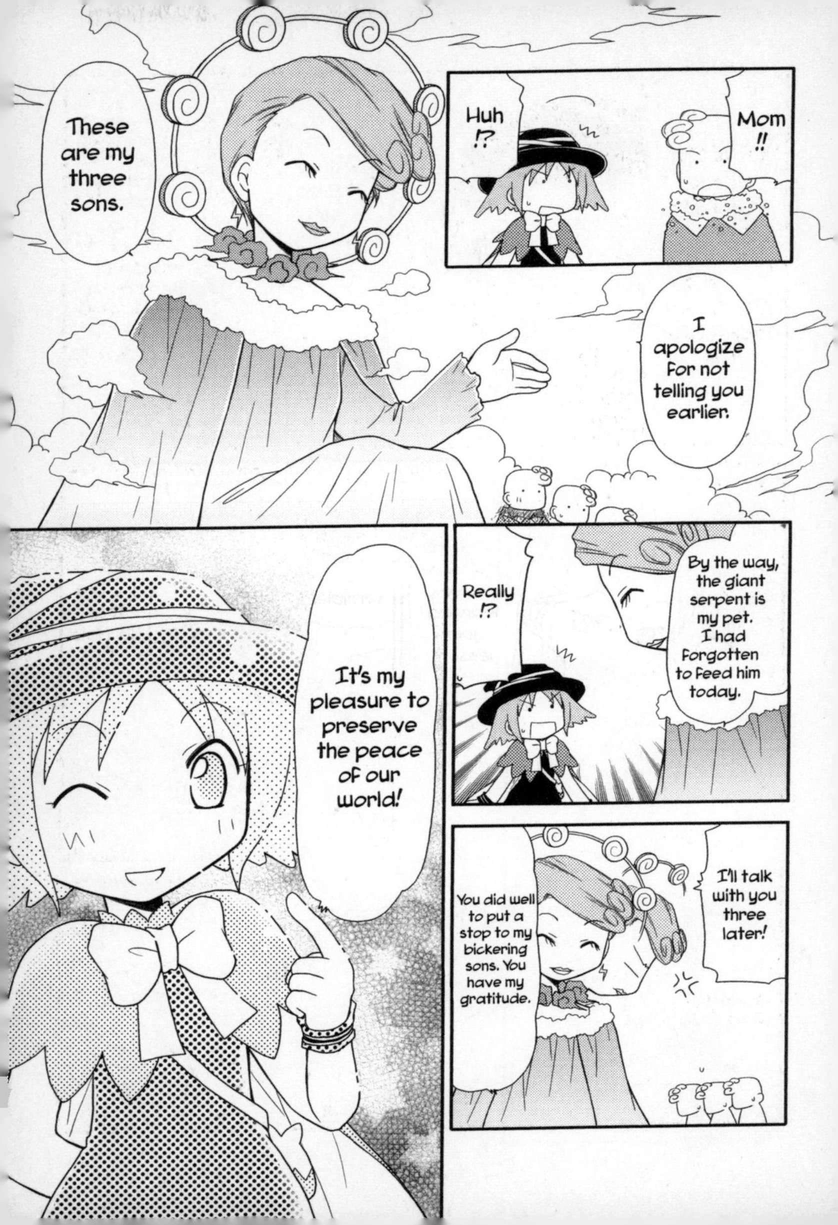
These are my three sons.
Mom !!
Huh !?
I apologize for not telling you earlier.
By the way, the giant serpent is my pet. I had forgotten to feed him today.
Really !?
You did well to put a stop to my bickering sons. You have my gratitude.
I'll talk with you three later!
It's my pleasure to preserve the peace of our world!

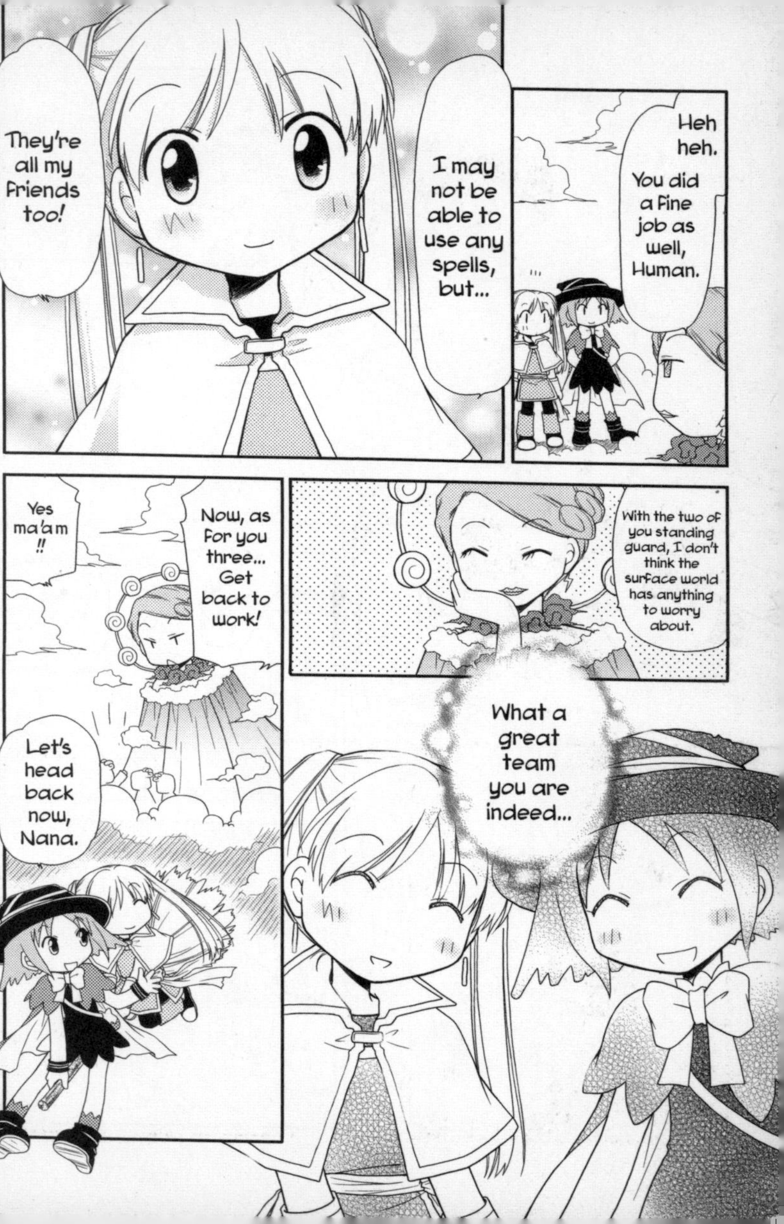
Heh heh.
You did a fine job as well, Human.
I may not be able to use any spells, but...
They're all my friends too!
With the two of you standing guard, I don't think the surface world has anything to worry about.
What a great team you are indeed...
Now, as for you three... Get back to work!
Yes ma'am !!
Let's head back now, Nana.

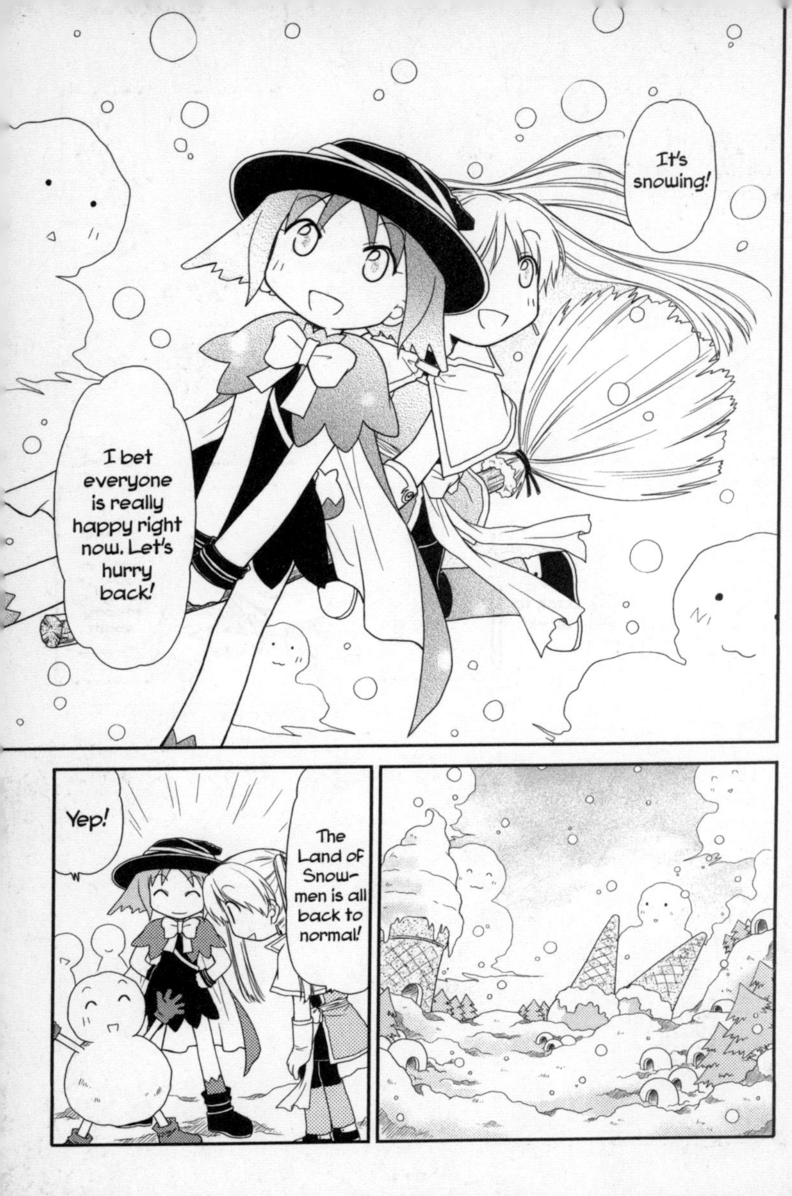
It's snowing!
I bet everyone is really happy right now. Let's hurry back!
The Land of Snow-men is all back to normal!
Yep!

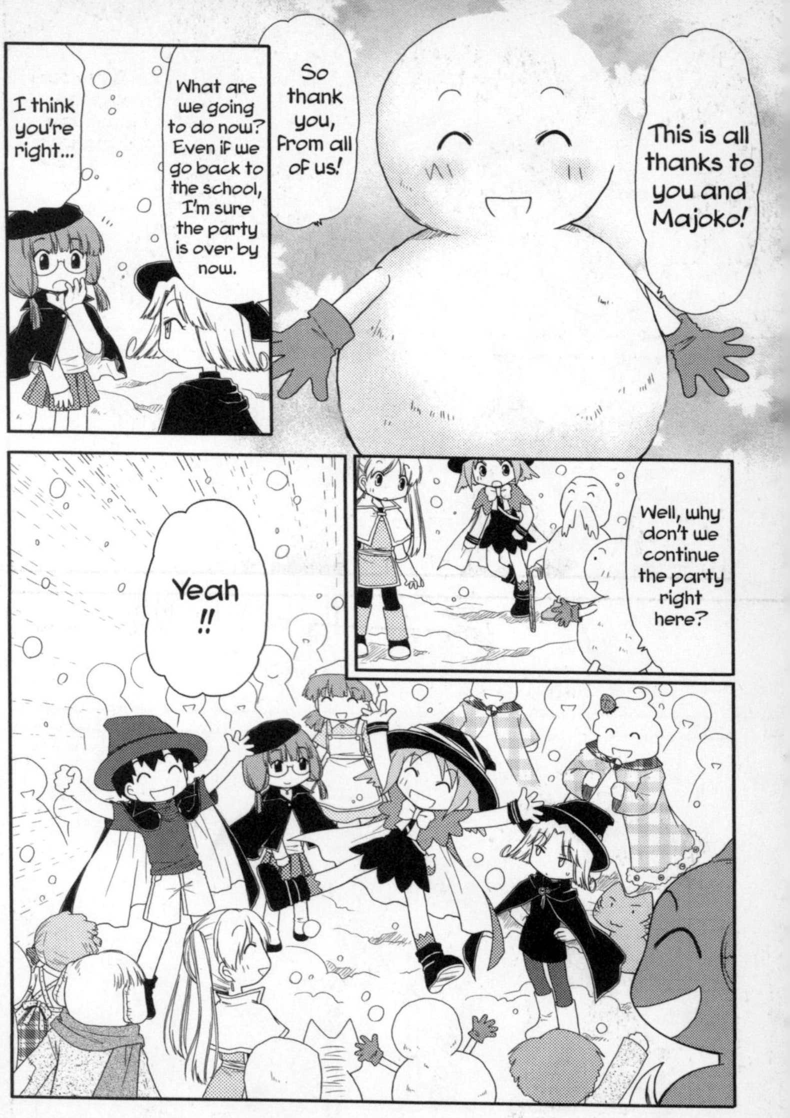
This is all thanks to you and Majoko!
So thank you, from all of us!
What are we going to do now? Even if we go back to the school, I'm sure the party is over by now.
I think you're right...
Well, why don't we continue the party right here?
Yeah !!

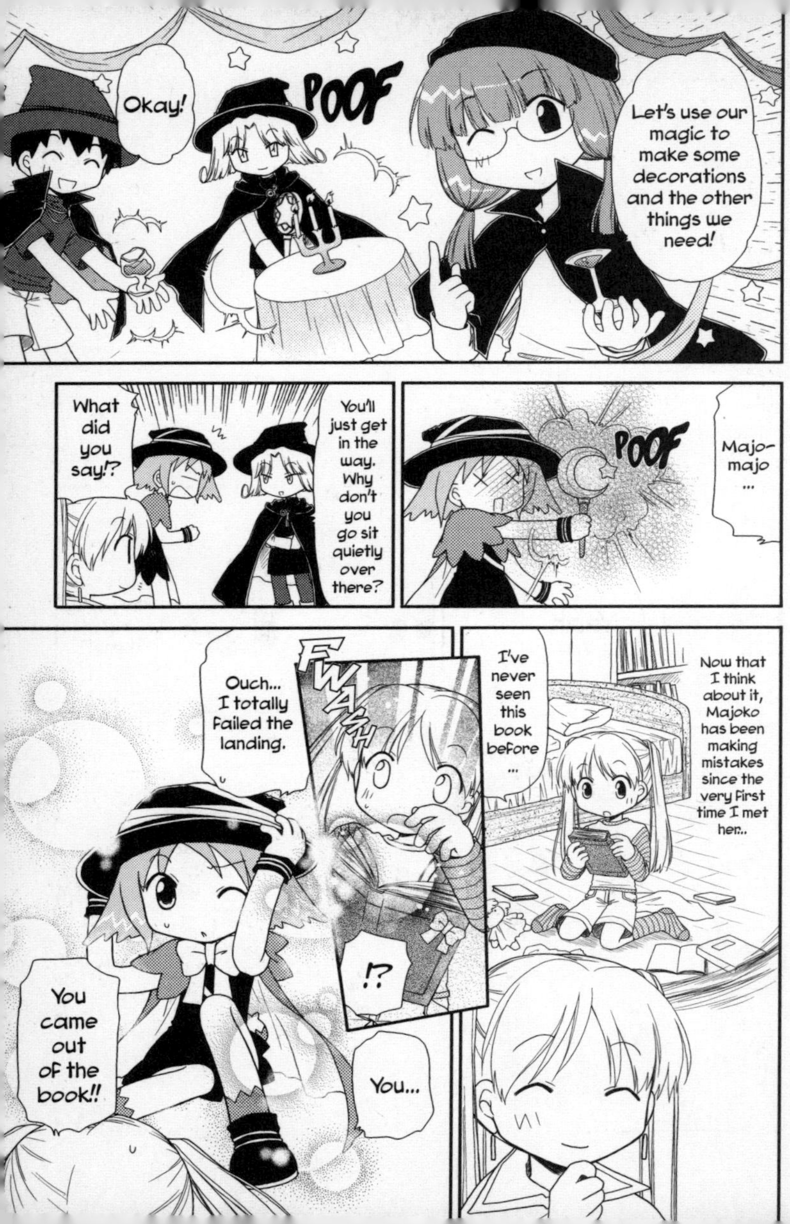
Let's use our magic to make some decorations and the other things we need!
POOF
Okay!
Majo-majo ...
POOF
You'll just get in the way. Why don't you go sit quietly over there?
What did you say!?
Now that I think about it, Majoko has been making mistakes since the very first time I met her...
I've never seen this book before ...
FWASH
Ouch... I totally failed the landing.
!?
You...
You came out of the book!!

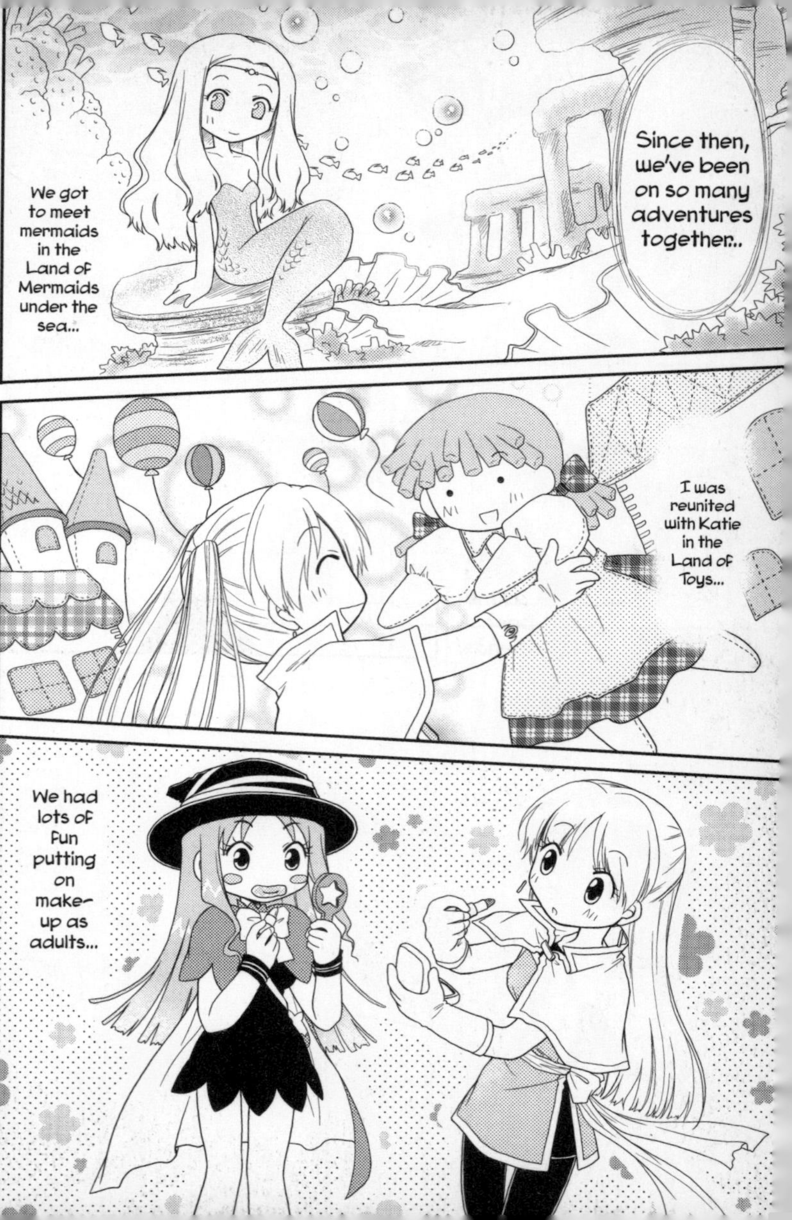
Since then, we've been on so many adventures together...
We got to meet mermaids in the Land of Mermaids under the sea...
I was reunited with Katie in the Land of Toys...
We had lots of fun putting on make-up as adults...

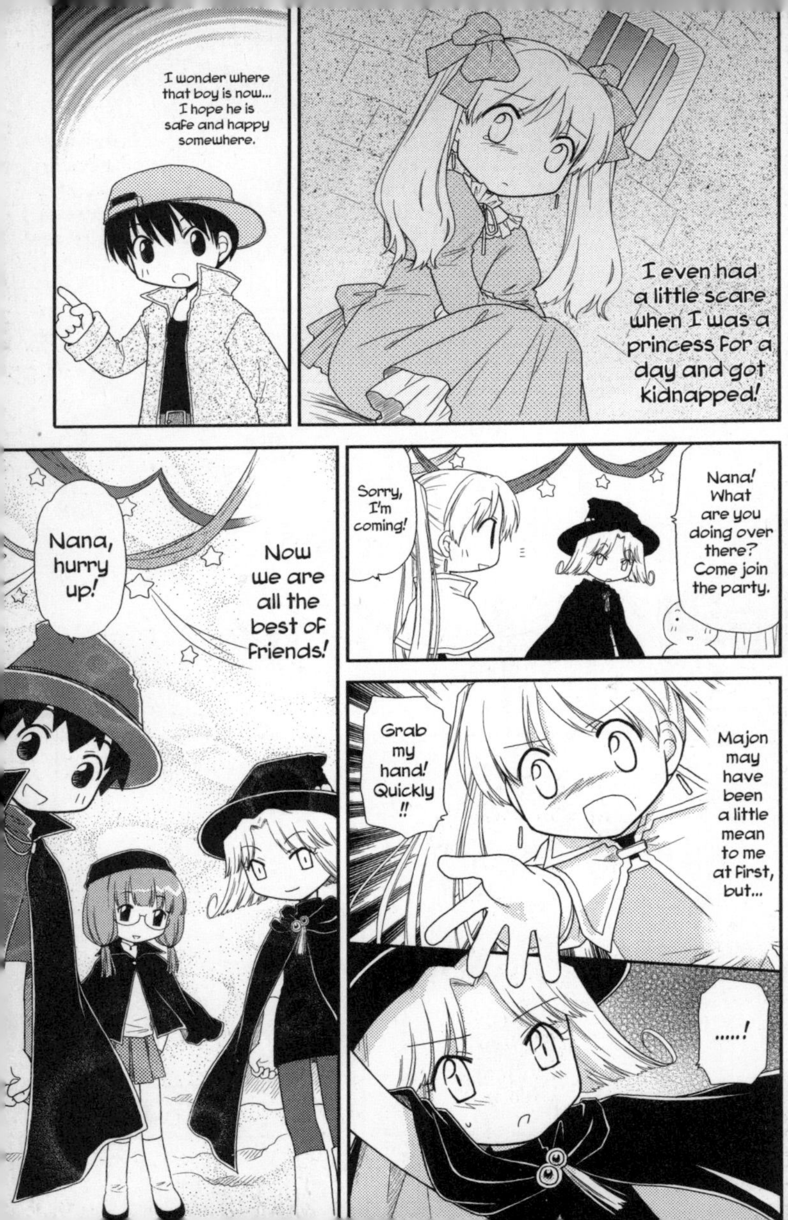
I even had a little scare when I was a princess for a day and got kidnapped!
I wonder where that boy is now... I hope he is safe and happy somewhere.
Nana! What are you doing over there? Come join the party.
Sorry, I'm coming!
Majon may have been a little mean to me at first, but...
Grab my hand! Quickly !!
.....!
Now we are all the best of friends!
Nana, hurry up!

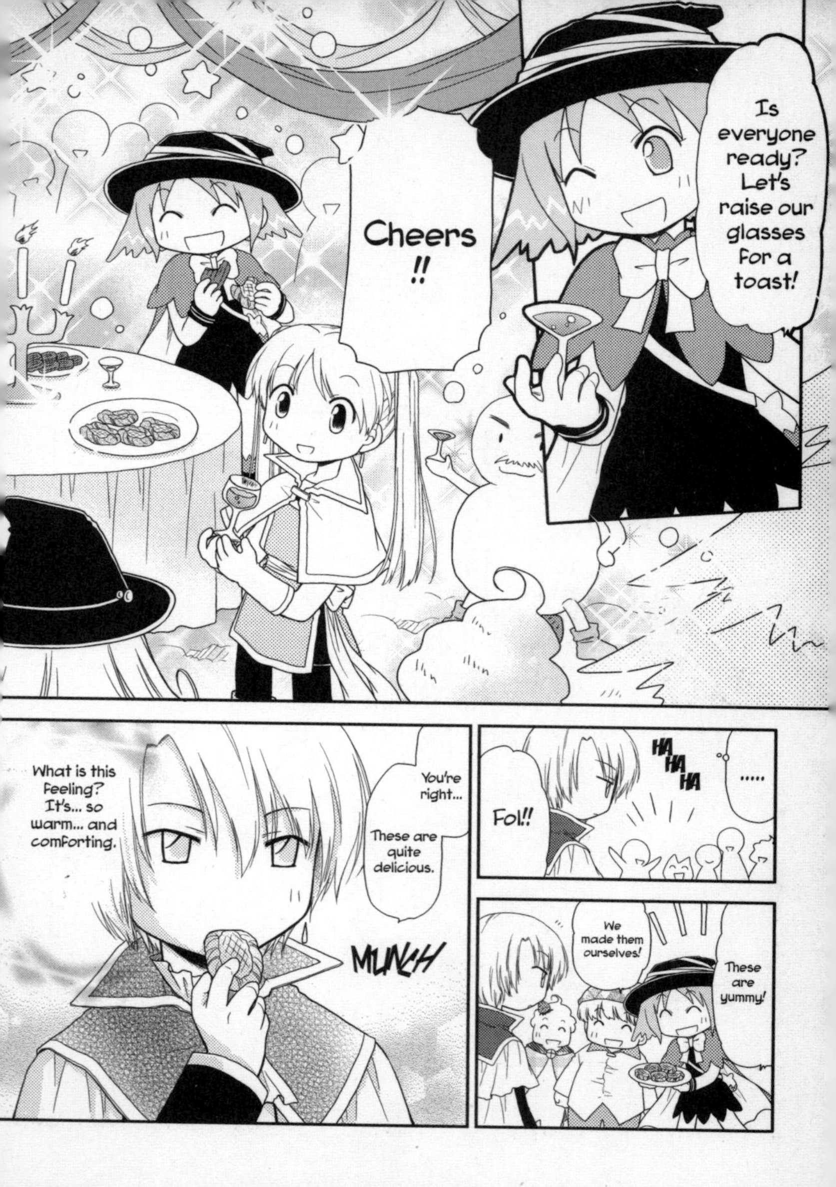
Is everyone ready? Let's raise our glasses for a toast!
Cheers !!
.....
HA HA HA
Fol!!
These are yummy!
We made them ourselves!
You're right...
These are quite delicious.
What is this feeling? It's... so warm... and comforting.
MUNCH

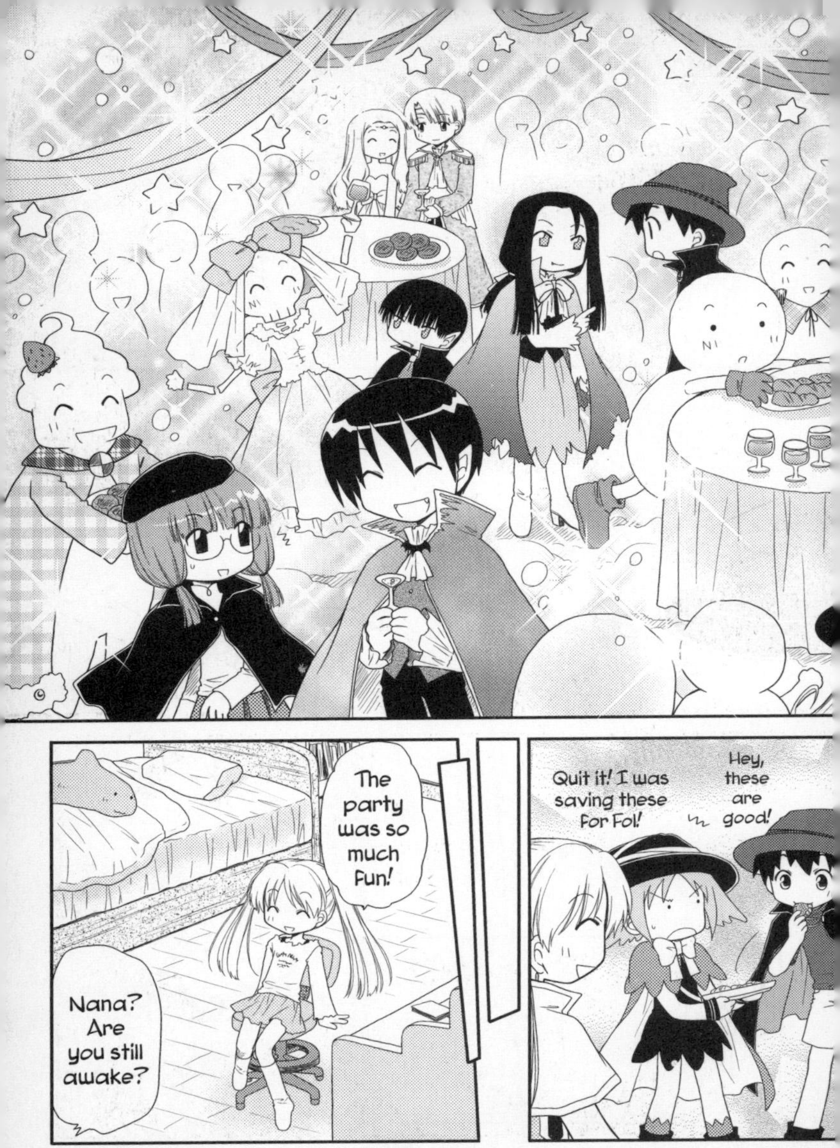
Hey, these are good!
Quit it! I was saving these for Fol!
The party was so much fun!
Nana? Are you still awake?

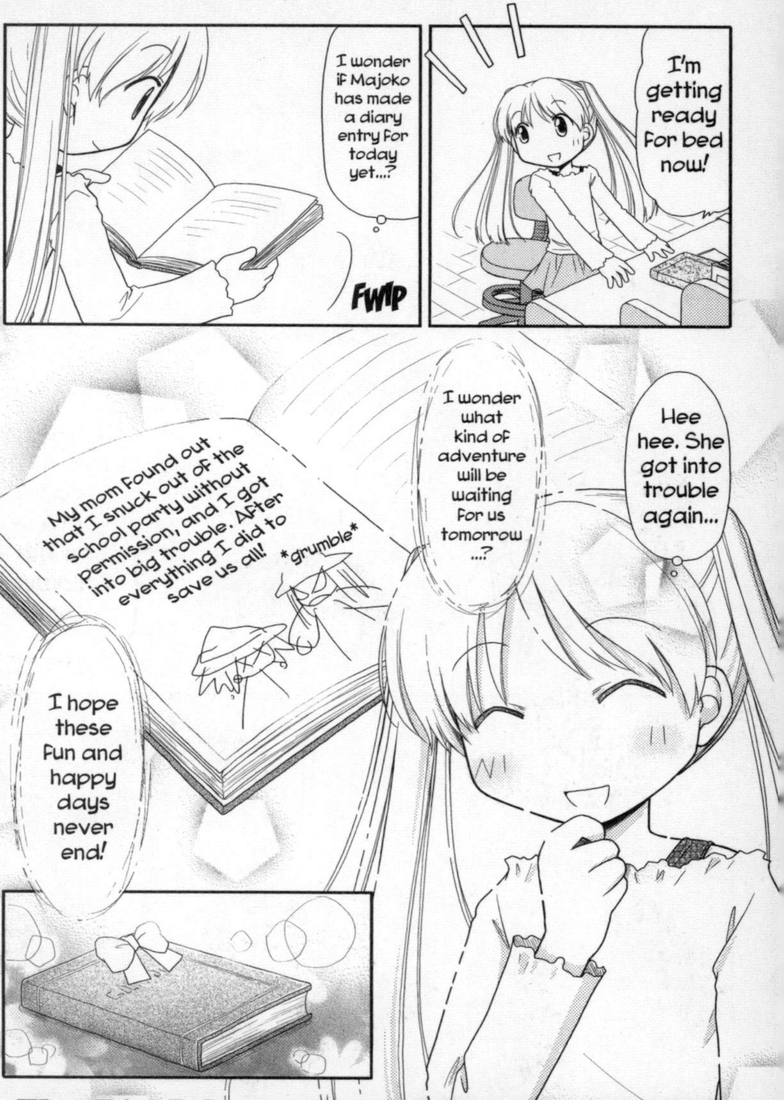
I'm getting ready for bed now!
I wonder if Majoko has made a diary entry for today yet...?
FWIP
Hee hee. She got into trouble again...
I wonder what kind of adventure will be waiting for us tomorrow...?
My mom found out that I snuck out of the school party without permission, and I got into big trouble. After everything I did to save us all!
grumble
I hope these fun and happy days never end!

The Big Adventures of Majoko [5] <Fin>

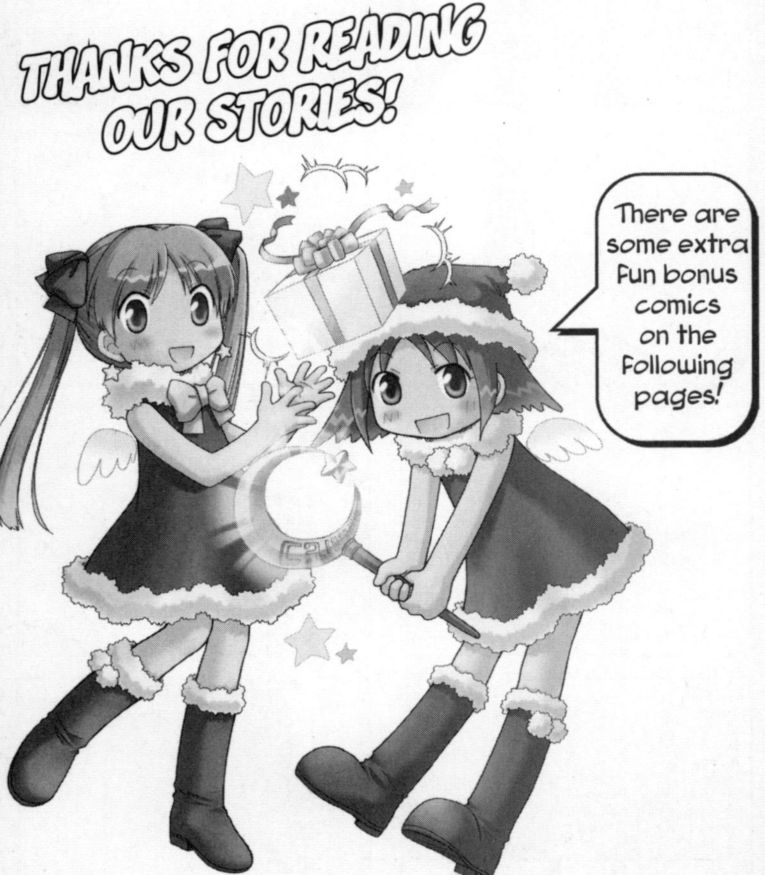
THANKS FOR READING OUR STORIES!
There are some extra fun bonus comics on the following pages!

MAJOKO'S SPECIAL SHORT COMIC THEATRE!

DON'T GIVE UP, KUUL

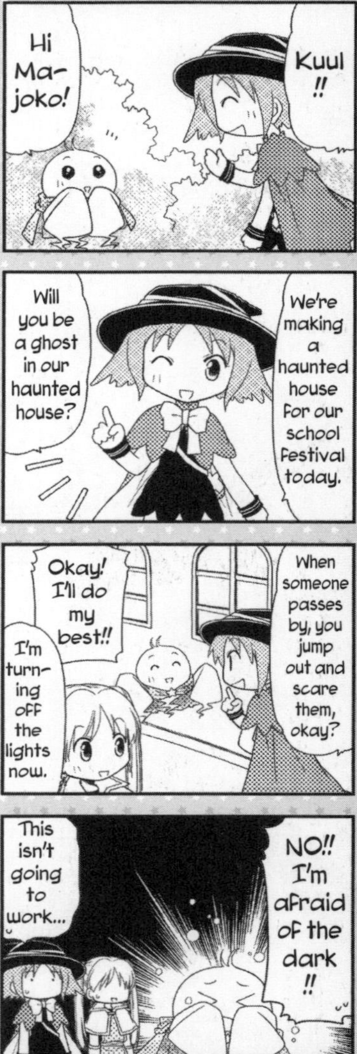
Kuul !!
Hi Ma-joko!
We're making a haunted house for our school festival today.
Will you be a ghost in our haunted house?
When someone passes by, you jump out and scare them, okay?
Okay! I'll do my best!!
I'm turn-ing off the lights now.
NO!! I'm afraid of the dark !!
This isn't going to work...

DON'T GIVE UP, FOL

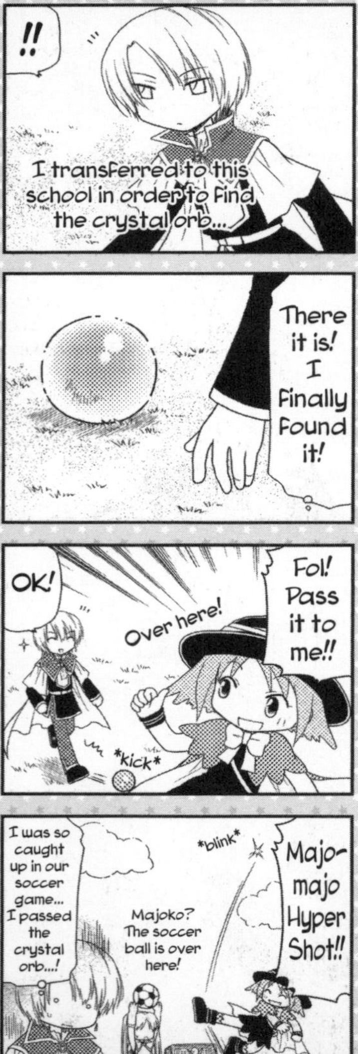
!!
I transferred to this school in order to find the crystal orb...
There it is! I Finally Found it!
Fol! Pass it to me!!
Over here!
OK!
kick
Majo-majo Hyper Shot!!
blink
Majoko? The soccer ball is over here!
I was so caught up in our soccer game... I passed the crystal orb...!

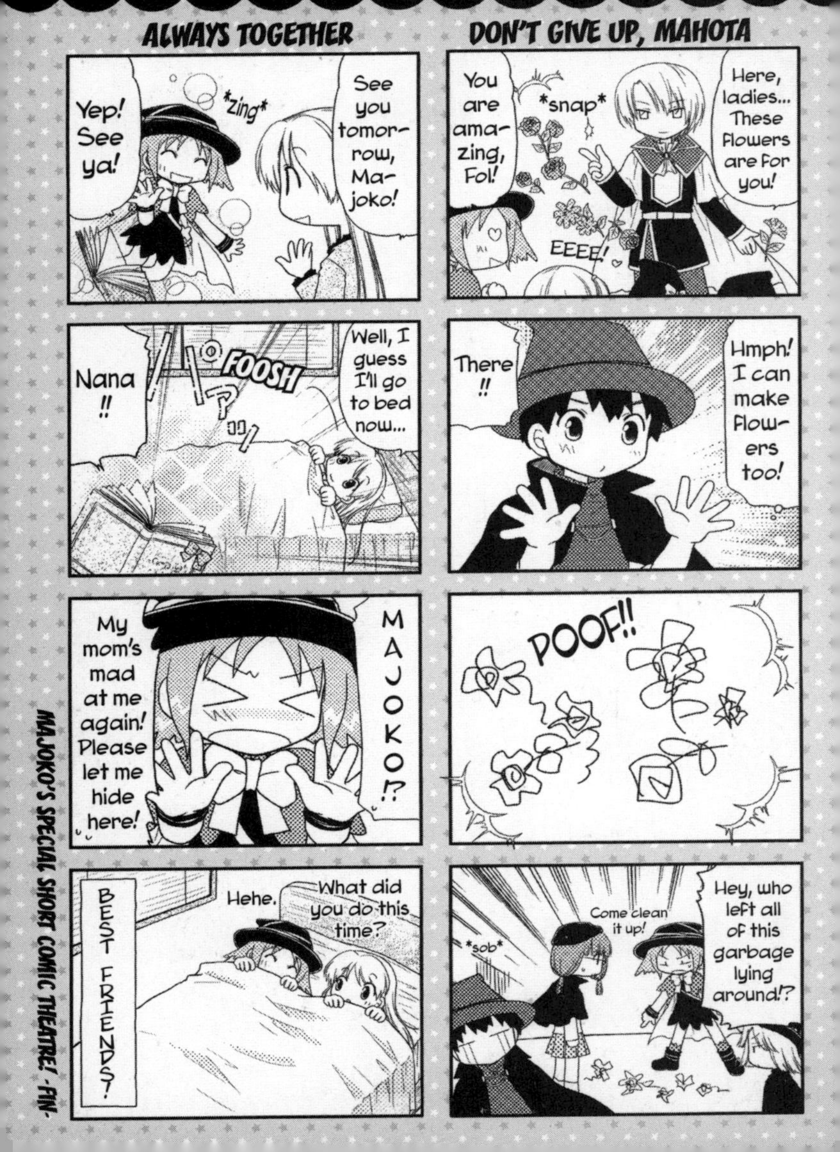
DON'T GIVE UP, MAHOTA
Here, ladies... These flowers are for you!
snap
You are amazing, Fol!
EEEE!
Hmph! I can make flowers too!
There!!
POOF!!
Hey, who left all of this garbage lying around!?
Come clean it up!
sob
ALWAYS TOGETHER
See you tomorrow, Majoko!
zing
Yep! See ya!
Well, I guess I'll go to bed now...
FOOSH
Nana!!
MAJOKO!?
My mom's mad at me again! Please let me hide here!
What did you do this time?
Hehe.
BEST FRIENDS!
MAJOKO'S SPECIAL SHORT COMIC THEATRE! -FIN-

SWANS in SPACE

VOLUME 2

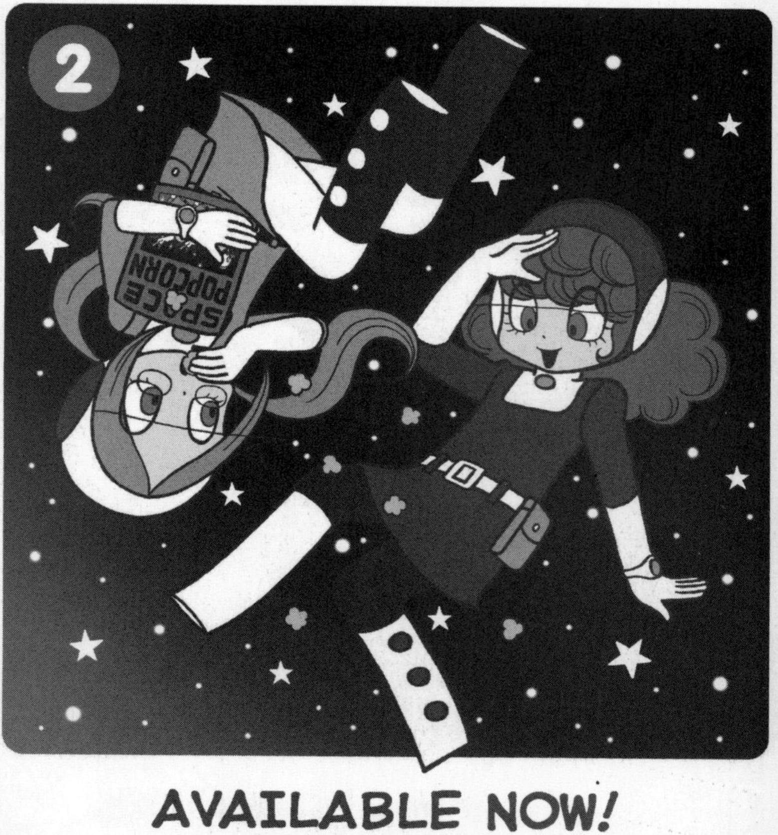
2
SPACE POPCORN

AVAILABLE NOW!

SWANS IN SPACE Vol.2
ISBN: 978-1-897376-94-2

COMING SOON:
SWANS in SPACE
VOLUME 3

AVAILABLE NOW!

SWANS IN SPACE Vol.3
ISBN: 978-1-897376-95-9

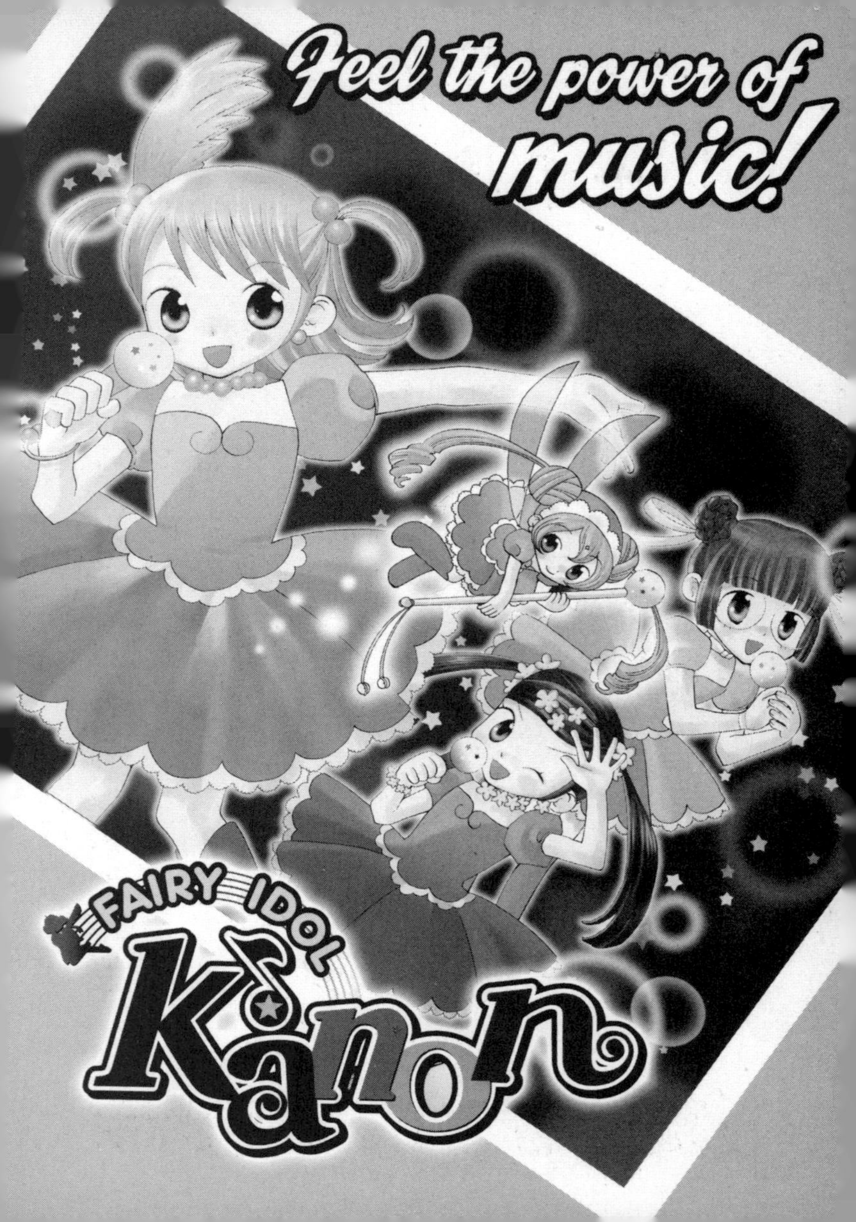

Feel the power of music!
FAIRY IDOL
Kanon

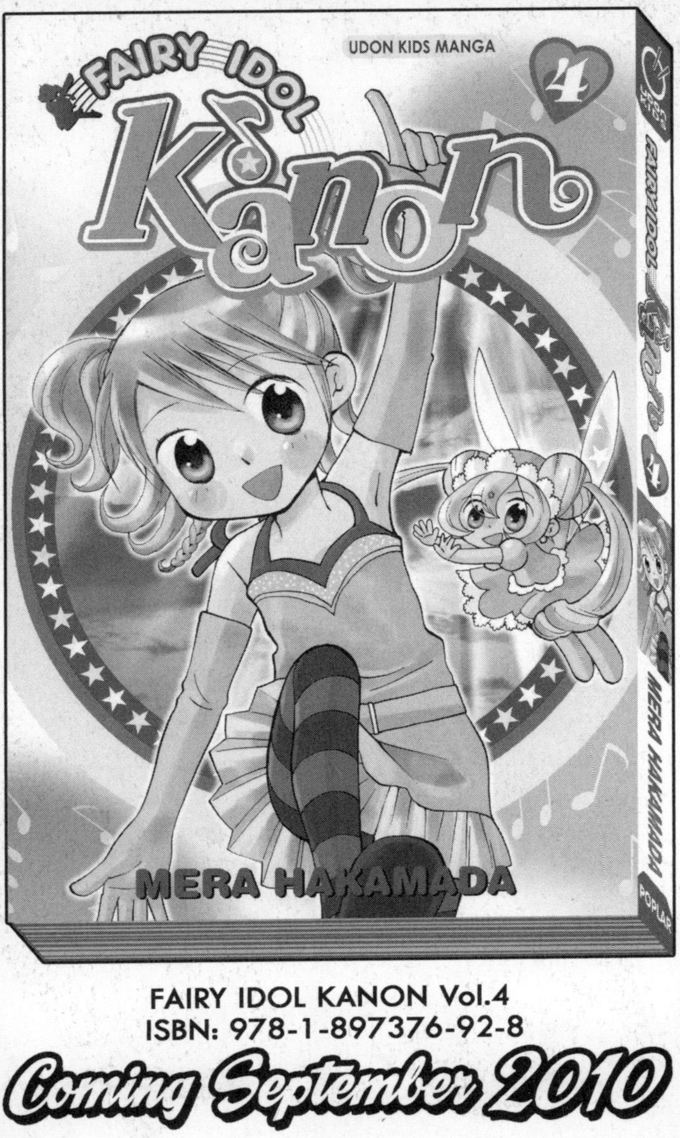
UDON KIDS MANGA
FAIRY IDOL
Kanon
4
MERA HAKAMADA
FAIRY IDOL Kanon 4
MERA HAKAMADA
POPLAR

UDON KIDS MANGA
The Big Adventures of Majoko
1
MACHIKO FUJI
TOMOMI MIZUNA

THE BIG ADVENTURES OF MAJOKO

Vol.1
ISBN: 978-1-897376-81-2

Vol.2
ISBN: 978-1-897376-82-9

Vol.3
ISBN: 978-1-897376-83-6

Vol.4
ISBN: 978-1-897376-84-3

Vol.5
ISBN: 978-1-897376-85-0

UDON KIDS MANGA
NINJA BASEBALL
Kyuma!
1
SHUNSHIN MAEDA

NINJA BASEBALL KYUMA

Vol.1
ISBN: 978-1-897376-86-7

Vol.2
ISBN: 978-1-897376-87-4

Vol.3
ISBN: 978-1-897376-88-1

MangaforKids.com

UDON KIDS MANGA
in SPACE
YAMAMOTO
1
SPACE PATROL
FULL COLOR MANGA!

UDON KIDS MANGA
1
FAIRY IDOL
Kanon
MERA HAKAMADA

SWANS IN SPACE

Vol.1
ISBN: 978-1-897376-93-5

Vol.2
ISBN: 978-1-897376-94-2

Vol.3
ISBN: 978-1-897376-95-9

FAIRY IDOL KANON

Vol.1
ISBN: 978-1-897376-89-8

Vol.2
ISBN: 978-1-897376-90-4

Vol.3
ISBN: 978-1-897376-91-1

Vol.4
ISBN: 978-1-897376-92-8

MangaforKids.com

NINJA BASEBALL
KYUMA Vol.1
ISBN: 978-1-897376-86-7

CAN A *NINJA*
LEARN TO PLAY BALL?

VOLUME 5

Manga: Tomomi Mizuna
Original Work / Supervision: Machiko Fuji
Original Illustrations: Mieko Yuchi

Translation: M. Kirie Hayashi
Lettering: Ben Lee
English Logo Design: Hanna Chan

UDON STAFF
Chief of Operations: Erik Ko
Project Manager: Jim Zubkavich
Managing Editor: Matt Moylan
Editor, Japanese Publications: M. Kirie Hayashi
Marketing Manager: Stacy King

ITAZURA MAJOKO NO DAIBOUKEN Vol.5

©Tomomi Mizuna 2006
©Machiko Fuji 2006
©Mieko Yuchi2006
All rights reserved.

Original Japanese edition published by POPLAR Publishing Co., Ltd. Tokyo
English translation rights arranged directly with POPLAR Publishing Co., Ltd.

English edition of THE BIG ADVENTURES OF MAJOKO Vol. 5
©2011 UDON Entertainment Corp.

English language version produced and published by UDON Entertainment Corp.
P.O. Box 5002, RPO MAJOR MACKENZIE
Richmond Hill, Ontario, L4S 0B7, Canada

www.udonentertainment.com

First Printing: July 2011
ISBN-13: 978-1897376850   ISBN-10 : 1897376855
Printed in Canada

This is the BACK of the book!

The Big Adventures of Majoko is a comic book created in Japan, where comics are called **manga**. Manga is read from right-to-left, which is backwards from the normal books you know. This means that you will find the first page where you expect to find the last page! It also means that each page begins in the top right corner.

START HERE!

PAGE 1

PAGE 2

WHEN YOU GET HERE, GO TO THE NEXT PAGE!

Now head to the other end of the book and enjoy **The Big Adventures of Majoko!**